A LIFE IN THE CINEMA

Mick Garris

ENCYCLOPOCALYPSE
PUBLICATIONS

To my wife Cynthia, the love of my life,
who always impresses and surprises me,
makes me laugh, and inspires me every day.
She is my favorite song.

Contents

Thank You

Being a writer is a little bit like being a vampire: you tend to sip the blood of experience and inspiration from those around you. I've been lucky enough to feed from some pretty amazing folks over the years, and I shall always remain in their debt. I've stood in the shade of so many talented people that I feel a little like the Woody Allen character, Zelig. There are many, many people whose friendship and inspiration have guided me over the years, leading to the publication of this book, and I'd like to take a moment to thank them, if you'll indulge me. After all, it's my first book, and I've got a lot of catching up to do.

In addition to the many friends, family, and folks I've been lucky enough to work and associate with, I'd especially like to extend my appreciation to: My mother, who would stay up late with me to watch scary movies when I was a kid, and tell me how well they held up.

My father, who regained his family late in life, and mended all the fences before he died.

David J. Schow, who was first to ask me to try my hand at fiction for his book *Silver Scream...* and wouldn't let me off the hook.

Jeff Gelb, for encouraging me to do it some more in the *Hot Blood* books.

Richard Christian Matheson, who put me together with Gauntlet in the first place.

Clive Barker, who unwittingly taught me a thing

or two about self-censorship.

John Landis, who was the first to get me to direct.

Steven Spielberg, the first person to hire me as a screenwriter, and the second to hire me as a director, and for his continuous encouragement and generosity.

And especially to Stephen King, who keeps giving me the rope, and whose friendship and inspiration means everything to me.

Mick Garris

Introduction

By Stephen King

By the early 1990s I'd written several films based on my own published works (some, like *Creepshow*, were pretty good; others, like *Silver Bullet*, were... Welles... not so good). Been there, killed that, as Mick Garris doesn't quite say in the stories that follow (but almost). I decided to take what I'd learned and write an original screenplay, and I had a bloody good time doing it. Adapting a novel like *Pet Sematary* for the big screen is tough—like swiping all the hotel towels out of your room and trying to cram them into a medium-sized attaché case. Compared to that, writing an original screenplay—something meant from the first to fit the movies' two-hour time frame—was a piece of cake.

The result was *Sleepwalkers*, a horror script about a race of beings that had been living with mankind since we crept out of the caves and climbed down from the trees. Living with us and feeding off us. It was also a story about a boy who loves his mother, and what happens to that boy when he finally falls in love with a girl his own age. (Well, the Sleepwalkers are actually thousands of years old, but true love turns us all into kids again, right?) Columbia grabbed the project and offered me two possible directors—let's call them A and B. Director A had done an arty-farty gangster film, and the studio was very high on him. Director B had done a couple of horror-franchise films that were good, but they had those *numbers* in the titles... *ewwww!* Probably for that reason, the studio wasn't quite so high on Director B; was nudging me, in fact, toward arty-farty Director A.

And I was allowing myself to be nudged, in spite of how much I liked Director B's *Psycho* film (I think it was III [note: it was actually *Psycho IV: The Beginning*]), which started with Norman Bates calling in to a radio talk-show, hosted by C.C.H. Pounder in a quietly ferocious performance.

Then I had a little talk with Director A, and the results were more horrifying than anything in the *Sleepwalkers* script. I wanted to tell the story of a thousand-year-old Sleepwalker lad who falls in love with a sunny California girl; Director A had visions of Art. To begin with he wanted a "Planet of the Sleepwalkers"—a kind of prequel, I guess—which he would film in Panavision and Dolby stereo, possibly with The Norman Jackoff Orchestra on the soundtrack. He didn't dismiss my timid objections that this wasn't what my movie was about; he simply rode over them without ever looking back.

I was reminded of my discussions about *The Dead Zone* with Michael Cimino, when Cimino was on board as director (a chore which was finally fulfilled—and admirably—by David Cronenberg) and I was on board as writer. Cimino wanted to change the locale from New England to New Mexico so he could use the world's largest truck in the show. The big truck just happened to be in New Mexico, y'see, and what the hell, they both started with New, didn't they? What's the big deal? And if you think all this has no bearing on the collection I'm introducing, it's because you haven't yet read the title story.

The big deal in both cases was that the director didn't want to make the story I wrote. I went with Director B for *Sleepwalkers,* and that turned out to be one of the smartest decisions of my life, because Director B was Mick Garris. I have worked with him on almost half a dozen projects since, and consider him my best friend in the business. There are only two honest men in Hollywood, and Mick is both of them.

As a collaborator, he has, from *Sleepwalkers* on, dedicated himself to bringing my words to the screen. He has often done it with flair—see, for instance, the scene which introduces Mädchen Amick in *Sleepwalkers,* a long, goofy-happy travelling shot worthy of Steven Spielberg's *1941*—but in doing so he has necessarily sublimated his own writing skills, which are formidable indeed. There are no Sleepwalker Planets in the stories which follow, but there's some damned fine writing. Director A, eat your heart out.

When people told Robert Bloch that he didn't look as if he could possibly have written all those awful stories—Norman Bates, Jack the Ripper, the hungry glass, the house of the hatchet, you gotta be kiddin'— Bloch grinned and delivered a line which has often been erroneously attributed to me (although I always gave Norman's creative daddy the credit). He said, "Actually, I've got the heart of a small boy. I keep it in a jar on my desk." Mick Garris sort of *looks* like the small boy Bob probably had in mind... if, that is, you think of a teenager from the late sixties or early seventies, into groups like Badfinger (and, later, Crowded House). When I met him he looked, in short, like the good-angel version of the main character in the title story and its grim sequel ("Starfucker"). He's a slender man who stands about five-eleven, with lots of brown hair falling around the sides of an intelligent (if slightly sardonic... as in Mr. Sardonicus) face highlighted by a pair of the most innocent blue eyes you've ever seen.

There's a little more gray in the hair these days (working with those studio types can age a guy, just ask the maker of *Words Without Voices* and the immortal *Gulp!*—you'll be meeting him soon), but otherwise he still looks that kid who was into Badfinger and the Kinks. It's hard to believe that this cheerful, smiling guy can possibly be the same fellow who created the new but not-so-improved Gramma of "Forever Gramma" or the sexual freaks and geeks that come posturing in and stumbling back out of the other stories in this collection. But the inside and the outside are sometimes two different things, and although Mick's one of the world's nicest guys (in fact the name of his company is Nice Guy Productions), he's got a few kinks of his own. Do I mind? Not at all. "Got a graveyard hand and a tombstone mind," the old song goes, and I admire that in a person. I really do.

Besides, this man can write. Check out the dreamy perspective work of "Chocolate," for instance, where the male narrator begins to receive empathic transmissions from a female somewhere out there in the great L.A. Mystic (and don't overlook the screenplay which follows, where Mr. Garris conducts a textbook seminar in the art and craft of adapting one's own work), or "Forever Gramma," in which a barefoot boy with cheeks of tan (so to speak) gets a sex-ed lesson from the dead. And don't dare miss "A Life in the Cinema" and "Starfucker," the stories which form this book's strong central core. Here is a real Hollywood insider writing about the real inside world of filmmaking: the good, the bad, and the cheesy. These stories are both erotic and cynical ("Give them guilt-free art-house erotica, wanking material for the intelligentsia," writes the narrator of both the central tales, "and the kilos to the kingdom are yours"), but they are above all well and fiercely told—when he's yarning about the tarnished tinsel underbelly of the town he knows (and clearly loves) the best, Mick Garris writes like a combination of Robert Bloch and James Ellroy, hardboiled *noir* with a ghastly little prink of the devil's own pitchfork. Gotta like it, my children; you have got to like that.

This is an entertaining and important debut collection, one likely to end up on a good many year's best lists, including my own. I felt fortunate to be tapped for the introduction. I just want one little favor from my little long-haired buddy, and that's an option to "Dream on Me." The only thing is, Mick, we're going to set it on

another planet, okay? Lots of frontal nudity and dig this:
we're going to shoot in New Mexico and feature *the
world's largest truck.* You'll love it, sweetheart, trust me.

Stephen King
Longboat Key, Florida
January, 2000

A Life in the Cinema

The Mexican woman's freak baby might have been the worst thing ever to happen to her, but it could have been the best thing in the world to ever happen to me.

I'd much rather show it than tell it, but that's just not the way things work out in this town. You hear all that shit about only being as good as your last picture, and all those other hoary old saws about the Industry-with-a-capital-I, but that's ancient Hollywood masturbatory storytelling. If you're smart, you get your next picture set up before the last one comes out. You're as good as your last *two*.

I guess.

It started with film school. We didn't have the kind of money you need to go to S.C. and use all that stuff Steven and George bought for them, but I did get a scholarship at UCLA. So you make do, right?

It was *great!* I mean, just imagine having all that equipment to use for nothing! Sure, most of the study work had to be done on video, but the thesis was always shot on film, with sync sound, even optical titles. I shot mine in 35mm 'scope and Dolby stereo.

One good thing about UCLA is the agent connection. You make a good film or write a good script, and every door in Century City suddenly opens up to you. It's like dogs smelling a bitch in heat. Make a short film on your own, and even if it's *The Fucking Titanic*, nobody's ever going to see it unless it comes from film school.

So that's what happened. It took me a year and a half to finish *Words Without Voices*, but it was worth it. I badgered my way into incredible locations, built weird, wonderful sets that represented every dreamscape you could imagine (and many you couldn't, I'm sure), got a full orchestral original score, and made my 24-minute epic.

If you know lighting, manipulation, composition, and you throw away the zoom lens, directing's easy.

After copyrighting the film in *my* name, and not the school's (they weren't going to make money off of my talent), I submitted it to film festivals around the world, and started collecting ribbons. First place at AFI Fest, first place at USA Film Festival, honorable mention in Seattle (fuck 'em. Who cares about Seattle?).

And then, you learn about taking meetings. I got calls from Endeavor, William Morris, CAA, the whole catalogue. The hungry young guys have the most hustle, but the old Jewish farts have the connections and the clients. Maybe you wouldn't want to eat with them, but they know how to get a deal greenlit. I learned quick that it's the agent, not the agency that makes the difference. The old guys are never too eager to take on the new clients, but some of them can be convinced. Eventually.

All of them wanted me to leave a cassette of my film—can you imagine that? I shot it in Panavision, spent weeks on the stereo mix, and they're going to glance at it through phone calls on a nineteen-inch screen. I know these lazy bastards all have screening rooms, so I insisted that they run the film in 35. I was nice about it and everything, but very persistent, so they'd know they were dealing with an artist.

Well, I got the pick of the litter. I made a couple of mistakes, first, like everybody does. One of these ten-percenters got real excited about getting me a "Homicide" meeting; as if I would even consider television drek. Another one thought getting me a sequel would speed things up.

Right. Do *Halloween 2000* and Hollywood spreads its legs. Then, who knows? Maybe *Hardbodies 4*!

So finally, old Rosen at Spectacular Artists and I reach an understanding. I mean, you don't want to watch this toothless clown take meals, but he knows how to throw his ninety-eight pounds around. We don't want to make development deals, he says, we want to make *Movies.* No TV, no cable. Theatrical features only. My scripts, full purchase only, no options. Pay *and* play.

It's good cop/bad cop time. I'm taking meetings in high-altitude offices on every lot, with Walter and Casey and Mike and Jeffrey and all the big boys, discovering how easy all of this can be.

Thank God for film school. These guys love to talk about how there's such a void left by Preston Sturges and Alfred Hitchcock and how there's never been an American equivalent to *The Bicycle Thief* and all that other dinosaur shit I flunked in Film History 101. And then I talk Carpenter, Dante, Hooper, Cameron: my gods. They like that, but only if you talk *Poltergeist* and not *Lifeforce, Halloween* and not *The Thing, Titanic* and not *True Lies.* The supreme measure of art is worldwide box-office.

So I pitch them my movies, and listen to their reactions. They give me their "thoughts", and I get all excited about some of their ideas, as though they just made my story better than I ever could have alone. Then I hang back and consider their "notes" a few moments, before telling them why those ideas don't work. They get a feeling of give and take, that I'm willing to listen to their suggestions, and yet that I'm strong enough to defend my own ideas. They like me.

My job is to charm them, then Rosen gets to be the asshole. But that's okay, he's used to that. He *likes* that. He wheels and deals, gets the studios fighting over me, the price goes into the stratosphere, and I get to make my movie in Burbank.

Now there's an experience. At UCLA, you've got everybody and his grandmother thrilled to death to be a part of a movie (tell them it'll be on cable, and you can hose any of the women who took their clothes off for free on camera). Everybody works twenty hours a day, just for the sake of making your movie. Commitment, creativity, drive: everybody wants to help out.

But the studio experience is something else again. First, there's the unions; you've never seen so many people to do so few things. You kick out a plug, a union electrician has to plug it in. You're just about to shoot the crucial shot you and the cameraman (excuse me— *cinematographer*) have been setting up for the last three hours, and the assistant director calls lunch. Of course, everybody dicks around when they get there, so you can't start on time, but there is no going over, or you're into triple golden time.

And then there's the twenty-seven teamster drivers who are assigned to the show, sitting on their asses in their air-conditioned station wagons, waiting around at $2,500 a week, in case somebody needs a Diet Dr. Pepper at the Company Store.

But that's the least of it. That shit I can understand. These guys make a living, they do their work, and they get paid. The Suits are worse. I mean, I wear a tie on the set; when you can still get into Disneyland on a Junior ticket, and shaving is an exercise in wishful thinking, you do anything you can to direct from a position of power. But these fuckers in their Armanis, with their illegal Cuban cigars and soft voices are the reason why all the movies you see are shit. Okay, here's how they think. What does "good" mean to you? Quality? Great. You and I think alike. But "good" to these guys is "familiar". Good is somebody else's hit. God forbid you make something unique, with an original vision. No, they want the "heart" *of Forrest Gump*, the "visual kinetics" of *Star Wars*, the "pacing" of *Lethal Weapon 4*, the "gloss" of *Armageddon*, shit like that. All they know how to sell is what they know how to sell. And that, not very well.

So once we're in pre-production, there are the fights. They want storyboards, and I don't work with storyboards. We hire a storyboard artist to keep them happy, knowing full well I'm never going to look at the fucking little cartoons once I'm on the set.

Then there's casting. Oh, God, you wouldn't believe the names they want in my movie. If it was up to me—and believe me, it wasn't—I'd cast all unknowns. I want you to see the characters I've created, not famous actors in the roles. But no. I write the scientist role patterned on an old high school biology teacher of mine, and they want Tom Cruise. Tom fucking Cruise to play a biogeneticist! For the social worker they can get Gwyneth Paltrow... but they'd have to give her dad executive producer credit. Ultimately, it doesn't matter who I want, because with money and schedule and billing and studio problems, nobody is available anyway. At least not until you get down to the bottom of the list. Dreg city.

And then, of course, there is the wonderfully creative hand of Mr. Flotsam, our esteemed producer. He "developed" this "package", and his involvement is primarily to bring in Mark Snow for the music, and he gets a presentation credit for that. For that he should get a black eye! This film demands a full orchestra, and I get a fucking synthesizer programmer from some wannabe "Twilight Zone" TV series!

Somehow, we get into production. Once the train starts, there is no stopping it. Digital Domain is already shooting plates for the effects shots, the dailies are coming in, the Suits are bitching about diffusion and coverage and boom shadows. They haven't the slightest idea how a movie is made. All I can say is Trust Me. I know what I'm doing. You're going to love it when it's cut. Of course, that's not enough for them. They're insisting on more coverage, at the same time they're bitching about going over schedule and budget. And this isn't *Godzilla* or *Waterworld*—this is just a lousy twelve million bucks they're talking about!

Okay, I admit I can be a bit tyrannical on the set. But do you blame me? My name is on the line. Written and directed by. Me. Nobody notices the accountant's name. Nobody cares about editor, or *cinematographer*. or the atmosphere, or matte artist. Nobody gives fuck one about costume design. So, yeah. If it's going to get done, it's going to get done right... even if it means a little more time and money. What are they going to do, fire me and replace me, twenty days in on a thirty-five day shoot?

So maybe a couple of *thespians* cried... it's the performance that counts, not how you get it. The only thing anybody can judge is what's on the screen. And actors! They'll do *anything!* Unless they're "names", of course. Then the fucking spoiled little prima donna babies won't even give you so much as a little nipple.

You've never seen a less cooperative group of people. I never set out to win a popularity contest; I just wanted to make my film.

So we made it. It wasn't that much over budget; I mean, it wasn't *Titanic,* or anything like that. So they sneaked my cut, like the Director's Guild requires. The preview cards were okay—not as good as we hoped, but okay. And it wasn't made for the carbohydrate crowd anyway. This is a sophisticated film, and they preview it for the horny-handed machinists and their toothless girlfriends in Long Beach. Brilliant. So the studio, of course, recut it and completely fucked the whole thing up, and tested their abortion in San Diego—my home town! Thanks, guys. Somehow the trades found out about the San Diego sneak, and they crucified us. I mean slit us up the middle and yanked out the entrails. Those guys like nothing more than shitting on an artist. If they know so much about making movies, let them try it! Fuck critics. If you ever met a critic, you wouldn't want to eat with him, either.

So much for flavor of the month. It plays the art house graveyard in four major markets, no TV support, no radio, just some print ads in the hip weekly papers that nobody pays for anyway. It plays in the 50-seat house at the Herpes Cineplex, and even Rosen doesn't answer my calls anymore. My one solace is that it killed Annamarie Longines' career in features. She got a sitcom last season, but it was gone after three weeks. They put it up against the last season of "Seinfeld". I gloated.

Okay, so the Brothers Warner (or, at least, their corporate equivalent) give me the boot. So what? There's six or seven other majors. Yeah, right, except that with the executive circle jerk that goes on, the VP assigned to your picture will be at Universal next week; his girlfriend is being hosed by an exec at Columbia, who's now at Tri-Star until his father-in-law makes him exec VP at Disney to keep him from telling about the episode in the private jet with the male lead in their new picture.

So the old grey fag gets protection, and I get a chainsaw right in the career.

Spectacular Artists dumped me, the development deals undeveloped, and before I know it, I'm sniffing around Gramercy, Dimension, Castle Hill, and the other independents. I'm hosing this 43-year-old Jewish American Princess agent who wants me to call her Mama. You should see the claw marks on my back. She's got an office with no secretary in Canoga Park or some god-awful place in the Valley, but the phone never rings. Never. She's hardly worth spilling my precious bodily fluids over. Or your time.

Sorry.

She calls in a few favors, and gets me a meeting with the Weinsteins on another *Hellraiser* thing; I go in, tie and all, and it's inevitably the same song: "I'm sorry, Mr. Weinstein's assistant was called out of town at the last minute. But he personally asked Mr. Fourth-String Pimpleface Nobody to hear your pitch."

Needless to say, my pitches were never home runs. The galling thing is that these guys are constantly hiring first-time directors—guys who've only made videos of their kids' birthday parties before wind up getting a hundred grand to do these coming-of-age-and-showing-teenage-tit arthouse indies that gross 67 million. I've done a studio picture, for Christ's sake, and get the bottom rung shoved up my ass.

By now my beach condo had flown to repossessionland. Ditto my SLK. I met Rebecca in a corridor at DreamWorks; I think we were both thinking of fucking the same producer. Her dream was jumping from soaps to features; personally, I thought she only made history by doing hardcore, but who am I to say so? Shacking up in Rebecca's West Hollywood apartment meant that I could dump Mama as a fuck-mate, but keep her on the string as an agent.

Rebecca also had a car.

By now, I'm starting to think that sitcom shit ain't so bad.

The door has slammed in my face so hard that "Just Shoot Me" starts to seem pretty goddamn funny.

I had to get out, go somewhere, anywhere. Get away from the TV.

Rebecca was out on an interview, so I jumped the bus downtown. It's not what you think. Downtown LA has no orange trees, no limos or movie stars, nothing you'd ever want to send pictures of to Mom. Just corporate high-rises, and a crumbling, decaying but lively city center, virtually 100% Latino: street vendors hustling in Spanish, salsa blasting from cheap, torn speakers, outlet stores, huge, fantastic old movie palaces now dowdy and rotting, showing three Spanish-language hits for two bucks, 24 hours a day. It's much more like Mexico City than the center of an American metropolis.

All I can do is wander and watch, chewing churros as the cops make the winos perambulate along. Gulping fresh Mexican juice from the vendors while a pimp opens his whore's face in a piss-scented doorway. I like it here; the street's like a 360-degree Dolby Digital Surround movie.

One of the things I like best is the collapsible green magazine rack on every corner. They're filled with weird Mexican adult comic books, bosomy romance pulps, and unbelievably bloody wrestling magazines—really great stuff. They cost next to nothing... and are worth every centavo. Even if you don't speak Spanish, like me.

But this time, I found more than masked wrestlers in bondage.

The old woman minding the stand had a basket in the shade, which she kept rocking with her foot. I saw the blanket in the basket squirm; she noticed me looking, and moved in front of it.

"Muchacho? " I asked, because I had nothing else to say.

"Muchacha."

Like it really mattered if it was a boy or a girl. A baby's a baby, right? They all look like Alfred Hitchcock, anyway.

Then the kid started to cry, this weird, soft mewling sort of sound. I sneaked a peek over the Santo magazine. The crying got louder, but the old lady wouldn't move. She just kept watching me like she was mad at me or something. I can't help it; I watch stuff. All the time. I guess I'm nosy... but show me a filmmaker who isn't a voyeur, and I'll show you a TV lifer.

The kid's catlike bellow was a primal screech by now, and even the old lady could no longer pretend to ignore it. She picks up the baby and lifts her blouse to release a stretched, hanging blob of a tit. She carefully lifts the edge of the baby blanket, and springs a leaking, incredibly long and erect nipple into the begging mouth.

She turns to see me watching her, and our eyes lock. I can't look away, and her grim face defies my stare.

Finally, the infant has taken its fill, and releases its hold on her breast. The leaking prong of her nipple springs up, and is quickly tucked away, after splashing drops of lactose on the baby's face.

As she wiped its face, I caught my first glance of it. This was no child. I didn't know what it was, but it was nothing I'd seen before. It was slippery-looking, completely hairless with dark, rubbery skin. It looked more like a human than any other kind of animal, but just barely. It seemed like it had been burned or something, except that its skin was wet, oily. It had lips like a fish, large and gasping, breathing like a rich fat man puffs on a Havana, wet and floppy.

I tried to get a better look, but she kept shielding it from me, covering it with the blanket and blocking it from view with her girth. I tried to wear as much sympathy as I could get on my face, a mask of soft, gentle caring. I had to see this kid more closely.

Talk was useless; she couldn't speak English, and Spanish is Greek to me. But I reached out with Allstate-sized helping hands to touch the baby. She was hesitant and defensive, but when she saw I had no intention of hurting or making fun of the thing, she let me lift the blanket, still watching my face the whole time.

Close up, with time to really see it, this freak baby was incredible. I knew immediately that I was back in business. And if you judge this thing the way you do a real baby, it was a girl. I had Rebecca's rent money in an envelope in my back pocket, and gave it to the old woman. I'm not sure why. I guess I just had to touch it. This thing would make the most incredible story ever; it all rushed through my mind in the time it took for the lights to flash around the marquee of the Million Dollar Theatre: all the words that had been shoved down my throat from the critics and the development meetings.

Heart. Story. Character.

All that shit.

I just wanted to hold the thing, feel its reality, touch it. But I didn't just want to do some latex life story. *Words Without Voices* had soured me on special effects. This thing was *real*, and *that's* what I had to show the world. No state-of-the-art Stan Winston special effect could ever hope to compete with the beating-heart, coursing-blood reality of this slippery, shifting-irised creature squirming in the blanket in my hands.

This baby was my movie.

I couldn't tell how old it was; how do you judge the age of something you've never seen before? It couldn't have been more than a couple months. When it realized that somebody new was holding it, its eyes locked onto mine, and we were both transfixed. The muddy irises seemed to swirl like whirlpools, clearing and changing to blue, then becoming so clear that I swear I could see the brain behind them. I could feel its heartbeat rippling through my hands as I stared into its cortex, distantly hearing it mewl, and seeing music deep within. Not like musical notes, but actually seeing the music itself. I don't know how else to explain it, except to compare it to the acid trips my stepfather always talks about.

This kind of eye contact seemed to tire the kid out, and the huge eyes filled with dead brown mud again, then slowly drifted closed. When I looked up, Mamacita was vamoosed.

Not that I minded. She had a chance to dump the freak, and jumped at it. If I had to sell year-old wrestling magazines to farmworkers on a street-corner, I'd probably have done the same thing.

But I lucked out. I had this incredible treasure in my hands; I would get another chance to thrill the world. And a month's rent for Rebecca's West Hollywood digs would pay for the old bitch's flop for five years. Later I would realize that she got the better end of the deal.

Rebecca was freaked but fascinated by the little slug in the bassinet in the kitchen. I decided to leave the details out of the story until later—especially the part about the rent money. I'd deal with that when the Arab came around asking for it.

"You said you always wanted a baby," I told her. She was not amused. But I knew how to handle her. She wouldn't have any trouble dealing with the freak if she knew she'd get at least a featured role in the picture at scale-plus-ten. We quickly discovered how simple the care and feeding of the little monster was; it sucked on anything and everything that found its way into its disgusting little smacking lips. Once Rebecca was leaning over it to get a good look, and the little sucker went for her breast right through the shirt. I tried to joke her into suckling it, but her sense of humor has its limits.

I named it Asta.

I gave Mama in Canoga Park the heave-ho, and set about scaling every bridge I ever burned. I bullied, badgered and blackmailed my way into meetings everywhere in town, from the sleaziest Troma to the most muscle-bound Paramount. At first it was always the third-stringers, like before; the studios are cautious. You can get the meetings; they don't want to close the door on anybody who might make a hit movie for somebody else, and not be able to get them back. The guy who flops with *THX 1138* at Warners might go on to do *Star Wars* at Fox. The door is shut, but not locked.

Anyway, I've got meetings with sons of mucky-mucks at *other* studios, and we talk "Heart" and "Story" and "Character", and we shoot box-office shit, and then I bring up The Idea. It's always the same reaction: "Yeah, but it's been done. The unfortunate baby is really more a Movie-of-the-Week, don't you think? But I'd be glad to put you in touch with our TV people." And that's supposed to signal the end of the meeting.

I won't let go. We talk *Elephant Man* and *Mask* and *E. T.* and all that other heartfelt mutant crap and my eyes go misty and caring and gentle. They start to get uncomfortable. I tell them how The Idea could be done so cheaply, and how much I learned by the last experience. Then I shrug like it's obviously brick wall time, and I say thank you, and walk out like a broken man. But they can't see my smile.

Before the door closes all the way, I pretend to spot the box I have sitting in the reception area, like I forgot about it. And before Mr. Pimple can finish punching up his next phone call, I scoop it up and swing around to face him, with Asta in my arms under a *Men In Black* baby blanket. "Oh, by the way... you want to see it?"

Of course he's too busy, and he has no idea that what I'm talking about is real, and he wants me the hell out of his office. Fruitless meetings never end. So I don't give him a chance to answer. I rush up, put the thing under his nose, and pull back the Alien.

The guy shits his pants. He wants to know if the guys who did the *Small Soldiers* made it, and I have to say over and over, no, it's real.

They don't believe me. I hold it closer, so close they can smell the acrid urine-stink that seeps from its skin, and invite them to touch her. Every single one I ever asked has declined.

It's amazing how quickly I get access to the ladder. I meet Sonny's boss, then her boss, then his boss, then his boss, and finally it's the rarefied penthouse office of Daddy himself.

At this point, Rosen's calling me back; he's caught wind of the tarbaby story, and he wants to break some backs at the majors. I don't blame the guy for dropping me; after all, I was poison. And Rosen doesn't give a shit about relationships or being my pal. He's a businessman. Right. He jerks my dick and I jerk his and we both come dollars. He knows I know he can negotiate the hell out of my deals, so I give him the nod. It's old home week, and he's got the studios beating each other up for the baby story.

Praise Jesus.

We set the deal up at Sony. I'm writer, producer and director; no presentation credit, but I'm not crying. We want to keep the budget low, shoot in some right-to-work state in the South, and I finally get to cast my talented unknowns, and throw Rebecca a three-line bone. Now that I'm producing, I can see the wisdom of keeping costs low, so that it's tougher for the studio to hide the profits if the film does business. We're talking a below-the-line of maybe five-point-three. And most of the above-the-line is me.

I decided early not to allow the cast and crew to see the kid until we actually shot the birth scene. I knew the reality of their reactions would make the scene really sing. I couldn't wait.

Everybody loved the script: even the Heart and Story and Characters. But wait until they saw Pee Wee. I was worried that during three or four months of pre-production, Asta might grow out of her weirdness. The freakishness might just be a stage. I held my breath every morning before checking under that bug blanket. But the thing wasn't changing at all.

In truth, I *did* learn a lot from the Warners experience. I'm prepared this time, I become the cast and crew's best pal, actually let them make suggestions, and pretend to consider them for a moment before I turn them down to do it my way. They like that.

Everything is going fine. We've run a day or two over schedule, but stay under budget, so the Suits are happy. They like the dailies, love the coverage and what we call the Look of Show.

I couldn't be happier. During breaks, I'm rocking my Winnebago with Cindy, my superstar discovery, chewing her implants and filling her with my goo. But the headier foreplay is thinking about the birth scene, scheduled for the Monday of week four.

Everybody's asking to see the puppet, who made the baby, when are we going to see the poor little thing. I just smile, playing the wise man with the secret.

B Day.

Crew call is 7:00 a.m., and I get there an hour early. Asta's been a little fussy, but seems okay. She's comfortable and well fed; I've got her in a basket that once held Snookie's Cookies.

Everybody's excited about the big scene. We'll be shooting Asta for the next three weeks, but this is her debut. I want to shoot the freak in continuity, just in case it changes at all during production. The locations that feature it are limited, so it's easy to shoot those scenes in order.

So we've got Cindy Starlet's belly as padded as Dr. Ellenbogen stuffed her breasts, and she's on her back, hyping up. For authenticity's sake she has been taking Lamaze classes at the clinic. Whatever works.

Rebecca's in the corner studying her line, looking sexy in her nurse outfit. She has no idea about me and Cindy, not that it matters if she did. I can afford my own place now.

Russell has just about finished lighting. I rush off and bring in the basket from my Winnie, and keep it hidden from view as I move onto my mark. I'm doing my cameo as the doctor who delivers the thing, so I'm in total control. I even gave myself a crucial close-up.

I'm mildly surprised to see that Cindy isn't wearing anything under the hospital gown. She winks, knowing I'm the only one in a position to know, and I give her little curls a tickle. She tries not to react in front of the others.

Then I bring Asta up onto the table, covered in her little blanket. Still, nobody but me has seen the thing, and my heart is pounding through the stethoscope hanging from my ears.

I place the baby thing between Cindy's legs (I like putting things between Cindy's legs). I'm the only one who can see Asta, and I enjoy watching it move wetly up against Cindy's private parts. Cindy tries not to react to the rippling wet pressure. Then, the inquisitive little beggar's lips seek out something that resembles a nipple down there, and starts to suckle.

"Quiet! Rolling!" Cindy can scarcely breathe... but she isn't about to blow the shot.

"Speed!" I can't believe what only I can see, but manage to stifle my laughter, and gently try to move it away from Cindy's happy button. Call me sensitive.

"Slate it!"

"Settle! Okay, Cindy... Action!"

And the camera makes its slow, relentless push in to the table. Cindy and I have spray sweat on our brows; I notice Rebecca watching me sneak a private grope under Cindy's sheet. But she won't bitch while the camera is rolling. It's perfect. Drama, tension, Cindy really making me believe she's delivering a difficult baby. Maybe this method shit isn't so bad; she was probably really dilating under there.

The camera is almost on top of us now, she's spasming with pain, and I'm struggling heroically to save the baby. Special effects releases the wash of fluid from hoses run through the table, and I lift Asta from between Cindy's thighs, holding the thing up in the blue light directly in front of the camera.

Asta played it beautifully, letting loose with that long, weak tremolo, spooking everyone on the stage into bug-eyed silence. I kept it rolling for a full two extra minutes, and when I finally yelled "Cut!", cast and crew alike burst into spontaneous applause. I bowed, holding the thing up in front of them, and Hollywood welcomed me home.

When I was sure that there was no camera bobble or sound problem, there was no way I was going to tempt fate. The take was perfect, and we wouldn't do another for Prudential.

I cleared the gawkers away, and set up for the close-up. Asta was no trouble at all under the lights. It just lay there, as if waiting for direction. Russ asked me if I wanted to use a doll for a standin to set the lights, and like a supreme dick, I said no. No doll is going to have the same reflective qualities of this kid's weird flesh. And it didn't seem to mind, anyway.

Well, I don't know how the word got out so quick, but Welfare showed up on the set before we even ran through the close-up. They were furious, screaming child abuse. There's some law about not being able to have an infant under stage lights for more than thirty seconds, and there must be a state welfare worker and a nurse and a teacher present at all times, or some shit like that.

I tell them there's no child here, that it's special effects. Or an animal. They want to know where the wrangler is. Right. Freak wrangler. By then, we're all yelling, so the First A.D. calls a break, and everybody else is glad to sneak away.

While the welfare bitch and I are getting close to fisticuffs, the Second A.D. gently taps my shoulder. What he whispers makes the whole argument moot. After biting his head off for butting in, I push him aside and rush over to the now-dark delivery table, where Asta is lying. I try to stand in the way, but the bitch in the grey suit is right behind me, wanting to see.

I let her.

Because the little freak wasn't moving, or breathing, or eating, or smelling, or fucking *living*.

Inside my head there were fireworks, suicide, guns and cacophony. But I stood stock still, my face a blank, vapid wall of I-told-you-so. While the woman was trying to puzzle out the rapidly rubberizing little torso on the table, I slowly turned to look her in the eye, and using all my power, said softly, "Is this really something that concerns you?"

We both turned to see what it was not: a glass-eyed, latex-skinned dummy prop. I remember being astonished at how phony it looked with its lights out, that devoid of life it looked like a castoff from *Critters* or something.

"There's your baby," I gloated, and she split, pissed off; even disappointed.

I called a wrap, and while everybody started to get ready for the next day's shoot, I took the little body and retired to the Winnebago. Cindy was waiting for me, looking all smiley and coquettish about the secret gumming she got under the sheet. I threw her out. She looked all upset and hurt, but fuck her. This was the end of my career.

I locked the door, and sat the little creep on the table and stared at it. The thing now looked ridiculously fake, its skin drying and looking like inner tube rubber— even down to the white dust of powder. The eyes were sightless, soulless, clear glass windows to a dark room.

Before I knew it, Rebecca was knocking on the door, but I just ignored her. She gave up quickly; she must not have been as pissed as I thought she would be.

I started yelling at the little pile of shit on the table, backhanding it to the floor. I'm sorry now, but you've got to comprehend the stress I was under. This little fucker was the key to everything I'd worked so long and hard for, and now all that was smoke. Fuck!

Suicide was an alternative, but I'm too much of a coward to pull the trigger, and not enough of a coward to go quickly. But as I stared into its ugly rubber mug, a simpler choice came to mind. We had the most important shot in the can already. The establishing shot of the monster was there. I could use the whole take. We'd already moved in to a good tight shot anyway, and there was no way the audience wouldn't buy it. Shot properly, maybe one of these effects tyros could help me pull off the rest of the show. Looking at the thing now, with its wick extinguished, the difference between life and latex was obvious... but there was no other way out.

We shut down the production for a few weeks while we sent out emergency bids to Rob Bottin and Steve Johnson and some non-union guys. When I showed them the kid the next day, they all thought it was nice, but a little simplistic in design. They all wanted to know who made it, and why didn't I just use them? I told them I'd made it myself, based on a dream I'd had, but I needed someone who could articulate and manipulate it better than I could. It had to be exactly the same look, I told them, only with more life. We thought about that digital shit, but I wanted something you could actually hold in your hands and get wet.

After the bids came in, we went with a local Texas kid who cost us a third of the big boys, and was willing to work thirty-hour days for the honor.

As I was waiting in the screening room to see the birth scene dailies, I held my breath. All the big cheeses were there; they knew it was the most important moment in the picture. I had only seen it on a shitty AVID output so far. But it was perfect. Everything in perfect focus, no bobbles, and the kid looked great. Unbelievable. When the Suits all gasped at the reveal, I started to breathe easy. By now, they all assumed that this thing had always been a special effect, anyway, and were almost glad to shut down for a couple weeks to keep the quality up.

All we had to do was hook them with the real baby footage, and they'd buy the rubber surrogate.

I went home that night feeling almost relaxed. New place, no furniture in it yet: just a bed, a laserdisc/DVD combi, and a projection TV. And a wicker basket with Asta in it. Once the latex clone was finished, I promised to give the thing a decent burial out back... but only if the rubber one was perfect.

I didn't have to shoot the next day, so I had my own mini-movie-marathon: *It's Alive*, *Rosemary's Baby*, and *Taboo VIII*, which put me to sleep, but with a raging erection.

It was an engorgement that would not subside in slumber, but rather kept time with my heartbeat until the door opened late that night. I opened my eyes. Unexpectedly, delightfully, Rebecca and Cindy entered in a shaft of light that penetrated the sparse, diaphanous nightclothes they wore. However unlikely, they seemed the best of friends, and got even friendlier when they joined me in the kip.

Our acrobatics were like a letter to Penthouse, and featured every erotic combination you could imagine... and six or seven more. It was a release I hadn't felt since pre-production began. I had a mouth at either end of me, and the two of them brought me to the most devastating, sphincter-clenching orgasm of my life!

But on the second jolt, I woke up, my little friend pumping, my eyes rolled back in abandoned ecstasy.

As the waves of orgasm died down, I gradually resumed consciousness. I opened my eyes for real... and almost threw up. That slippery fucking maggot kid from the cookie basket was between my legs, impaled on my divining rod taken so deeply down its throat that I must have fertilized its stomach. The thing was ravenously sucking my milk until I was dry. Its skin was slippery again, oily and alive, as it slid hungrily over my flesh.

Barely conscious at four in the morning, and dazed from the force of the orgasm, I could only stare through slitted, puffy eyes at the monstrosity devouring me. The incredible suction slackened as it sensed there was no more juice to be had, and I weakly backhanded the thing. It didn't even react; gathering my strength in disgust, I hit out with full force, knocking the piece of shit against the wall, where it hit with a splat before sliding stickily and lifelessly down the wall.

I stood up, my head throbbing with every heartbeat, and walked dizzily across the room, following my still-extended wand until I was right over Asta. There was a trail of blood on the wall pointing at the gooey little heap that lay on the floor. Guilt, disgust, and horror welled up in the pit of my stomach, and lurched out of my mouth and onto the dead heap.

First with the stage lights, and now, literally at my own hand, I had killed the thing again.

I jumped into my sweats, and scooped the horrid pile into a plastic bag, then carried it out into the yard.

There was no moon, which was fine with me, so I took the mess and buried it deep behind the barbecue pit. Blood-blisters on my hands, I rushed back into the barren house.

I stayed in bed the whole next day, just thinking about the little monster. There was no innocence there. This was no child, no infant. In the months I had been in possession of it, there had been no sign of growth or maturity or change. The thing is what it is, not what it's going to be. What that is, I don't know, but I soon would make an educated guess.

All I know is that day I was as fucked up as I've ever been—my ecstasy had been linked end-to-end with extreme revulsion. I'd been blown by the ghost of a monster baby. Not recommended. And then the fucking toilets backed up. I know that may seem mundane in this perspective, but it has everything to do with it. When I tried to flush, there was merely a gurgle, and I knew at once the damned machine was playing with its food. The lid was lowered and the plumber called.

I forgot about it until I had to go again that afternoon. Ready for relief, I lifted the lid, only to see that fucking squirmer Asta settled in the bowl, basking in dinner. I tried to flush it down to greet the legendary sewer gators, but the plumbing just backed up, spewing fouled water onto the bathroom floor.

Again, in anger, humiliation, and disgust, I beat the shit out of it, mangled the tortured little body, and killed it a third time. Big fucking deal. It would be back... no matter how often, or distant, or deeply I buried the thing.

The old Mexican woman knew I was her salvation the first time she saw me. I know that now. I must have destroyed the baby two dozen times by now, but it'll keep coming back.

To feed.

I can only imagine how long its last host continued to lactate and suckle the parasite that had claimed and

controlled her. It's like giving a stray cat a dish of milk—
you'll never shake the fucking thing. My lust to own it
was the closest thing to love it ever felt, and now we're
paired. Mated. For life.

It comes, each day after I kill it, to partake of my
body's castoffs—my cells, my essence. It sweats my
saliva, lives on my excreta, rejuvenated by my
spermatozoa.

God help me if it tastes my blood.

In the months since we shot the birth scene, sleep
has been only a distant dream that comes fleetingly. The
phone used to ring before I pulled it out, and many
people have come to the door and given up trying to find
me. Whenever my defenses drop, it comes home to
ravage me. I fade into exhausted sleep, knowing I'll
wake to find it devouring me, my sex slid deep into its
female region, another slippery appendage behind and
inside me, taking, not wasting anything, not even tears.

This thing will live as long as I do.

Maybe longer.

I had to have the little fucker to exploit. It was the
strongest emotion I could feel, and now I'm paying up. I
know of one sure way to end the torment. I can't believe
I've put it off so long. Asta may be indestructible, but I
am not. I have only a single regret.

I know I'll never make another movie.

Joy

The window-shaped box of honeyed sunlight crept its way up the body, incrementally traversed the length of the bed with a warming caress and met his smile with a kiss. Wrapped in the innocence of sleep, smoky tendrils of dreams taking leave for the day, Jon seemed every inch the peaceful, content Buddha in a blanket.

As the earthly world beckoned him from dreamland, gently nudging him awake, the beatific smile only broadened. A new day opened its arms and folded him into a loving embrace, and his face shone more brightly than the new sun that woke him. Shrugging off the cowl of sleep, he breathed deeply of the morning, sucking huge draughts of the world inside. He was the happiest man in the world.

That Jon woke and lived with such joy was not so surprising; that others didn't perplexed him. The complexity of his very being so overwhelmed him and filled him with an awe and respect for the creator that his life was lived in His honor. He cast off the bedclothes and stood naked at the window. The city below had already yawned and rubbed the sleep from its eyes, and was abuzz with people: in cars, in busses, in shoes, in hats, in love.

It all worked so well! People needed air to breathe, and air was there! It rained the water we needed to drink; plants and animals were in plentiful supply for food. How could anyone not live in gratitude of God's wondrous plan? He gave us wisdom, knowledge, the ability to fend for ourselves. If the weather turned inclement, he gave us animals to skin, stones to build with, hands to fashion, and minds to create the mortar.

The city was a monument to His gifts. Jon reached out of the window to touch life, felt it touch him back and shivered with the thrill. He watched nature and technology (which was, itself, borne of man's mind, which in turn was borne of nature, and therefore natural) shake hands under a grey-orange shawl that turned to an icy blue, scudded with cotton candy. He saw the street below, and craned his neck to see the towers of the skyscrapers that were built to raise the level of the earth to meet Him.

It made him smile. Life made him smile. He was filled with joy.

He became aware of the life around him: first, of course, the teeming masses on the streets and behind the windows around him. Then the pets, the dogs, cats and gerbils. The moths in his closet, the ants in the pantry that had no right to his Lucky Charms. They were obvious and evident. But he was aware, too, of the invisible life around him: the microbes, the germs, the little one-celled beasties that he was no doubt breathing in and out of his own body now. He was happy to host them, celebrated their house party inside him. It tickled, made him laugh.

Just standing naked as a newborn in the eye of God, a bright light to the moths of life, sent an electrical charge through his body that prickled his skin in gooseflesh, and shrank his scrotum so tight that his testicles grunted in protest. He knew he could be seen by anyone who chose to peer beyond the eighth floor window, and the thought renewed the delightful shiver. There was nothing dirty about the vessels we'd been given; they were beautiful adorned or unadorned. And besides, his penis was mostly hidden by his girth.

The thought of his penis made him aware of his suddenly overwhelming need to urinate. As he relieved himself in the superhero peanut butter jar, he marveled anew at the human mechanism. We eat, we drink, our systems process it and reject what we don't need. The miracle of elimination, experienced on such regular occasions, gave him so many opportunities to thank the creator for the blessed life he lived.

He filled the jar with hot, gold thanks, and walked it over to the window and poured it onto the thriving marigolds, making steam in the morning coolness. "This is for you," Jon said to heaven, "with all of my love."

Suddenly stroked by the brisk morning's fingers, Jon slipped into loose-fitting clothing and out of his tight-fitting room.

The Child of God walked among the people, and they were oblivious to his love. But Jon didn't need to speak his love to them; it radiated from his every pore. He was but a cell in the massive creature that inhabited the earth. He was a part of the machine He'd created in His image; and so were the others. Where was their joy? How could their every thought, their every waking moment not be dedicated to the euphoric appreciation of His bond, His will... His glory?

It lay all about them as it did about him. Everywhere one looked—even with closed eyes—He was present, His magical, wonderful plan ubiquitous and evident. He could hardly keep from laughing out loud with the joy.

But *Them*...

They were joyless, empty husks, littering the planet with their worthlessness. He was immediately sorry for the thought that anything He created was worthless, and he didn't really mean that. It's just that they should be more grateful. That's all. He felt guilty.

He was surrounded by them, a cherub bobbing in a sea of expressionless faces. When they did flash expression, it was invariably anger, hate, viciousness.

Faces on fire with resentment barked and howled and spat at one another, and he knew when night fell it would only be worse. Under the blanket of darkness, they scurried off into secret places, groping, tasting, using, and fighting one another, rending the night with flashes of gunfire, the glint of knives, a river of life flowing into the soil at their feet. And He let them do it. He gave them the choices, but They had to make them.

And so Jon walked among Them, loving Them through their hatred, giving Them his life. But all they gave him were their backs. The little round man in the ill-fitting clothes might well have been the Invisible Man for all the notice he was given. He knew he wasn't the sort of man who solicited looks, but he looked at them, marveling at their magnificence and variety. They were an endless array of artful flesh sculpture, and they didn't seem to even know it. And he... well, he wasn't handsome, really, but he was pleasant enough. And certainly they could feel the joy he generated. Perhaps it was the scars that made them—not really look *away*, since they never looked in the first place. They weren't disfiguring; they were barely noticeable pale lines etched on his face and body.

But even though he moved through Them like an unwelcome virus, he knew they shared the planet, the organism, and he was, as ever, at peace. His face, despite the thin white lines, was innocent, ageless, rosy, and devoid of the crevices left by a life lived. He could be in his thirties or his sixties; it was hard to tell. But he was forty-six.

But even though his innocent sweetness and love were ignored, they would continue to be broadcast. He was in love with them all, these walking, talking, hearing parts of God's body. He wanted to crush them in his embrace, smother them with the love and passion he felt for them, feel flesh against flesh in an act of global communion, feeling the blood of life coursing through their bodies together.

But all he could do was watch them.

Even though he couldn't hear them, he knew people whispered about him behind his back. Even that made him smile. *Everyone* else had the mechanism that allowed hearing; it was ordinary, everyday, average. But Jon was special; he had been chosen to possess twisted clots of solid flesh in place of the cochlea. He didn't have to hear all of the uglinesses multiplying around him. Words could never hurt him. They could say what they pleased, but they could not steer him from living his life for the One Who Counted. He'd never hear them fire their hateful guns, their lovers' quarrels, their corruption of their limitless gifts.

No, it was chosen that he should not hear. His head was wrapped in celestial, blissful cotton, and even a nuclear blast would go unnoticed. When he spoke—which was rare—his deaf-man baby-talk earned him special treatment; speaking made people over-play their acts of kindness. He would ask the lady in the convenience store for an Annabelle's Rocky Road, and she would puff and coo with a big, waxy red smile about how they were the best. And sometimes he didn't have to pay for it. He knew people thought he was stupid because he was deaf, but he wasn't. He knew the truth, and that made him smarter than all the others. And he got to be deaf.

Jon walked the same way every day, up and down the city streets by rote. His route was automatic, mindless, unchanging, yet no one ever noticed him, despite the twenty-some years of regularity.

His first stop was always the schoolyard. The joyful innocence of children brought him the closest to God. Their newness and freshness and incompleteness gave him hope and filled him with passion. Winter was best, because when they played foursquare, or tetherball, or hopscotch, or dodge-ball, the sight of their breath in the chill air coming out of their little bodies delighted him. Seeing the blood rise to crimson their cheeks thrilled him.

Though he couldn't hear their exuberant cries as he clutched the chain links of the fence, he could feel their energy, their youth, their Life. He wanted to play, too.

But he just watched.

To Jon, watching was participating. He was with them on the broken blacktop, skinning his knees and flushing cherry bombs down the toilets. His joyous reverie had its own peculiar deaf man's music, swelling his head with its cadences. His heart pounded a march that he shared with them, and gave him hunger.

But his heartbeat fluttered when he saw the New Girl. He thought it was Angela at first, but even he knew that wasn't possible. If Angela were still alive, she would be nearly his size now. But she was with Him, now, and had been for nearly three decades. Of course, He could have given her back to him, but Jon knew He didn't work that way. Besides, the New Girl's eyes were brown.

Angela's ice water eyes were the first thing anyone noticed about her. They had a depth and serenity that belied her five years; he could see Heaven in her eyes. Two years her senior, he'd been in love with his sister since her birth, teaching her the Piggy game when she was a baby, helping Daddy give her a bath, teaching her to walk, and sharing a room with her.

He saw Angela in the New Girl, and the House came back for the first time in years. The little house with Daddy's room, Jonny and Angela's room, the kitchen, and best of all, the concrete patio with the cardboard Pictsweet Train on the other side of the sliding glass door.

He had just finished painting her name on the engine when he used his Jerry Mahoney dummy to call her to see. She never hesitated; from the bathroom, her bright-eyed grin leading the way, she ran to her special big brother...

And through the sliding glass door.

It was a spectacular crash, and he didn't even take cover as it rained shards of glass, which shattered into smaller prismic crystals as it hit the concrete, showering her in rainbows of colored light as she stood before him in shock. She was motionless, uncomprehending on the patio, staring pool-eyed and questioning at him, as an atlas of crimson highways slowly appeared across her face.

He watched her ice water eyes go crimson as she spilled red lava tears down her face. She wilted before him into a pool of her own blood, slowly taking leave of Jon's world. She got to be with Him, and Jon didn't.

Though he couldn't hear it, Jon knew the bell had rung, because when he returned from the pool of Angela, the playground was empty, and the New Girl was gone. And so he continued to walk.

His hand brushed his face, and he could feel a few random, spiky whiskers reaching from his skin. There weren't many, and he never considered shaving them— that would be an affront to the Creator—and he wanted to see them. He had never cut his hair since his parents died. He'd never had the need; it had all fallen out the day of the accident. Even his brows and eyelashes. His body was as hairless as a newborn's. But just in the past couple of weeks, there was the trace of a beard.

He wandered into the subterranean public restroom, breathing deep of the natural scent of man as he entered. It was a real, unalterably natural scent that couldn't be hidden with deodorizers and perfume. He liked that. He didn't like chemicals.

As a wino kneeled in confession in front of the porcelain altar, Jon stood in front of the mirror, his image shivering in the flickering neon light. He could see his beard, and counted twenty-seven hairs—not just dark pores, but actual *hairs*—on his face.

The neon light made the tiny white scars on his face stand out, and he raised his pudgy fingers to trace them. They were artfully random, almost like the decorations carved into the faces of African tribesmen. He liked to feel them, and his sensitive fingers caressed the slightly raised lines with love and devotion.

He ran his long thumbnail across the numb lines, and found a new space under his eyebrows. Hooking the nail under the hairless brow, he cut into his flesh, and drew the nail across the brow beneath the skin like opening a letter. He repeated the cut under his other brow, and his eyes were awash with his blood. He leaned over the sink and let it dribble down the drain, where it would eventually meet his Maker.

"I love you," Jon told God as he gave him his blood, letting it drool into the basin until it congealed on his face.

Then he cleaned up, blotting the new wounds with toilet paper, and heading back into the sunlight.

Back on earth, Jon imagined the sounds of the birds and the trucks' air horns, and the chattering of mankind, invented sounds for them in his mind as he melded with the world. He could grant them any sound, and chose colors for them. The old woman was surely talking a blue streak. And the silent squawk of the crow that sat and shat in the tree overhead: almost certainly purple. The blast of the Mack truck that almost crushed the bicycle had to be red. Deep, dark, blood red. Crimson.

He never chose a path. Every day Jon let himself into the world, and let its tide drift him where it would. Today, its pattern was as random as any. It took him to school, to the park, and eventually to church.

He stopped in front of the church. It made him laugh. He watched the old ladies scurrying in and out of the mouth of man's massive testament to himself. They struck him as germs being breathed by the church. They built these monstrous gargoyles of guilt so they could celebrate their lives with He Who Granted Them Life for—what?—maybe an hour a week? Jon just could not understand their selfishness. Who needed to build a temple when there was no escaping its edifice? To merely be alive was to be worshiping at God's feet. These rationalizers, excuse-makers, mere *men* with their Holy Bible and their curliqued architecture were beside the point. It was so *obvious.*

The Invisible Man grew corporeal, unable to keep from chuckling at the folly of mankind. And faces turned to look at him as they skittered past, self-consciously racing into the church, eyes pink with tears, rheumy with age and regret, clouded by cataracts they hoped He'd rescind. They wanted to give back their gifts.

He watched a young mother and her infant skittishly approach the church, and he stopped smiling. The baby magnetized him with the perfection and innocence that came with the new child warranty. Their eyes connected, and Mommy turned to see what made her baby stare so.

Jon was not used to having attention paid to him when he was watching others. His mouth hung slack and dumb as he saw the baby's tomato face brighten and balloon into a toothless grin. Mom flushed with a proud smile at him, but he didn't see it. He and the baby both had expressions that climaxed with saliva drooling from the shiny lower lip.

The baby laughed, gleefully acknowledging another unformed, unstructured, incomplete flesh sculpture, and the wide baby's mouth made Jon gasp in horror. He never expected to see teeth in the infant's mouth, but he *did* expect a roof. Inside, where you would expect soft, pink membranes hooding the mouth, there was a gaping black cavern. If the child had had no chin, he could kootchie-koo her all the way through her cleft palate to her soft little brain.

Though she was at least fifty feet away, Jon's hands reached instinctively up, as if to caress this special, chosen child. Mother reared like a skittish pony, and whisked her daughter into the church. After reeling in the sunshine for what must have only been a minute, but felt like a good chapter of his life, Jon walked with lumpen disorder into a church for the first time.

It was a little different from what he had expected. Not nearly so grand or ethereal. It was scuffed and a little grimy, more earthly and real than he had anticipated, with the patina of life all about him. But he was taken aback by the vertiginous height of the ceiling overhead. The sun draped him with images of stained-glass angels; Jesus Christ himself, bleeding from his crown of thorns, lay across his back. Unaware of the whispered prayers that drifted smokily through the church, Jon wandered up and down the pews, eyes to heaven, forgetting for a moment what brought him in.

It was a grotesque manse, founded on fear and obedience, delighting in meting out violent punishment for breaking the sacrament. This was no palace of love and devotion. His God did not live here.

He glanced around at the frightened little mice who lit their candles. This was the home of their last hope, not their first. With his heightened sense of smell, Jon breathed the stench of death, of decay, of hopelessness. It was a joyless building. He didn't want to be here.

But then he saw the Baby again. It had been watching him since his entry, and he had not even been aware, despite the sixth sense that had linked them.

Mommy was kneeling, lighting a candle, and didn't notice the silent communication going on. Jon stared at the child with wide, loving, possessive eyes. He needed to own it, to get closer to God. It was so new and perfectly imperfect, so chosen, just as he was. They belonged together.

He made a decision. His eyes never breaking from the child's, he dashed up the aisle, thinking quietly but unaware that his lumbering footfalls echoed mushily through the stone walls. The Mother turned just in time to see Jon's ox-like visage loom up in front her as he took the googling child in his ham fists. Frozen in senseless un-understanding, her mind finally told her what was happening, and she screamed as she ran alter him.

Jon had never run before, and was not good at it. The fear of this house of a wrathful God washing over him, he felt the child's mother on his back, ripping at his face and eyes with her fingernails. Like a frightened bull, he kicked at her behind him, throwing her onto the pews, not hearing the resounding snap of her spine as it ripped apart.

Her screams of agony and despair filled the church, and the baby in his arms filled Jon's heart as he raced it outside.

As all things come to he who waits, the curtain of night fell over the city. Jon stepped out of the shadows and into the moonlit park, still cradling the baby in his arms. He loved his child, tickled it under the chin, and the babe chuckled with glee, and drooled on his finger. Jon stuck the wet finger in his mouth, savoring the newness.

He sat on the earth under a huge tree, the baby in his lap, and rocked back and forth, basking in the moonlight. From the center of the park, the lights of the city seemed a million miles away. They were surrounded by trees and brush and clean, black air.

As they smiled at one another, Jon could feel the beating of the child's tiny heart. He unbuttoned his shirt, just to feel this living thing against his skin. It was so warm, so alive, so foreign. Where hairless flesh touched flesh, there was a sheen of sweat. He slid the baby across his stomach, like running a pat of butter over a hot skillet.

As he held the child against him, it tried to suckle his sizable breast. He let it.

Jon looked from the baby's face to the face of the moon. To him, they were the same. They both reflected God; they were both His handiwork. The Child was the seed, and Jon knew he must plant the seed.

He removed a shoe, and dug through the new dew into the soft soil at the base of the tree. He would plant the seed, and give it nourishment, and in its place would grow a tree. He would tend God's tree, and it would reach high up into heaven, and finally up to God himself. And Jon would climb that tree, and sit at God's feet with Angela, and give him all his love.

Sweat began to drip from his hairless brow as he continued to dig, the child now asleep in his lap. The hole for the seed grew as the sole came off his shoe. But it was big enough. Jon lay the child in the dirt, and as he began to fill the hole over with dirt, the baby—for the first time—began to cry.

He patted the soil into place, muffling the cries that he couldn't hear anyway, lovingly planting his gift to God. Removing his clothing to stand naked over his gift in the moonlight, he could not hear the voices shouting at him.

But they were only words—only *men's* words—and it wouldn't have mattered to him. He didn't hear the frantic warnings through the bullhorn. He didn't even turn when the policeman fired a warning shot over his head. He was too busy offering his Gift to acknowledge mere mankind.

So the bullets took him by surprise. He felt the fist of God rip through his heart, and saw the geyser of blood explode from his chest and rain down on the newly planted soil. He felt one useless ear ripped from the side of his head, and was glad God had chosen to take it.

He smiled as he collapsed to the earth, blood dumping from the cavity where his heart used to be, propelled by its ghost rhythm. He saw his life spill onto the soil, and watched capillary attraction draw it down to fertilize the mewling, muffled seed that lay crying underneath.

As the Blue Men rushed to his monument to unearth the baby, Jon never even saw them. As his vision went dark, his spirit went bright; moonlight glinted off his toothy grin as his corporeal body emptied itself of life at the base of the tree. Before being completely enveloped in night's cowl, the Jon in his head climbed hand-over-hand up its branches, to sit with Angela at the feet of their creator.

But he never got there. There was no there to get.

And somebody turned off the moon.

Baby Shower

It wasn't like me to just take the girls and go, but I'd just had all I could take of her bullshit. No, she never lied to me about Paul (though she never mentioned Terri, but my sister Sally filled me in on that); I just couldn't live that kind of life with her any longer. Jesus, we've got kids now, or doesn't that mean anything?

It's the nineties, now, and we've long since graduated from the paisley VW van to a more discrete eggshell Volvo wagon. It was one thing when we were on the road with the band in our twenties; the bed-hopping stuff was required activity in Rock'n'Roll 101. But we've both made jump off the Lover's Leap of the Big Four Oh now, and the three-ways and psychedelics have given way to lid lifts and tummy tucks. Yes, my monthly Greenpeace pledge is up to date, and I even marched to protest Operation Rescue at the Family Planning Center, but I had to leave early for a client lunch at Harry's.

It's one thing to see your old lady gyrating under your drummer through a marijuana fog, and quite another to see her making goo-goo eyes with the principal across the cafeteria at a PTA meeting. I don't know... to me it kind of smacks of the depressing classifieds in those sleazy sex papers: you know, the over-sexed, under-toned pitifuls who hide their eyes under black bars while revealing their dimpled whale-flesh in column inches.

So while Sunshine (yes, Sunshine; she was christened Bernice, but the spirit is eternal) was at Whole Earth shopping for wheatgrass juice and chromium picolinate, I scribbled a note heavy on hurt and blame and four-and five-letter words, threw together some clothes, and ushered Tina and Chastity into the station wagon. I told the girls their Mom would meet us all at the desert, and that Memaw and Gramps couldn't wait to see them.

I savored Sunshine's eventual anger, losing myself in the rubber and asphalt freeway symphony. Fine; it was her turn to feel something other than lust. I knew if I had confronted her, she'd have talked reason, and I'm sick of reason. It was time for a little impulse for once in my life. Okay, call it cowardice if you like. I call it survival. But then it dawned on me that a more likely reaction was passive acceptance, and I got more pissed, with the Volvo cruising at a cool eighty-five down Freedom Road.

Tina had her head out the window, her cheeks balloon pockets for desert wind. Her sister, the sensitive one, was throwing up in a bag. I guess she got the neatness trait from me; some might call it anal retentive, but I call it tidy.

The first few hours on the nearly deserted Sunshine Highway were bliss. The sky was blue, the howdy-waving clouds fluffy, and the tranquility of family, however splintered, comforting. The choice was made, and being right felt righteous. The white line hypnosis set in, and despite the UV protection of my Foster Grants, Sunshine flooded my brain.

Married in the park by a Universal Life minister cum hash broker, our life was a succession of crashpads and fleshpole vaulting. Our first house, a converted turn-of-the-century bakery with a giant plaster donut on the roof, was the Big 0, a perfect symbol for our relationship. Even though the bakery had lain fallow for over a decade, we still had occasional Sunday morning tourists knocking on the door and ordering jelly donuts. Saturday nights, Sunshine stayed up late making acid crullers to give out free to unsuspecting families.

Our couplings were frequent, all the way to the end. It was not the frequency, merely the variety and satisfaction level that waned... for both of us. But while for me the pronging was replaced by ambition and breadwinning, hers was supplanted by school teachers, the Maytag man (not so lonely in *our* neighborhood), and even a *cop*... though in truth, it was his wife who inspired Sunshine on a labyrinthine maneuver worthy of Lucy Ricardo. Admittedly, Mrs. Bacon was a knockout, maybe even worth sleeping with a pig to rub up against... and Sunshine was definitely an equal opportunity bed partner. At least she didn't sleep with our Labrador, Roach, though she spoke about the possibility more than once on the brink of orgasm.

So maybe it's age, or growing up, or the shifting of morality, or the fear of death, or the encroachment of parenthood and the fucking legacy of the Reagan-Bush years, but I just couldn't subject the kids to any more of her sexual irresponsibility.

I looked over at the girls, the beautiful, miniature beings so lovely and trusting and adorable. Mine. The amazement I felt over them was overwhelming. Yes, it's been going on as long as bipeds have trod the earth, and anyone can have babies, rich or poor, black, yellow, or green, but *my* children! Parts of me made them, formed them, and despite the lack of my Y chromosome, you could see my genetic material passed on to the little squirmers. Their innocence, trust, and unconditional love made me their willing prisoner. Of course, they'll hit their teens and hate and reject me, but now, all they feel for me is love and respect... and I for them. Life was beginning to feel meaningful to me for the first time in years.

Chastity had stopped puking, and Tina was whisper singing to Doobie, her imaginary friend. She had my voice, I was proud to note. Maybe it would serve her better than it had me. My folks hadn't seen the girls since Christmas, and I knew they'd be thrilled by them. There was always a kinship there; Tina had her Memaw's eyes: sheer black and white windows of intelligence. No visible irises, just whites punctured by ebony pupils, haunting and piercing. Chastity had her mother's eyes: green and gold, one of each. Mine were like my father's, if it matters. Ice water blue, pale and failing. His glasses were so thick his eyes seemed the size of baseballs behind them, and I resigned myself to his fate. You couldn't get contact lenses if your eyes were that bad: the lenses would be so thick you couldn't blink over them.

So I thought it would be fun to sing together on our vacation, and belted out some Beatles. The girls didn't know any of the words, and didn't seem particularly interested, either. Same with CSN&Y. Gentle Giant. The Move. And I sure as hell didn't know any songs by *their* fave raves, the Butthole Surfers. Sublime? Give me a break! How can you sing that crap anyway... that's not music, just a bunch of noise. What happened to songs you could *sing*? Of course, they didn't get that from Sunshine, either. Her taste runs to the folkie bores: Joni Mitchell, Richie Havens (in fact, one of her most alluring attributes when I met her was the claim that she had just aborted a Richie Havens fetus the week before).

So, I let them play a Snot Rag tape until they spotted a Jack in the Box and the Hunger Zone kicked in. We drove Gila Bend Jack crazy with our shouted orders, feeling a little electric zizz of guilt for the mountain of cholesterol that lay before us. Back home, the girls and I would sneak out of Sunshine's macrobiotic jail cell every week or so to indulge in deep-fried fantasies, some good old American processed sugar, heavily breaded and salted. Tina, the practical one, did order the chicken sandwich, though, because it came on a whole-wheat bun.

We ate and I drove. It got dark, and they slept. It felt like we were surely losing our way, that there couldn't be civilization way out here in the dunes and two-lane blacktop. But no, Mom's directions were quite explicit; the Volvo bisected the desert, and eventually nosed the ruby dawn sun into the sky. There it was, like the opening titles of *Close Encounters:* "Now Entering Ponce de Leon, Nevada, population 213".

I wanted to turn around. Ponce de Leon was sand and pool supply stores and health food parlors and mobile homes and sand and a church and a post office and sand and old people. *All* old people, bustling about the little clot of civilization like the Disneyland at the doorstep to Saint Peter's gates. If any of these morning folk were under eighty or so, you wouldn't know by looking.

I pulled off the Fountain of Youth Presidio and onto Rejuvenation Road. Dad was right; I couldn't—and didn't—miss it. The Volvo wheezed and crunched up the rock driveway in front of their mobile estate, and I was suddenly aware of silence. The hours of engine hum burrowed through the headcheese of my brain and left its ghost within. The silence took time to adapt to.

I reached for the seatbelt, and noticed for the first time that a roll of flab lay over it. I actually had to lift my belly up to unbuckle, and the quease of embarrassment and self-loathing welled up underneath. Of course, Dad wouldn't say anything; he's as wide as he is tall, and, from what Sally had said, not in the best of health.

The girls were coming to life, but before they could get out "are we there yet?" Mom and Dad were out of the trailer and onto the quartz.

I wasn't so sure I was at the right place at first. And then I thought that pod people had replaced my parents with a frightfully malformed simulation. But as they grew close, baseball eyes asparkle, there was no doubting. Oh, Mom was Mom: you know, silver hair hennaed orange, polyester stretch pants, black bustier, and that roadmap face, creased by decades of cigarettes and after-hours living. Old, but still Mom.

But Dad was another story. If he hadn't been squeezing Mom's butt with excitement, I'd have guessed she was flinging with the Carnation man. It looked like he'd just unzipped and stepped out of a Dad suit! He was no longer the egg man... not even the walrus; he'd shed his Siamese twin and become downright skinny! Old-man skinny, leathery from the sun, his dentures glinting against the brown, dry skin that crinkled into a jolly smile. I looked down and sucked in my gut, but they didn't seem to notice. They were too busy beaming.

"Look at those babies!" Mom squealed, and grabbed the girls, rubbing their apple cheeks against her crepe paper face. The girls looked at me with big Keane-painting eyes, and I gave them a nod. They gingerly hugged back.

Dad saw me checking him out. "Noticed I dropped a couple pounds, did you?"

"You look great... both of you!" Mom was sensitive.

Mom didn't even look at me; she was squeezing the love out of her granddaughters. "Oh, these little girls!"

Chastity was offended. "I'm a young lady," she pouted.

"Well, oh my yes!" It was the first time I noticed that my parents were old. Yes, they were in their seventies, but they were always just Mom and Dad, forever thirty-five. But I saw them as strangers and found them old. Elderly. Aged. Seniors. And they said Old-People things like "oh my yes!"

"Well, for gosh sakes—" Dad's old man impression again—"come on in and get some grub! Memaw's been cookin' it up since before sunup!"

Old people always start doing things before sunup, don't they? And they go to bed before the news, and keep the thermostat up above 80. Mom and Dad were *old*. What a concept.

Breakfast was a concept that made me uncomfortable, after hefting the spare tire to unleash myself from the front seat. I really wasn't hungry. "I've put on a couple pounds..." I hemmed, rocking on rounded heels, hoping no one would notice. Hope sprung eternal, and we were soon gathered 'round Mom's repast.

Well, the mobile home dining room looked like the brunch at the Royal Hawaiian, the table groaning under a repast that could feed the proverbial troops: tropical fruits, omelets, sausages, steaks, muffins, and every other bowel blocking masterpiece Mom could conjure up... all under the fishnets and flowers of The Islands. Mom (Dad called her Naniloa now) was on her King Kamehameha kick now, and the garden isle was everywhere. She seems to go in king cycles; when I was a kid, it was Midas. She spray-painted everything gold.

Since Attila and his Huns weren't expected, we correctly assumed that we were expected to consume the ingestibles. My stomach gurgled, and Tina's eyes widened. She tippy-toed up to whisper in my ear: "I'm concerned about my cholesterol intake, Daddy."

My Dad, even without the hearing aid, picked up on it. "Then you just stick with the fruits and the turkey sausage, PeeWee." She liked PeeWee.

He turned to Chastity. "How you doin', Princess?" I could tell that "Princess" was pretty lame to the Nickelodeon-and MTV-addled, but her gap-toothed grin through masticated hash browns showed she liked him anyway. I always called her Chas, because Sunshine couldn't resist calling her Titty. I guess even Princess beats Titty.

The wicker chair grunted like a rusted gate when I took my seat, and my best friend, old Mr. Guilt, reared his ubiquitous head. "Don't go off your diet for us..."

Mom smiled a mommy grin. "What diet is that?"

More guilt; a faux pas, a foot in mouth. "Well, you and Dad have dropped some of that excess baggage, so I thought... you know..."

It was Dad's turn for laughter, despite the lack of a bowlful of jelly to shake. What was so fucking funny?

"Nobody diets in Ponce de Leon! It's that good desert air, clean living, late to bed and early to rise, activity, wholesome food!" But his real wink-wink keep-this-to-yourself secret to everlasting health? At least one good B.M. every day.

Chas and Tina knew from B.M.s, and giggled. Even I was starting to relax. The meal progressed, and I began to remember family. The blood link that bound us, and the happiness it provided. Its fragile, handle-with-care glass was shattered on the kitchen tile by Sunshine, and all it took was dinner with Memaw and Gramps to glue it back together.

I watched them eat; they blossomed in the role of hosts, and despite their age looked more beautiful than I remembered them. As all of us dive-bombed the steaming platters of conspicuous consumption, I sneaked the occasional peek at them. I saw Mom flush and give Dad an embarrassed, loving wink. And Dad's hand slid under the tablecloth, staying under and spraying Mom's apple cheeks an even brighter shade of crimson. I had to look away... they were my *parents!*

Ponce de Leon agreed with them. I was happy for them and their marriage—they never acted like this when I lived at home. They seemed so close and loving and life affirming that it brought me back to the dark side of Sunshine and the depression she wrought.

Soon I was ready for my own good B.M. and a nap, so the folks took the girls out for some frozen yogurt.

The long drive from California, coupled with the gargantuan meal, suddenly hit me like a time-release Valium, and I went in to lie down.

It felt spectacular to slide naked under a clean, white (non-tie-dyed) sheet in the crisp, dry Nevada heat. It was too dry to sweat, and my pores prickled into excited gooseflesh as they made contact with the slick cotton. My nerve endings were puckered and heightened, and despite the exhaustion, my body felt covered with sensitive, erectile tissue.

Alone in the goldening desert sunlight, an erection raged as never before. Perhaps my little partner sensed his release, and stood proud and independent. But I was slipping in and out of slumber, and when my hand found it and fumbled, it melted.

When my faltering dream brain realized nothing was going to happen, I dropped it.

I woke up in the dark, not quite sure where I was, my brain smothered in molasses, my fist clenched around my penis. Then I remembered where I was and why, and the irrational fear gave way to another attempt at self-gratification. I squeezed a few times, but the effort was noncommittal; too much like work.

And I looked up to see little Tina's silhouette watching me from the doorway. "Want some, Daddy?" she asked me in that adorable little cartoon-girl voice. "It's peach." Oh, yeah... yogurt.

"No, thank you, Teen." My face burned red, but with luck it didn't glow in the dark. "Dad's taking a nap, okay?"

Sunshine used to dance around the house in the buff all the time, saying how it was so healthy for the kids, but even under cover of the sheet, I was embarrassed. Besides, even though she never exercised, Sunshine had a perfect body, the bitch.

And I had this spare tire.

"Can I watch you sleep?" In my haze, I had forgotten my little girl was still there.

"No, please, honey, it's not polite. Just let me sleep a little while longer, okay?" She understood polite, and left me alone. I just couldn't wake up, and didn't really want to. I was out immediately, to dream of standing fat and naked in a beauty contest with Chippendale dancers... and Sunshine was the judge.

I awoke in a puddle of my own sweat, drenched as if I had just climbed out of a swimming pool. The heat that put me to sleep now hung oppressively over me in the night.

The trailer's darkness was pierced only by the blue light of the television, the silence broken only by its high, dog-level electronic squeal. It drilled through my groggy head.

I got up to find the girls asleep in their sleeping bags in front of the Playboy Channel. The sound was off, as if they thought they could get away with something... and they did. But the squeal of the picture tube was an ice pick through my brain, and I switched it off.

The room was totally dark now, and I just stood in the middle of it, feeling the darkness blanket me. Everything was still and quiet in the desert... so far removed from life in the big city. It felt like there were earplugs in my ears, as if silence can only be achieved through muffling sounds out, not by eliminating them. It felt claustrophobic.

Mom and Dad were gone, and with the girls sleeping, I felt very alone and melancholic. Careful not to trip over them, I walked outside.

Shaking the dumb fog of sleep from my brain, I stood under a magnificent sky, lit by a full moon and a buffet of pinprick constellations. I found myself breathing deeper out here than in the city, filling my lungs with the rich oxygen mix of the desert, the cilia that lines my lungs screaming out for more and more of the intoxicant.

After hours of driving, and more of sleeping, my muscles had contracted, and it felt good to uncocoon them. I stretched and walked, and my feet tingled as blood filled them. My mind breathed and wandered as I walked with my hands in my pockets, kicking the loose gravel that was the street. It was a stroll blessed by solitude and reflection, and bitterness dried up with my sweat in the light, palmy breeze.

Turning onto the Presidio, blissful isolation also evaporated into the night heat. Ponce de Leon's main drag was buzzing with night-lifers! All two hundred and thirteen raisined citizens were out on the street, drinking, dancing, carousing, and just having one hell of a time.

Disneyland to the contrary, this was the happiest place on earth. I stood at their periphery, alone, apart from them more than just geographically, and envied them their joy. Drops splashed on the gravel at my feet, and I wondered if it could rain from a clear sky. But the rain was falling from my eyes.

I felt like an illegal alien.

The dress code was the elderly inevitable: plaid walk shorts with Hawaiian shirts and black socks with brown shoes for the men, tight polyester pedal pushers with stirrups and short-sleeved white blouses for the ladies. The bolder amongst them wore only bras on top, acknowledging the heat and liberalism of the desert.

But one thing took a little while to become apparent... there wasn't an overweight soul among them.

I had to chew on that for a moment or two. Have you ever been in a group of senior citizens where no one was at least a little pleasingly plump? You know, it's not their fault, metabolisms change and all, but it seems to me that old folks are always either over—or underweight. These were the slimmest, trimmest oldies I'd ever seen.

My age made me an outsider, but it was my paunch that made me most uncomfortable among them.

Not that these were all fitness fanatics, mind you. Some of them were downright skinny, their flesh hanging from their skeletons like crepey draperies. And they were eating and drinking like there was no tomorrow—and from the looks of some of them, there wasn't. Somehow, these folk could down all the yogurt banana splits, strawberry daiquiris, and grasshopper pies they wanted, and never pay for their Epicurean sins.

I can indulge occasionally, but not without a visit from old man Guilt... or his brother Mister Pounds.

But the elderly citizens of Ponce de Leon flourished in a kind of Grey Sin City of overindulgence. It was as if that desiccating sun melted their fat and evaporated it. I didn't want to be there when it finally rained.

I was sweating again; it ran in salty rivers off my body, only to dry in the breeze. I really wanted to take a shower, especially now that I found myself entering this hot spot.

A particularly jolly group stopped me and smiled with recognition. "Say—" the old man said, poking me in the chest, "you're Dick and Paula's boy, aren't you?" Oh, good, they were expecting me.

The man had a good-looking older woman on each side, and he winked conspiratorially, knowing I'd noticed. How could I not? One of the women was particularly well-endowed, and kept them holstered only in a sheer brassiere that showed her nipples. I tried not to look, especially because they cleaved in papery creases, but exposed nipples are exposed nipples, and they are made for eye contact, elderly or otherwise.

She knew I noticed, could probably feel the heat from my scorching blush, and her nipples puckered with her smile. I remembered a time in the fifth grade when my ancient teacher leaned down to chastise me, and I peeked down her dress at the creased, hanging, deflated water balloons that dangled from her chest in wrinkled sacs. I was disgusted by the sight, but stimulated by the idea of bare breasts. Pavlov's dog barked, and I could feel swelling down below.

The other woman was dressed more chastely: she actually wore a blouse. She smiled, too, naughtily blinking giant come-hither eyes behind her inch-thick eyeglasses. I wondered if the bright sun could accidentally burn her face through the lenses. Maybe these were just her nighttime glasses.

But it was time to speak. "You folks having some kind of festival? What's the occasion?"

The three of them giggled. "Occasion?" the old man said with some surprise. "Hell, it's Tuesday! That a good enough reason? We kick up a fuss every night, 'cept Sunday. Never on Sunday. We're as irresponsible as all get out, aren't we, girls? Especially Susie, here!" Susie—with the boobs—giggled, and actually *goosed* the old guy, I swear to God. And he squealed like a stuck pig.

The goosing grandma's lascivious smile told me it was more for my benefit than the goosee's. The townlet was really jumping now, a geriatric Woodstock under a vast, deep blue tapestry of night. Lots of lights, friendliness, and despite the awkwardness I felt here, everyone was doing their best—in their own way—to make me feel welcome.

I scanned the horizon. "Have you seen my parents?" Lascivious Susie Boobs gave a nasty sort of grin: "Who hasn't?"

The old guy seemed to cut her off. "Not tonight, son." He gave Susie a look.

"No, not tonight," Susie agreed.

"Not tonight, uh-uh," The Eyes echoed.

"But I'm sure they're around," Pops said. "Have yourself a time."

And they rejoined the party.

I wandered through Ponce de Leon, amazed by the overwhelming *joie de vivre* in the air. Under other circumstances, this could be contagious. But I was busy chewing my anger and hurt, savoring and nursing some festering hatred, and that felt better to me then than any love of life could.

But I partook of the town's pleasures nonetheless: a yogurt shake here, a margarita there, a couple shots of tequila somewhere else. And frankly, I could not keep the anger in place. Before long, it fizzed and went flat, like an open bottle of Perrier in the fridge. Or in the oven, more precisely. At any rate, the pain had worked itself to a dull throb, and even that was getting hard to feel. Damn it.

So I continued to walk the boulevard exchanging howdies, a yogurt sundae in one hand, a grasshopper in the other, and a shit-eating grin plastered across my face. I was a mirror to all those smiles that walked up to me, near-perfect, man-made porcelain choppers that spoke to me, welcomed me, chattered, birthed tongue-snakes and jolly sounds and big, enveloping funhouse laughs that drilled through my alcohol overcoat and into my dying brain.

Faces were watching me everywhere—don't tell me they weren't—and I'd have climbed the high dive to jump into their pit.

I reached the end of the main drag, becoming one with the citizenry of Ponce de Leon, and stood in front of a mysterious, black concrete box structure. No sign, no lights, but it looked like a bar, and there was a steady stream of customers entering... and very few finding their way out. Looked good to me. I love a mystery.

There was a heavy black curtain blocking the doorway, and the thought that there was something to hide inside made it all the more appealing. I hefted the curtain and stuck in my head, only to come face to school-cafeteria-worker face with a grumpy looking lady with her white hair pulled back in a netted bun. She greeted me brusquely: "You don't want to see this, son."

On the contrary. I really did want to see this... especially now. She protested; this is a private club, and blah, blah, blah, blah. I think it was the tequila that shoved her aside with the ten-dollar bill in her D-cup; it couldn't have been me. It all seemed so seductively seedy that I couldn't resist its irresistible force.

This was hardly one of those roadside sucker traps with a cage and a "Baby Rattlers" sign that turns out to have toy rattles inside. No, this place offered more than its money's worth.

I made my way down a long corridor that emptied out into a dark, smoky den, filled with hot-blooded oldies groping one another. Something more than the desert air had heated these reprobates to the point of spontaneous combustion; the Fountain of Youth emptied out into this primordial pool, and men and women had their hands and mouths behind zippers and buttons, in places you'd wash before and after touching.

It must have been three hundred degrees in there... and it was getting hotter.

The faces of the groping groupers were not on one another; no, their eyes were all aimed in one direction as they fondled their way to heaven. They were all watching a tiny, intimate stage at the front of the room.

My head turned in 100-frames-per-second Scorcese slow motion, and my heart stopped. This was the show to end all shows, the greatest show on earth, quintessence, the *piece de resistance*.

My mother and father, the Ward and June Cleaver of the Carpenter household, were buck naked, rutting like missionary weasels, wide open for business. I was staring into the conjoined plumbing that launched me into orbit on Spaceship Earth, rocking to a steadier beat than Charlie Watts ever hit. My mother and father, Dick and Paula, all flesh and hair and perspiration, were fucking onstage for an audience.

Dad looked up at me in mid-stroke with an expression that I may have mistook for embarrassment, and said, "I thought you were home sleeping..."

I wished. Keeping down my gorge, I ran outside, crashing clumsily through the dry, scraping sound of elderly applause.

I tore through the streets, my head spinning, and felt the sky growing around me. It grew dense and heavy, pregnant with something spectacular as I ran through the staring faces along the Presidio.

Grandparents were turning their faces from me to the gathering thunderheads, and the town, or merely my senses, hushed into funereal, expectant silence. I continued to run from them.

The time-lapse sky was black with wet, spongy nimbus clouds, which ripped open with a frightening roar, suddenly dumping sheets of bath-warm water to the parched, sandy ground. Old people were screaming in my wake back in town, like they thought there were the Wicked Witch of the West, afraid of melting like they do in Oz.

Lightning cracked and arced overhead, igniting the night sky, and leading me back to the mobile estate. The girls are terrified by lightning and thunder, and I had to get back to them, and their real world, and hold them in my arms, and feel them breathe, their little hearts beating a double tattoo against my chest, and smell their little-kid fear scent, and make everything real and okay for them... and them for me. I had to forget what I had seen.

The street behind me emptied of life in moments, and was soon the Fountain of Youth River. It slowed me, sobered me (like I needed that), and I followed the lightning to Grandma's House.

When I crashed through the front door, the girls were hugging in front of David Letterman, terrified. They looked up at me and leapt into my arms, shivering, their little bodies covered in gooseflesh. I really felt like a Daddy as I held them, kissed them, and told them rain stories. It may have been the most intimate family gathering we'd ever had.

The rain was relentless, the cats and dogs long since graduating to elephants and giraffes. The girls went to bed with me and we all fell asleep pretending to be lying under Yosemite Falls.

Somebody kicked the dream reception unit into overdrive, and as the torrents of rain battered the trailer's metal roof, visions of Sunshine battered my brain. She was lying on a giant round waterbed, birthing our babies and licking them clean, the ultimate earth mother. She nursed the still-wet Tina as Chastity was sliding out the canal. But there was more to follow...

Me. I watched my own adult head come gasping out from between her legs, and saw the fluids gushing out around me. I emerged, naked, wet and crying, five-foot-ten, balding and with a prominent spare tire.

Then I was the other me, the one crawling out from between her legs, and saw that we were on the little stage of the weird club on the Presidio, and an excited, masturbating audience of toothless senior citizens made wet, gummy noises of approval. I cried and turned to Mother Earth, but there was a baby at each breast, and no teat for me.

Suddenly, my face purpled, and the heat was overpowering...

As it was in the trailer, when I finally awoke in the middle of the next afternoon.

The rain had evidently ceased some time ago, leaving in its wake a stuffy, sultry afternoon. The soft silence in the otherwise empty trailer was soothing at first, but grew intimidating, almost frightening.

When I stood up from sweat-soaked sheets, my head spun, and I almost had to collapse. Surrendering to an overwhelming call of nature, I retreated to the bathroom, and let loose my own river of no return. I felt relieved of several pounds by the time I flushed, and looked in the full-length mirror.

What happened to my love handles?

I mean, it wasn't Arnold Schwarzenegger staring back at me from the glass, but it seemed my paunch of insecurity had fled, leaving me svelte around the belt.

Overnight.

Light-headed and lighter-bodied, I felt as if I might float as I made my way to the ethereal silence of the living room. My mom and dad weren't there.

And neither were the girls.

No problem, I told myself, though my intuitive self was less reasonable. Nausea rode up my gorge, and I went outside.

The silence was overwhelming. The air was still and heavy, the desert stands motionless, the sun cradled in a cloudless blue frame. But the arid wasteland of Ponce de Leon, Nevada, had been transformed,

•

had become a wonderland of tropical fauna! What was quartz sand was now something green and ubiquitous, a feathery, tendrilled vine, an Instant Kudzu—just add water!—like those Magic Rocks you grow in fishbowls.

In the hot sun, you could actually see steam rising from the thick jungle stuff, and my jaw lolled several inches down my chest. And if you watched closely enough, you could actually see the stuff growing.

There was not a living soul to be seen in the trailer park. In the middle of the afternoon. In the middle of the jungle.

Intuitive me took command, and I panicked. Where was my family? The Volvo was still there; maybe they walked into town. It wasn't so far; I'd done it myself the night before. I jumped behind the wheel, and tried to start the car. Without success. It didn't even bother to growl at me before giving up the ghost: just a *click!* and that awful desert silence.

I got frantic, and started running house to house— I mean trailer to trailer. My parents and my babies were gone, and so were the other inhabitants of Ponce de Leon. No one was home, and I ran down the gravel road into town. It was a jungled ghost town, devoid of any but vegetable life. And mineral death. Not an animal in the mix.

The creeping greenery breathed its steamy exhaust over the dead and drying community as it enveloped it, covered it, dressed it for dinner.

Where were my babies?

I broke into shops and homes and already rusting cars and RVs, but the town had been abandoned. It looked like a 1950s nuclear test site, but without even the Ozzie and Harriet dummies standing in the kitchen for the illusion of life.

My throat was raw from screaming for the girls, and I felt the hundreds of square miles of desert surrounding me closing in, squeezing my jigsaw brain, baking me and basting me in my own juices. My scalp sizzling and scrambling in the late-day sun, I trod back that long road to the mobile estate.

I stood looking at my parents' trailer, without the heart to enter. It was a desert tomb, and waves of heat rose from its roof as it reflected the slowly setting sun. And then, a face appeared at the window. Two!

Chastity and Tina!

I ran in and they ran out, and we collided at the door in a roundelay of hugs and frightened kisses.

"Where is everybody?" Tina asked me, and I couldn't give her an answer. I couldn't be a real father. All I could tell her was the truth: "I don't know." And I couldn't fix it for her. But anything else they needed, well, I was there and theirs...

And we went back inside, where they had turned the air conditioner on high, and I held them for hours, until we fell asleep, waiting for Memaw and Gramps.

The next day fell on us, finding us alone and deserted. We had power, color TV, food, and a roof over our heads, but no phones, and no way out. We were stuck in the middle of nowhere, pioneers, prisoners of the sun, surrounded by its sea of dunes. All we could do was wait, and watch the desert kudzu creep.

Dad had a huge stock of Dos Equis, and I made a ferocious dent in his collection.

I don't know how many days we spent making do, but I remember that even the kudzu was beginning to go brown and crispy in the heat when I discovered the girls' new secret. I was nursing Dos Equis *numero cinco* in the Beer Chair when I heard them talking and giggling outside. Something told me they were talking to *someone,* not to each other. I tried without success to hear the third voice.

Curiosity picked me up by the scruff of the neck, and I dipped around the side of the trailer, crunching through the thick groundcover. They heard me, and their little heads jerked around guiltily, and I knew they were hiding something. I stood at full, intimidating Daddy height in front of them and asked what they were hiding.

The power play was successful; they silently parted, and revealed something *squirming* in a bundled blanket on the foliage. I looked at them, cautious. "Will it bite?" So much for intimidation.

They just giggled. "Of course not, Daddy," said a very sophisticated Chastity. So I hesitantly crouched down and opened the bundle.

It was alive. It was pink and sweating in the heat. It was a *baby:* a beautiful, perfect, baldheaded, weensie-fingered little boy. I marveled at his perfect, miniature fingernails, his wrinkled little tootsies, his toothless gums, and his crystal clear, ice-water blue eyes. Just like mine. And Dad's.

But the biggest marvel was its very existence.

"Whose baby is this?" I needed to know. "Where did he come from?"

"It's ours!" Tina announced, a little petulant.

"This is not your baby!"—I knew they weren't *that* precocious—"Where are his Mommy and Daddy?"

"Ain't got none!" said Chas. "No grown-ups around here but you!"

"Don't say ain't," Tina scolded, then, giggling: "it ain't proper."

I had to put this back on track. "I mean it, now! Where did your little friend come from? Where did you get him?"

Chas sighed. "From the New Forest, Daddy," as if it were the most obvious thing in the world. Of course, the New Forest.

Then Tina posed a curious question: "Do you think storks come here for vacation, Dad?"

I had to see this New Forest, and the girls led the safari. I carried the baby, wondering what kind of forest could exist in this reconditioned bombsite.

But there we were, Lawrence of Ponce de Leon and his family, out on the green-but-browning dunes, zigzagging across the desert until we reached the oasis. It was a little valley, lush with vegetation, suddenly twenty degrees cooler than the hundred-and-six-degree hike.

We sat in the shade of a strange, pink tree that reached out to give us comfort with branches, which waved in a growing breeze. The baby was wriggling like a little worm, and I let him crawl across the vegetation. He moved to a soft mound at the base of another tree, and rolled around in the thick clump of baby tear that grew green and moist in the shade.

Then he stopped and gave a drooling giggle of excitement. The little mound *moved!*

Tina and Chastity squealed with excitement; they knew what was going on, if I didn't. "It's happening!" Chas shouted. "Another one is coming up!"

The baby just giggled and goo-gooed, as the mound continued to rumble. The girls ran closer, and I reached up to pull them away. They ignored me, and ran right back. I just stared at the mound with them, bewildered and expectant... and a little scared. The sod puckered, then ripped open from within. Crumbles of soil came from underneath; something was climbing out of the dirt!

Tentatively, I moved closer, then immediately jumped back as something thrust up through the soil, reaching high into the arid sky:

A tiny, shriveled pink-white human hand!

Shivering with excitement, the girls started to dig the dirt away, while the baby at my feet just watched and gurgled happily. Tina and Chastity swaddled the new baby in an old T-shirt, brushing the soil from its skin.

"Oh, boy!" Tina exclaimed. "It's a girl!"

"Look at her eyes," said Chas. "They're like Tina's!" Yep, black-and-white eyes, just like Tina's. Just like her grandmother's. The little boy just looked up at us with his calm, ice blue eyes and smiled, like he knew us. He was happy to have another like him, and waddled over to be with the new little baby. They both looked at us, and it was obvious that they would be a part of the family. There was certainly a familial resemblance you didn't even need to look close to see.

It took some getting used to. The girls seemed relieved to not have to keep it secret any longer. What could I do, punish them? So it wasn't long before they told me about the others, the dozens of babies they were watching over in other homes scattered throughout the community. And there were no doubt more on the way.

We have the two living with us in the trailer, and they are handful enough; imagine what it's like tending to all the others. There is no time for boredom. But Richard and Paula are the best and the brightest. They are family, and united we stand. The girls love them, have their own pet names. Richard is Pee Wee, and to Tina, Paula is Naniloa.

Every so often, when the night is blue-black and pocked with stars, we tell the little ones the story of how the rains fell on Rejuvenation Road, and washed it clean for us.

But I think they knew the story better than we did.

Dream On Me

"It's not my fault!" he said through the chill that dried his sweat.

"Of course it isn't your fault. It happens sometimes. I understand."

He was startled to look up into Martika's eyes as she cradled his head in her lap. He expected to see Linda, though he should have known better.

Martika, of course, didn't understand. This wasn't about tumescence defeating penetration. The blood that had pounded through his veins had stalled out, defusing any active organs. The passion had been sapped by Linda, who had invaded their lovemaking, even from the grave.

He looked up past Martika's breasts and into Linda's face, crushed by guilt and nausea. It was Martika who continued to speak, but Linda who stared. And Linda who understood... and tried to blame him.

But he was the Blameless Man. He couldn't bear the guilt, never had. Not only over Linda. Ever. He couldn't bear fault, and was expert at rationalization that relinquished him from responsibility. He was unable to shoulder hurt feelings or pride, and unwilling to accept fault for pain.

Martika leaned over him, the brown nipple of one breast brushing his cheek. "You're shivering. You cold?" She stroked his face, which broke out again in a chilly sweat. He wanted to open his mouth and nurse away the pain, let it draw out a lust that would overpower his memories with carnal bullets, to pull her legs open and part the red sea with his Moses.

But Linda sat on his shoulder.

He was back in the Audi; Linda had insisted on driving the new car. Bob's Big Boy and a drive-in movie: let's play teenager. He honestly didn't care. "Whatever you want" was the refrain. It had become a joke to him. He meant it; when it didn't matter, he said it: "whatever you want," even though he knew it made her defensive, as if a spoiled little princess being indulged, getting her way. He could tell that this night it pissed her off. They sped down Ventura as he hid in the Calendar section.

"What do *you* want to see?"

"Whatever you want..."

"Don't you have an opinion? Doesn't anything *matter* to you?"

But he didn't have time to answer. He saw the pipe truck before she did; his scream made her crush the brake pedal to the floor, and the car made a screaming doughnut before righting itself just in time to slam head-on into the flag-tipped pipes jutting out of the back of the truck.

Miraculously, they missed him; predictably, she had been impaled. The half-inch aluminum javelins made webs of the windshield and a pincushion of the bucket seats. She was spiked to her leatherette seat like a butterfly pinned to its velvet showcase, the anger still gripping her face. Her blood watered the asphalt through the feeding tube that pierced her heart, first in beating gushes, soon in a weakening, dribbling flow.

She was still looking at him, her eyes sightless but filled with blame and fury, her hand a claw, digging into his thigh so hard that blood was drawn: his only injury from the accident.

And then...

"It's not my fault."

"I can't do this any more. I'm not going to share you with a ghost."

He could see Martika with sudden clarity, as if the camera operator had suddenly racked focus. And what he saw shook him. She could see through him, see the deceit, the wicked core he'd gone to such lengths to keep secret under a hide of humanity. His heart of guilt was lain bare to her.

"I'm sorry," he said, feeling doubly naked as she watched with the lidless brown eyes that suddenly saw all. It was all he could say.

"So am I. If I'm going to be with you, I want to be *with* you. I mean, I know you don't want to hear this, but I love you, Andy. I really do care about you. But Linda is dead! Get her out of my bedroom!"

Or he'd lose her. As he'd lost them all since Linda.

Martika was the first who really mattered. Her sweetness was genuine, deeply rooted, not a ruse to be dropped when he'd been captured, only to be replaced by ball-snipping PMS madness. Her temperament was steady, intelligent, nurturing; she forgave easily and without battle, and seldom considered the imagined hidden agenda. And she never sought out the hidden dark side; she seemed blissfully oblivious to his shadows.

But now, she allowed herself to see beyond the shell, that he was agonized by Linda's spirit. He couldn't bear it if Linda pulled them apart. He had never told her, but he probably loved Martika even more than he had loved the dead one. And now she'd found him out. He couldn't let her leave him.

Martika watched him; he seemed so weak and vulnerable, hardly the man most people saw. He needed her so much, and—she had to admit—she him. But even as she held him, she felt his skin go clammy and prickle into goosebumps. The conjoining of their flesh had been more than physically rewarding; she loved the feeling of being entered by his warmth as she wrapped him in a blanket of her arms and legs. They were a flesh sculpture, a Japanese puzzle box that only became two separate pieces when taken apart.

But it was not only fluids and a mutual heartbeat symphony that they shared. There was a level of sanity above and beyond the world outside. Their eyes locked during sex, the shared gaze broken only by the occasional blink. It was a silent communication that allowed them to see directly into one another's brains, to see the electrical impulses at work. It surprised them when one day they noticed they were both making the same sound when they made love: a Zen sort of hum that seemed to place them on clouds, looking down at the earth before they fell back to the planet.

Martika never wanted to notice the gradual change that crept into their love life. They still looked into one another's eyes, but she could see a vacuum forming behind his pupils. The connection was not being made. There was a distance she could sense... an obstruction. He was looking beyond and through her now. At someone else? At Linda?

It was his charm and strength and confidence that had first attracted her, and that dreaming thing, but now that she could sense something hidden, his weaknesses were becoming increasingly obvious. She knew about Linda, indeed had nursed him through recovery. But these were darker secrets within him, a guilt and melancholy that were becoming increasingly difficult for him to hide. And for her to ignore. She would do almost anything for him, but he had to do for himself, too.

She couldn't carry his burden any longer. She didn't care about a former lover; what in the world did she have to do with his life before they ever met? But she would not let their life together be spoiled by a third party. Even if it meant losing him.

More than anything, she wanted to feel him touch her, not only with his hands. She wanted their bodies to pretzel together; she needed the Vulcan mind-meld that happened on their best linkages. But, knowing it wasn't going to happen that way tonight, Martika knew she had to sleep alone. Without him. And, goddamn it, without *her*. Even if she *is* dead.

He lay on the couch, staring at the door, dreading the breach in his Good Guy Suit that Martika had at last detected. He couldn't sleep, not after Linda's visit, and certainly not after he'd driven a wedge between himself and Martika. Well he hadn't done it himself. It was Linda, really. Why wouldn't she just leave him the fuck alone? He couldn't let her push Martika away.

He just looked at the door, saw the little slice of light underneath go out, and remembered the feel of Martika against him.

It hurt Martika to sleep apart from him. Just knowing that he was on the other side of her closed door felt wrong, as if she were punishing a child for hurting himself. The bed felt too big, too empty, but she lay in it, knowing that she was right this time. She could only see clearly from a distance.

She looked at the door, could hear his even breathing. She knew what his breath felt like against her ear, his scent still lingering on her pillow. She was tired, worn out but wired. Her eyes flickered and the bed did a high-seas dance as she watched the closed door.

She pressed her thighs together, flexing the muscles, wishing her legs were wrapped around him. The area between remembered him, and was wet. She wished they had finished, and drew her legs up against her chest. She wasn't about to touch herself

As the bed swam, the door opened, revealing his silhouette in a wedge of moonlight. She couldn't speak, though she felt she ought to turn him away. He stood strong and tall and naked. And he spoke.

"I really do love you, you know. And I don't want to fuck that up."

He came closer to the bed, kneeled on it. She wanted to say "not now", but her voice wouldn't work. She wanted to stop him because she knew she should, but she wanted him the way he was and the way they were.

"I need you, Martika."

He'd never said *that* before, though she'd craved hearing it.

And he lay behind her fetal ball, spooning from behind. He kissed her back, his hands strong, working their way in a walking massage that began at her neck and led to her ass. He followed his hands with his mouth, and reached around to feel the front of her.

She was gratified that he didn't reach first for her breasts, as every man before him had. He caressed her face, her shoulders, her stomach, and by the time he discovered her goose-pimpling breasts, he found them wanting and pointed. He turned her onto her back and tasted her. She sat up in front of him, and he nursed.

She wished she had milk to feed him, but all she could give were body and soul. And they were his. He rolled her onto her back, grabbing her wrists and holding them tight against the bed, and she opened up to him, wrapped around him, and clenched him, rocking, in her vise as he took her. She rolled him over, taking control for the moment, thrusting him into her as deep as she could take it. They gave and took and gave and took, the overpowering becoming the overpowered, and met in the fabled Land of Climax with a heaving sigh.

And she dared open her eyes, knowing even before she saw that she was alone.

The bastard had dreamt all over her again.

He stared at the door, the Puppetmaster of Dreamland, hoping he'd made things right. He felt like Barbara Cartland, or one of those gothic pulp novelists, creating breathy women's romances of seduction and submission, and the guilt bore on him. Martika deserved more than that. So he had let her get on top for a moment before being overcome. He knew what she liked by now, he hoped.

He waited on the couch for her invitation to return to the bed. The dreams always woke her up. He didn't wait long. The door opened, and she stood there in her chenille robe. That wasn't a good sign. He'd hoped to see her naked.

"You don't play fair."

He knew that. He would if he could... but he didn't know any other way. She stayed in the doorway, keeping her distance.

"It used to be that way for real, you know." Her tone was wistful, yet broken. Caved in. "A long time ago..."

"I want it to be that way again," he said. "It can be."

"I don't know. I'd like to think so. But when things start to slide, I don't know if they ever get better." And then, hopefully, because she wanted it, too: "Do they?"

"They can with us."

She took a deep breath, gathering the strength to say it, to take her position and stand her ground.

"Not as long as you keep Linda alive."

She expected a defensive reaction, but got silence in its stead. He was actually considering what she'd said. He looked so hurt that she wanted to hold his hand and apologize... but she realized she'd done nothing wrong.

"I know how hard it was; I know what you saw. But you're with me now. You say you love me; you used to show me."

He looked up and their eyes locked. "I'm sorry. I do love you. And I need you. More than anyone before. Linda is gone."

She wanted to believe him, saw new strength in his eyes. No, the *old* strength, the confidence. Now, if only he would come to her, and show her he meant what he said.

He stood up and went to her, taking her in his arms. "I don't want to lose you."

He wouldn't.

They embraced, they went to bed, they made love, and the clouds behind his pupils parted. He was home.

In the afterglow, he refused to roll off and surrender to the sleep that dogged him. He could see she was watching him, almost dared to call her expression inscrutable, but she would have slapped him for it. Even though she'd have laughed afterward, she'd have meant it.

He tried to read her face. "What?"

"See? You didn't have to dream on me."

"I think maybe I did. This time."

He watched her consider that for a moment. "Please don't dream on me unless I ask for it. Okay?"

"Okay. I love you."

"Parrot fashion..."

She watched him fall asleep.

The defenses tumbled, and his youthful, unlined face cried innocence. He lost a good ten years as he slept, and every experience that lined his visage fled. He was newly minted in repose.

But now Martika was wide awake. Wasn't that always the way? He conked, she buzzed. It was hard not to resent it, but of course, it wasn't *his* fault. She lay on her side and watched him sleep; his breathing was deep and even, with a light whistle through the hairs in his nostrils. He fell deep and quick. His eyes did a REM-dance under their lids. His hand spasmed; he was dreaming.

She could only wonder what he dreamt. He swallowed, his hand clutched, jerked, scratched her, so she pulled away. His breathing came harder, and the breath deepened, soon dropping down into a trance-like hum, just like the best times they made love... just like only half an hour ago.

She saw another spasm; a wet spot was growing on the sheet. He was dreaming that they were making love. It made her smile. Maybe things would get back to where they were... where they should be. Maybe they would be okay.

Suddenly his eyes snapped open.

"Linda?"

The fantasy crashed to earth, plummeted to hell.

"No! Not Linda! Martika! Say it! Martika! Remember me?"

Even as she screamed at him she knew she was being irrational, knew that he couldn't control his dreams... only hers.

But she just...

Couldn't.

Take.

Any.

More.

Linda!

He saw her clearly, and his eyes shone with regret. "I'm sorry. It wasn't—"

"I know it wasn't your fault! It's my fault!"

"It's nobody's fucking fault!"

She knew that. But she wanted him gone. She needed to be alone. She sent him home... to a hollow shoebox apartment he visited only occasionally to pick up his mail.

He walked through cobalt moonlight. We wasn't sorry he'd run the dream thing. It was the only way to restring the broken web of their faltering relationship. But he didn't dare tell her he'd learned it from Linda. Martika wasn't jealous of Linda, not really, but she'd certainly feel like a third-generation lover knowing he'd used Linda stuff on her.

He'd tried it professionally for a while, actually made some money manipulating people's dreams. But he could see little future in sitting in the homes of the lonely, the depressed, and the depressing, watching them sleep and giving them their own Indian Jones and Pamela Anderson fantasies. He grew to resent them, and didn't want to get as close to these strangers as he needed to be to dream on them. And even though it was only fantasy, he didn't want to share in their sex. He'd certainly had his fill of watching soft-bellied mommy's boys sleepwalking as they Errol Flynned around cheap apartments and squirted in their slumber.

He wanted to teach Martika to power dream, but she didn't possess the guile and cynical bitterness it seemed to require to reach the plateau. Not that it was ever a problem for Linda; she specialized in cat-claw resentment. He was glad that was beyond Martika.

Linda's beauty was in her imagination. The dreams they shared traveled the universe, and their waking hours seemed mundane by contrast. They were far happier in the controlled world of sleep than they were when the fantasies ended. How could real life ever compete?

But she sure knew how to dream on him.

Martika felt guilty. She'd turned him away, even after he'd told her he'd loved her, needed her, cared most of all for her. But, Goddamn it, if he loved her, why did he dream about *her*?

She'd never get to sleep that night. Not without help. She gulped down two dry Halcion and turned on the TV. She stared at the set for several minutes before realizing she was illuminated by ceramic dogs marked down to three payments of $14.65 on the Home Shopping Channel.

An electric current pulled her attention to the curtains; she rose, reeling as she stood, the Halcion marching to her brain, and pulled the gingham open. Andy was on the street below, and their eyes connected for the briefest of moments before he turned away in shame and she let the curtain fall closed.

Her face heated as the sedative stirred her mind of molasses with anger and confusion. She had to sit down... lie down... let him go... just let him walk away... just stop the bed from spinning, stop the laughter from the closets... and just hitchhike to Dreamland. Martika wound down like a grandfather clock. Nobody pulled the chain, and she sunk deeply into sleep.

Andy finally stopped walking, surprised to find himself standing—once again—before Linda's grave. Why the surprise? A little metal plaque in the sod with her name on it: that was Linda. The sight of her resting-place, her name coldly inscribed, made him shiver. Now, as he stood before Linda his mind—a fickle grey muscle—turned to Martika. Martika loved him as he loved her; Linda only wanted somebody to take responsibility and blame. The dreams were almost worth it; her temper and her death were not.

He suddenly felt depleted, exhausted. He needed to lie down on the grass and let his whirligig brain slow down. The earth rocked and reeled under him as he stared up at the sliver of moon peeking through the clouds. The moon was shaped like Martika's face... but it had Linda's expression.

Martika's hands clutched in her sleep, her face darkened, troubled. Her closed eyes danced in drugged REMerobics.

He'd closed his eyes in the cemetery, and opened them in bed. With Martika. The Woman in the Moon. He saw her clearly, unfiltered, and found her irresistibly beautiful. Her skin was an even bronze, her black hair cut blunt and glossy, her crescent eyes an even and piercing brown as they opened up to him. Her face gave its apology, and he climbed on top of her, needing to press the full length of his body against her skin.

They met with cool fire: night skin burning hot a couple layers lower. He tried to enter her without hands, but was unable. To his surprise, his groin ended in a thatch of soft hair. There was no divining rod to join them.

But another body pressed against him from behind. He didn't need to look over his shoulder: the pressure of the tiny breasts that were all erect nipple gave Linda away at the first zap of their electric contact.

He looked over his back anyway, when he felt her enter him with his penis.

He tried to fight her off; but she was intent on impaling him as she'd been impaled, hoping to draw blood as she'd spilled it to the highway pavement. He felt his flesh tear, and tried to throw her off. He screamed like a girl until Linda used him up, and rolled him off the bed and onto the floor.

Not finished, Linda dropped onto Martika and entered her, too. The dark-haired one gasped as she took the full length of his penis from Linda, bucking it deeper, not wanting to like it as much as she had to. And the room spun into darkness, with laughing voices coming from under the bed fading into her ears.

The alarm made Martika's heart club her awake the next morning. She was hung over from the drug, and her eyes felt swollen and sandy. At first she was surprised to be alone in bed, but it didn't take long to reach a high enough state of consciousness to remember the events of the preceding night.

Another dance with Dr. Guilt. How could she have treated him that way? He'd been through some heavy times; the guy had watched the woman he loved die, hadn't he? Would she deny him his feelings? She felt selfish and shrewish, and wanted him in her bed with her more than anything, to hold and rock and caress and nurture and help. She was so, so sorry.

She grabbed the phone, and called. And got the machine. And didn't leave a message. And called again, and did.

When she stood up, she almost toppled over again. She needed some coffee, at least. The night before the morning after had ripped her up and spit her out. She had to sort it out; she'd make it up to both of them.

He was waiting for her in the living room, and her heart leapt at the sight of him. Until he didn't move.

"Andy?"

His naked body was huddled in front of the fireplace .. . motionless... cold... dead. She ran to kneel in front of him, and her knee skidded across the gelatinous curdling puddle of his midnight blood. He was impaled on one of the andirons... a cold satay, skewered from behind, basted in his own blood. Horrified, she slid back against the wall, urging down her bile as she remembered the night's events... the fight, the Halcion, the hurt and anger...

And the Dream.

Her Dream.

Her taste of the Power.

"I don't want it!" she screamed. "No more fucking dreams!"

Andy was in no position to argue.

His Insignificant Life & Very Important Death

At a particular moment nearly forty years ago, the bowels of the earth moved and shat fourteen billion lives. Not particularly impressive compared to other moments that gave birth to five kazillion lives, but of particular significance to Dane Carslake.

To a planetary cantata of bursting larvae, cracking eggs, and the ripping open of amniotic sacs, Dane's mother's body, having suffered a full ten days of agonizing labor, was finally allowed to pop the pup and serve up its final child.

The earth chose to celebrate the birth in its typical fashion: it continued to turn on its axis, had a hundred million creatures draw their final breaths, and birthed a trillion more.

That's how special Dane was, by golly.

And he knew it. As a child, he wondered if the other kids actually thought as much as he did. It didn't seem so. They just seemed to do, not to ponder. And they seemed happy doing it. But Dane never considered whether or not he was happy. He thought and did and turned in his homework on time, but if anyone ever asked if he were happy—which, fortunately, they did not—he would have to have thought about that. But he wasn't *un*happy, if that counted.

But significance was always a more important consideration to him than happiness. Once he realized he was capable of independent thought and action, he became obsessed with the concept. There was an infinity of lives and personalities abuzz around the globe, in countless phyla and species, and the fact that nature's random science project chose to assemble *him*—and allow him the wherewithal to consider the process— taught him to appreciate the pride of man.

He became obsessed with the remarkable uniqueness of every individual, and bored the shit out of his pre-pubescent peers with his fascination. It seemed all they ever wanted to do was put boogers in girls' sandwiches and watch Stevie Neff drop his corduroys and squeeze out a butt snake from the crook of a tree twenty feet above them.

At a fart-lighting session in the underground tunnel they called The Fort, Dane wondered aloud, "I wonder if blue looks the same to you as it does to me..." Nobody else cared. They just measured butt-torches and ignored him.

Dane began to grow up just weeks before a junior high summer, with the ill-timed and nearly concurrent discovery of several facts of life that would have been better left unrelated: nostalgia, puberty, death, and personal insignificance. It was a heady explosion of education for an adult, let alone a new twelve-year-old... and most of his peers did let Dane alone.

He lay in his bed, hearing the otherworldly theme of the forbidden *Twilight Zone* drift like Eden's snake through the heater vent. It very nearly killed him that he was not allowed to watch what he knew would be his favorite show. The music and that clipped, matter-of-fact narrator's voice bound him in gooseflesh, and held him in its thrall. He didn't need to see the Zone to love it.

Then it was gone again for another week, and he would ache inside when he heard his classmates talk about it with excitement the next day. And worst of all was that a *girl* liked it best. Cindy didn't talk stupid girl talk about dolls and makeup and Elvis and stuff. She had a subscription to Famous Monsters! And her parents gave it to her for Christmas! They didn't just *let* her read it, they *bought* it for her!

Dane's mom was okay when it came to comic books, figuring at least he was reading *something*, but she would never knowingly let him bring a magazine in the house that reveled in man-made monsters and hatchets through the head.

But Cindy's did.

And so Bernard Herrmann's theme always brought Cindy to mind: a round, green-eyed face that hid behind a fading mask of spray-paint freckles that spattered her squashy little nose. A face framed with rings of gold rope that hung over her shoulders, dangling at her chest. Her chest that, he realized on his back in the bottom bunk under his younger brother, Jack, had swollen to the fifteen-year-old level.

He drew the image out of recent unconscious documentation. He hadn't really thought about it before, but... Cindy Thompson had a bosom! With that revelation came another: Dane Carslake had a stiffy.

He reached and grabbed it with both hands, and his body spun upon its axis and shot the sheets, washing Cindy's face from the screen of his mind.

He realized after the fog cleared that the orchestral crash that greeted his first orgasm was not a heavenly choir of naked, Cindy-faced angels, but rather a woman screaming.

His mother.

Frightened and spattered with guilt, he quietly leapt out of bed, and almost collapsed on the floor as the blood rushed from his head. Giving the blood a moment to climb back into his cranium, he crept into the short hallway and looked into the living room through the slats of the wall heater.

He saw a depressingly familiar passion play well into its second act. Mom was screaming at Dad, and Dad was taunting her with wordless grins, a provoking skull of cruelty that drove her to increasing violence. Uncle Eddie, Mom's brother, was trying to intervene, but Mom and Dad ignored him, dancing the Sour Marriage Tango to a familiar beat.

Tiring of the lead, Dad grabbed her by the shoulders and shoved her against the wall, and she crashed into the heater, kicking dents in the slats right in front of Dane's face and making him jump back.

So far as the boy was concerned, marriage was about staying together for the sake of the children, so that everyone in the family could keep everyone else from having to suffer happiness. Resentment and exploded dreams and broken promises and "we'll see"s were what family was about. *Leave It To Beaver* and *Father Knows Best* might as well have been *The Twilight Zone* to Dane, as fantastical as those families' lives seemed to him. But it must be that everybody else's families were like that, because there was nobody like his Mom or Dad or his retarded brother Jack on TV.

Mom cut her ankle on the heater slats, and it brought her to a boil. She launched like a rocket at Dad, cocking her arm to bring it across his face: a face that must have once held some kindness for Mom to ever have married him. But now it was lit with defiant hatred as he easily grabbed her arm in a meaty hand, and slapped her face with the other.

Shocked but reflexive, Mom bit hard on the arm in her face, startled to find a chunk of bleeding, hairy Dad-meat in her mouth. As she spat it onto the carpet, Uncle Eddie raced over to her, and Dad charged out the front door.

She shoved her brother out of the way, yelling "If you go now, don't you ever come back here!" as she stumbled across the living room and out the door in

Dad's wake. Uncle Eddie followed her outside, begging her to let her husband go, but she was out of control.

Shivering as the cold wet spot on his pajamas made contact with his leg, Dane made his way through the tear-blurred ocean of the living room, and stood behind the front door, gripping it with white knuckles as he peered outside.

Dad was already in the car gunning the engine, ready to peel out, but Mom had gone around to stand in front, her hands on the hood, blocking his departure.

"Don't you dare leave now!"

"Get out of the way, or I swear to God I'll run over you!"

"Dammit, get in the house and let him go!"

"I'm not moving!"

"I'm warning you!"

Then, slow motion as Dane's mind slipped into overdrive. The car jerked as Dad dropped it into gear, his foot still on the brake. Uncle Eddie drifted through the quicksand night, throwing Mom onto the lawn and taking her place in front of the car, his eyes going so wide they seemed to bulge. The differential went *clank!* as the transmission connected, and the Chevy wagon gave a behemoth roar as the accelerator hit the floorboard.

Dad's skull face locked in a smile as the car bounced over Uncle Eddie as if he were a flesh and bone speed bump at the drive-in.

Dane watched Dad pull the car to a halt, never dropping the horrid smile as he looked back to see Uncle Eddie's body jerking as if the driveway were a hot griddle. Then, he *backed up over him!* He knew it was Uncle Eddie, but Dad didn't care. His bloodlust had exploded just like Dane's penis did moments before, but Dad was making a different kind of wet.

Drive, bouncing over the body.

Reverse, bouncing again.

Drive, reverse, drive, reverse, then the wheels just spinning in the crushed, jellied remains... a smoking, tire-rubber barbecue of Uncle Eddie burgers.

The next thing Dane knew, the police were taking Dad away, and Mom had him in her arms, hiding his eyes. He had discovered through his father man's seemingly limitless capacity for cruelty, and through his uncle, his capacity for goodness and protection. Both examples were vivid, but one was far more potent than the other. And cynical-making.

Dane coped. It was just another thing that happened, another example of how individuals responded differently to the presentation of life. He actually thought it was interesting. For the first time in his life, Dane developed a sense of past. The glow of nostalgia was new to him; he began to remember what it was like when he was little, and his Dad used to tell him what to do. And what the all-night drives to Yosemite were like every summer. And when he was in grade school, when he only had one teacher for the whole school year, and no PE.

After Dad left, Dane was out of school for about two weeks. When he came back, just a few weeks before summer vacation, he found that the yearbooks had already been delivered and were still circulating. Excited, he got his copy in homeroom, and flipped through the miniature seventh-grade mug shots.

He wasn't in the book. Anywhere. Not even in pep rally or camera club shots. Not even at the lunchtime sock hop. He wasn't even there. And worse...

Nobody even noticed.

Oh, he was asked to sign other kids' books—after all, he had achieved a special level of celebrity when the gruesome details of his uncle's death began to make the rounds and gather fictive weight. It wasn't as if nobody knew who he was. They just hadn't noticed that he wasn't in the yearbook.

So for all the importance he placed on the significance and uniqueness of the individual, he now realized that it just *didn't matter.* Nobody cared about what made you different from the others. They only cared about what made you *like* them. Friendships, romances, conversations were founded on similarities, not polarities.

And so Dane set out on a personal quest for worldwide significance.

In a quarter-century of attempting to matter, Dane discovered he only excelled at insignificance. It was not that he was talentless, merely that—regardless of what he and his mother thought—he just wasn't special.

He drew mediocre pictures of uninspired subjects. Even the attempts at joining the *avant-garde* were depressingly familiar. In an attempt to shock his grey visions into bold, paint-spattered life, he merely made a mess. The work was not incompetent, merely boring.

He was equally proficient at music. Beatling away on a Silvertone special he saved a year to acquire, he stepped like a mastodon into the world of rock'n'roll. Though his fingers bled greatness, his amp spoke mediocrity. Or just noise. He was almost good enough take a peel-deep bite out of the sixties in a succession of cruddy bands that were destined for obscurity.

Though the life he lived as a musician in the Haight was chronicled as a hotbed of communal sex, mind expansion, and free-spending tours in psychedelic schoolbusses, it seemed that Dane had blinked and missed it. He read about the orgies in TIME, saw the Summer of Love spread before him in full color in the Sunday supplements, even played twelfth-billed at the Fillmore one night in 1969, but he had yet to experience the multi-coupling flesh pretzels he read about in the letters to *Penthouse.*

He didn't sing well enough for leads, but did just fine with backing vocals. Just fine. And though he played in over two dozen bands over the years, he never played lead guitar. He was the rhythm player, the guy you notice *after* you check out the bass player.

The lead singers, the guitarists, the drummers were constantly having their flesh Popsicles nursed by begging bearded toothless smiles, but Dane was somehow passed by the Love Parade. His hair fell to his ass, his bell bottom paisleys hung from slender hips, and his mother felt he bore a striking resemblance to Rod Stewart, which he could not argue. But his relationship with his left hand was far more rewarding than with any of the women he encountered.

After years of garage symphonies and junior high dances—where the 14-year-old girls' crushes were too dangerous to consummate, and besides, their love was truer than could be reached on the yucky physical plane—he was asked to tour with Dr. Hook. He bit. Okay, it was as a guitar technician, a roadie who made sure their instruments were in tune and well strung, but it was a tour. The sixties were struggling to hang onto the middle seventies, but polyester, John Travolta Mach II (after *Welcome Back Cotter* but before *Pulp Fiction)*, and Soul Train were doing their best to pry loose its grasp.

Dane and his decade had one last chance to make good. It was four weeks of sex and drugs and rock'n'roll. For Dr. Hook. For the Medicine Show. For their groupies. And on the last night of a grueling month of lugging two-ton amps and sound machinery... for Dane.

He found himself in the fabled land of the Big 0, rock style. Musicians, roadies, groupies and hangers-on were in a homecoming Continental Hyatt suite, a recreational pharmacy spread out buffet-style for the indulgence of all at hand. Satin record company jackets were draped like ghosts from a dead decade across the floor, as legs spread, jaws gaped, lips licked, and lily-white buns played clench and release to the Wall Street Shuffle. The seventies were a vampire sucking the Peace and Love from the blood-beating stalwarts in the room, replacing them with Hugo Boss changelings and Italian shoes without socks.

But even if blood were all he'd get sucked tonight, for Dane it was enough. He walked into the party, leaving the ignominy of a decade that forsook him in his wake, and spread his arms in the sign of the cross, and surrendered.

He was unable and unwilling to hide the erection that stretched his jeans as he tiptoed over the pistoning minions to the smack bar. The sight of all this flesh, much of it still tight and youthful, some of it jiggly and dimpled, all of it shiny with heat and false passion, made him hungry: for food, for sex, for life, for humanity. For eternity.

As usual, they were all doing and he was watching. He stood at the wet bar, doodling pictures in the expensive powders laid out for the guests with his finger, when she stood up and made eye contact. Her spider eyes ran tears of sweat and mascara down her cheeks, and her mouth was smeared with crimson, mostly left behind to decorate the throbbing stalk on a desperately graying record executive panting on the floor. She wiped her mouth and her crotch on a towel, wrapped it around her waist, and walked toward Dane.

Certain she was coming for pharmaceuticals and not for him, Dane gallantly looked away, trying not to stare at the tiny sweaty tits that were all nipple as they stared at him. But she knew the difference between man and woman, and knew he noticed. She fished in a huge snifter filled with parti-colored drugs, gulped down some windowpane, then shoved Dane's hand in, placing another hit between his fingers. Helping him, she led it to his mouth, pushed it in with her own fingers, leaving them inside his mouth as she made him swallow. And suck.

His erection tested the Levi's guarantee as she slipped her fingers out of his mouth and into her own, tasting him, then using her insect digits to remove his shoes and socks. She stood wordlessly before him, silently daring him to make a move, and they were standing tall, two trees in a pygmy forest.

He could feel each of the fibers in the shag carpeting under his feet, exquisitely aware of their polyester texture wriggling, struggling to live beneath the crush of his flesh. He looked down to see the fibers reaching up between his toes, and binding him solidly to the floor.

But that was his only heightened experience. He looked at the flesh locomotive that was chugging to oblivion around him, and it was suddenly desaturated of all color. Sound muffled in cottoned reverence, he stared dully at the monochrome movie that lived at his feet. He'd heard about the colors on acid, but it figures that for him they'd been purloined.

He saw his reflection in his twin tree's eyes, then noticed her bark turn up into a sexy smile. She reached to release a sturdy root below his waist, but as she leaned in to devour it, it shrunk protectively from her attack. No matter how much she coaxed, its retreat was final.

So Dane bade farewell to the Stratocaster, Plaster-Cast world of music, as unfulfilled there as he was in love, life, and creation.

He slept through the eighties, waving goodbye to that decade with ten years' seniority at Shearson Lehman as an eighth-class drone, a festering, childless marriage under his belt, and a growing paunch hanging over it. Bored to somnambulance by a noncommittal and disinterested planet, he grew plates of armor made up of equal parts bitterness, resignation, and alcoholic indifference.

It was not always so. His marriage began with a frantic coupling and a mutual taste for sweat on skin. He and Andrea coupled often and eagerly, experimentally and exhaustingly, with the laughter, passion, and abandon that signified the non-physical, spiritual side of their relationship as well. Sexually, they were oral obsessives, always eager to fill one another's mouths with one another's flesh. Devouring themselves, they kept an uncaring world at bay, and for the first year or so, it was never allowed to intrude.

But it's a persistent old planet, ain't it?, and it kept reaching out and grabbing for them in little pinches that over the years turned into big, jawing bites. Sweat and semen gave way to mortgages and taxes, and eventually to sleep, ne'er to dream.

Their mutual fascination with one another became another thing, a sick-making thing, a gradually creeping cloud that slowly darkened their lives. The unannounced sprinkle turned to deluge before anyone noticed.

Those differences that so charmed and charged one another became irritants, that which made them individuals kept them from becoming one, then drove an iron spike between them. Joy turned to boredom turned to anger turned to bitter resentment.

They were no longer married; they just kind of hung around the same house. Not that they didn't share; on the contrary, the cathode glow of home shone equally on them both, saving them from the monster god, conversation.

Tiptoeing the eggshell floor of their existence, they hid behind the leering wink of Jerry Springer to keep the bullet words at a safe distance. Anything spoken could and would be misconstrued.

It seemed Andrea was always pissed off, and treated each word as an invitation to do battle. They infected one another with a cranky, world-hating disease that brought out the worst in one another, a defensive pit of discontent that masqueraded as polite hatred. Easily ignited, they seldom spoke to one another. Dane had seen the dead hole behind Andrea's eyes take over what once held the excited light of dreams fulfilled. So he worked to extinguish his own fire with sips of Remy that made him cozy. Well, he never reached cozy, but the blanket wrapped him nonetheless.

Jerry turned into Jay into Conan, then into lights out and better-get-some-sleep. But even with the gentle coaxing of Remy Martin warming his dead stomach until it burned, sleep found only uneasy purchase on Dane's pillow. Contact with Andrea's body, once so electrifying and magnetic, now made for cranky grunts and I-was-just-about-asleep!s. Trying to keep still but wanting to wiggle his foot in his nervous wakefulness, he glared at his wife from behind closed eyelids. And the longer he lay awake, the more okay it seemed to die. He wouldn't mind it right now if it *were* just lights out, if he just kakked, right here, right this minute. It would be so much easier. Just to die, and not have to worry about getting some sleep. If the heavy pounding of his heart would just stop. If it would just burst, and quit shoving blood through his veins in such a noisy rush. If he had a gun, it would be so easy to just shove it in his mouth and pull the trigger, spattering an empty, septic mind all over Andrea's pillow. If it could all just stop, and let his blood run down her face with her tears, and wouldn't she be sorry then? And the weight could be lifted, and the pain could stop. Then they both could be happy. Please, God, sleep or death.

Finally, the Xanax unconsciousness, black and dreamless.

L'chaim...

And with grim inevitability, Dane's life continued its statistical course with a divorce, a depressing bachelor apartment near the office cubicle, an allergy to the milk he needed to fight the festering ulcer that had seized his gut, and an addiction to the alcohol that deadened the fire and fanned its flames at the same time. He felt like a cigarette butt, slowly being ground out by the Birkenstock of life.

He worked and drank and tried to sleep, his paunch broadening, his hair thinning on top. His part slipped lower by the month, until soon he combed it from his ear in long strands over the shining desert that was his scalp, waxing it in place and avoiding winds that would lift the stiff hair-hat into a wave of greeting. He knew it wasn't fooling anyone—certainly not himself—but he couldn't bear a hairless reflection in the mirror.

The night his divorce was final, he didn't need the Xanax to sleep. Not even the Halcion. As soon as he flicked on the bedroom TV, his own lights went out. The entertainment was far superior that night on the dream-o-vision that spun laughing faces around his careening bed. When it settled, he was with Cindy Thompson again, for the first time since school. She was a freckled twelve, but with a high school body, and it was all in his hands. Hands that rolled the socks from her ankles, slid the Catholic plaid skirt up legs flecked with fine little sunny-gold hairs; hands sneaking under a thick white bra that offered no resistance, pulling long crumples of toilet paper from the wads underneath. Fingertips burning as they made contact with the hiding alabaster bulge that had never seen the sun. The jolt of contact with tiny nipples, hardening under his touch into miniature towers barely larger than good-sized goosebumps. Then, his own flesh tower, hidden by the girth of encroaching middle age, plunged into hitherto unexplored territory, exploding within as soon as it is engulfed.

Then, awake.

And he remembered another time many years back when dreams of Cindy Thompson soiled his sheets. Pavlov's dog barked, with Uncle Eddie's dying face and skid-mark body. Cindy Thompson, semen and blood. Death and taxes. Time and tide.

For the first time in a quarter century, and under circumstances depressingly similar to the last, Dane wept, washing away a life unlived, unearned. Though the tears eventually dried, his pain never did. He bolted back a shot of Remy to soak up the blood.

It was the next morning that, despite the rain, shone sunlight on him. He got the morning mail, still rubbing the sleep-crust from his eyes, brought on by the duct-draining of the night before. The notice was there: an invitation to his high school class's reunion. His mind immediately vacated the present, dumping his work, his divorce, his alimony, his ubiquitous bottle of Remy, and the crush of the planet itself on his shoulders into a subdural dustbin.

The headcheese of his brain grunted memories, painted them with a rosy watercolor, and convinced Dane that he was being transported into a better time. An easier time. A happier time. And better than that was the signature of the reunion committee chairman at the bottom of the invite: Cynthia Thompson.

Cindy Thompson.

Not Mrs. Cindy Wiederhorn, or even Cynthia Thompson-Applewhite.

Cindy Thompson. Singular. His silent partner in two of the most important solitary orgasmic experiences of his life. He had two months; he would lose weight, buff up, and see Cindy Thompson. And go back to when he was happy. He'd forgotten that there was never such a time.

The plane spat him onto the parapet, and he knew he was coming home. Tonight was the big deal on Madonna Street. The city had grown and blighted, just like all the others in the world. Emptied of life and filled with activity and industry, it belched in his face, replacing the scent of spoiled cantaloupe from his youth with the choking diesel air-wick that darkened the sky. But Dane was oblivious. All he could smell was the carob-tree-and-Clorox musk of Cindy Thompson wet dreams. He was going back to school, back to his friends, back to his innocence, and back—for the first time—to Cindy Thompson. His step was sprightly, his body ten pounds lighter than it was eight weeks before.

He let Hertz put him in the driver's seat, and headed to the hotel where the gala was to be held, checked in, and began to get ready. Six hours early.

He was sit-upped and showered and blown dry and tied and polished and raw-silk-jacketed by four, and the soiree was not until eight. He fidgeted with the room service cracker-dough pizza, and let himself be bathed by the magic glow of Spectra Vision as he popped a Diet Sprite from the mini-bar and kept from drinking. There would be enough of that later.

Party time.

His heart pounding a pre-detox Ginger Baker solo, he stepped into the crepe-paper and winking-white-light past, and found himself in the progeria ward.

The faces were all familiar, and mostly corrupted by time's passage. The recognition was immediate, but each of them looked like children painted over with practical joker's dust of time. A layer of wrinkles, a jacket of fat, powdered grey wigs. They were not adults, they had not grown; they'd merely been dipped in age.

The men had suffered the worst. Shining pates, broad beams, thick glasses. Dane actually felt he had survived the ravages of the past two decades better than most as they pinned his senior picture to his lapel. But many of the women had actually taken care of themselves. There were many who were unable or unwilling to combat the bodily backfires of multiple births, but a surprising number had nipped, tucked, and aerobicized to look even better than they had in school.

He smiled as he recognized faces, scanning the crowd with hopeful eyes for Cindy. He walked up to old chums with a grin and a greeting, and made a remarkable discovery. Each one reacted the same way: a quick, sneaky glance at the picture on his chest, a vacant lack of recognition, a glad-handed howdy, and an excuse to move on after an awkward, conversationless pause.

No one recognized him.

Not merely that their reminiscence was vague... they truly could not for the life of them remember him. Apparently, Dane was a master of the delible impression.

As the band played Beatles, Badfinger and Beach Boys, and graying, overweight slobs embarrassed themselves with a drunken jerk with a side of mashed potato, Dane wandered like a ghost through the strangers-by-choice. He had stepped from the time machine, and been ambushed by Morlocks.

And still no sign of Cindy Thompson. But who cared? If she weren't married, she'd probably be fat and bald and saddled with a dozen brats. Or more likely, she'd be more beautiful than ever, tantalizingly available, and when their eyes met... that same light clicking off. She wouldn't know who the fuck he was, either, the bitch. And he sat down to nurse a drink, hating her. Wishing her dead.

The band stopped playing, right in the middle of "Without You". Danny Turner stormed the stage and took the microphone for some no-doubt earth-shattering announcement. Dane's eyes were going rheumy as he glared at the former A.S.B. president, Mr. Track-Star-With-A-Hundred-Girlfriends, Mr. Handsome-Glad-Hand-Superman-Smile-And-Spitcurl-Straight-A-Valedictorian-Dickhead-Voted-Most-Likely-To-Succeed. Dane was getting drunker. Fucking self-important jock with the 170 IQ gained fifty pounds, four kids, and more chins than a Chinese phonebook. Dane gloated about the creep's fall from grace. Okay, Daniel T. Turner, esquire. High school was the best time of your life. It's all downhill from here. You manage the garden section of the Sears at the mall, pulling down—what?—a cool 25K a year? Bitchen. Dane gloated, watching the chins warble, but not hearing the song. Quivering, even frightened. What the fuck was this feeb blathering about now?

The room had gone silent, and the RA. rang with feedback around the words: "... is dead." Big gasp, Dane perking up. "... friend to all of us, and worked so hard to make this event such a special one for us. But her limo crashed through the guardrail on 248, and by all accounts, it was all over very quickly."

Dane went white. No.

"Who among us did not love Cindy?"

No! Not that Cindy!

"I know we'll all wish the Thompson family..."

My Cindy! Dream lover, wet sheet, heart-squeezing, happy-making, death's head Cindy Thompson. Dane killed her.

He was suddenly at the center of a very tiny universe, and it revved up into a wavering spin around him. Centrifugal force tried to throw him against the far wall, but to protect himself, he threw up all over the table in front of him.

And that led him home, clicking his heels and hoping Toto would join him. Off the plane and back into town. Making a choice. Not going to the house, the unbearable shrinking prison. Going to a better place, a more important place, a more spectacular place... for a spectacular act. He went downtown, riding the elevator in the tallest high-rise to heaven.

Monday, lunch hour, traffic, both on foot and on wheels. The streets choked with zombies that lived on carbon monoxide and anal-retentive schedules. Clockwork automatons that clocked in at eight and out at five, melted microwave meals blocking their bowels and clogging their arteries. It was time for Dane Carslake to be noticed... if not in life, then surely in death.

He stood out on a ledge on the library tower, forty-six stories above the insect grid. Acrophobia whirled about him, tugging at his clothing, and he felt a King Kong surge of power. Wind whipped at him, and he felt strong, decisive, conclusive. He would matter with a splatter.

Wind rammed up his pantlegs, cooling his erection, frigid but proud. The city ran its business, oblivious to him. But not for long. An animal inside him made Dane howl at the top of his lungs: no words, merely raw emotion. But the city drowned him out.

He reached into his pocket and pulled out his wallet, and let it drop to the sidewalk below. Generating forty-six stories of momentum, it nearly cracked the newsboy's skull when it hit. The kid fell unconscious across a bundle of the *Times,* making crimson headlines.

An old woman rushed to help the boy, picking up the wallet and pocketing the cash before she looked up.

Even from his height, Dane could see activity below. The ants were pointing up: a bird? A plane? No... it's street-splatter man!

He pulled off a loafer and gave it a toss. It crashed through the windshield of an uninsured '69 Datsun, which screeched across three lanes in startlement, ramming a Mercedes and a school bus into the sidewalk. Score: 1 unemployed wife-beater, 3 upper-crust matrons, returning from group-rate lid lifts and tummy tucks at the finest plastic surgeon in the city, 5 pedestrians— including one in a wheelchair that should have been worth at least double points, and 14 students from a school for the mentally retarded.

Now, people were looking up, pointing at Dane. Already there was a Metro Traffic report on the unusually heavy downtown backup. Gridlock spread out at Dane's feet, widening across the city's expanse, and his satisfied smile at its fulcrum beamed across his face.

Hell swarmed in the streets below, much to his delight. He knew it was time to act, that there were no doubt cops and shrinks in the elevators now, rising to the occasion to talk him down. And he could hear the chuffing of the waspy helicopter in the distance.

High in the sky, he could hear the honking, the voices, the city symphony that was composed just for him, and he prepared to dive. But another sound caught his ear.

Pop.

And a scream.

Pop. Pop.

And even more madness below. Running, screaming, cacophony.

Pop.

And Dane spotted its source. Across the street, a full three stories below him in a window in the Citibank tower. A sunburned gunman was firing randomly into the crowd... a red sniper.

As if he could feel Dane's eyes on him, the sniper looked up, and their eyes locked. The gunman smiled as he raised the gun and framed Dane's face in the crosshairs. Dane leaped... but not before the bullet crossed the street and dove into his body.

Unbelievable force threw Dane against the huge glass plate that shone indirect sunlight on the Members of the Board within. Executives looked up just in time to see the safety glass shatter into spiderweb cracks as Dane's body bounced off the window. His head cracked like a soft-boiled egg on the concrete ledge, and his body flailed gracelessly through the air.

Never had Dane been more aware of his environment; his brain catalogued every detail, his nerve endings scrabbled to the surface, magnifying everything. As death beckoned, his life was heightened. Blood was rushing from the crack in his skull, rosy eyewash that prettied the view of the smog-choked concrete city. The bullet had blasted a hole the size of a Granny Smith apple through his diaphragm, just below the heart. He was aware of the wind whistling a C-sharp through the tunnel wound. The hole played a scale as unfamiliar body parts found the exit hole and came to the surface.

The fall was endless and unglamorous, as Dane's body fell against ledge after ledge, bright lights of concussion when his head met concrete, hot rips of pain as limbs shattered, shards tearing through the flesh. And always the electrical current of awareness turned up to 11.

So slow. So endless. Until the end.

Then, the pavement rushed at his face at a million miles an hour, shoving his teeth through his brain and out his back. It all went black as he swallowed his palate.

It took nearly ten hours to clear the gridlock. Drivers cursed one another, praying for each other's death so they could get home a minute or two earlier. And a chorus of radio reports sang a round of the day's events, a new tragedy to tabulate, a new mass murder to chronicle, prosecutorial careers to make, fodder for a new book, six-figure TV-movie rights, agents, and other ghouls picking their teeth.

There was a new name to add to the list: Jack the Ripper, Charles Manson, Juan Corona, Angelo Buono, Ted Bundy, Henry Lee Lucas, Ed Gein, John Wayne Gacy, Charles Whitman, Richard Ramirez, and now, ladies and gentlemen, please welcome our special guest, Andrew David Bigelow, the Citibank Sniper.

A piker in the mass murder game, really, a tally often dead, and merely by bullet, no sex, no direct contact with knives or axes or chainsaws; hell, he didn't even eat any body parts or hail Satan with their blood. Just got dumped by a girlfriend who was sick and tired of being beaten up and fucked raw whether she liked it or not, and ol' Andy just got pissed and blew off a little steam.

An unspectacular showing in the big-time human hunt, and soon forgotten. But at least he was there in the news morgues, interviewed in an HBO documentary on multiple murderers on death row.

But what of the victims? Okay, there's Sharon Tate and the LaBiancas. But she was a movie star and they were a part of the evening's festivities. Dane Carslake was merely the sheet-covered foot, out of focus way in the back corner of the picture on the newspaper, one of ten victims whose identities were being held pending notification of the relatives.

In fact, Dane was never identified. His wallet was now in the possession of a sweet old lady who welcomed lonely old men into her guest house, fed them homemade wine laced with battery acid, and collected their social security checks for them. Accordianed by the Main Street trash compactor, Dane's features were far from recognizable, and the truth of the matter is, the cops really didn't give a shit.

So they scraped him off the street, slopped him into an anonymous pine box, and laid him to rest under six feet of earth.

And a miraculous thing happened: the body decomposed, bacteria bred, worms fed, and his body broke down into a primordial jelly that made very good baby food for the million and a half new lives that were spontaneously generated within him.

Forever Gramma

Folks think that what I saw happen to Gramma when she died when I was little might mess me up for the rest of my life, but I'm almost a teenager now, and that's a long time since I was nine, and I'm okay. Nobody ever believed me, of course, because I was just a little kid—except for one guy, and he ain't telling nobody nothing... least so far as I know about it. So I just stopped telling it. I mean, what's the point of telling if everybody thinks you're a liar? I ain't no liar, no matter what you hear. Anyhow, they always get all het up about the gooshy dead and dying stuff—if they knew about the sex, they'd right have a hissy.

It takes a while for word to get to Juniper Hill, and that suits the folks around here just fine. There ain't many of us in the first place, and they like that, too. Juniper Hill is mostly a bunch of houses the folks made for themselves, or their great-grandfolks did, anyway, and kind of handed them down to their kids, and to their kids, and like that. I guess I like it being so pretty and natural and all—and there ain't even a church or nothing, except for the Baptists, so I like that—but I sure wish we had the cable. Old Mr. Cootie Man—I mean, Mr. Cooperman down to the General Store's got one of them satellite things, but it got knocked down in the big storm when I was really little, so we ain't got no TV at all. He keeps meaning to fix it up, but for close to five years now it's just been playing pigeon pond.

When I think about Gramma, I don't think about the gooshy stuff, anyway. I think about peach cobbler. Mom and Dad got their own memories about her, but to me—and I bet to most people who knew her—it's that thick glass deep dish, with juicy yellow peach parts with the heat bubbles you can see coming up through the sweet crumbly stuff on the top. When Gramma was making cobbler, you could smell it far as the eye can see. Once I even smelled it from in the underground fort all the way out in the field, and I came running.

I love my mom and dad, but they got their problems, like most folks, and they get to fighting. There's a lot of what they call cabin fever on the Hill, especially when it's snowing, and folks kind of get their backs up, and you really can't blame them. Being cooped up kind of gets you antsy, particularly if you ain't got moving pictures or the TV or even a library to keep your mind off it. Dad kind of takes any excuse to make the thirty-mile trip to the post office to check the mail, even though all that's ever in there are coupons for stuff you can't even get at the Cootie Man's.

Gramma's the only person, male or female, that I never seen get cranky. She's just like the Gramma they got in that Dick and Jane book, you know, with them apply cheeks, kind of plump and old-fashioned like, with salt-and-pepper hair pulled back in what you call a bun, and always in her flour-dusty apron. When you see a picture of a grandmother, that's my Gramma. I think she looks that way on purpose. Anyway, she's always got something cooking, or she did, and was always smiling and happy and seeing the silver lining in every cloud, and looking for the silk purse in every sow's ear. Everybody liked Gramma, but I think I was her special favorite. She always had something special for me around the house, like warm chocolate chip cookies, and a bottle of Dr. Pepper, or a not-too-old issue of The X-men that she got from some mysterious place, and she never told me that comic books would rot my mind.

When Mom would bitch at me, Gramma would just tell her, "At least he's *reading*," and give me a crinkly old Santa Claus wink. Kind of like we were spies on the same side.

Gramma didn't shop at the Cootie Man's too much, because she had a pretty good garden of her own. She had all them fruit trees and vines and vegetables, and she didn't mind the neighbors picking them if they wanted to just help themselves. And that drove the old Cootie crazy. She said store-bought stuff was all full of chemicals, and she liked her food the way God grew it. So the only time she went to the Cootie Man's store was for them police magazines she liked so much. It's kind of funny how an old lady could get so much pleasure reading about silk stocking murders and shotgun killings and stuff, but that was Gramma.

But what kind of cracked me up about the Cootie was that he had this big crush on Gramma. He was an old guy, but, as he told Gramma, "not a stranger to romance". So she called him "Stranger", but always with a little twinkle in her eye so she didn't hurt his feelings. So here's this old guy who's just crazy about this old lady, and she never buys his groceries, and only goes into his store once a month. Not long before she died, whenever them magazines come in, he'd close up the store and come out himself, all personal like, and bring them to her.

Everybody on the Hill knew the Cootie had a crush on my Gramma, and they all thought it was real cute. It just cracked me up, because he was this crabby old guy, always yelling at you if you wanted to see if you'd already read one of the dusty old books on his rack, and grouching if you didn't have the right change or nothing. He was just a lonely unhappy old guy who took it out on kids, because the grownups wouldn't take any of his guff. But when he was within spitting distance of Gramma, he turned into Mr. Google, all sweet and nervous and fumbly, with a bobbing Adam's apple and a voice that cracked more than the Pembertons' teenage son Mackie, who's got the Down's Syndrome, which means he's retarded.

When Gramma died, I cried a whole lot, but remember, I was just a little kid back then. Even still, I still felt embarrassed to soak my pillow. I didn't know how hard it hurt to love somebody and lose them. It was kind of like there was a piece of her in me, and some crazy doctor came in and took a slice of Gramma offa me without any of that anesthetic stuff. It may have been my heart that was hurting, but my whole body felt the pain. Nobody'd ever died on the Hill since I was born, and I didn't know much about the system.

Did you know that when you die, they take out your blood and your guts, and all your insides, and sew you up and pump you full of stuff called formaldehyde before they buried you?

It's true. Well, you might guess that they don't have no mortuaries in a place as little as Juniper Hill to do that gruesome stuff, so they was just about to make arrangements to send her off to Steepleton before the Cootie raised his hand to volunteer.

Back when he was a young man, which I don't believe was *ever*, seems he was an animal doctor. Fact is, when Grampa died, and this was before I was even born, the Cootie was the guy who got him ready for the Big Sleep. It turns out that most of the folks that passed away on the Hill in the last twenty years or so got put to rest at the hands of the Cootie. So somehow it seemed natural that if he took care of Grampa, he should take care of his widow, too.

So he did, even though I hated the idea of his hands on and inside my Gramma. But they didn't consult me on this matter, so the dirty deed was done. It made me sick to my stomach—not a good sick like too much of Gramma's bread pudding, but an ugly kind of sick, devil sick, like something mean and ugly's tugging at your innards.

114

They had the funeral at Gramma's house. The Baptists said we could have it their place, but Gramma always said if she had a drop of Baptist blood in her veins, she'd cut her wrists and let it all run out. I know that don't sound like the sweet old granny I been telling you about, but that's what she said, anyway.

Everybody on the Hill showed up, and even some folks from Steepleton. It was a grand affair, and I think it was so crowded not only because everybody loved Gramma so much, but also because there was nothing much to do around here anyhow. Everybody made one heck of a hissy, and there was lots of big love words and tear-wet shirts and dresses. Even my Daddy cried, and that kind of scared me, because I never saw him do that before. Once when he was chopping wood, I seen the head come flying off the hatchet and stick with a bone chop plunk into the cradle of his arm, and all it made him do was yell a bunch of F-words and their cousins. He even watched the doctor in town sew it up so's you couldn't see the raw meat inside no more, and his eyes never ever even got watery.

I try not to let nobody ever see it, but there's something wrong with my eye plumbing, cause it's real easy to get the river to flow. Sometimes just stubbing my toe will set them to stinging and they'll get all wet and shiny, and I'll act like it's my allergy or something, but it ain't. One time I remember just seeing a hawk way up there in the top of the old spruce feeding her baby hawks, and the sky was so blue it was almost purple, and the clouds were like cotton balls, and it was all so darn pretty that it started again. I feel like a baby when it happens, but there ain't nothing I can do about it, the Lord just built me a little off-kilter. It don't make me queer or nothing, just a little wet-eyed sometimes. Some folks is like that.

So I hated that old funeral. There was people everywhere, and Gramma looking like a wax dummy in a wood box, and it didn't even look like her. But they was baking Gramma's recipes for all the folks, and I guess that's what really did me in. I smelled that peach cobbler, and it just made my belly do jumping jacks. I felt all yucky and queasy, and my eyes just started running. No way I was gonna eat no imitation cobbler some old lady thought she could make like Gramma. She could copy the spices and the recipe, but nobody could put in that little pinch of Gramma.

I pretended to start sneezing, even though lots of other folks—mostly the ladies—was bawling their hearts out. I just wandered outside and sat under a tree by myself. There was a big crowd up by the casket, and I watched them through the doorway. Like I said, everybody loved Gramma, and they all wanted to pay their respects. I don't think it was so respectful to be eating at her funeral, and trying to copycat Gramma's food, but adults got different ideas from kids, and they run stuff, so I just sat and missed her.

It was kinda creepy how they all kept walking up and saying how natural she looked. It seemed kinda ghoulish to me, all of them talking about her corpse like it was some kinda pretty new wallpaper or something. And the Cootie Man was there, soaking it all up like he was the Leonardo da Vinci of dead folks. They was telling him what a genius he was, and ain't it awful how the Lord called her home, and he was just all puffed up and not looking sad for real at all.

When everybody else was jawing over the cookies and coffee, I saw the Cootie Man look real close at Gramma, kind of a gooey romance movie kind of look, and then he stroked her face real gentle with the back of his hand. Then he leaned down, and—I couldn't really tell for sure from my place outside—he either whispered some private secret to her or kissed her on the ear.

Either way, it gave me the willies, and if she was alive, she'd have smacked him a good one right across the face. He turned around real sneaky like to make sure that no one was looking, and he saw me looking back at him, and turned the color of his bow tie: bright ugly red, with pink spots. I looked away, wanting to throw up. I didn't want to feel such a—what do you call it... *intimate?*—moment with that old crabapple. But it was too late. I glanced back, and his eyes were burning holes in my head, and we was both embarrassed. Then he brushed at her face like there was a smudge or something, and that he was doing business, not swiping a kiss off my dead grandmother. But he didn't fool me. I hated him, and I bet he felt the same about me.

Gramma always wanted to be buried out under God's eye, so everybody got together to make the trip out to the meadow where they buried Grampa. Mr. Cooperman had a van because of the store, so he loaded the casket inside, and took off to meet everybody at the field for the burial. We all waited a long time before he finally showed up. He said he had to get gas, and so everybody else had been waiting there, wiping their shoes on their pantlegs, and talking about what a perfect day it was, and how happy Gramma would be about it. I hated how they talked about how Gramma used to be. She still lived in my heart—I mean I was just talking with her a few days before, and she told me a joke and gave me a Pepper Free—and to all these people she was like Abraham Lincoln and Marilyn Monroe and John F. Kennedy and all them other dead history people. Grownups got weird ways to handle their problems; they push them away and put them in a box with something like their problems, but not exactly the same, and not painful, so that what hurts them don't hurt them no more. If you know what I mean, and I bet you don't.

Well, that was the longest day of my life, even up to now, and I was glad when it got dark and I didn't have to look at the masks everybody wore on their faces. It took me a long time to get to sleep that night, I remember, because I kept thinking of Gramma, and the Cootie kissing her gave me a real nervous headache.

It was a long time later that the creepy stuff started happening. It must have been the end of summer, maybe a month or two later, because I remember it was a real hot dry day, and the evening was still kind of what Gramma would have called sultry. Mom and Dad just declared war for the eighth time that week, and I was just outside walking and hiding my leaking eyes. My chest was hurting, but I knew little kids didn't have heart attacks so I wasn't going to die. But my heart sure did give me pain.

I just wanted to get lost, but that was easier said than done on the Hill. I spent my life roaming the area, mostly because there wasn't nothing else to do. I'd been out for hours, and never even had my dinner. My stomach was howling like a coyote, but I didn't pay it no mind.

I started thinking of Gramma, and just plain missing her. I never knew how close we were until she died, and now she just left a big chunk out of me. That old lady took up a lot of space in my heart, and now that Mom and Dad were at it again, I had no place to take it but the woods. I thought about the way she sang to me when I was a baby, and those big red cheeks, and the little veins on her nose, and the dark blue dresses with white polka dots, and stopped and sat under the tree, my heart weighing a million tons.

All of a sudden I knew why I started thinking about Gramma, I mean more than the missing her, and my folks' fighting. My nostrils started doing a dance... Gramma's peach cobbler was in the air! I kind of shook off the jacket of walk-around I was wearing, and found myself on the dirt road that circles the old Cootie's place. I never would have come there on my own, but somehow some secret autopilot in my brain hooked into the cobbler scent and brought me here.

There was no mistaking it: there was a pinch of nutmeg, and just a whiff of ripeness that Gramma waited for to make her cobbler the juiciest. Nobody made cobbler like Gramma, even when they tried to like at the funeral. But I smelled Gramma's cobbler now. And it was coming out of the Cootie's window, and that just didn't seem right.

Well, I ain't no peeping Tommy, but I hiked up onto my tippytoes, and Indian-walked quiet as I could through the crackly leaves and up to the window. The scent of the cobbler was so strong now you could almost *see* it hang in that summer air.

Now, I never been inside the Cootie's before, and I didn't right know what to expect. I couldn't see a whole lot, because the windows were real crusty, you know, old man bachelor dirty, and there was some girly looking lace curtains hanging kind of half-assed in the way. The whole place just seemed kind of dark and messy, a *lot* cruddier than my room at its very *worst*. There was junk all around that I couldn't really see, and a stuffed duck-billed platypus on the mantle by the stove.

The Cootie was even creepier at home than in his store, and I guess he was some kind of animal lover, because the platypus wasn't the only stuffed animal I saw there. There was a pile of old-fashioned teddy bears lying all over the floor, and over by the front door, I swear to God, there was a big stuffed black bear, full-sized, standing up and posing like he was a ballet dancer. If it weren't so goose-bumpy, it might have been funny.

Now that I'm remembering it, it seems like I saw more than I thought I did at the time, because of the windows and the curtain. But the main thing I remember was seeing Mr. Cooperman himself sitting at the table, a big old poop-eating grin on his face, eating a dish of what looked to me like Gramma's cobbler. He didn't have a shirt on, and he was all red and pink-dotty in the face, all sweaty like he'd been cutting wood or something. He might have been naked; I couldn't see past the table, and didn't want to. It was bad enough seeing that he had titties, almost like a lady. It was disgusting.

Anyhow, he was just talking and laughing, and acting all happy and weird. I couldn't see if there was anybody else there that he was talking to, or if he was just crazy and talking to his own self. I suspected the latter.

Well, by now, as you might guess, I was getting mighty creeped out. I couldn't see nothing more, so I just kind of hauled ass. Even home seemed better than Mr. Cooperman's nut house at that point, so I ran home and climbed in the bedroom window so's I wouldn't have to interrupt the parental argument that was still happening in the front room.

Well, the old creep that I tried to steer real clear of was now becoming a center of intrigue. I just kind of lay in my bed, turning it over in my head, wondering what any of this meant. The Cootie ain't no cook, that much was sure. And that cobbler was Gramma's, no doubt about it. Maybe he had some in the freezer, and popped it in the microwave. I doubted that Gramma would have encouraged him by baking him cobbler. That was her special dish, and she just didn't give out her special dish to Cooties, least not to my knowledge.

But the thing that kept sticking in my mind like a ghost story was his face, all blotchy and purple and sweaty, with a big, cobbler-choked smile, and his hair all oily and mussed up, and them big man-titties shaking when he laughed.

Yuck.

I knew I had to go back to the Cootie's, and the next time I did, I was as sorry as much as I was glad. Maybe sorrier.

It got real cold real fast; I thought it was gonna be sultry like that other night, so I didn't wear a jacket. It turned real cold after dark, and I was shivering when I got there. It looked like nobody was home at first, and I remember saying a dirty word or two to myself. But the van was in the driveway, so even though there weren't any lights on that I could see, it was obvious that he must be home. Where else could he be on Juniper Hill?

I stalked the place, real sneaky like, and went back to the same window I stood at a few nights before. Nothing. Just moonlight making scary shadows on the stuffed animals. But everything was real still, not even a breeze to lift the dying leaves off their branches. It felt like a ghost town. A *cold* ghost town.

There was really nothing much to see, though it looked creepier in the dark than it did the other night, so I started to make a circle around the place. It was real secluded there, just a bunch of grandfather trees and a wagon wheel fence around the house, and that was no big deal to step over. He didn't have no living animals, which seemed kind of weird for a guy who used to be an animal doctor. But what about the Cootie *wasn't* weird? But it got weirder, just the same.

The next window I came to was the bathroom. I guess when you don't live next to nobody, they don't put that ripply knobbly glass in so folks can't see you pooping. The Cootie just had plain old glass there, and I could see right inside. I couldn't see nothing happening in there, and it was so cold I was getting ready to go home without a story, until I saw the yellow light.

Way down at the far end of the hall, there was just a flicker, a little sunburst of firelight coming from under the door. He was home, after all.

I finished the circle around the house, and ended up at the bedroom window. Even before I got there, I could see the light peeking out into the night through the crusty window... I sneaked over there, stretched up on my toes, and played spy vs. spy.

My eyes had to adjust, because the moon was real full and bright that night. All I could see at first was silhouettes, because the fireplace was at the other side of the room, with a big, hot fire crackling. I saw it all through the lace curtain, which ticked me off; and my breath in the cold night air kept fogging up the glass. At first, it was just shapes kind of squiggling on the bed, but before long, I could kind of bring it all into focus.

It's kind of hard for me to make my brain remember this stuff, because it really don't want to. But I think I'm gonna feel a whole lot better if I get it all out, every bit of it, because not a whole lot of it made sense to me. The stomach-ache that always comes with the memory always goes away, anyhow.

The first thing was seeing that old Mr. Cooperman was lying naked on his belly on top of the bed. That was almost enough to set my gorge to rise, and once again, I almost turned around and headed home. He was kind of moving and humping, sort of like doing the Bottom Ups, but not in the bathtub. It was like he was trying to drill into the bed with his middle section.

It was kind of half-disgusting and half-fascinating and educational watching them two big white moons of his butt moving up and down, clenching and jiggling like Jell-O molds with a muscle inside. He was all hot and bothered, and because I was just a little kid then, I didn't know what the heck was going on. I just thought he was rubbing his tummy on a pile of pillows, like some weird grownup hobby or something, but you probably guessed that he was sexing.

Well, it weren't pillows he was sexing with, and this is the hard part. He was grunting and puffing like the 9:15 through Steepleton before he rolled over and fell onto his back. He had that same purple sweaty smile on his face I told you about when he was eating that cobbler, and that's the first thing I noticed. That and his little wet and gummy pecker hiding under his big fat belly.

But my brain made my eyes move across the bed to the white puffy pile that he rolled off of. It took a while for me to make it out through the grime and the curtains, but that was a body he was humping. He had himself a woman, and I never seen a naked woman before, so I looked.

She wasn't moving, it seemed like, and certainly not heaving and out of breath like Mr. Cooperman. She had a big old tummy, kind of stretched tight looking, like a water balloon, and real yellow, though that could have been from the firelight. And then, I saw my first naked boobies... leastwise the first ones since when I was a nursing baby. They was real big and kind of saggy, and fell onto the bed on both sides of her as she lay on her back, with big long stretchy creases on them. They just kind of hung there and settled into bowls of titty under her arms. She had long hair down around her shoulders, salt-and-pepper grey, just like Gramma's, except not in a bun. And candy-apple cheeks just like Gramma's.

My soul got caught in my throat, and I felt my body scream like a little girl... Old Mr. Cooperman was sexing with my dead grandmother!

I could see juices running out between her chubby thighs, making her grey hair down there get all sticky and shiny in the firelight, and I thought she was peeing in her sleep, like little kids sometimes do. But somehow I knew, even at age nine, that he had been poking his wiener in there, and he got his wet in her.

And then, that old horse-crap pig that invaded my Gramma looked up at the window, right into my eyes, and I saw the fear of God move in.

Well, the thing inside me that set me to screaming took hold of me and threw me on the ground, and wouldn't let me move. I suddenly felt the cold get a million times colder, and I finally started to shiver so hard it wouldn't stop. My body was shaking, and my eyes were running, and my mouth just wouldn't stay shut. I know I screamed some more, and couldn't stop screaming. The old Cootie came running out of the house, buck naked in the night, his baggy old skin turning into baggy old gooseflesh, and he picked me up by the scruff of the neck and shook me real hard to try to shut me up. It was like he had to tell me excuses, make me think he was a good guy, instead of a creepy old pig that fouled my Gramma.

He was yelling at me, but scared like, not mad, but I was too messed up back then to understand what he was saying. "I brought her back!" he kept yelling, like it made any difference to me. "It was the seed! The seed!"

Well, a nine-year-old kid don't know dick about no seed, I'm here to tell you, but he went on about how potent his seed was, and the power of the reproductive organ, and how much his love for my Gramma brought her back to life. I couldn't look at him, my eyes just dropped and fixated on his shriveled up little pee-pee, all sticky and matted and ugly. I didn't want to see it, but it was right in my face.

The Cootie tried to pull me up, but I just yanked away; I didn't want the son-of-a-bitch to touch me. He smelled all sour and filthy, and I just wanted to upchuck all over him and his darned house. And he just kept trying to "explain" to me. I didn't want to hear it. I know now that he was even crazier than I thought, with all his talk about his "seed", but to a little kid, he was just a big, weird, scary grownup.

He looked like a big old bald-headed polar bear out in the moonlight, and without his glasses his face looked all beady and dim-witted. The goosebumps made him look like a plucked turkey from some angles, and my brain must have thought it was real funny-looking, because it made my mouth start to laugh and wouldn't let it stop. My body was still shaking from the cold, and my breath was steam, there was tears running like rivers down my face, and he's trying to tell me his side of the story.

Finally I got myself together enough to pull away from his fat guy hands that couldn't get a tight grip anyway, and turned and ran...

Right into Gramma!

It right scared the cider out of me. My dead grandmother was standing in my way, naked as a newborn, her boobies swinging side to side, her eyes staring holes through me. I waited for her to say something, or do something, or help in some way, but she just stood there, her mouth falling open and a long string of saliva dribbling out across her lip. Her eyes were kind of half-mast, somehow stupid, and it looked to me like there was nobody home. Her body was all swollen up, ripe looking like a melon, but dry as summer dirt. It's funny how even though I knew right away that it was Gramma's body, it only seemed just barely related to her with her spark extinguished.

She was dee-ee-double-dee dead, without any doubt. And she smelled real bad, and I knew where the Cootie had gotten sour. She smelled like something the dog dug up, and in a way I guess she was. The look on her face told me she didn't know much of what was going on, but as she watched me, I saw something flicker in her head, and her jaw started to rock from side to side. Her lips, all dried up in a roadmap of wrinkles, were working, moving. She was trying to talk.

Her words were as dusty and corroded as she was, and it took a while for me to figure them out. It was more the rhythm I recognized than the actual words; it was a familiar, singsong refrain I'd heard many times at her house...

"All I've got is diet."

Not all of Gramma's lights were out, but they sure had gotten dim. She stared at me from under leaded lids, but there was no connection. This wasn't the way I wanted to remember Gramma. I blinked, and the tears blurred her, and for just a flash I saw her at the oven, dusted with flour, a polka dot apron with peach juice on it, carving me out a big hunk of cobbler.

But old Mr. Cooperman's voice brought me back home. His voice was real high and girly now, and it was like some kind of monster was talking through him. "She's still with us, boy, don't you see? Stay here, she'll make cobbler! Won't you, Emily?"

I felt like I was going crazy with him, standing between these bulging, naked old bodies, one sweaty and drooping, the other dry and swollen, rotting.

I tried to run, and Gramma turned to look at me in an empty, vacant-barn stare. I ran into a tree, and it was like somebody took a flash picture in my face. I fell again, and Gramma was coming after me, like maybe to put a Band-Aid on the boo-boo. The Cootie freaked, and grabbed at her, afraid she was leaving him. His hand caught onto her titty, and it just kind of burst with a little pop, and slid off her body into his hand. I saw a bunch of little worms and crawly stuff wiggling out of the hole on her chest and in the flesh soup in his hand.

My head hurt, and the ground started to tilt and spin, and I could hear laughing from far away, kind of like from people who lived here a long time ago in history. I was real dizzy, and I saw Mr. Cooperman start to cry.

Naked Gramma turned to face him, cocking her head from side to side like a curious puppy as she stared at him. The Cootie called out her name real soft and romantic like, and reached for her hand. She took his hand in both of hers, and brought it up next to her mouth, just staring at it for the longest time before sticking it into her mouth.

The Cootie was smiling until the bite, which I could hear real loud from the garden. Her dentures crushed the bones in two of his fingers, and she sucked on them, ignoring his screams. I think she was eating the marrow out of them. Then she pulled away, and I saw the skin from his fingers in her mouth stretch like rubber bands and snap with a final tug.

Blood was spurting from his finger holes, and she looked like she was wearing old-time lipstick as she chewed his fingers like Fritos. Old Cootie Man couldn't move; the blood was gushing and his eyes was bugging out like they was like to pop out of his head and into the garden. But they didn't till later.

Gramma just kind of swooned and fell on top of him, and their bare bodies chafed together like fingers on a chalkboard, making my skin crawl. My head hurt too much to move, and my eyes wouldn't look away as Gramma's hands worked their way down the Cootie's flesh, just like an old lady checking for the ripest peaches in the store.

She found what she was looking for; both her hands wrapped around his sticky little wienie and balls. He stopped screaming for a minute, and her red lips kind of gaped apart real slow, like a wound that wasn't quite healed splitting open, with blood getting thick in strings across the opening of her mouth. She took his peter and balls into her mouth like a fifty-fifty bar, and started to chew.

Gramma didn't even open her mouth when she looked up at me, and the hairy skin around his peter just tore and spurted like a butchered buck. The ground was still spinning when our eyes locked, and she stared at me with a mouthful of Mr. Cooperman. His screams went real far away as I threw up and passed out.

It wasn't till right after sunup the next day that I woke up to my Dad picking me up and carrying me to the pickup. I saw what was left of the old Cootie on the ground, big rib bones sticking out of the chewed-up skin, a big chunk of his head missing. Dad kept turning my head away, but I had to keep looking back to see. There was no sign of Gramma anywhere.

I couldn't talk much for a while after that, and I was scared that I was gonna be in trouble because nobody'd believe me about my Gramma coming back. But I was nine and the Cootie man was mauled up pretty good. Folks figured I saw *something*, but I was little and they wanted to protect me or something. Everybody was scared there was some kind of crazy killer or renegade bear for a while, and after a while I just let it go. Nobody ever even thought twice about Gramma. Far as they knew, she was at rest in the field next to Grampa. I wanted to think so too.

But every now and then, when the nights go all sultry and we pop open the Dr. Peppers, I think about the Gramma who loved me, and made me stuff to eat, and saved me the best parts of the chicken, and my eyes go all wet and girly. But I have had occasion—more than once—to make my way past the Cootie Man's house, still abandoned after all these years. And I swear on all I hold holy that I've smelled peach cobbler cooling just inside the window. But I ain't had the guts to go up close and look.

Now I never knew you could come back after you die, and folks say you can't. Even real smart teacher-type folks.

But I know different, and I know true. I don't know what brought her back: the Cootie Man's seed or her own will. But I do know that if she came back, it wouldn't be to go sexing around with him. And I also know one other thing... wherever she is, part of her has a little house in a chamber in my heart, where she is forever. I love you, Gramma.

Starfucker

I was the bastard son of Art and Commerce. Hollywood chewed me up and swallowed me whole, and when it had digested me, evacuated me like watery excreta from its overloaded bowels.

You'll have to excuse the unlovely imagery; I have no reason to be bitter. Everything that happened was my own damned fault.

It wasn't just the studio system. The independent world is almost as dire; it's just a smaller list of talentless moneychangers who have to justify their existence. The only reason you don't get rewritten by a list of hacks is not because of some kind of integrity inherent in the scruffy independent system; it's because they'd rather not pay all those dogs to piddle on your papers.

Well, there's no Movie Police forcing you to lie down and spread 'em for Hollywood. You don't like it, go back to the night shift at Vidiots.

There are many reasons to love an industry unburdened by morality. Primary among them is Forgiveness. A Hit forgives us all our trespasses, in fact, *rewards* us for them. One *Titanic* and you're allowed to scream and rant and fire and pull guns and fuck anybody who'll prance to the crook of your finger. And they forget all about *Piranha II: The Spawning*.

I had my big shot, my X-wing Fighter to Alderaan, my major studio break... and I bombed out big-time. It wasn't big-budget, but it was high profile. The trades were filled with the saga of the film school prodigy who jumped right out of the gate and into studio features, even without a load of music video shit on his resume. And how that first-time Hollywood Helmer never even finished the movie. The studio wouldn't even Alan Smithee the damned thing; they just flushed their investment away... and I followed it down the drain.

I learned a big lesson, and I'm ready to share it with you, free of charge.

Never work with puppies, kids, or mutant babies.

My own mutant kept me underground, feeding off my bodily fluids like Bernie Brillstein before meeting its untimely end as In-Sink-Erator chum for the Studio City sewer gators. As Asta's grue spattered the rusted porcelain of my kitchen sink, so did I. But I got over it. I even began to bathe again.

And work.

Well, when I say work, you won't find it on my resume.

I wrote and wrote and wrote some more. And when I finished, I wrote some more. But the padlock had rusted shut. Nobody wanted to buy the stories I had to tell. Fair enough. Again, nobody's forcing me here. I serve of my own accord. So I wrote and wrote and wrote some more.

But I never sold any of it. And I can't blame anyone but myself. I thought that my experience had deepened me, and that my writing had matured, and reflected new reaches of insight into the human psyche. In truth, I was just jacking off.

But between then and now, I *did* shoot another feature length film, though I haven't told my new best friends at CAA. And it made a fortune, though not for me. I say film, but it was shot on MiniDV video, for a Valley company called Vivid. The San Fernando Valley is the red-rimmed sphincter of "Adult Entertainment", and for a shining moment—though I hadn't sported an erection in close to two years—I was its king. If you've spent way too many nights alone with your VCR and your left hand, you may be intimate with my timeless classic, *Gulp!* Yes, the exclamation mark is part of the title, your guarantee of artistic merit.

The two-day shoot had only one real disaster, though "disaster" is a subjective term. Patty Petty had just been implanted eight days before the shoot with massive bags of mammarian come-hither, topping her slender frame with enormous globes that stretched her fine alabaster skin so tight that, during a particularly energetic (and award-winning) coupling that involved five men, two women, and one excessively randy orangutan, her breasts just split right open, dropping the silicone bags to the floor like unwanted Gerber's from a baby's mouth.

It was beautifully lit, and the camera was in the perfect position to see it all. It may be my most memorable scene.

With an investment of eight thousand dollars—and one thousand of those crispy green boys were all *mine!*—*Gulp!* has grossed close to eight million dollars. Thank God for insurance. It swept the Adult Film Awards (Best Feature shot on Video, Best External Orgasm, Most Orifi Filled, and a host of others) and almost made me wish I'd used my own name on the damned thing. Almost.

Gulp Two! was a certainty. But I left that to other hands. Been there, porked that.

It's funny, if not really all that amusing, how one thing leads to another in this berg. In the afterglow of *Gulp!*'s transcendental performance, Patty was cast as a Wise-Beyond-Her-Years Stripper, a featured role that required Tasteful Nudity in an otherwise unmemorable Artistic Endeavor known as the Untitled Independent Feature. The Sterling Stripper Story crashed and burned before the first week was in the can, but pretty, petty Patty introduced me to its producer, who had actually seen and enjoyed *Words Without Voices,* and he hired me to write his Magnum Opus... for the princely sum of two thousand American dollars. That was exactly double my *Gulp!* fee, so I wrote my little telltale heart out. It was a grim, violent, Urban Drama, spattered with Red Humor and brotherly love. Well, our Masterwork of Renegade American Cinema stepped into mucky post-Columbine legal entanglements that kept it from even being midwifed on video.

But two years after it was collecting dust on the Payment Due shelf at the lab, Mr. Producer highjacked his finest hour (and forty minutes) and managed to book it illegally into the Slamdunk Festival. For the uninitiated, Slamdunk is the scruffy alternative to Sundance and Slamdance, where loft-living men in black get their tawdry little celluloid stories that no legitimate human will have anything to do with projected onto the big screen once before being consigned to a K-mart video transfer with felt marker labels that sit with pride on the apple crate next to the dying Korean TVCR and the Tarantino collection.

Luckily, Sundance stank on ice that January. People had grown tired of the sensitive as well as the insensitive. Cinematographic ennui blanketed Park City with eleven inches of dull snow. And, with a bit of help from unnamed sources, word began to creep out about the lesbian nipple-tonguing scene in our Masterwork. It is said in the Bible of American Independent Cinema that if you blanket raw Eros in artful light and gorgeous surroundings, they will come. Give them guilt-free art-house erotica, wanking material for the intelligentsia, and the kilos to the kingdom are yours.

We played to a full house, breaking the legal logjam and leading to an eleven-week run at the Nuart. It's still running midnights at the Angelika Center, even though it's been on video for months. Sure, most of the attention went to the snotty little auteur in the backward cap and the baggy Hilfigers, but you know, somebody writes this shit. And this time, that somebody was me, and that shit was *mine.*

So now I'm working again.

I mean, I'm not Kevin Williamson, but I'm doctoring a couple of Gramercy scripts at ten grand a week, sold a spec to Fox Searchlight for the low six figures, and made an overall with Bob and Harvey over at Miramax that includes directing my third script for them. If and when.

But I've been through this before, and if you can't learn from experience, you are less than human, and consigned to a life as detritus. You exist to fail and provide an example to those who *can* learn from your mistakes.

So... no Porsche and big house for me. I'm driving a TT, with a condo at the Marina City Club. Leave the pretensions to the backward-cap crowd. I'm even letting my hair grow out brown.

There's even been a rebound in the social world. Invitations to screenings and parties are ubiquitous, and I don't even bother to RSVP. I haven't paid for a meal since Slamdunk. And that was a year and a half ago.

I wasn't even going to bother with the American Cinemateque opening party, except that I'd never seen DeMille's silent *Ten Commandments* before. Hell, I'd never seen *any* silent film before... or any DeMille, either, for that matter. But I'd heard about the grand old Egyptian Theatre, and there was a live orchestra, and my tickets were free, but they'd have cost *you* a hundred bucks apiece... *if you* could get them. I was at a meeting at Paramount in the neighborhood anyway, and it was better than fighting traffic to the Marina. Well, the Cinemateque completely ruined Hollywood's first and greatest movie palace, cramming a hideously ugly high-tech architectural disaster into its beautiful shell, and I slept through the dusty old harridan of a movie.

But the party afterward made the evening more than worthwhile.

Oh, it was littered with the usual suits and poseurs and perfect specimens at both ends of the Hollywood rectum spectrum. There were the witty and famous, the witless and gorgeous, the rich and the stitched, the sparkled and the spackled, the cream and its curdle. Milling about the cramped, crimson lobby were Golden Age Movie Star lookalikes serving drinks and the latest trendy biblical edibles from Along Came Mary. It was mildly clever. They did, however, manage to find some pretty good doubles: a Gable and a Lombard, a magnificent Monroe, a mammarian Mansfield. There was a remarkably unhaltered Harlow sheened in a *Platinum Blonde* satin gown that chilled and hugged her alabaster breasts with static electricity that made her nipples point shamelessly all the way to heaven.

It was almost enough to make me give a shit about Old Hollywood. It was fully enough to feel my first post-Asta stirrings Down There.

The tight marcel of her white-hot hair, the anachronistic, unathletic voluptuousness of her unfettered hips, the sea-bottom near translucence of her milky—no, *creamy*—skin enraptured me in unexpected ways. Everything old was new again. My fascination did not go unnoticed. A publicist for the Cinemateque, ever alert to the needs of Her People, smiled at my obvious rapture, sidled up to me and gripped my elbow with her manicured claw, sipping champagne from a plastic flute from the other. Her lipstick smeared the rim a muddy, dried-blood color.

"Pretty, isn't she?"

Pretty. Meg Ryan is pretty. A nice day is pretty. A fucking *nose* is pretty. Harlow II was something way beyond that. I don't know that they've even got a word yet for what she was. Really, it's been a couple of years since I last gave a shit about sex. I mean, it was ruined for me, I thought, for good. And Madame Publicité only bittered the batter. Though her high, domed forehead was stretched tight and shiny, her telltale hands were creepy and crepey. Her thinning hair was course and wiry, her collagen lips bloated like a flounder's, her eager eyes trapped in a look of constant surprise. She was the sexual Antichrist.

But what the Antichrist taketh away, Harlow II gave back a thousand-fold. Hallelujah, I am reborn.

The publicity monster stroked the inside of my arm with her talons and released a string of intimate words in my ear in a voice I know she felt was sultry, but to me was a gaseous nicotine croak.

"You can have her, you know," she exhaled, wilting the rented flowers around us. "Let me introduce you." And the Publicity Pimp, gripping me so tight I feared blood loss, led me to the Goddess.

Well, suddenly realizing the woman was a professional wilted me a bit... until we were face-to-face. It turned out I was the proverbial man who needed no introduction. She knew who I was, had seen the Masterwork during its Nuart run, even *bought* the video, though it still hasn't come out at sell-through. She even knew about *Words Without Voices*.

Had to be an actress. Damn it.

But who else works these Hollywood gigs? Professional servers? Beautiful People entirely uninterested in the performing arts? What the fuck did I expect? It was a disappointment, though it did nothing to fade her glory. She was magnificent, one of a kind. And the wattage from her smile could run a thirty-plex projection booth for a year and a half.

The Pimp winked and left us, with a smutty exit line that dangled huskily in the air of her wake: "If you need a third party, you know who to call." I'd rather lick Michael Jackson's star on the Walk of Fame clean.

When the tendrils of her reeking Giorgio finally receded and I could draw the semblance of a breath, I laughed uncomfortably. "Seen any good movies lately?"

Her smile never broke, even with her simple answer. "No."

I was falling hard. They haven't made a good film in years. All they make are Crybaby Movies, no real guts or glory. Tobe Hooper can't get a studio picture set up. Gus Van Sant reshot fucking *Psycho*. It's all crybaby shit or comedies that aren't funny or send-ups. There hasn't been a real movie in the 90s, and the new Millennium seems just as bleak.

But she had an addendum: "Not since your picture at the Nuart." And then her smile went sideways with the extra-added attraction. She whispered, "Gulp." Not like a title, or anything. Just the word. Gulp. Without the exclamation point. Just to let me know that she knew. And still, she never lost her smile.

I could only stare at her in admiration. "Same to you, but more of it." It was a lame retort, I know, but I had to say *something*. And she laughed, a tinkling shower of delight that prickled the hair on the back of my neck. Gulp, indeed.

"If you weren't an actress, I'd ask you to marry me." Chicks dig that.

"If you weren't a director, I'd slap you for that." But I was, so she didn't. "I like directors... especially the young, talented ones."

"If I meet one I'll be sure to introduce you." The self-deprecating stuff always hooks them. And I wanted her hooked. Gaffed. Boned.

"Oh, we've already met."

Her wet, crimson lips glistened, and I watched them stick together and peel apart as the "m" made its way through her mouth in slow motion.

"Will you be at the after-party?" she asked. After-party? What after-party? Was that on my invitation?

"Will *you*?"

"I have to be."

"Then so do I. When and where?"

"It's a secret." And then she leaned close, offering a bud-tipped alabaster view, and shared her secret with me.

The rain was biblical, but the directions very specific. The little roadster and I headed up Laurel

Canyon, past Joel Silver's Frank Lloyd Wright masterpiece on Hollywood Boulevard, turned left on Wonderland, and slid through an aquarium of eely estuaries and sobbing oaks. We groped through the rare midnight storm, ever upward, evading the cracks of lightning that drew closer as we drove higher. At the applause of a particularly splendiferous hand of electrical fingers in the sky, I turned to look down at the Basin below and behind, just in time to see its voracious maw go dark.

It made little difference to my slithering drive. Here in the jungle of the Hollywood Hills, there were no streetlights. The moonlight was my guide. I was so close to my destination, I could not give up my quest, even if the party was called off when the lights went out.

So I continued, the heart of Indiana Jones beating within my chest.

At last I emerged at the crest of the mountain, and I saw Xanadu. Not the Olivia Newton-John bowl-filler, but the Orson Welles original, done Southern California-style. It was vast and pink and Spanish-tiled, probably built in the twenties when this acreage could be had for pocket change. And though the dozens of windows were dark, red-vested car chimps were jockeying the Benzes and Beemers into place. I parked the TT myself, and let the rain submerge me as I walked to the door.

Cool.

Security was tight, but I didn't need a ticket. The enormous Polynesian totem at the door let me right in without even a word passing between us. Either a fan or he'd been primed.

I walked inside this Old Hollywood mansion, and found myself submerged in darkness. I squinted through the twisting hallway, choking on the musk of history, and stepped into the spider's parlor. It opened up into a giant room filled with overstuffed furnishings and the glow of pale candlelight. It was a step into another era, one you only see on the screen, and even then only in black-and-white. This place was an education in early cinema, the kind I flunked out in at film school: an education I did not want, but could not avoid. The whole house was dressed in the elegance of a Hollywood long gone, like an Ernst Lubitsch drawing room comedy, dressed by William Cameron Menzies. The ceilings were high and scalloped, the maroon velvet draperies belted into place by gold ropes. It all looked so wrong in color.

This was a Hollywood for which I had no nostalgia. It had grown long in the tooth on quaintness and manners and dust and censorship. It was far removed from real life: cornball artifice with heavy makeup and jerky special effects. It looked like Cary Grant should step in and offer me a drink.

Which is exactly what happened.

His black hair oiled into a perfect, shining part, a pearly grin that rounded the dimpled chin into an undersized apple, he poured me champagne and wished me well before disappearing into the candlelit gloom.

As my pupils adjusted to the light, I realized that I stood in a room filled with perfect specimens of an age gone by. Elegant in their evening clothes, many of them had been at the Cinemateque gala. But none of the icons from the fifties or beyond were here. These replicants were strictly of pre-war vintage. Most of these had *not* served at the Egyptian; they were *special:* the very most beautiful recreations of Hollywood's so-called Golden Era. Not really being a student of celluloid history, there were a lot of lookalikes I didn't recognize at the time. You know, if a movie was made before the birth of Michael Bay, I wasn't interested. But some of them you just couldn't avoid, so great was their status as pop culture icons.

Even the new generation of filmmakers that comes after me would have recognized the young John Wayne, that woman with the big monkey in *King Kong*, Kate Hepburn, Jimmy Cagney, Jimmy Stewart, Lana Turner in a bright red sweater, that woman who always had her blond hair hanging over one eye, that Thin Man guy with the moustache, the old lady from Big Valley, who was a lot better-looking young, but still no babe. Except for Lana's showoff sweater, all of them were in the most elegant evening clothes of the era: white tie and tails, satin gowns, real classy stuff.

But what really looked out of place, even more than seeing these facsimiles in full, living color, was watching what they were *doing*. The place was fetid with body heat. Those elegant clothes slid off of bare shoulders and dropped into elegant little pools of silk at the feet of the guests being serviced. I mean, it wasn't like everybody was whanging and banging in the middle of the room or anything; it was a little subtler than that.

But the Hollywood Hills were alive with coupling. Each massive easy chair, divan or settee was occupied with at least one gorgeous specimen treating the guests to a taste of Old Hollywood. A hand cupped a puddle of breast here; a flesh probe reached between tight buttocks there. Lips met teats and groins lubricated to the gentle strains of the string section in the other room. This glamorous repast of bodies on bodies was still elegant, passionate yet ethereal. It was my first appreciation of Hollywood Past.

I felt out of place, like a child, apart from the party, a guest but not a participant... until tapered porcelain fingers rested on my shoulders from behind. I turned, and joined the celebration. Harlow II touched her scarlet lips to my cheek and gently slid her fingers between mine. "I was waiting for you."

Jesus!

The words eased over me on her gentle breath, and every body hair prickled to attention. In the candlelight, she was even more luminous, practically digitally enhanced. Her fingers wrapped around mine, and it was as if we had melted together at the hand.

"Nice party," I managed, but my voice cracked the "nice" into two syllables. I couldn't imagine a modern woman as beautiful as my Jean... and I told her so.

"You should see me on a weekday."

I shuddered. The veil of imagination lifted for a moment, and for just a slice of that moment I could see past the platinum hair and the period lipstick, and saw her as just another beautiful actress in LA. Everything suddenly darkened in a crash of artifice, and my pulse dropped. The arousal waned, and I struggled it back in time, but without success. Jean was a working girl, another gorgeous face in the Academy Players Directory, with a wannabe resume and an attraction to randy directors. I went limp.

She noticed.

"What's the matter?"

"Nothing. I just imagined you without the wig, having lunch with your agent at the Ivy and checking your pages every hour on your cell phone. In the real world."

She looked at me, figuring me out. "This is my real world. Here. Now. With you. This is no wig; go ahead, feel it."

I did. I ran my fingers through the curling-iron waves, and she closed her eyes, enjoying the journey. "Pull on it." I gave it a little tug, and her lips parted, releasing that intoxicating breath. It was not a wig.

"I don't have an agent, I eat lunch at Musso and Frank's every day, and I hate cell phones. In fact, that's how I tell good people from evil people. If you talk on a cell phone in a restaurant, you're evil. Period. No way around it, no second chance. One strike and you're out. Cell phones in restaurants or talking in a movie theater: the true signs of human slime." I hoped nobody would choose this moment to reach out and touch me via the PacBell digital in my coat pocket. "This is me, the real me, the ever me. Just a little less dressy on weekdays. So mind your manners, or you'll have to be spanked."

Oh, please, not that. I apologized, and she forgave me.

"What would you like?"

"Are you kidding?" Uncharacteristically, her face flushed and she looked shyly down under my hungry gaze.

"You want something to drink?"

"Cary Grant gave me champagne, which I don't drink. I'll take a Coke, if you've got it. But I just want to be with you."

She smiled at me, all girlish and genuine. "That's so sweet." And she led me by the hand. We walked through dim caverns of candlelight, each containing bodies in rhythmic heat. I was not startled to see Cary lying beneath an energetically hyperventilating Madame Publicist, her eyes rolled back in her head in ecstasy, her nails gouging red rivers down Cary's chest. I tried to sneak past, but her eyes found me, and she gave me a yellow wink. Her words reached me on a wave of dragon breath: "Have a nice time..." And then she came. Loudly.

Ugh.

Other couplings were more visually appealing. There were fantasies fulfilled throughout the house, animus cloaked in an historic glamour. Dead movie stars brought back to life by the vigor of our desire. I can't tell you how exciting these violations of the Hays Code were to watch.

Laid out in the elegance of the location, the perfect grooming and formal wear intensified the heat to an amazing degree. The power may have been off, but the house was filled with electricity. I had always seen that Old Hollywood shit as dull and historic and musty and grampy. But now it was making me sprout wood.

I'm a director, so I observe. I felt no guilt staring at the couplings as Jean led me through them. It was a symphony of flesh, and each of the players was first chair. And I was being led to the podium to conduct a little ditty of my own.

I couldn't believe that the dark room she eased me into was anchored by a heart-shaped bed. That image would have worn a beard even in one of those old thirties movies. But it did, and the bed was made up in pink satin, as if art-directed to set off Harlow II's peach gown. The high-ceilinged room was lit only by a shaft of blue moonlight through a curtain of rain. The chill of the moonlight was tempered by the heat of our bodies. When she slid lightly onto the corner of the bed, tiny arcs of static electricity crackled between her and the sheet. As she sat in the shaft, highlighted by the moon, I could only gasp. She lifted her arms to me, and I dropped down next to her. I knew this had to go slow. It had to be drawn out. This might only happen once.

She stroked my face with her delicate fingertips, a Mona Lisa grin tugging at her scarlet lips. Those lips moved slowly in, and I wanted them to just devour me: wrap around my head and work their way down to my toes until I was dinner. Instead, they eased against my cheek, pausing there before peeling wetly away and leaving their crimson imprint. She grinned at the lipstick she'd left on my face, and lunged in to lick it off in a swift wipe of her tongue. Then she laughed.

I put my hands up and gently held her face in them, as if it might shatter. Her skin was as smooth and white as an egg. She let me draw her face close to mine, and finally we kissed. No suction, no open mouths, just our lips touching each other, gently at first, breathing each other's breath. I kissed her upper lip, her lower lip, then tilted my head to kiss them both at a vertical angle. Then I got hungry. I started to pull her lower lip into my mouth, nursing on it. Soon, the tiny pink tip of her tongue ventured into my mouth, tracing my teeth and gums. There was the faintest taste of chocolate on her tongue, and I savored it. I wrapped my mouth around her tongue, and she slid it deeper inside, soon moving it to a samba rhythm. Then she took my tongue and nursed on it. I'm sure my eyes rolled back in my head in idiot abandon.

When finally we broke for air, we just looked unbelievingly into each other's eyes and breathed. And then we both just broke into laughter with the delight of it all. She nestled into the base of my neck, kissing it wet and warm, and I carefully lowered the satin strap that held in Nirvana. But I wasn't about to go right for the good stuff. I wouldn't be the pig with the hands that only wanted to grasp the tits and the clutch. For the first time in my life, I pleasured in the getting there. I felt the rich gloss of her neck and shoulders, stroked the clean, perfect whiteness of her deliriously long back. I kissed down her neck, tasted her wrists, even lifted her arm to cradle my head under it and kiss her pit. I tasted the slightest hint of salt and loved it. There wasn't even a trace of stubble.

And she, too, was happy to take her time with me. Her lips brushed lightly over my neck as she unbuttoned my shirt. I could feel the heat of her breath as she nuzzled my chest, her teeth lightly tugging on the hair around my nipples. She sucked easily on mine as I wanted hers. But I'd get there soon enough.

My hands went all exploratory, gently excavating the secrets of her body. I eased the satin down off of her breasts, and there were little sparkles of static electricity introducing them in a fanfare of tiny fireworks. Her happy little breasts were as white as the rest of her body, not surgically enhanced, and capped with tiny pink roses that almost disappeared in the moonlight. I first felt their heft with a light stroke of the underside with the back of my hand. I slowly closed in, palming them, holding them, clutching them. I nuzzled them, but that was it. Soon I had drawn them hungrily into my mouth, and I wanted to feed off of her: milk, blood, anything. I just wanted to swallow her fluids.

At that point, it wasn't long before I was atop her, the globes of her ass clutched tightly in my hands. Her legs scissored me tightly as she chewed voraciously on my earlobe. And as her body was wracked in orgasm, I was pumping two years of dormant seed endlessly into her. I thought it would never stop... but finally it did.

When the new sun peered into the bedroom window, the old movie was over. Jean was gliding into jeans and a T-shirt, and brushing her hair out of her eyes. She wasn't Jean anymore. I bet she lived in the Valley. I heard the leaden thump-thump of techno-disco booming through the old house, and a ripple of nausea curdled me. It took me a while to come to. The 2000s had fully replaced the 1930s. And I didn't like it.

I watched the muscles of her chest heave as she brushed her platinum and tried to figure out what came next. "Um... what do I owe you?"

"Don't worry about it. Last night was all taken care of."

Nice party.

I couldn't take my eyes off of her, and she winked at me in the mirror.

"When can I see you again?"

She turned to me. "Anytime you've got fifteen hundred bucks. Or a part you might think I'm right for. I'm a very versatile actress."

I tried to smile back, but I'm sure she saw my face crash. Jean was gone. This stranger gave me a mock pout. "Aw, baby misses Jean Harlow, doesn't he? I can be Jean anytime you can afford it." And she handed me a business card with her pager number on it. She kissed me hard on the lips and toodled.

What a crash. I don't know why I felt so devastated, so abandoned, so cheated. But here I was, hollow and deflated, still sticky from last night, inside and out. All I had left was the drive home.

Home.

I stared out at the sewage bobbing along the beach from my 10th floor condo. I hated the present. A second stage smog alert hung heavy over the effluent, and the traffic on the boulevard below was blocked like a bowel. I had the Criterion *Armageddon* on the DVD player, enveloping me in full Dolby Digital surround, but even that couldn't bring me out of it. Normally its twenty-cuts-a-minute exhilarated me; today it merely enervated me. It just felt like a bunch of frantic, noisy crap, a cinematic nagging mother-in-law, screeching in my ear. I missed the past... and I'd never even been there.

So I decided to visit.

I made a sojourn to the dreaded San Fernando Valley to Dave's Video, a beacon in the midnight of Ventura Blvd. I loaded up on every black-and-white DVD made before the Great War and charged it to my Gramercy account. Research, you know. Let them pay for my education in the classics.

I lugged the tonnage of my cinema booty back to the Marina, and vegetated in front of the new HD screen from the Good Guys. Tendrils of beard sprouted as I reached back into the ghosts of the past. First, I made my way through every Jean Harlow film I could find, from *Hell's Angels* through *Saratoga.* She'd made a couple dozen pictures in the course of a half-dozen years, then up and died. But Jesus, what a legacy she left! Through Harlow, I discovered Howard Hawks, William Wellman, and Victor Fleming. The movies spoke to me in an eloquence I'd never known before. They just plain *spoke!* The words sparkled, the scenes played out without cuts, the camera observed, rather than led the characters! What a revelation!

I worked my way through the Harlow collection, hungering for her crumpled little expression, lusting after her pale, ever-braless form. *Dinner at Eight* led me to George Cukor; Cukor led me to Ernst Lubitsch, who led me to Preston Sturges, who led me to John Sturges, who led to me John Ford, on to Hitchcock and Huston, David Lean and Frank Capra, Tod Browning and James Whale. And through the filmmakers I met some new dead friends: Jimmy Stewart, Robert Donat, Gene Tierney, Donna Reed, Ava Gardner, Rita Hayworth, Jean Simmons, Glenn Ford, Ann Savage, Veronica Lake, Boris Karloff, Fay Wray.

Who knew these creaky old grinders would be so filled with wit and beauty and humor and tension and revelation? Who knew that a film could be more than a barrage of flash-cut imagery, digital animation, and DTS explosions?

Maybe you did, but I didn't.

I know, I'm sounding like some old fart film instructor who can't let go of a past that's practically been buried alive, but it's true. I don't mean to preach here—I really don't—but I was born again. I guess I'd only seen the old shit. I didn't find the jewels. That would be like judging today's movies by the latest Adam Sandler.

The best of the old stuff was elegant and smart and breezy and entertaining and, well, *engaging*. And the worst of it was... well, the worst of it was like most of the movies today. Bankrupt and boring.

I got it.

Bleary-eyed and exhausted but also wonderfully recharged after a dozen weeks of non-stop watching, I turned off the set. I'd forgotten the world was in color, and it startled me. The cleaning lady had vacuumed around me for the last couple of months, and thrown out all the food delivery cartons, but the place was still a litter of videos and detritus. As I stood, my head reeled. My eyes had stared at a fixed focus for so long that they found it difficult to hone in on anything else. My hair was a couple inches longer, and I had the semblance of a Fu Manchu beard tickling my chin.

I slid the glass door to the balcony open and stepped out onto the cusp of the real world, and let it breathe on me. It was noisy and argumentative and its breath stank. I liked the movies better. Reality bathed me in ugliness, and I shivered. It reeled around me and my mind drifted away to beauty.

I remembered what brought this on in the first place. I opened up my wallet, and pulled out her card. It didn't have a name on it, just a number. I dialed it, got the system's nervous beep-beep-beep, punched in my number and waited. This time, as I looked out into the vast Pacific, I couldn't discern the turds floating out there. Maybe they cleaned them out again; maybe they were just hiding. But the sea was as blue as the veins on Cher's forehead. If only the sky matched. Instead, it was congealing into a disgusting mauve solidity.

Her call booted me out of my coastal reverie. She knew who it was from just my "hello." She was good. I needed to see her. I wanted to share what I had found with her, and needed to siphon some of it off of her, so I invited her over. She came.

By the time she called up from the lobby, I was showered and shaved and reborn. My eyes could focus near and far again, and my breath was kissing sweet. My expectant erection tugged me like a divining rod to the door at the sound of her gentle rap. Oh, my lovely embodiment of the past, my alabaster testimony to all that once was beautiful and elegant and witty and desirable. My link to another, better world, the only world that mattered, a world without corruption or darkness or despair.

My Jean.

I pulled the door open... and wanted to cry.

This was not my Jean. This was that girl in the Jeans and the T-shirt and the Reeboks and the backward Nike cap, fresh from the gym. This was all the girls I'd read and dated and sampled and discarded and been discarded by. This was now, and I wanted—*needed*—then.

She saw it and knew. She lifted a shopping bag from Trader Joe's and pulled out a bottle of wine. "I brought wine." I tried not to look so let down, and she dug deeper in the bag. "And Jean."

She held up the peach satin gown with a twinkling little smile that did its best to win me over. "Which way to the bathroom?"

Unable to speak, I merely pointed, and she scurried through the condo and locked herself in. No matter what she looked like when she emerged, I had seen behind the facade. I knew it was fake now, and that it wasn't going to work. It was so perfect that night at the Cinemateque, until the fateful morning after. I wouldn't see Jean anymore, merely the actor playing her. It wasn't the same thing.

Still, when she emerged, the gown clinging to her like hot breath, she was stunning. The lips were sanguine, the hips unfettered, the breasts at full attention. But now, having experienced the real Jean Harlow in every one of her films—even the one with Laurel and Hardy—I realized she didn't really look all that much like Harlow. Beautiful, desirable, yes. Harlow, no.

"Forget about that girl at the door," she told me. "I sent her away. I want you all to myself." She gave me a sharp little bite on the lip. I tasted my own blood.

She stepped into the middle of the living room and appraised the place, knowing I would appraise her in the light of the picture windows. The room basically consisted of open space, the giant TV system, and a view of the murky Marina. And now, her. She startled me with a sudden squeal of delight. "Look!" she said as she knelt at the pile of silver discs littering the floor. "You've got all my movies! Let's watch one!" She picked up a copy of *Red Dust* and held it out to me in front of the stack of electronic hardware. Then, in a baby-doll voice: "How do you work this thing?"

I popped the disc into the machine and fired up the monitor, filling it with the true Harlow and Clark Gable.

"Do you have any popcorn, Clark?" she asked me. I had to disappoint her, but she was good-natured about it all and pulled me into a pile of pillows with her. It was a strange experience looking from the screen to the siren curled in my lap. She mouthed all the dialogue that Harlow spoke as the sun outside sank into the Marina.

As the movie continued, she slid up against me like a cat, and the contact was all warm and comfy and even arousing... but that's not what I wanted. I wanted the woman on the screen. The Jean in my lap started to purr, her engine ignited and accelerating. She pushed me back into the pillows and climbed atop me; I drowned in her body.

Her skin as smooth as the discarded satin gown, she flowed against me like butter on a frying pan, melting on me. Her talents spread throughout her body, but mine resisted. I tried closing my eyes, but could not keep the girl at the door out of my home. She drew me into her and we coupled ferociously, but it was nothing like that night. And I know it wasn't her fault, but I couldn't help but focus on the tiny red pimple sprouting on her chin. The *real* Harlow would never be so blemished. We united wetly and energetically, and our mutual release finally jettisoned enough unspilled juice to cramp my sphincter. But I was not satisfied, and she knew it.

"You know, I try my best to be her for you, but I can't really *be* her."

I couldn't say anything. I was spent and sweating, and just couldn't come up with an answer. I felt like the king of movie geeks, pining for a movie star who died before my parents were even conceived. What a fucking goober.

She just watched me, her mind working, and I felt like a twelve-year-old. My heart had been broken by an image on television. Her gaze just embarrassed me. Mama, make it stop. She just kept looking at me, judging me, shrinking me with her eyes. Meanwhile, the movie had come to an end.

Without saying anything, she walked across the room, still spectacularly naked, and picked up the phone. Her eyes still pinning me to the floor like a butterfly specimen, she started dialing and walked into the kitchen. I heard her dulcet, off-screen voice, but not the words. I heard her sign off before she re-entered the room and cradled the phone, shameless in her sheath of flawless ivory flesh. She gently took me by the hand and took me to the glass doors overlooking the water. She stared out for long silent minutes before speaking.

"How much would you pay to spend the night with Harlow?"

I figured it was time to pay up. I guess fifteen hundred wasn't a lot to pay to discover what a retard I was.

"I'll get your money."

I went to the desk and brought her the cash.

"I didn't mean me," she said as she took the bills and folded them into her dainty Bakelite purse. "I meant Harlow."

"I think you're as close as I'm ever going to get."

That made her laugh. "I'm not."

I was sick of her laughing at me. Think again about me casting you in anything, I thought.

"I mean Harlow, Jean Harlow, exactly who we were watching on the screen."

"What are you talking about?" I didn't want to play this game.

"What would you pay for a night of connubial bliss with Jean Harlow?"

"The real Jean Harlow? If it were possible?"

"If it were possible."

"I don't know. I can't go that far into the abstract."

"Come on, think about it. If you could have one night with her, how much would it be worth to you?"

I thought about it. "Fifteen hundred?" I thought it would compliment her.

"Shit, you can get *me* for fifteen hundred. Come on, for real. An entire night with Jean Harlow, exactly as you've seen her in the movies. How much?"

"I don't know... ten thousand dollars?"

"Cheapskate."

"Twenty."

"Jesus."

I gave up. "Then let's stop doing this. I couldn't fuck Jean Harlow for all the money in the world, so let's just stop this. She's been rotting since 1937."

She just smiled sweetly and shook her marcelled little head. "*I don't think so . . .*"

Where the fuck was this going? "Well, if she's a hundred years old and living in Argentina or something, I don't think I want a piece of her."

That fucking smile again.

"Would you pay a hundred grand to spend the night with the Jean Harlow of your dreams? The 1937 Jean Harlow? If you could. For real."

Just for the hell of it, I thought about it. Would I? The decision was a bit more difficult in the wake of the powerful orgasm I'd just experienced minutes ago. But with the Gramercy and Miramax deals set in hard copies, I had some disposable income. Is that how I'd dispose it? A hundred grand? Hell, I could spec out a script in a month for double that. So that's like two weeks' pay. Of course, you can't crank out a dozen scripts a year, but Jesus, even if it's a couple months' pay... would it be worth it? I didn't have a wife or kids or anything: just me and my TT. I'd pay a hundred thousand dollars to sleep with Harlow.

If it were possible.

So I said yeah.

And she said really? And I said yeah, I think I would. And she said that was interesting and slid into her jeans and that fucking T-shirt again, kissed me goodbye, and fluttered away.

It was another week before she called me back. I was immersed in *Saratoga* when the machine picked up. I never answer the phone, especially not when I'm viewing, and *especially* not when it's Jean onscreen. But it was her voice: "Are you there? It's Jean."

The voice, I had to admit, was perfect. I picked up.

"Hi."

She giggled, sounding like New York in the thirties. "Go to the bank," she whispered.

"What for?"

"It's time."

"Time for what?"

"You know. Hundred-thousand-dollar time. Cash or traveler's checks."

Well, you and I both know what that meant. But what it meant was impossible. I didn't know how to respond to her, and just sat there with that porcelain face basting my brain, probably breathing funny.

"Are you still there?"

"I'm here."

"Can you get to the bank today? And meet me at Union Station tonight at eleven?"

I didn't understand. "I don't understand," I told her.

"Like heck you don't." And then, with another tinkling little titter, she hung up, as the real Jean smiled at me from my 62-inch Pioneer, enhanced for sixteen-by-nine.

I'd spent a couple of nights sharing skin with this phenomenal creature, reaching a Nirvana Kurt Cobain never dreamed of, but what did I really know about her? That she could set me to palpitating was a given... but what kind of idiot would go to the bank, pull out a hundred grand, and meet this angel in the middle of the night at a train station in the cesspool of downtown Los Angeles? Surely this was a setup; obviously this, well, I'll say it, this *prostitute* had found a malleable mark, a sucker just dying to toss off his ill-gotten gains. She and her pierced and tattooed cohorts would beat me up and take my cash. *You* would never have gone for a crackbrained scenario like this one, and I would never have dared writing such a silly plotline. If I'd turned it in to Sid Fields, I'd have flunked Screenwriting 101.

But, you know, I did have a hundred grand. It was pretty much all I had at the moment, but, you know, I had more coming in. And I was unburdened by investments. What was the worst that could happen to me? Other than having my money stolen and my throat slashed, what did I have to lose? My soul? Yeah... *that's* worth a lot.

Was it really that preposterous to think that I might be able to have... *Jean*?

Well, the answer was obvious, but I sped down to Washington Mutual anyway.

Still grand but aging and missing a few teeth, Union Station reached coldly into the scuffed, blue-brown night sky. Mine was the only car in the desolate lot, and I parked as far as I could from the three creased, ruddy faces sharing hits off a bottle of violet rotgut. The sound of their retching was a perfect contemporary counterpoint to the timeless architectural elegance that reached out to embrace me. I was, as usual, anally punctual. Eleven distant chimes hung sweating in the muggy night air.

As I stepped into the empty vastness of the old dowager, it was like stepping into an evacuated Capra epic. I could imagine the postwar homecomings, the reunited sweethearts spotting one another through the teeming masses of humanity, the brass-band sendoffs to the senator's last hurrah. But the monochrome crowd evaporated, and the cracked leather seats and the gang-gouged woodwork brought me back home. It was an empty Art Deco barn strangling on its memories. I would be one of them.

Then, the tip-tap tip-tap of high-heels echoed around me, and I turned just as an unmistakable silhouette rounded the corner. She stepped into a shaft of light, and its reflection off of her platinum hair ignited the room in yellow fire. She stood there, letting the spotlight caress her perfection.

"Hi."

"Hi back."

I walked to her, my heart suddenly racing in anticipation, the cash in a shoulder bag, suddenly weighing a hundred pounds. What the fuck was I doing here?

"What the fuck am I doing here?" I asked her.

"Dreaming. Give me your keys."

"Where are we going?"

"Heaven."

I followed her out of the cavernous, empty building and back to my car, unable to pull my eyes from the lift and ripple of the perfect globes of her rear as she walked.

The thick summer night laid on us like an oil change, even with the top down. She caromed through the dank darkness, the empty downtown Los Angeles streets choking on their past. Broadway was a desiccated corpse, the klieg lights of the grand Million Dollar, United Artists, and Los Angeles Theaters long extinguished. A handful of zombies lumbered like cancerous cells through her clogged artery. We were on our own Fantastic Voyage through Innerspace when Jean suddenly pulled off behind the old Times Mirror building, and guided us down a long, dark, seemingly endless alley.

That alley led to the decaying backside of a once-grand edifice, a cracked granite frown slowly settling into the sinking subway horizon. She pulled us into its gaping, festering maw, and kept driving like a drill into the ground. The corkscrew drive was seemingly hellbound as it dug us deeper into a quakephobe's sweatiest nightmare. But as we plunged down beneath the city, lit only by headlights and the dim, browning sconces that studded the concrete wall, the temperature grew much cooler.

In moments, my grinning little TT peered into a grand open lobby, its flawless white-veined black marble gleaming in the shine of its headlights. A giant stone Thinker sat contemplating us in the middle of the vast room as Jean killed the engine and tip-tapped across the gleaming mirror of marble floor to the center pair of sculptured brass doors. The elegance of the lobby was impressive, and of another world: overstuffed leather and cherry sofas and chairs, vast WPA murals of noble working people on the job, a heavy walnut reception desk the size of a Beverly Center screen. It had all of the chi-chi quiet snootery of a Beverly Hills face-tightening clinic.

Jean said "I'm here" to nobody and nothing in particular, and the giant, wizard doors opened up to Oz.

The hallway was of impressive length and faded grandeur, lit by the dull Cocteau glow of faux lantern sconces. It was a soft, warm, but dim light... and in it, Harlow II was even more ravishing. She led me down the length of the hallway, and as we reached its end, the dark wood double doors opened up to us, revealing the Man Behind the Curtain.

The man was tiny, certainly not over five feet, with a venerable, dried-apple countenance tightly sheltered with a thick, pomaded landing strip of artificially boot-blacked hair. A ghost of cataract and eyelids that drooped like sagging breasts almost hid the sparkle of his rheumy grey eyes, and his osteoporosis curled him into a tiny question mark. He looked up at Jean, apparently unwilling to make eye contact with me until getting her approval.

"He's good," she told him, and the little lawn gnome finally looked up at me, manufacturing a smile that revealed perfectly straight white teeth that were way too big for his crepe-paper mouth. He reached out his right hand—which was missing the thumb—and I shook it. I don't know if you've ever shaken hands with a guy without a thumb, but it just doesn't feel right. His other hand was tucked out of sight in his pocket, and I wondered if the little gremlin was born without opposable thumbs at all.

After I shook his hand, he kept it reaching out at me. I thought he was stuck on pause or something until I realized that he was waiting for me to hand over the shoulder bag with the cash in it.

"Who are you?" I asked, and he looked back up at Jean, who turned to me with a smile.

"No names."

That made the little homunculus grin, and his smile, even in the dim light, was blinding. I handed over the bag to Pee Wee, who zipped it open and started carefully counting the bills. This was going to take a while. Jean leaned in to stick a kiss on my cheek.

"Have a great night." And she turned back down that long, lonesome hallway.

"Wait." She turned back with an expectant look. "Can this guy even talk?"

That made the withered little manikin testy. I thought he was going to bite my kneecap. "Of course I can talk! Oh, shit, I've lost count!" And he started over. From one.

With a "Nighty-bye," Harlow II was down the hall and out the door, leaving me with my own private Dr. Loveless. I waited in the doorway while he counted it all out: one hundred thousand dollars in hundred-dollar bills.

Eventually satisfied that I wasn't a piker, Mr. Subspecies turned and led me down the newly revealed corridor. I had to move slowly to keep from overtaking his baby steps.

We took another turn and he reached up on tippy-toes to flip a light switch, revealing a long, antiquated chamber that opened out onto several apartments. Each of them had a large picture window that looked into the central chamber, and each window was draped with ornate wine velvet curtains on the inside. Most of the curtains were closed, but not all of them. As I followed in my Munchkin's eensy steps, I was able to see into a drape that lolled lazily open. Inside was an ornate bedroom, decorated as if by Menzies: heavy wood pieces, a high molded ceiling, and a vast silk-sheeted bed against the wall. The only light was cast by the dim chamber sconce, but even in the shadows I could see that the bed was unmade.

Just as we passed the window to the clip-clop of teeny feet echoing through the otherwise silent chamber, a face suddenly appeared like a spotlight in the opening of the curtains. I jumped, I admit it, startled by its abrupt appearance, and the golden halo that surrounded her familiar face in the struggling, limp light reflected off her bottle blondness. But most unnerving of all was how her eyes were locked on mine, just a foot or so away from me. This was most definitely not Jean.

The face was enormous, a round, fleshy visage under a marigold mane, exquisitely painted in white-hot Helena Rubinstein beauty. The eyes, though—they were huge and liquid pale, drilling right into my own. But the spark was out behind them; they were gorgeous but empty, lifeless, shining husks of eyes. I wasn't sure she could even see me through them.

But boy, could I see her.

Striking in her red satin wrapper, she was an uncaged housefire. That huge moon of a face rose over an alarmingly ample décolletage and a waspy little waist I could circle in two hands. This was a woman you could only see in color: the red of her lips, the electric gold of her hair, the flamingo pink of her tongue, and—even though bound behind the thin red wrapper—the evident, nursed-dark muddy brown howdies of her vast, reaching nipples.

The Little Man gripped my hand in his gnarly, four-fingered tug, trying to pull me down the hall, but I couldn't move, not now that I recognized her. This incendiary explosion of boobs and blondness had been immortalized most spectacularly by Frank Tashlin in *Will Success Spoil Rock Hunter?*, but that's not how I recognized her.

No. The little relentlessly yiping dog at her feet was a clue, but what finally led me to put it all together were the tiny, nearly invisible telltale sutures that circled her neck.

I was eyelocked with Jayne Mansfield.

Obviously, some assembly had been required, since she was decapitated in a car wreck in 1967. But that was Jayne. The real deal. Alive. Breathing. Her impressive water wings heaving with each breath. I could barely even blink as I riveted into her glassy, vacant orbs. She didn't blink at all, not once. It was unsettling, at the very least. I'd only seen eyes like that once before, and I didn't want to remember it, but now she made me.

When I was five years old, my dad was teaching me how to ride a bike without training wheels for the first time. He'd just taken them off without even telling me, and I was roaring down the street, oblivious to my new mastery of two-wheeled travel, when he shouted out for me to look, that I was riding without training wheels. I looked down, saw that it was true, and panicked. The handlebars shimmied and I lost control. Dad came running to help me, just as an ancient, wheezing Impala roared around the corner on a tail of grey exhaust, and slammed him into the phone pole. I skinned my knee through my jeans as I fell off the bike and ran to see my father, who was shattered and pinned between the empty grin of the Impala's grille and the cracked Phone Pole Tower of Pisa. Our eyes were cinched as his life beat away with his slowing heart, leaving the flesh husk and the glazed, sightless eyes reflecting my own. I could see, even then, when his life had left him, and his eyes gone blind.

And now Jayne gave me the same vacancy sign before pulling the curtain shut.

"Come on," the tugging little gnome croaked as I allowed him to pull me from the blockaded showroom. "She's not for you."

"Was that Jayne Mansfield?" I asked him.

"No, it was Jane Pauley. What the fuck do you think?"

"You're a cranky old asshole, aren't you?"

"I'm actually very sweet once you get to know me."

I didn't believe him. But I followed him down the seemingly endless chamber anyway.

He stopped me at the very last room.

"You didn't bring flowers, did you," he said in a judgmental sneer. "She likes flowers."

"Nobody told me."

"It's breeding, common decency to bring a woman flowers. Now... you know the rules."

I looked at him. How should I know the rules? "Not really."

"Just be gentle. Thoughtful. And no rough-housing."

And then he was off, no doubt back to his place behind the curtain. His walk took him forever.

I gently rapped on the ornate door and waited, my heart trying to climb up my throat. I kept waiting, the mystery and marvel and anticipation shriveling my nerve as well as my manhood. I felt like a turtle pulled back in its shell. When it became evident that no one was coming to answer my knock, I reached out and gripped the doorknob. It was greasy with palm-sweat, but wasn't locked. It opened, and I entered in quiet, tiny steps.

The room was hushed and dark, but so were my desires, I guess. But the dim light from the candle guttering on the nightstand couldn't extinguish the glow that Jean Harlow—the real Jean Harlow, alive and in full living breathing color—cast. She sat on the edge of the peach satin bed, draped in shadow and a fine silk chemise. She turned to face me, but the curtain of shadow blacked out her features. I was frozen in place, my mouth gawping; I hadn't the strength to take a breath. The hairs at the nape of my neck curdled and a shimmer of gooseflesh traversed my body. Jean. Jean. Roses are red. And all of my guts have gone green.

After a big slice of eternity, I made the next move, taking a step toward her and the bed. Jean glided back a few inches on the satin quilt, lifting her face into the warm, gentle caress of the candlelight. It was at that moment that it became obvious that Harlow II looked nothing like my Jean, the real Jean. *The faux* Harlow had been sandblasted by modernity, corrupted by the modern age, while Jean—milky, creamy, elegant Jean— was above all that passage-of-time nonsense. I don't know how she was here sitting on this bed in this room with me after dying in 1937, but she was. This was no imposter. Somehow, she had been rescued from the ravages of death, had earned a station in eternity, and for a hundred thousand dollars I had bought a share of that station. A night with my forever Jean. A taste of eternity. Whatever science or magic made it possible, I was its slave.

And Jean's.

Unlocking the invisible shackles that bolted me to the floor, I moved to the bed and looked down at her longingly. She looked up into my eyes and gently patted the space on the bed next to her with her palm, once, silently inviting me to sit. Her eyes, though pure and startlingly blue, were ringed in black mascara, and as vacant and unblinking as Jayne's, though larger and more inviting. Her mouth was painted in a rose red so dark it was almost black, and shone in the pale candlelight. Her lips eased open, just a sticky little fraction of an inch, releasing the softest, curious sound from within. She was purring a constant, sensual little rumble, her own internal combustion engine.

"Jean?"

Without blinking or moving her eyes from me, she nodded. I sat next to her and took her pale ice cream hand in mine. The hand was cool and soft, limp, barely motivated, and I drew it to my face. I touched the back of her hand with my lips, I couldn't help it, and she let me. Her skin tasted like vanilla and fresh hand soap. She watched me kiss her hand through barren, staring eyes, and I laid my hand on her cheek and turned her face toward me. Her eyes turned sluggishly to mine, and we were face to face. Her purr was more distinct now, though no less sensuous. I could feel her breath stroke my face in cool even waves. Its scent was a bit pungent, but no more than it might be after a plate of penne arrabiatta. But it sure didn't smell like vanilla.

She neither resisted nor encouraged me, so I bent in and kissed her. She kissed me back, and my eyes closed in exultation. Her full, soft lips parted, and her chilly pink tongue sought mine. She sucked it into her mouth and began to nurse off of it, and there's no way I was going to stop her. I sneaked a peek as she milked my tongue, and her eyes were wide open, still unblinking, her mouth sucking mechanically, almost painfully, on my tongue.

I pulled away to look at her, and she looked back, gorgeous but empty. No resistance, no encouragement.

"What would you like?" I asked her. She just looked back at me. No words. Never any words. I knew the lights were out, but it didn't keep my libido from raging. My fear was that, presented with a dream, my physiognomy might recede and that junior might chicken out; but *au contraire, mon ami, au contraire.* The passive, alabaster icon on the bed with me ignited my hormones and overcame my stupefaction. The ample voluptuousness of one of Hollywood's greatest stars awaited me; the dream of a lifetime was at my fingertips, and if it wouldn't come to life to a symphony of Preston Sturges dialogue, if it would instead be my own personal silent epic, well, shit, so be it.

I reached out and gently lifted the strap of her chemise from her shoulder and let it drop, revealing the delicate sundae of her breast to me. Her eyes locked shamelessly on mine, and I reached over to cup it in my palm. As her feline engine accelerated, I bent down and took her breast in my mouth. It yielded, its cool marshmallow vanilla a creamy treat. The nipple stayed relaxed, unresponsive, never flexing to attention. Her arms curled about me and limply came to rest on my shoulders. I looked up from her breast and she watched me nursing on her with those clear blue unblinking eyes. It stopped me. I raised my face to hers, tried to see beyond the pupils, but was blocked by absence.

She moved in, eyes still wide open, and kissed my mouth. The hum from within was soothing and welcoming. I let her kiss me, closed my eyes, and ran my fingers through the tight marcels of her platinum hair. Her hair felt like weaves of satin, glossy and slippery, and my fingers got lost in it. My thumb tangled in one of her waves, and I gently tugged it free.

Her breath caught in a gasp and I opened my eyes, afraid I hurt her. Her eyes were even wider now as I lifted my hand from her hair... pulling a patch of it away with my thumb! There was a clot of grayish reddish brownish skin at the base of the tangle of spun gold wrapped around my thumb, and she reached for it, unable to take it in her own sleeping fingers.

"Oh, God, I'm so sorry, I'm so sorry!" I tried to calm her, but she just kept quietly and unsuccessfully reaching for her curls. There was a dark brown square on her scalp where the patch had pulled free, and a few drops of a dark fluid that could only have been blood wept to the surface.

"Are you okay?" She didn't answer me, of course. She had given up trying to retrieve her hair and was suddenly reaching for my groin with curious, less-than-dexterous fingers. I couldn't help it; the boy had a mind of his own. As she fumbled to release me, I helped her with the zipper, quickly forgetting about our little experience with the hair. The same mouth that had locked so successfully to my tongue now found succor in the netherworld.

The suction was remarkable considering the fragility of her other movements. I had never felt anything like the cool, muscular, rhythmic suction her mouth incurred. I couldn't help but grip her hair in my hands as I approached a bucking, uncontrollable orgasm that jolted through my body, emptying me of weeks of celibacy.

I jerked violently in fulfillment, and her head bobbed off and back onto my convulsing tissue. It was irresistible impulse; I didn't mean to pull away the handfuls of flaxen hair and grey, preserved flesh. And when she screamed—the first vocalizing she'd released since I entered her room—I looked down to see that one of those fragile, ice blue, vacuous eyes had been punctured, and wept a clear tide of thick tears.

Her inhuman screech echoed through the silence and in moments the little gnome was charging into the room in hunched-over horror. *"Jeeeeeaaaaaaaaannnnnnnnn!"* he howled. It was the longest single-syllable word I'd ever heard. He yanked me away from her in an incredibly powerful four-fingered grip, and in a cloak of guilt I climbed back into my khakis.

The little professor tended Jean with incredible gentleness, his own eyes going glassy as he dabbed her leaking eye socket with his hanky. *"I said no rough-*

housing!" he told me as he soothed her delicate body. "You'd better get out of here."

I agreed. As I made my way to the door, I heard his plaintive, melancholy words evaporate into the velvet night: "Daddy fix, Baby. Daddy fix again."

My hundred-thousand-dollar half-hour was over.

I've tried several times to return to the House of Harlow, but it is long gone, and without a trace. I've called and called Pseudo-Jean, but that number is no longer in service, and there is no new number. Now all I have to remember Jean are her movies. I've seen them so often that I know them all by heart, but it isn't just the movies themselves that so entrance me. It's the time long past, the dream long remembered. And I had a piece of that before I put its eye out.

Chocolate

X woke up wearing someone else's smile.

It was chocolate. The smell, the flavor, the unmistakable texture of the good stuff... creamy, dreamy and dark, so rich that it woke me up. As it dissipated, it left in its place an overwhelming rush of disappointment, bordering on depression.

Now, I'm not a guy who salivates at the mention of a Hershey bar—I've always prided myself on my clear thinking and level-headedness—but in my dream state that morning, I'd have killed for a hollow Easter bunny.

I never dream .. . not so I remember, anyway. On the rare occasion that I *do* dream, I never remember the dream, merely the dreaming. I'll wake up, my head filled with the most amazing bubbles and shadows of boundless nocturnal thought, only to have it vanish as I dredge myself into the waking world. Dreamland and I remain perfect strangers.

But this chocolate heaven stayed with me into the light of the morning sun. The purity of its taste, the milky calm of it melting down my throat, the gentle caffeine rush flowed through me with such sensual pleasure that I immediately understood why our great-grandparents considered the stuff a powerful aphrodisiac.

Since the divorce led me into the gym and a macrobiotic diet all those months ago, this was wish fulfillment I never knew I desired. I can take sweets or leave them. I *thought*. But if I take them, I can hire out to Macy's on Thanksgiving Day.

But the diet isn't so tough. Nothing ever used to be much of a problem. Sure, the marriage was less than successful, but we handled it in a civilized manner. We didn't hit each other, or scream all night, or fight endlessly. It just didn't work, so we ended it. It was a passionless affair, from the time the vows were said, and we're better off now apart than together. And Babette and I are still friends.

The day The Dream woke me, I had to go shopping. Since the Schick Center aversion therapy, it's no big deal. I could guide my cart past the beckoning candy and cookies with considerable ease. But today, the lingering taste made life more difficult. With fierce determination, I loaded the basket with the required rabbit food: sprouts, spinach, pao darko tea, you know the stuff. But it was when I headed to the meat counter for the ground turkey that I heard their little voices.

A Nestle's Crunch called me by name; the Cadbury with hazelnuts was trying to crawl into my cart; the M&Ms—plain and peanut—were trying to melt in my mouth, not in my hands. I turned away from the meat counter, and went looking for Mr. Goodbar.

I raced home with my bounty, and tore into the candy with a voracious desire. Stuffing it into my mouth, where there should have been a surge of sensual satisfaction, a chocolate itch scratched by Godiva, there was only letdown.

It was creamy, rich and sweet... but *meaningless*. I could take it or leave it. Even though alone, I went pink with embarrassment; it really wasn't worth the hypoglycemic rush I knew I would have to endure. I didn't crave that shit.

I gagged down a salad, and washed it down with unfiltered carrot juice.

Yum.

Senses are important to me. I create artificial flavors for the food industry, and my first fear was that the olfactory was acting up, and my career might be jeopardized. But the Chocolate Experience was an isolated one, and it was soon forgotten.

It must have been two weeks later when the sneezes blasted me from slumber at about four in the morning. It was the damned cat. In my sleep it hummed and sputtered in my lap, as I stroked it, loved it, cuddled it as if it were my closest life-long chum.

But I'm allergic to cats.

Okay, I love animals, am a member of Defenders of Wildlife, PETA, *and* the Cousteau Society, but I just hate cats. They're sneaky, annoying, leave their hair all over the furniture—which they've clawed to shreds—and make my eyes go red and teary. My deviated septum packs up and explodes when one of the little darlings is near.

So what in the hell am I doing cuddling and cooing Puff in my sleep? And with all deference to the wisdom of my allergies, since when does *dreaming* of a cat make me sneeze?

Something was going on here that I didn't understand. It struck me that perhaps I was dreaming someone else's dreams.

But it turned out to be more than the purloining of slumber fantasy. What was happening to me was much more than a dream.

One night, while driving home from a particularly tiresome day at the lab, the dream spilled into my waking hours. I was overwhelmed with affection and warmth, overflowing with a rush of romance that would have made the Bronte sisters blush. Somehow, I was a human radio tower, receiving emotions of such depth that I nearly crashed the Mazda.

Here I am on the way home from Consolidated Flavor Enhancement, looking forward to choosing from a variety of at least half-a-dozen boxes of Lean Cuisine in the freezer, a light beer, and a stroke magazine I hid in the evening Examiner, and I was nearly knocked senseless by this rush of true love so inestimably foreign to me.

I thought I'd been in love a hundred times—I know I told a hundred women I loved them, and I sure meant it at the time—but I'd never known true love. And from this experience, not even a reasonable facsimile. With a crescendo of sudden shame and embarrassment, I realized I didn't know shit about love. I was suddenly hit in the face with my shallowness, so incapable of emotional depth that I never knew such feelings—at such depth—even existed.

When the transmission ended, it left me drained, and unbelievably sad.

Supposedly you never miss what you've never had, but now that I'd felt this exhilaration, I was left deflated and so depressed that I actually cried my way home.

Even as a child, I never cried. I used to lie in bed at night, trying to summon up the image of my dead grandfather to make myself feel enough to spill tears, usually without success.

And now, caught in the valley-bound gridlock of rush hour traffic, my anticipation of Pritikin bread and Cookin' Bag chicken was trespassed by the swelling and spilling of heretofore arid tear ducts.

To a newcomer, feeling is pain.

But it was a glorious pain, and once felt, I needed to experience it again. What was happening to me? And why?

Over the ensuing weeks, the transmissions were random. Somehow, I was a psychic burglar, stealing someone else's senses. Without warning, I would suddenly see through someone else's eyes, taste with their mouth, or—by far the best of all—feel what they were feeling.

But nothing I could do could will the transmissions on. They struck at random and always alone: smell without sight, touch without hearing, emotions without vision.

However, now that I seemed to understand what was happening, and looked forward to receiving the signals, they were denied me. I *wanted* to feel the emotions of a *true* human being, someone who felt deeply and passionately, and seemed to take a proper place on the planet. I felt like a welfare tenant in Hearst Castle, that I deserved to be evicted from the planet for impersonating a human being. I wanted to be allowed to grow.

But days passed, and the only emotions to roll about in my head were, disappointingly, my own. I kept occupied at the lab, made myself so busy that it kept me from wishing on the empathy rush.

Just an ingredient or two from perfecting an imitation honeydew flavor for Jelly Bellies, it struck again. No longer confined to dream infiltration, the transpositions chose to attack in my waking hours, and usually at the most inopportune of moments.

Like the first time, it began with a smell. It was almost-roses. In my business, I knew immediately that it wasn't real roses, but a very good simulation. I've since identified it: Tea Rose perfume. And then, the feeling. I covered myself with my arms, suddenly standing naked in the middle of the lab, toweling myself dry, powdering my body, softly, luxuriously, sensually pampering myself.

It was a *woman!*

And as swiftly as she was there, she was gone, and the heavenly scent of almost-rose on her skin gave way to the syrupy stink of near-honeydew. A bad bargain, but it left me with a raging erection.

Though I hadn't seen her, I knew she was beautiful, judging her from the inside out. She was filled with love and goodwill, and her abrupt departure was painful. I needed to know her better. I needed to know her at all.

That was the day. From that point on, it was all I could do to live my own life. I thought about her endlessly, wondering who she was, where she lived, what could be the sonnet that was her name. What did she look like?

The next phase was paranoia.

Was she receiving me? Was this sensual exchange a two-way circuit, or merely a party line on which I was invited to listen in? And if she were receiving me, she could see how relentlessly superficially my life had been lived. Before finding her, my deepest thought was the perfection of imitation top sirloin, and I was sure she'd found me out. She *must* know about the men's magazines that littered my bedroom and bathroom... and in turn be aware of the inordinate amount of time spent with my left hand. Even *before* the divorce. I suddenly felt very lonely, in the most literal sense of the world, knowing that she deserved better than *me*.

And so did I.

For the most part, what I received from her were the most beautiful and pure thoughts and feelings that I had ever experienced. They were so good, so generous, so giving that I could but envy her. I threw out the beaver books, dusted and vacuumed the house, and even scrubbed the toilet. I even began to make the bed every morning. You never know...

Perhaps my attempts to impress her through the two-way mirror I imagined existed between us was a little overboard, but I had to be my best for her, and thereby for myself. I wrote checks to wildlife organizations; I began to compose hopelessly romantic poems; I had fresh roses around me at all times; I even went so far as to buy a cat. If she knows, it is worth the sneezing and the watery eyes.

I tried not to consider the more likely possibility: that she was blissfully unaware of my existence. I needed to find her, to see her, to talk to her, to make her a living, breathing soul mate, who would no doubt find me her ideal companion for the rest of our lives. I knew that it had become obsession; I needed her to know it, too. My most fervent hope was that she would transmit while writing the return address on an envelope, or while giving out her phone number. Was that too much to ask? After all, didn't there have to be a reason for our psyches to become entwined in the ether?

She just kept doing little things that drove me more and more madly in love with her. She *sang* in the mornings! Can you imagine a soul so bright and cheerful that it could start the morning with a song? She laughed a lot. And when she cried, it was for joy. But it broke my heart to feel the wet of her tears. She needed my shoulder.

You'd have fallen in love with her, too. But I was there first.

In bed one night, I drifted off to sleep in her bubble bath. The water in her tub was so bubbly and relaxing that I just couldn't keep my eyes open. I hoped she slept as easily as I.

It was only a couple hours later that I bolted awake.

There were hands on my chest. Rough-hewn and horny, they gripped and kneaded our breasts, twisting, massaging, pinching extended nipples, and I felt overpowering heat in my loins. I realized in aroused horror that she was sending again, and this time...

It still embarrasses me to even think about it.

I felt our breasts get hard with the rough handling. I felt a hot, wet mouth circle the nipple, the tongue tickling the hardened teat into a miniature pagoda of flesh. My heart thudded with fear, confusion... and excitement that I hoped I could attribute to her. I didn't know how to react; he was playing rough, but it felt... *good*.

I could feel wet heat working its way down my body, and before I knew it, I felt penetration! My body had by now completely given way to hers, and I felt things I'd never felt before—nor wanted to! The first stroke was absolutely the most shocking experience I'd ever known. And it kept going.

And then, before taking leave of me, the experience reached its apex, and I experienced my first vaginal and clitoral orgasms. And to complete the set, my rocket launched, making a mess of the newly washed sheets.

After the physical devastation, I just lay there in bed, sweating, feeling guilt and shame, and a curious sense of empathy that no other man can know. I was nauseous with post-coital confusion, and didn't sleep the rest of the night.

Sleeping never got any easier. She was constantly on my mind, the thought of her constantly gnawing at me. I needed her as much as I wanted her, and I'd never wanted anything so much in my life. Even though I only received flashes of her for a few minutes total during the course of a week, I felt that I knew her better than any man has known any woman. And for some time, there was no reason to believe that it wasn't true.

Who chooses their soul mate?

Would that it were so simple: to meet all of the available potential partners, and using mind and body, making the most intelligent decision for a life partner. No, love chooses us, not the other way around. And once hooked, there is little turning back. I was in love with a nameless woman I'd never seen, who quite probably had no idea I even existed. Had I known it was hopeless, I might have been able to stop it. Or I might not. But I didn't, and I didn't want to.

And neither would you.

A few days later, she was sending again. I looked down, and we were painting our nails. Her hands were long and tapered, and the polish was a wet, blood red. The polish was applied slowly, gracefully, peacefully, and her thoughts, as ever, were loving and calm. When she finished, my view followed her hand as it grabbed the door of the bathroom medicine cabinet, and pulled it open.

Her image whooshing by in the cabinet mirror was so casual and inevitable that it took me a moment to realize I had actually *seen* her! Instantly, the transmission fled, freeing my own senses to realize what just happened. The vision settled in the lightning flash of memory permanently embedded on my cerebellum, and my fury with the brevity of the vision gave way to tides of joy. In my mind, at least, I had grasped the Holy Grail, if only for a fraction of a second.

She was breathtaking!

That was no surprise, having known her as I did. But she was nothing short of a goddess. Her hair, still damp from the shower, was brown, and fell to her bare, milky shoulders. Her pale green eyes were huge and innocent. And she was naked. Her firm, small breasts acted as proud hosts for her attentive, brown, eraser-like nipples.

She was truly all that a human being could be. And then, she was gone.

It was fully three weeks before I heard from her again: three weeks of the most intense loneliness I'd ever felt. I wanted her so badly that I couldn't eat, which suited my waistline if not my heart. It was the cruelest form of impotence I could imagine; I needed her to know that she was the most important thing in my life.

I kept putting in the hours at work, but my heart and mind were far away. I managed to bring the Honeydew Project to a reasonable end, and the Jelly Belly people were happy, but I knew it wasn't perfect. But I didn't care; that shit didn't mean anything to me now. I wanted to share my good fortune with *her*.

I found myself riding an emotional roller coaster, and I was never sure if it was hers, mine, or ours. My spirits would soar to the heights of ecstasy, and in moments plummet to the depths of gut-churning despair. In one moment I'd share a smile with everyone

I'd pass, and in another be screaming at the slightest misdemeanor that encountered me. I'd gone from a man whom few had ever seen angry, to a veritable amusement park of emotions.

The next time she visited me was embarrassing, but at least it was a visit.

As a child, did you ever dream of going to the bathroom, only to wake up and find that you'd wet the bed? I did it a couple times when I was little, lying in the top bunk over my older brother. Boy was he pissed!

Well, that's what happened. But it wasn't a dream; it was her! She must have gotten up in the middle of the night, and I woke up peeing in my bed. It was the weirdest eliminatory experience I've ever had; I was pissing for her, and it felt like it was coming from someplace it wasn't. And then, when she wiped, it *really* felt strange.

When she went back to bed, we couldn't sleep. Something was bringing us pain, and I couldn't bear her hurt. She deserved only joy, and there was nothing I could do about it. And, with random rancor that too often typifies those things over which we have no control, this transmission lasted longer than any previous one.

But I didn't mind; it was time together. And perhaps she was reaching out to me for help. I would have died to keep her from hurting, and I hope somehow that she knew that.

I felt tears splash down on my naked chest, but when I looked down, my skin was dry. I ached for her, and she was gone.

All I could do was worry about the woman I loved. I wanted nothing more than to block out all of her pain, to bring the boundless joy back into that beautiful, uncluttered, loving intelligence. I called in sick the next day, for even though I was no longer receiving, I was nauseous with her anguish.

Later that day, it came in a brief flash of incredible anger, and was gone. It was a shock getting this unannounced flash of temper stabbing through me in the middle of my Weight Watchers whole-wheat pizza like that. The strength and nastiness of the emotion was devastating; it was something of which I thought she was incapable. Something must have pushed her to the brink to ignite such horrible fury, and I wanted to destroy it for her.

By night, however, it appeared that all was well. I was watching a heart operation on PBS, when suddenly I broke into a gale of her melodious laughter. It was a joyous, cleansing experience for us, and I knew that she must have crossed that bridge over troubled water. I actually cried with the joy of relief that the gorilla on her back had been shot and killed. God, I never wanted her to hurt like that again! She was gone quickly, but I went to sleep happy. I probably dreamed about her.

A few days later, I knew she was still happy. Her next transmission was uncluttered and clear. She must have been lying in a meadow somewhere beautiful. I could feel the prickling of the grass, and took deep breaths of the cool, fresh air, scented with just the faintest touch of real carnations. We were completely at peace, and I happily wore her smile again. Now that my fear for her happiness was put to rest, I could go back to needing and wanting her again. If only we could meet, I thought, I'd give her anything she wanted: all the love and support she could stand, and then some. But I wouldn't smother her, I promised aloud.

Though I ached to be with her, I was sleeping better. I knew she was untroubled, and that made my life better as well. I knew that someday soon, somehow I would find her. That's all there was to it.

And then, several days went by without so much as a smell from her, and I worried anew. I would panic on those occasions, *certain* I'd lost her, that I'd never hear from her again. Hurt and crestfallen, I never allowed the feelings to become anger or resentment. That was beneath me and the purity of my love. I would try to convince myself that I was lucky to have had as much of her as I did, that she had made my life better and more complete just by existing.

But that didn't cheer me. I missed her terribly.

Then came Saturday. I was lying on the couch watching *The Seventh Voyage of Sinbad* for the first time since I was about twelve. Trust me, it doesn't hold up. In fact, it lulled me into a sleep so deep it was as if somebody had flipped a switch and turned off the world.

Then came the rush, and I slept so soundly that nothing made any sense. My hands gripped something tightly, and I was completely confused. I was lashing out, poking, slashing. The blanket began to lift, and I felt like filth.

We were killing.

I felt the long, phallic blade in our hands hit flesh. It slowed at impact, then ripped through the living meat in sickening penetration. We hacked repeatedly through the squirming, helpless flesh, hitting bone with jarring abruptness, then tearing through. The vibrations of flesh being rent moved through my hands and into my body, settling in the acid pit of my stomach, and I shivered with the hideousness of it. I felt the warm, wet spray of blood like tears on my face, felt it run down my arms in hot, pulsing rivers.

Then, the slashing stopped, and she was gone. The next emotions were my own. I felt indescribably dirty and savage, with a sense of degradation I had never known. I wore a bloody sheath of sickness and depravity I'm certain will never come off. If you haven't felt it, you can't know it... and I never did before this. I was red with shame and humiliation, sweating a foul stench of guilt. I retched repeatedly over the side of the couch until I went limp, my stomach empty. And then I couldn't stop the tears that splashed into the puddle.

That was months ago. I haven't heard from her since. This is the longest time by far between transmissions, and I'm resigned to the likelihood that there will be no more. She lied to me, cheated on me, used me. I want to hate her, flush her from my mind.

But I can't. Love chooses us. And I can't stop thinking about her. So I'm still waiting, just in case.

I need someone to tell me how to feel.

FLESH AND FANTASY

A Screenplay

Based on the Short Story

"Chocolate"

FADE IN:

INT. ROOM - NIGHT

It is dark, anonymous. We can't really tell where we are, because we are tight on the ravaged FACE of JAMIE EVANS, a man in his thirties who would look appealingly boyish, if not for the drying spatters of BLOOD on his face and clotting his hair.

We don't know whose blood it is, but we catch shocking glimpses of it throughout the room's shadows.

This was quite a BLOODBATH.

The only LIGHT in the otherwise black-shadowed room WASHES OUT his FACE. He SQUINTS when he looks up, then away, as an anonymous BODY, covered with a blood-soaked SHEET, is carried through by two UNIFORMED OFFICERS. Jamie appears broken, exhausted, as if telling a story he can't bear to repeat.

                    JAMIE
               (directly into camera)
          Have you ever been in love?

His answer is a patronizing sigh, and a billowing gust of rancid, blue CIGARETTE SMOKE. Jamie SQUINTS.

                    MAN'S VOICE (O.S)
          I've been married for
          seventeen years.

                    JAMIE
          I asked if you've ever been
          in love. Really in love.

                    MAN'S VOICE
          Sure.

Jamie just looks at camera for a moment, then shakes his head.

                    JAMIE
          Not like I have.

                    MAN'S VOICE
          Oh, no. You're special.

                    JAMIE
          I mean it. No man ever loved
          a woman like I loved her.

                    MAN'S VOICE
          I can see that by the blood
          clotting on your shirt.

                    JAMIE
               (disgusted)
          Okay, fine. If you want to
          call it murder, that's fine
          with me. I just don't care.
               (beat)
          I'm tired.

The CAMERA PULLS BACK and AROUND to REVEAL
the BACKS of two other MEN facing him. Jamie
halfheartedly waves away another GUST of
BLUE SMOKE.

                    MAN'S VOICE
          We're all tired. Let's back
          up a little bit. I'm not
          clear on how this whole thing
          started.

                    JAMIE
          What difference does it make?
          You don't believe anything I
          tell you anyway. How often do
          I have to tell it?

                    MAN'S VOICE
          'Til I think it starts to
          sound like the truth, God
          help me. You'd better just
               (cont'd)

                    MAN'S VOICE
                     (Cont'd)
          humor me, okay? Start from
          the beginning; a little
          background might help.

                      JAMIE
                   (sarcastic)
          Fine. I got up, got dressed,
          and went to work. I don't eat
          breakfast.

                    MAN'S VOICE
          Where do you work?

EXT. COUGAR CHEMICAL LABORATORY - DAY

San Antonio, TX... but not the high-tech
corner. This is the other side of the tracks,
not exactly seedy, but not MIT, either.

It doesn't look like you'd expect a science
lab to look; the building is a faceless block
in a line of faceless blocks in the downtown
warehouse district in the heart of a big
city. Lots of ancient, crumbling BRICK, some
trying to hide under IVY and style.

                    JAMIE (O.S)
          Cougar Chemical. I create
          artificial flavors for the
          food industry.

INT. COUGAR LAB - DAY

We MOVE with Jamie along a ROW of BEAKERS,
TEST TUBES, BOWLS, and a jumble of other LOW-
TECH lab and kitchen UTENSILS. The LAB
appears fairly SLAPDASH... bordering on
GRUNGY.

We barely recognize Jamie in his natural
state: clear-eyed, energetic, natural good
looks hiding behind the round, owlish

glasses. He has energy, humor, and if he's not exactly overflowing with happiness, he is at least comfortable in his surroundings. He is dressed in very unscientific jeans and rolled sleeves, loading WATER from the COOLER into a BEAKER... until he notices that some jokester has put MAGIC ROCKS into the drinking water. They have GROWN into spiky towers overnight.

                    MAN'S VOICE (O.S)
          White lab coats, germ-free
          lab, that kind of shit?

                    JAMIE (O.S)
          Not exactly...

                    JAMIE
          Who put the Magic Rocks in
          the Sparkletts?

JEANETTE, a Selma Diamond-type in her fifties with a CHEROOT dangling from her mouth, a bag of chili-cheese FRITOS hidden behind her elbow, and the ubiquitous CRYSTAL dangling from her neck, is stirring a BUBBLING CONCOCTION on her HOTPLATE in the corner of the lab, trying not to chuckle. She is bright but crusty, refreshingly bullshit-free.

There is a "NO SMOKING" sign prominent on the wall behind her.

There are little piles of CRYSTALS, a couple PYRAMIDS and other NEW AGE ITEMS on her desk.

A long ASH drops from the end of her CHEROOT into the pot. She looks around, sees no one is looking, and quickly stirs it into the mixture. What they don't know won't hurt them.

Jamie SMELLS something from all the way across the lab.

                    JAMIE
              (without even looking)
          Chili-cheese Fritos? I
          thought you were on a diet...

Jeanette turns, busted.

                    JEANETTE
          Maybe you didn't know that
          the Frito is nature's perfect
          food.

                    JAMIE
          Particularly the chili-and-
          cheese variety.

                    JEANETTE
          Particularly. Look it up.

Jamie continues to mix some ingredients in a
glass bowl with a popsicle stick. As the
mixture THICKENS, he takes a TASTE. He SAVORS
it expectantly for a moment, and when the
FLAVOR hits his TASTE BUDS, he GAGS and SPITS
it out.

                    JAMIE
          Yuck! There is just no way to
          perfectly synthesize honeydew
          melon. It's impossible!

                    JEANETTE
          I been tellin' you that all
          week. The General and I came
          close in '77, but the test
          rats gave birth to two-headed
          offspring. Legal felt that
          was a considerable drawback.
          So how much call do you get
          for artificial honeydew
          melon, anyway?

                    JAMIE
          It's the challenge!

                    JEANETTE
          Challenge schmallenge. Give
          'em cantaloupe!

Suddenly WALLY comes charging into the lab
from around the corner. He's a little dynamo
who's just hit 40: balding and a little rat-
like, he's a real upper, enthusiastic and
funny without realizing it. He's the only
one in a LAB COAT; he likes the COSTUME.

                    WALLY
          Jamie! Jeanette! Tongues!

Jamie and Jeanette sigh in unison, and
exchange a tired, resigned look. They've
been through this before. A lot.

               JAMIE AND JEANETTE
                    (in unison)
          Again?

                    WALLY
               (in Bullwinkle voice)
          Nothing up my sleeve...

And the grinning, excited mad doctor rushes
over to them, dipping an eyedropper into a
steaming mug of vile-looking LIQUID.

                    WALLY
          Close 'em!

Jamie and Jeanette look at one another, then
they CLOSE their EYES in unison, throw back
their heads, and stick out their tongues.

Wally SQUIRTS the repulsive-looking GLOP
into Jamie's mouth first, then Jeanette's.

                    WALLY
          The Golden Tongue first.

They are prepared for anything... but not
for this.

                    JAMIE
                 (surprised)
          Hey! Wally... this is
          really... good!

Jeanette nods surprised agreement.

                    WALLY
          You're surprised?
                 (grinning proudly)
          Come on! Analysis!

                    JAMIE
                 (savoring for a moment)
          Okay, let's see... roast
          beef... medium rare...

                    JEANETTE
          A little smoke...

                    JAMIE
          Mesquite!

Wally nods, as if having found a cure for
cancer.

                    JAMIE
          Just enough marbling for
          flavor... wait! Not roast
          beef! Prime rib! Right?

Wally is unable to contain his proud glee.

                    JAMIE
          Wally, this is perfect! The
          General's sure to give you a
          raise!

                    JEANETTE
                 (in awe)
          Prime rib! I didn't think it
          was possible!

                    WALLY
          Thanks!
            (tasting some, because he
            likes it, then sobering)
          Seems a shame to waste it on
          Gainesburgers.

Jamie and Jeanette join in his slightly
depressed nod. But Jamie looks for the silver
lining.

                    JAMIE
               (brightening)
          But you did it!

                    WALLY
          Yeah. I did it, huh?

Jamie turns, sensing someone coming before
the others notice. Almost as if he smelled
the approach. Off Jamie's look, Jeanette
stuffs out her cheroot, waves away the smoke.
But it is too late.

GENERAL COUGAR ENTERS.

He is the head of Cougar Chemical, and
despite his affection for military-style
Everett Koop epaulet shirts, is a nice, if
eccentric, scientist-turned-businessman.
Approaching seventy, there is still a
twinkling of Peter Pan about him, and an
excited joy-to-the-world attitude.

                    GENERAL COUGAR
          This is a tobacco-free
          environment, Ms. Rogers.

                    WALLY
          If you call that shit
          tobacco...

                    JEANETTE
          Sorry, General.

                    WALLY
          Welcome, O Great Olfactory.
          What brings you to the
          dungeon?

The General thinks Wally's a riot. He claps
his hand onto Wally's shoulder.

                GENERAL COUGAR
          Come on, everybody, it's
          here! It's time for the
          unveiling!

And he LEADS them out of the lab and into
the corridor. Confused, Jamie, Wally and
Jeanette hang back a bit, whispering in his
wake.

                  JEANETTE
          That guy could be in a
          crowded stadium and tell you
          who farted.

                   WALLY
          And what they had for dinner.

INT. LOBBY - DAY

All of the company's two dozen or so
EMPLOYEES are gathering in the lobby when
the General leads our group in.

                GENERAL COUGAR
          Hi... hello, everybody. Just
          a minute.

A ten-foot-square SOMETHING is being put
into place against the back wall, hidden
under a DROPCLOTH. As WORKERS are putting it
into place, the General rushes over with an
excited smile, taking a PEEK under the canvas
before he begins.

He is very excited to unveil whatever is
behind the canvas, and proceeds to do so with

great ceremony.

                    GENERAL COUGAR
          As you know, I've
          commissioned a new logo for
          the company, and it's finally
          here. I knew you would all
          want to be here for its
          formal unveiling, and...
          so... um . Let's unveil the
          son of a gun.

With a giant grin, the general gives the
signal, and the workers pull off the
dropcloth to reveal the new canvas.

It is a giant, stylized snarling COUGAR, very
dramatic, and in decided contrast to the
drabness of the distressed brick walls. The
EMPLOYEES look at one another, and,
realizing a reaction is expected from them
by the eager General, they APPLAUD the
painting.

Jamie, standing nearest to the canvas, takes
another step closer, intrigued by the
powerful image. As he STARES at it, we PRESS
IN ON HIM, and IN ON THE PAINTING.

The CHATTER and AMBIENT SOUNDS grow distant
and MUFFLED to Jamie, as we move relentlessly
CLOSER.

ANGLE - THE CAT

When we are unbearably close to it, we
suddenly match it with a FLASH CUT of a REAL
COUGAR SNARLING: a shocking split second.

INCLUDE JAMIE

He jumps back, terrified, and immediately
embarrassed when everyone REACTS to him.

                    GENERAL COUGAR
          Jamie, are you all right?

Jamie WHISKS his HEAD around to the VOICE.

ANGLE - JAMIE'S P.O.V.

The view SWINGS across Wally and Jeanette,
not settling on the General, but rather on a
close, SUNLIT VIEW of a STRANGER: a handsome
young man, almost MALE-MODEL looking,
laughing with delight. A complete non
sequitur.

RESUME JAMIE

He is looking right at the General, wide-
eyed. JAMIE'S P.O.V. Merely the General.
Normal.

RESUME OTHERS

                    GENERAL COUGAR
          Jamie?

Jamie's HEART is POUNDING. He doesn't know
what just happened. And he cannot see any
sign of the HANDSOME YOUNG MAN. Gone.

                    JEANETTE
          What's the matter?

Jamie looks around sheepishly. He doesn't
understand the hallucination, either.

                    JAMIE
               (not so sure)
          I'm fine. No problem.

                    GENERAL COUGAR
               (proudly)
          Do you like it?

                    JAMIE
          Love it, General.

                    GENERAL COUGAR
          Please don't kiss my ass,
          Jamie.

                    JAMIE
          No, I mean it. It's really...
          special.

                    GENERAL COUGAR
          It is, isn't it?

INT. RESTAURANT - DAY

It's high noon in a crowded blue collar
steakhouse, bustling with the lunchtime
crowd. Wally and Jamie have a corner table,
and are settling in behind their meals.

Wally is digging into a big STEAK, a mountain
of FRIES, and a BAKED POTATO with sour cream
and butter, lots of butter on his three
rolls, etc.

Jamie picks at a puny, wilting CAESAR SALAD,
mooning enviously over Wally's real food.
Wally looks at Jamie's plate.

                    WALLY
          How can you eat that rabbit
          food?

                    JAMIE
          I have to eat that rabbit
          food. If I don't watch it I
          turn into the Goodyear blimp.

                    WALLY
                (his mouth full)
          Funny. I can eat 'til I puke,
          and never gain an ounce. High
          metabolism or something.

Jamie looks from his own plate to Wally's.
Depressing.

192

                    JAMIE
              (good-natured)
          Fuck you.

                    WALLY
          Still, Mr. Newly Single, "be
          all that you can be". How's
          the love life?

                    JAMIE
                  (joking)
          Oh, me and my left hand are
          going steady now.

                    WALLY
          So long as the right hand
          knows what the left is doing.
          All newly fit and fabulous,
          and no place to go, huh?

                    JAMIE
          I just need a little time to,
          you know, think about stuff.

He takes a bite of his delectable salad.
Mmmmmm...

                    WALLY
          My band is playing at the
          Stand Friday night. Why don't
          you come? You might meet some
          nymphomaniacal rock'n'roll
          animal!

                    JAMIE
          I don't think I'm ready for
          that. Give me a decade or
          two.

                    WALLY
          Don't give me that divorce
          depression shit. Come on,
          man, let's play grown-up!
          Anna's got to watch the twins
                  (cont'd)

                    WALLY
                  (cont'd)
anyway! Come on... Bachelor
Night! It'll be great!

                    JAMIE
I don't think so. Not
tonight.

                    WALLY
It beats an evening alone
with the left hand.

                    JAMIE
Don't be so sure. The new
Penthouse came today.

                    WALLY
Funny. Come on; it might be
the last time I ever play!

                    JAMIE
Yeah, right. You'll be
strapping on a Stratocaster
'til the day you die.

                    WALLY
Don't be so sure. I just
turned 40 on Wednesday.

                    JAMIE
Happy birthday.

                    WALLY
Hardly. What's more
depressing than a 40-year-old
failed rock'n'roller?

                    JAMIE
Child support and alimony.

                    WALLY
I'm serious. I've been in
bands since I was 16, and
                  (cont'd)

                    WALLY
                  (cont'd)
never even come close to a
deal. That whole time, you
know that one day it's going
to happen, that you're
finally going to cut the
album, go on tour... and then
you turn around and turn 40
on Wednesday. When do you
realize that it just might
not happen?

                    JAMIE
Come on, Pollyanna! You're
the one who's always telling
me about luck and timing.
You've got to hang in there!

                    WALLY
What, for another 40 years?
                  (mock announcing)
"Ladies and gentlemen, please
give a warm Home for the Dead
and Dying welcome to Wally
and the Hardening Arteries!"
I'm ready to take the hint. I
mean, it's great to do a show
and have everybody tell you
how wonderful you are, and
have women kiss your bald
spot, and sleep real late on
the weekend... but I'll tell
you... I got more excited
about that fucking prime rib
dog food flavor than about
any song I've written in the
last five years.

                    JAMIE
It's okay not to be a
rock'n'roll star, you know.
Maybe you were meant to be
the world's greatest designer
of artificial flavors.

Wally shakes his head.

                    WALLY
               (meaning Jamie)
          Second best...
                    (beat)
          You know what's scary? I look
          forward to going home to Anna
          and the twins and a big bowl
          of popcorn and a Disney
          video. You want depressing?
          Try turning 40 watching
          "Pinocchio"!

Jamie doesn't know what to say to that. They
both look down at their empty plates,
thinking. Wally calls out to their WAITRESS.

                    WALLY
          Bring me two slices of the
          chocolate cake.

                    JAMIE
          You know I can't eat that
          stuff, Wally!

                    WALLY
          Who said anything about you?
          I'm still hungry.

The waitress uncrates two enormous slices of
CHOCOLATE CAKE; Jamie's stomach GROWLS as
Wally digs in.

                    JAMIE
          Just let me smell it...

And Wally graciously allows him a deep,
savoring draft.

INT. JAMIE'S APARTMENT - NIGHT

That night. The apartment is tidy, if
depressingly barren. This is the domain of a

newly-divorced man: a couch, a TV, a cheap
coffee table littered with bills, a
Penthouse, a deck of cards, and some boxes
that still, after all these months, need
unpacking. Jamie ENTERS, turning on the
LIGHT, making it even more empty, hollow and
depressing when you can see it.

                    JAMIE
          Lucy?

We TRACK WITH HIM through the living room to
the TV, which he flicks ON.

                    JAMIE
          (impersonating Ricky Ricardo)
          Honey, I'm home.

A big, uninterested-looking cat (lucy) comes
to the edge of the room, looks up at jamie
without expression.

                    JAMIE
          Hi, Lucy.

When the cat sees him, she ignores him and
goes back to napping on the couch. Jamie
makes a mock CRABBY FACE back at her.

We FOLLOW HIM into the adjoining...

INT. KITCHEN - NIGHT

His stomach GROWLS again, and he heads to
the refrigerator, opening the door. It looks
much like Old Mother Hubbard's cupboard. We
see some WILTING LETTUCE, a CHUNK of WHITE
CHEESE, an OPEN PERRIER BOTTLE, a WEDGE of
LIME, and a half-bottle of NATURAL CATSUP.
Yummy.

He takes what's left of a loaf of whole-grain
BREAD from the cupboard and unwraps the
cheese, ready to attack it with the KNIFE.

INSERT - CHEESE

Patches of charming GREEN MOLD adorn it.

RESUME JAMIE

He grimaces and tosses it into the trash. He gets a glass, fills it with ice, and squeezes the LIME into it. It's completely dry, nary a drop of juice. He tosses it, and pours Perrier into the glass.

It might as well be tap water. Completely FLAT. He pours it down the drain.

He valiantly CHEWS on a slice of the dry BREAD, which CRUNCHES between his teeth, and heads back into the

INT. LIVING ROOM - NIGHT

He goes to Lucy's COUCH.

                    JAMIE
          Move over.

Lucy gives a glare of disdain, and clears his spot. Jamie drops onto the couch, which HONKS at him, making him jump.

He pulls a SQUEAKY TOY out from between the cushions, and tosses it to Lucy, who gives a so-that's-where-it-is! look and begins to chew on it.

Jamie picks up the remote and turns to the TV as a COMMERCIAL ENDS, and "Pinocchio" comes on.

                    JAMIE
          No thank you.

He changes the channel; JULIA CHILD is preparing an outrageously fattening meal.

It's too much for Jamie to bear as he chews his Dickensian slice of stale bread. He THROWS his piece of BREAD at her, and changes the channel.

Julia is replaced by a tempting, lovingly gooey shot of a BASKIN ROBBINS HOT FUDGE SUNDAE. He whimpers softly in frustration and changes the channel.

A sweating NAKED COUPLE is CREATIVELY COUPLING, huffing and puffing their undying devotion as they reach an impossibly violent mutual orgasm on a cable channel. He can't take it.

He turns off the TV and faces Lucy, who watches him with detached curiosity.

                    JAMIE
          You know, you and I never
          really seem to talk.

Lucy gives a low, soft MEWL.

                    JAMIE
          Just talk. Just you and me.
          About things that matter.

Lucy just looks at him.

The apartment is quiet. Jamie looks around, and the depression is starting to get to him. He stands up, not quite sure which way to turn. He heads over to an uncrated BOX marked BOOKS, and begins to rummage through them.

INT. JAMIE'S BEDROOM - NIGHT

As empty and depressing as the rest of the apartment.

On the NIGHTSTAND is a small framed SNAPSHOT of Jamie and a beautiful four-year-old BOY, his son BOOTH. There is a WOMAN with them,

but she doesn't fit into the frame, and is
cut off down the middle. She is Jamie's
estranged WIFE, VANESSA.

Jamie climbs into bed and OPENS the BOOK;
some TORN PAGES fall OUT. At first annoyed,
he picks them up, then notices...

INSERT - BOOK AND PAGES

A young child has scrawled a primitive crayon
DRAWING of a KITTY all over the page.

RESUME JAMIE

He lovingly TRACES the CRAYON MARKS with his
fingers, wistful, and looks over at the
PICTURE next to him. He picks it up, the sad,
loving daddy.

ANGLE ON PICTURE

Jamie's face is reflected in the glass over
the picture.

                    JAMIE
          I miss you, Baby Boy...

                              DISSOLVE TO:

WIDE ANGLE - LATER

It is after two a.m. Jamie is heavy into REM-
sleep, the BOOK face down on the pillow next
to him in the dark, which is trespassed only
by the red glow of the clock's numbers.
Something makes him MOVE.

He licks his lips, TASTING something in his
sleep. MUSIC indicates the IMPORTANCE of
this MOMENT. Slowly, groggily, he comes
AWAKE, opening his eyes, looking pleased at
first, then confused. The TASTE is still in
his mouth, even after leaving Dreamland.

                    JAMIE
          Chocolate...

                              HARD CUT TO:

INT. INTERROGATION ROOM - NIGHT

CU Jamie, rubbing tired eyes and addressing
the CAMERA and the INTERROGATING DETECTIVES.

                    JAMIE
          I just thought it was some
          kind of wish fulfillment
          dream about Wally's cake,
          after all those weeks of
          nothing but rabbit food, but
          the taste was still in my
          mouth after I woke up. I
          could smell it, too. This was
          no Hershey bar, either. It
          was really good stuff.
          Custom. Bittersweet, with
          just a touch of orange.
          Really special stuff.

                    MAN'S VOICE (O.S)
          I don't know how you can be
          sure it wasn't a dream...

                    JAMIE
          It wasn't a dream. I just
          kept tasting someone else's
          chocolate.

                    MAN'S VOICE
          Look, does this really have
          anything to do with anything?

Jamie just looks right into the CAMERA. He
doesn't give a shit whether he is believed
or not. He doesn't expect to be.

                              CUT TO:

INT. COUGAR LAB - DAY

Jamie, still boyish in his glasses and work
manner, despite an obvious lack of sleep, is
going through papers in the file cabinet when
crusty old Jeanette sneaks up from behind
and GOOSES him. He JUMPS, scattering PAPERS,
and her LAUGHTER becomes a RATTLING COUGH.

                    JEANETTE
          Boy, Jamie, you look like
          shit. Those wild bachelor
          nights are taking their toll.

                    JAMIE
          I had a hard time getting to
          sleep last night.

                    JEANETTE
          Next time call me. I'll come
          over and read you Mother
          Goose.

                    JAMIE
          And what'll you tell Mister
          Jeanette?

                    JEANETTE
          That I went to an orgy. He's
          very understanding. The old
          Polyp's been trying to get me
          to join a swing club for
          years.

He doesn't react, as she helps him gather
papers.

                    JEANETTE
          You used to have a sense of
          humor.

Wally ENTERS.

202

                    WALLY
He needs a woman. Know
anybody?

                  JEANETTE
What're you talking to,
chopped liver?

                    WALLY
Let me put it another way. He
needs a girl. Know anybody?

                    JAMIE
I just need some sleep. I'm
just a little cranky.

                    WALLY
The twins get cranky.
Grownups get testy.

                    JAMIE
                 (testy)
I'm not testy...

                  JEANETTE
Why don't you go home and
take a nap if you're going to
be such an ogre?

                    JAMIE
God, I'm okay. I just didn't
get much sleep last night,
all right?

                    WALLY
I can go three days without
sleep and still run six
miles.

Jamie just glares at him.

                  JEANETTE
Would you do us all a favor
and go home?

                    JAMIE
          I'm fine, Jeanette. Besides,
          can the world wait another
          day for artificial honeydew?

               WALLY AND JEANETTE
                  (in unison)
          Yes. Go home.

Feeling tired, Jamie realizes that might not
be the worst idea in the world.

                    JAMIE
          You guys sure?

Jeanette takes a CRYSTAL from the piles on
her DESK and puts it in Jamie's PALM.

                    JEANETTE
          Here. Keep this in your
          pocket. You'll feel stronger.
          Guaranteed.

                    WALLY
          Go. If the Great Olfactory
          inquires, you were puking red
          dye #2 all over your bench.

                    JAMIE
          Thanks for your concern.

                    WALLY
          Fuck you. I just want to use
          your Mac.

EXT. CITY STREET - BUS STOP - DAY

Jamie climbs off the BUS and walks along the
street, losing himself in the crowd.

EXT. ANOTHER STREET - DAY

Jamie steps into the a RESIDENTIAL ROW of

proud old BROWNSTONES, and he seems hesitant
to continue. As if forcing the issue, he
heads up the STREET.

EXT. BROWNSTONE - DAY

He STOPS at the base of the nicest-looking
HOME on the street, and looks up at it,
seemingly with some PAIN. After a few
moments, he nervously goes up and PRESSES
the BUZZER. A WOMAN'S VOICE comes over the
INTERCOM.

                    WOMAN'S VOICE
          Who is it?

                         JAMIE
          It's me.
                    (a beat)
          Jamie.

There is no answer, and for a moment he is
sorry he RANG. Then, the DOOR BUZZES loudly.

He takes a BREATH and ENTERS the FOYER.

INT. HALLWAY OUTSIDE APARTMENT - DAY

The FRONT DOOR OPENS, and an attractive WOMAN
in her 30s looks at Jamie. It is his
estranged wife, VANESSA. Intelligent,
earnest, hers is an unadorned beauty that it
takes some time to discover. Warm, but at a
distance, she is HOLDING a SWEATER in her
hands.

They are silent for a long, uncomfortable
BEAT. They make each other NERVOUS. Before
any words are spoken, Jamie suddenly
SNEEZES.

                         JAMIE
          You wearing Tea Rose again?

                    VANESSA
          No reason not to...

She realizes how that sounded, and changes
course. She doesn't want to hurt him, but
sometimes she just can't help it.

                    VANESSA
          You off work today?

                    JAMIE
          I wasn't feeling well. I kind
          of got off the bus at Fifth
          by habit, so I thought I'd
          check in on you and Booth.

                    VANESSA
          You're not coming down with
          anything, are you?

                    JAMIE
          I'm just tired.

She opens the door wider, and STANDS BACK to
let him awkwardly ENTER his former home.

INT. LIVING ROOM - DAY

It is neat, comfortable, lived-in and homey,
everything Jamie's place is not.

                    JAMIE
          Place looks nice. So do you.

                    VANESSA
          Thanks.

She looks down with a forced, uncomfortable
smile. He finds himself near a BOUQUET of
ROSES and SNEEZES again. He steps away from
the flowers.

                    VANESSA
          Gesundheit. You want a
          Kleenex?

JAMIE SNIFFS, shakes his head "no", and she
crosses the room, continuing what was in
progress when the DOORBELL RANG. She slides
OUT of her BLOUSE, revealing her CHARMS in a
tiny, lacy BRA for a moment before she slips
into her SWEATER.

Jamie LOOKS AWAY, even though they were
married for some years, but can't help taking
a peek. Maybe that's why she did it. Or maybe
it's no big deal changing in front of her
ex-husband. But it is to him.

As she pulls the sweater over her head, Jamie
notices a MARK on one cradled BREAST.

                    JAMIE
          (despising his jealousy)
          Is that a hickey?

Vanessa's HEAD pops out through the sweater,
looks up at him with an expression
threatening to flower into a Mona Lisa grin,
when suddenly, the four-year-old WHIRLWIND,
BOOTH, comes CHARGING out from the back of
the apartment.

                    BOOTH
          Daddy!

He takes a flying LEAP at JAMIE, wrapping
his arms around his father's legs and
knocking him to the floor. JAMIE is LAUGHING
now, the ice broken by the little boy who
looks so much like him.

                    VANESSA
          Careful, honey. Daddy's not
          feeling well.

                    BOOTH
          You got the flu? Get plenty

of rest, drink lots of
fluids, and above all, take
Bayer aspirin.

                    JAMIE
          Thanks for the advice, doc.
          Hey, have you been washing
          behind your ears?

Booth covers his ears self-consciously as
jamie reaches over, seemingly pulling a
silver dollar out of booth's ear.

                    JAMIE
          How long has that been in
          there?

                    BOOTH
               (giggling)
          Magic Daddy!

Vanessa can't help but SMILE, herself.

                    BOOTH
          Are you moving back home now?

Jamie looks at Vanessa.

                    VANESSA
          Daddy's just visiting.

                    BOOTH
          You said you were just
          testing...

                    JAMIE
          That was a long time ago. The
          test part is done now, and
          lucky you! You've got two
          places to stay now, just like
          rich movie stars!

                    BOOTH
          Do rich movie stars have a
               (cont'd)

                    BOOTH
                  (cont'd)
          mommy in one house and a
          daddy in the other one?

                   VANESSA
          Most of them. Come on, honey,
          You'd better get ready for
          class.

                    JAMIE
          Class?

                    BOOTH
          Dance class. P.U.!

Jamie shoots Vanessa a look.

                   VANESSA
                 (defensive)
          What's wrong with dance
          class?

                    BOOTH
          Mr. Toad says even boxers
          take dance class for their
          co-ordinaries...

                    JAMIE
          Mr. Toad?

                   VANESSA
          Todd!

                    BOOTH
             (giggling, pushing it)
          He's a fairy!

                   VANESSA
          Stop that, Booth. Mr. Todd is
          not a fairy!

                    JAMIE
          Relax. He doesn't even know
          what it means.

                    BOOTH
Uh huh! It means like a lady
with flypaper wings and a
magic wand!

                  VANESSA
He is not—

                    BOOTH
He dances like a fairy.

                    JAMIE
Well, you know dancers...

                  VANESSA
He's not.

Jamie is about to ask how she knows, but the
final look in her eyes answers the question
before it is asked. She knows. And we know
where the HICKEY came from.

                  VANESSA
Look, Jamie, I'm glad you
stopped by, but we've got to
go. He can't be late.

                    JAMIE
     (nodding, getting it)
Sure, I understand. Can't be
late. Listen, Skeezix. You
want to play ball, maybe go
hiking this weekend? Do some
man stuff, okay?

                    BOOTH
Yay! No dancing!

                  VANESSA
'Bye, Jamie.

He leans down and gives Booth a hug and a
kiss.

                    JAMIE
See you Saturday morning,
Moose. Here's a key. If I
don't answer, just come in
and get me up. Love monster
hug.

They HUG and GROWL like MONSTERS.

                    BOOTH
'Love you, Daddy.

                    JAMIE
          (turning to Vanessa)
I'm sorry, Nessie. I don't
have any right to be jealous.

                    VANESSA
Sometimes you just make me
want to hurt you. I'm sorry.

                    JAMIE
Oh, no, Alphonse. I'm sorry.
Friends?

                    VANESSA
          (smiling, nodding)
Good friends. Sorry I'm
crabby—

                    BOOTH
She started her period today.

                    VANESSA
Listen, if you want to come
over tomorrow night... you
know, we'd be glad to see
you.

                    JAMIE
          (really?)
Well, maybe so. I'll call
you.

Jamie smiles, leans forward to kiss her
goodbye, and she TURNS to offer her CHEEK.

EXT. STREET IN FRONT OF BROWNSTONE - DAY

Jamie EXITS the building. Booth yells and
waves goodbye for the window above. Jamie
turns with a warm smile to wave back, and
walks into a STREETLAMP. Booth thinks it's a
riot.

EXT. THE STAND ROCK CLUB - NIGHT

Wide angle. We BOOM DOWN to find the rather
YUPPIESQUE Jamie looking out of place in a
LINE of devout rock'n'rollers milling into
the club. We ENTER the club with Jamie.

INT. THE STAND - NIGHT - CONTINUOUS

We FOLLOW Jamie into the noisy club, seeking
our way through the rowdy patrons, in search
of Wally. MUSIC BLASTS over the P.A., but
only ROADIES are on the STAGE.

We FIND the STAGE DOOR with Jamie. He knocks
timidly, and we FOLLOW HIM IN.

INT. STAND DRESSING ROOM - NIGHT - CONTINUOUS

Wally is glad to see Jamie. He jumps up and
gives him a big BEARHUG, looking
outrageously different in his HEAVY METAL
STUDS and LEATHERS.

They are surrounded by other—younger—members
of the band, all of whom are either TUNING
UP or TOOTING UP. The room is littered with
the usual assortment of GIRLFRIENDS,
GROUPIES, ROADIES, and HANGERS ON.

The BASS PLAYER offers Jamie a toot.

                    JAMIE
          No thanks; I'm on a diet.

                    WALLY
          Help you lose weight.

                    JAMIE
          I'll just say no, if you
          don't mind. I've lost three-
          and-a-half pounds this week.
          Look!

He lifts his shirt to show Wally.

                    WALLY
          Svelte. Hey, Jamie. Do that
          thing with the quarter! Watch
          this, everybody, this is
          great! That thing with the
          quarter, Jamie!

Jamie is uncomfortable being put suddenly on
the spot like this. He shakes his head,
trying to shut Wally up.

                    JAMIE
          Another time. This is your
          night, Wally.

                    WALLY
          No, no! Go ahead!

                    JAMIE
          Really—

But he is saved by the bell. A very
managerial-looking type enters and points at
his watch.

                    CLUB MANAGER
          Ten o'clock!

They all turn their attention from Jamie,
grabbing their instruments and heading out
to the stage.

                    JAMIE
          Break a leg, Wally.

                    WALLY
          God forbid.

INT. STAND - NIGHT - STAGE

The RED SPOTLIGHT REFLECTS majestically off
his BALD SPOT, as he LEAPS into the air and
CUES the first HEAVY METAL NUMBER with a
crashing CHORD.

Jamie makes his way through the crowd,
feeling way out of place here. He hasn't been
to a rock club in a long time. He watches
the crowd as much as he watches the band.
He rests his ELBOWS on the TINY TABLE,
sneaking his fingers into his EARS,
embarrassed to let anyone see that he can't
take the NOISE.

We MOVE IN ON HIM, now HEARING the way HE
hears, the sound slightly muffled, but still
almost unbearably LOUD.

To his EMBARRASSMENT, an attractive, tall,
thin, bleached blonde WOMAN SITS directly in
front of him.

                    WOMAN
          Do that thing with the
          quarter.

He jerks his hands from his ears; he didn't
hear her, but we did. Now the MUSIC is
unbearably LOUD. They have to shout into one
another's ears to be heard.

                    WOMAN
          I said, do that thing with
          the quarter.

Doubly embarrassed now, he sputters, trying

not to look at her cleavage. It sounds so
dirty when she says it.

                    JAMIE
          It's just a little magic
          trick, just, you know,
          silly...

          WOMAN
               I want to see.

CU JAMIE

Something is happening. Her voice, the
crashing ROCK'N'ROLL, the AMBIENT SOUND is
all being sucked away into a black velvet
vacuum. He REACTS; the SILENCE is
horrifying.

But the sound doesn't just evaporate. It soon
gives way to the perfectly recorded strains
of romantic CLASSICAL MUSIC—real champagne
and candles stuff.

JAMIE'S P.O.V.

The woman talks, her face close, a little
distorted, but all we can hear is the
CLASSICAL MUSIC, and now a POP, and the sound
of CHAMPAGNE POURING.

HER P.O.V. - JAMIE

He feels a touch of panic. He is CRYING OUT
like a DEAF man over the rock'n'roll, unable
to even hear himself.

                    JAMIE
               I can't hear you! I can't—

JAMIE AND WOMAN We HEAR what he hears:
hushed, romantic VOICES under crystal-clear
CLASSICAL MUSIC, the very present FIZZ of
champagne. And, in the background, a soft
CHIME sounds... EIGHT TIMES.

He shouts soundlessly to her, and she, getting a little FREAKED, backs away.

ON JAMIE

She's gone, and he is near panic in deafland, when suddenly, the soft velvet is pummeled to submission by Wally's wall of dinosaur MUSIC. He quickly covers his ears with his hands.

He looks around, sees the woman looking away from him from another table, striking up a new conversation. Everywhere else, life is normal, but it takes a moment for Jamie's terror to pass.

EXT. HIGHWAY - NIGHT

A ROCK'N'ROLL VAN careens down the empty late-night highway.

INT. VAN - NIGHT

It is Wally's. Jamie is driving, due to Wally's obvious flirtation with illegal substances.

Wally punches on the radio, and a truly obnoxious metal song rends the night. Wally grimaces, PUNCHES UP a NEW AGE STATION, relaxing to the synthetic AMBIENT SOUNDS.

                    WALLY
          Thanks for driving, Jamie.
          Anna will appreciate it.
          It'll be close to two before
          I get home now, and she
          always waits up.

                    JAMIE
          No problem. I mean it, Wally;
          you really kicked some ass
          tonight.

                    WALLY
          We were pretty fucking great,
          weren't we?

                    JAMIE
          Next thing you know it's MTV,
          lots of smoke and babes in
          bikinis. Wearing leather
          pants with your buns hanging
          out.

                    WALLY
          Anna says I've got cute buns.

                    JAMIE
          I never said you didn't...

                    WALLY
          Anyway, I'm quitting.

                    JAMIE
          Not this old song again.

                    WALLY
          I mean it. I'm too old.
          Rock'n'roll sucks. It's all
          business... no more passion.

And he goes glum. Jamie doesn't want to get
into this again. He leaves Wally to his
thoughts, concentrates on his driving.

ANGLE - OVER JAMIE'S SHOULDER - THROUGH
WINDOW

The van ZOOMS along the highway. A BUS
WHOOSHES by them, its LIGHTS blinding. Then,
save for the SYNTHESIZERS, silence.

ON JAMIE

We slowly MOVE IN ON HIM.

ANGLE - JAMIE'S P.O.V. THROUGH WINDSHIELD

Something is happening to Jamie's VISION! Little SPOTS begin to appear, POPPING like champagne BUBBLES all over the FRAME. A haunting SOUND/MUSIC gives a sense of foreboding as the FRAME begins to OPTICALLY SHIFT!

ON JAMIE

He's getting scared, his eyes wide. We keep PUSHING IN until his EYES fill the frame.

RESUME JAMIE'S P.O.V.

The view of the highway is changing, running away like watercolors in the rain through the bubbles and colors. It is now the VIEW of a PARK!

There is a quiet POND, a young couple walking along a LIT GRAVEL PATH under a CLOCKTOWER that reads 11:30... two hours earlier than it is in the van.

City buildings reach high into the skyline over the trees that line the park.

RESUME JAMIE AND WALLY IN VAN

WALLY IS REACHING TO CHANGE THE STATION WHEN HE LOOKS UP TO SEE THE BLIND FEAR ON JAMIE'S FACE.

                    JAMIE
                 (screaming)
          Wally!

                    WALLY
          What's the matter?

Jamie is frantically jerking the wheel,

trying to maintain control, but he is flying
blind! The van SCREECHES crazily!

                    JAMIE
          I can't see!

RESUME JAMIE'S P.O.V. as it keeps dissolving
from the PARK to the HIGHWAY and BACK!

EXT. HIGHWAY - NIGHT

The VAN is STRADDLING the middle two lanes,
WEAVING crazily.

RESUME JAMIE AND WALLY IN VAN

They are being thrown about the van. Wally
tries to grab the wheel, but is thrown aside
at each jerk of the wheel. Jamie tries to
slam on the BRAKES, frantically yanking the
wheel!

RESUME HIGHWAY

A huge DIESEL GROCERY TRUCK looms toward them
from the rise ahead! It BLASTS its HORN!

RESUME JAMIE AND WALLY

Jamie's blind eyes BULGE WILDLY.

                    JAMIE
          Take the fucking wheel!

The TRUCK is getting closer, the horn more
frantic!

Wally LUNGES across Jamie, GRABBING the
WHEEL just as Jamie jams and locks the BRAKES
sending them into an insane skid!

RESUME HIGHWAY

Tires SCREECHING and SMOKING, the VAN dances
in a mad pirouette across the blacktop,

directly into the path of the DIESEL!

The TRUCK tries vainly to maneuver out of
their path, horns blasting, as both vehicles
skid on a COLLISION COURSE!

RESUME VAN

Jamie and Wally are screaming, frantic,
trying to steer, their hands fighting at the
wheel!

RESUME HIGHWAY

The TRUCK SMASHES INTO the tail end of the
VAN, throwing it into a SPIN, and off the
side of the highway.
The VAN BROADSIDES a TREE, and everything
goes quiet, as the truck's horn fades into
the distance.

INSIDE VAN

Quiet, except for New Age Shit. Jamie's face
is cut and bleeding, his eyes closed. Wally's
AMP has tumbled into the front seat, with
Wally seemingly underneath.

Jamie's eyes open, and he realizes what has
just happened.

                    JAMIE
          Wally! Wally, you okay?

We HEAR some whimpering from behind the amp,
and finally, Wally rises up, his face in a
shit-eating grin. He's laughing, as if he
just got off STAR TOURS.

                    WALLY
          That was great!

Jamie didn't think so. He looks very worried.

INT. COUGAR CHEMICAL LAB - DAY

It is early, and Jamie is the first one
there. He looks haggard, tired as he pores
over a stack of papers, notes, vials, and
other tools of his research, filled with
anxiety.

He is so deeply into studying whatever
chemicals might be bringing on his insanity,
that he is oblivious to the arrival of Wally
and Jeanette.

                    WALLY
          You should have been there
          last night! You really missed
          a spectacular show.

                    JEANETTE
          No thank you, Mr. Mike
          Jagger. I'm too old for
          rock'n'roll... and frankly,
          sweetheart, so are you.

                    WALLY
          Not that shit, the wreck!
          Real E ticket stuff! The
          van's a total write-off!

Then she notices the BANDAGE on Jamie's
forehead.

                    JEANETTE
          Oh, my God! Jamie, what
          happened last night? Are you
          all right?

Jamie LOOKS UP, startled, noticing them for
the first time.

                    JAMIE
          What?

                    JEANETTE
          The accident!

He is pale, a bit tortured, afraid his sanity
is slipping away.

                    JAMIE
                  (scared)
          You guys haven't had... um...
          any strange... experiences
          lately, have you?

Wally and Jeanette look at one another, not
sure what's next. Wally assumed everything
was okay.

                    WALLY
          What do you mean?

                    JAMIE
          Like... hallucinations.
                  (beat)
          I've been... um... seeing
          things... hearing things… .
          that aren't there...

                    WALLY
          That happens to me all the
          time...

                    JAMIE
          Well, it doesn't happen to
          me! Something I'm working
          with is pushing some buttons
          I don't want pushed!

                    JEANETTE
          We don't work with anything
          like that. It's all natural
          ingredients here...

                    JAMIE
          Uh huh... as if nature can't
          hurt you. Toadstools,
          strychnine, sumac, peyote...

                    WALLY
          Where?

                    JEANETTE
          Knock it off, Wally.
                    (to Jamie)
          What's it like? Blackouts?

                    JAMIE
          Not really. I'm still awake,
          but, I don't know, in the
          middle of some other reality.
          Somebody else's reality.

                    JEANETTE
          Like seeing through somebody
          else's eyes?

                    JAMIE
          Sort of...

                    JEANETTE
          You ever have an out of body
          experience?

                    JAMIE
            (emphatic, disbelieving)
          No.

                    WALLY
          Oh, God, here we go with the
          New Age shit.

                    JEANETTE
          It's a hell of a lot better
          high than pharmaceuticals...
                    (to Jamie)
          Is it like somebody ancient
          living in your body?

                    WALLY
          You mean, like you?

She ignores him; Jamie's losing his patience
with this bullshit.

                    JAMIE
          Jeanette, I appreciate your
          concern, but I am not
          astrally projecting, and I'm
          not a reincarnated Aztec
          prince. I'm just tasting
          things that aren't in my
          mouth and seeing things that
          aren't in front of me, and
          it's scaring the shit out of
          me!

                    WALLY
          Artificial honeydew can do
          that, you know.

Jeanette is a little miffed at not being
taken seriously.

                    JEANETTE
          Or it could be that you're
          just losing your mind. You
          seen a shrink?

That's what Jamie is most afraid of. He looks
at her, frightened, so vulnerable that it
scares her.

                    JEANETTE
          Joking...

                    WALLY
          You feel okay now? No
          hallucinations or anything?

Jamie has to think about it for a moment.

                    JAMIE
          Yeah. I think so.

                    JEANETTE
          Look, you might think I'm
          just a crazy old broad, but
          this stuff is for real. I
                    (cont'd)

                    JEANETTE
                    (cont'd)
          wouldn't screw around with
          things you don't know about.

                    WALLY
          You're right, Jeanette. We do
          think you're a crazy old
          broad. Jamie... how many
          fingers?

                    JAMIE
          I'm okay, Wally.

And with the sweep of an arm, he shoves all
the chemicals he's been working with into
the trash.

                    JAMIE
          Fuck honeydew!

INT. JAMIE'S BEDROOM - NIGHT

It is very DARK. The only illumination is
the LIGHT from the CLOCK RADIO in a soft WASH
over Jamie's sleeping FACE. His eyes are
REMMING as he DREAMS.

Suddenly, something DISTURBS his sleep, and
his EYES JOLT OPEN with a GASP.

Jamie, confused, STARES into the pitch
darkness of the bedroom, his PUPILS dilated
in the blackness, his HEART POUNDING.

Dead, dark SILENCE. Nothing there. But
still... He doesn't trust his own senses, or
the calm. He peers more deeply into the
night, as we PULL BACK to reveal his softly-
lit face as the only visible object in an
otherwise invisible room.

ANGLE - JAMIE'S P.O.V. - THE BEDROOM

Darkness. Until, suddenly, a MAN'S FACE

flashes into the black as he LIGHTS his
CIGARETTE with a LIGHTER. Then, as the FLAME
is extinguished, the FACE goes with it.

RESUME JAMIE as he JOLTS UPRIGHT.

                    JAMIE
          Hey!

The RED ASH of the lit cigarette flares for
a moment in front of the FACE again, and then
moves away, disappears, and the curtain of
darkness cloaks the INTRUDER.

These two brief flashes are just long enough
to allow us to recognize the intruder as The
Man Who Wasn't There at the Logo-Unveiling
earlier at Cougar Chemical!

                    JAMIE
          What are you doing here?

He climbs out of his bed, frightened, and
CROSSES the ROOM toward the Intruder, on
edge.

                    JAMIE
          Who are you?

His anger held in check by fear and caution,
he reaches out blindly into the darkness,
stumbling for... SOMETHING. He GRABS a LAMP,
lifting it up as a weapon, and FLICKING it
ON.

The ROOM is LIT by the lamp as Jamie CHARGES
FORWARD at...

No one.

He stands alone in the room, just in his
shorts, his heart leaping into his throat.
He looks over at the window, shut and locked
behind the curtain. Leading with the LAMP,
he approaches the CLOSET, notices that it is

AJAR. Oh, shit.

He GOES to the CLOSET, quietly as possible, barefoot across the rug, the lamp his torch and club. Reaches for the CLOSET DOOR, fear choking him, and WRENCHES it OPEN.

In the BACKWASH, a COAT tumbles out of the closet, onto Jamie, scaring the shit out of him. Frantically, he fumbles it off, only to REVEAL that he is still ALONE...

Where is the Intruder?

He sets the LAMP back in place, and we FOLLOW Jamie out into:

INT. JAMIE'S APARTMENT - NIGHT

as we STEADICAM with him down the HALLWAY in his search, building tension as we SEEK the mysterious STRANGER. We play it in real time, suspensefully and methodically searching the few ROOMS of his bachelor apartment, moving through darkness and shadow.

At the KITCHEN, he REACHES for the LIGHTSWITCH, fumbles it ON. Nothing. But something. He stands ALERT for a moment. It is the middle of the night, but distant MUSIC filters through the apartment.

Curious—and still frightened—Jamie heads back down the corridor. He stops at the BATHROOM. Flicks on the light. Nothing. WINDOW LOCKED from within.

There is only a single room left. Jamie ENTERS the LIVING ROOM. Turns ON the LIGHTS. Can't see anything amiss. Goes to the door. Chained from inside.

He RELAXES, releases a long SIGH. It had to be a DREAM. After standing in the middle of the empty room for a moment, he TURNS OFF

the LIGHTS, and heads back to the BEDROOM.
However—he no sooner STEPS into the HALLWAY
when:

ANGLE - JAMIE'S P.O.V. - XCU THE INTRUDER'S
FACE!

Jamie is staring right into the Man's FACE!
His EXPRESSION is startlingly benign, even
SMILING as he looks right into the CAMERA
and SPEAKS.

                    MAN
          Did I wake you?

Jamie JUMPS a mile, lunges for the HALL
LIGHT, flicks it ON, but the Man is GONE!
Never there. No way he could have gotten in.

Jamie stands there, certain that he is
starting to LOSE his MIND.

                              SHOCK CUT TO:

INT. JAMIE'S BEDROOM - MORNING

The CLOCK RADIO suddenly BLASTS ON with
MARIACHI MUSIC at full volume, and Jamie
JOLTS AWAKE. We see a bottle of Halcion on
the night stand next to the clock radio.

                    JAMIE
          Jesus!

Barely able to open his eyes, he fumbles for
the obnoxious radio, finally slapping it
OFF. A BASEBALL BAT he had lying on the bed
next to him for protection FALLS to the FLOOR
with a loud, startling THUD.

INT. JAMIE'S BATHROOM - DAY

He FLUSHES, then turns to his groggy

reflection in the MIRROR. He GRIMACES, then turns on the shower. When it starts to steam, he CLIMBS IN.

INT. SHOWER - DAY

He starts lathering up, coming to life. The hot needles of water are having an effect, and he's looking a lot better. He even starts singing.

But as he lathers up his HAIR, everything changes. He GASPS, almost choking on the WATER. He suddenly is in great PAIN, almost as if having been kicked in the balls. He doubles over, GRIMACING and PANTING, his arms across his abdomen!

JAMIE'S P.O.V.

Very wide angle, very unsteady, VERTIGINOUS VIEW. The SHOWER STALL seems to be revolving like some kind of twisted CAROUSEL. We LOOK DOWN to see WATER and SHAMPOO running down the drain at our feet, and the CAMERA continues to TURN, slowly ACCELERATING and LOWERING, as if being drawn down the drain!

And then, the strange SOUND/MUSIC, - and the bursting BUBBLES change things.

We are looking down another drain, and the REVOLVING CAMERA slowly comes to a halt. Something RED flows into this drain with the sudsy water. BLOOD?

RESUME JAMIE

Gasping, but returning to normal, he feebly reaches up and shuts off the water. He takes long, deep BREATHS, and that seems to help the PAIN go away.

As he STANDS TALL, we FRAME HIM in CU.

INSERT - X-RAY HEAD SHOTS

With each CUT, there is a joltingly loud SOUND. They are SKULL SHOTS, matching the angle of Jamie's face perfectly. We go through a series of BRAIN SCAN X-RAYS of Jamie's HEAD from every angle.

INT. DOCTOR'S OFFICE - DAY

Jamie is chewing his nail as DOCTOR SCHOW pulls the last of the X-RAYS down. The doctor is twice Jamie's age, but as physically fit as Jack LaLanne.

                    DOCTOR SCHOW
          Well, if you're looking for
          an organic explanation,
          you're not going to get it
          from me. No lesions, no
          inexplicable shadows, nothing
          we can see. That doesn't mean
          it isn't there, but a
          physical cause in my opinion
          is highly unlikely.

                    JAMIE
          Which means I should be
          wishing my sanity goodbye...

                    DOCTOR SCHOW
                  (smiling)
          Well, I did just get a new
          Porsche 911, and much as
          another 5-day-a-week patient
          would help, I'm afraid I just
          can't justify it. Of course,
          this is just a cursory visit,
          but there is nothing to
          suggest delusional behavior,
          and certainly no
                  (cont'd)

                    DOCTOR SCHOW
                     (cont'd)
          schizophrenia that I can
          detect. You don't drink?

                    JAMIE
          Not at all. Never have. I
          can't stand the taste.

                    DOCTOR SCHOW
          Recreational drugs? I won't
          tell.
           (Jamie just shakes his head)
          How about diet?

                    JAMIE
          Macrobiotic. I'm trying to
          lose a few pounds, get in
          shape.

                    DOCTOR SCHOW
          Well, don't do anything too
          radical. If this is a big
          change from the way you used
          to eat, you might not be
          getting enough protein or
          carbs. Your brain and your
          body don't get enough fuel,
          they sometimes try to fight
          back. Every symptom is your
          body trying to tell you
          something.

Jamie just nods as if being lectured by a
teacher.

                    JAMIE
          So, basically you're saying
          you don't know what's wrong
          with me.

                    DOCTOR SCHOW
          Well, if you're talking about
          stats and readings and
          physical evidence, you're fit
                     (cont'd)

                    DOCTOR SCHOW
                     (cont'd)
          as a Stradivarius. You tell
          me you've experienced a set
          of hallucinations. That's not
          really uncommon, you know.
          You keep having them, then
          we'll draw some more blood.
          Don't mean to disappoint you
          with the news that you aren't
          sick or crazy.

Jamie just sighs.

                    DOCTOR SCHOW
          Go get yourself a good steak.
          You'll feel better when you
          feed your mind and body...

                    JAMIE
          I don't eat red meat.

                    DOCTOR SCHOW
          Exactly...

INT. SUPERMARKET - DAY

Jamie strolls the produce aisles, his CART
filled with WHOLE-GRAIN BREADS and other
HEALTHY FOODS.

He doesn't look very enthusiastic about the
vegetables and fruits he's selecting, and
his STOMACH GROWLS embarrassingly.

The OTHER SHOPPERS are mostly MOTHERS
pushing huge CARTS laden with FROZEN
DINNERS, ICE CREAM, big CHUNKS OF BEEF, and
family-sized PACKAGES of JUNK FOOD that make
TWINKIES seem like Adele Davis food.

Jamie looks at their stuff with envy,
practically DROOLING over the delectable
poison.

ELAINE, a younger, attractive WOMAN who is
filling her cart with the same kind of RABBIT
FOOD as Jamie, SPEAKS and STARTLES him.

                    ELAINE
          I don't know how they can do
          it, either.

Jamie turns, thrown off guard, thinking he's
hearing things again for a second.

                    JAMIE
          What's that?

                    ELAINE
          I mean, it's so easy to eat
          food that's good for you...
          it even tastes better. But
          they raise their kids on
          Twinkies and Count Chocula,
          so that's what they like.

                    JAMIE
             (getting his bearings)
          Right. Sausage and eggs and
          Froot Loops for breakfast,
          chili dogs and Fritos for
          lunch, and a steak with
          'tater tots for dinner, with
          a banana split for dessert.

Elaine doesn't notice the dreamy, wishful
quality in Jamie's voice.

                    ELAINE
          Then again, Adele Davis did
          die of cancer...

                    JAMIE
             (confidence growing)
          And Froot Loops are part of a
          balanced breakfast.

She flashes a sweet, disarming smile, and
Jamie is getting increasingly comfortable.

                    ELAINE
          You know what else is
          terrible?
                    (licking her lips)
          Mile-high chocolate cake.

                    JAMIE
          And pizza with sausage,
          pepperoni, and black olives.
          Yech!

They are really getting into it now,
torturing each other good-naturedly with
their favorite garbage foods.

                    ELAINE
          And chocolate chip—no, double
          chocolate chunk cookies,
          still warm so the chocolate
          gets all over your fingers
          and mouth. Just awful.

                    JAMIE
          You know what's the worst?
          Swiss orange chip and
          chocolate raspberry truffle
          ice cream, double scooped on
          a sugar cone.

                    ELAINE
          No, in a cup with whipped
          cream, nuts and a cherry.

                    JAMIE
          And chocolate jimmies!

                    ELAINE
          Poison!

Jamie pauses for a moment, and observes her
shapely figure.

                    JAMIE
          So how long have you been on
          a diet... and for God's sake,
          why?

                    ELAINE
          Ninety-six days.
          Hypoglycemia. Paying for the
          sins of twenty-six years of
          double desserts. What about
          you?

                    JAMIE
          Forty-seven days. Vanity. I
          could pinch more than an
          inch.

He is surprised at the ease of their
conversation. It's not usually this way for
him.

                    ELAINE
          Forty-seven days on this
          stuff is pretty good.

                    JAMIE
          Ninety-six is incredible. You
          wanna celebrate?

INT. JAMIE'S KITCHEN - NIGHT

We PAN ACROSS a litter of junk food WRAPPERS:
PIZZA REMAINS in a cardboard box, an empty
wine BOTTLE, CHIPS, FRENCH BREAD, etc. We
END UP ON JAMIE, ripping open a bag of
FRITOS. There are two big bowls of ice cream
with all the toppings in front of them.

Lucy the cat watches protectively from a
distance.

                    JAMIE
              (putting chips in her mouth)
          Ah, nature's perfect food:
                    (cont'd)

                    JAMIE
                 (cont'd)
          the Frito...
                 (beat)
          How do you feel? Is your
          hypoglycemia—

                    ELAINE
          I feel just fine.
           (sharing a salty Frito kiss)
          You cured me!

She starts to GIGGLE and he joins in,
realizing he feels better than he's felt in
a long time: no transposing, high, happy
spirits. He laughs.

                    JAMIE
          No, you cured me.

The laugh melts into a gentle smile, and they
take a beat to look into one another's eyes.
A soft blush of shy embarrassment passes
between them before he finally calls up the
courage to reach over and KISS her gently on
the forehead, SHIVERING slightly from
nervous anticipation... and the cold.

                    ELAINE
          You cold?

He shrugs, and she pulls her SWEATER over
her head. Her SILK BLOUSE underneath gives a
tantalizing glimpse of her shape. She drapes
the sweater around him, tucking him into it.

                    ELAINE
          That better?

Well, it is at first. But he starts to ITCH,
almost immediately, and has to take it off.

                    JAMIE
          Wool...

                    ELAINE
          You allergic?

                    JAMIE
          Sorry...

                    ELAINE
          You don't have to
          apologize...
                    (beat)
          So sensitive...

She takes his hand to kiss it, then stops.

                    ELAINE
          Are you married?

The question startles him, coming from
nowhere.

                    ELAINE
          The white band on your ring
          finger... where a wedding
          band would be.

                    JAMIE
          I was. The divorce was final
          a few months ago.

                    ELAINE
          Hence the diet.
                    (beat)
          I'm sorry.

                    JAMIE
          It's okay. Seven years of a
          monogamous relationship. At
          least I'm safe.

                    ELAINE
                    (coy)
          Really? For what?

                    JAMIE
          Here. Have some of this.

ANGLE - CLOSE TWO-SHOT PROFILE

He scoops some of the melting SUNDAE in to spoon and brings it up to her mouth, and we MOVE IN to frame them tightly.

There is a moment of silent tension, and then she leans slightly forward, and her LIPS PART.

She takes the spoonful of ICE CREAM into her mouth, looking into his eyes as she savors it.

She SLIDES the spoon from her lips, leaving some ice cream on the spoon, and puts it in Jamie's mouth.

They repeat the process, their lips ashine with melting ice cream and chocolate sauce. A little CHOCOLATE dribbles onto her chin, and he wipes it away with his finger, then licks off the remains. It is inevitable that they move into a long, deep KISS, amidst the litter of sinful GLUTTONY that surrounds them...

INT. JAMIE'S BEDROOM - NIGHT

Jamie and Elaine are NAKED, MAKING LOVE in each other's arms on top of the tangled sheets. It is gentle but sweaty, tentative and intimate, actually rather sweet and friendly. As it ENDS, Jamie SMILES, holding her in his arms.

They trade a friendly, sweet KISS, surprised at how easy it is for them to be together. She SNIFFS, and he sees that TEARS squeeze out from the corners of her eyes. She is CRYING. He gets nervous, afraid he did something wrong.

                    JAMIE
          What's the matter?

She just shakes her head, unable to say
anything. Concerned, he strokes her face,
speaking gently.

                    JAMIE
          Elaine... what's wrong?

                    ELAINE
          (looking at him through tears)
          Nothing's wrong. I'm just
          feeling... emotional.

He wraps his strength around her.

                    ELAINE
          It's real easy to be with
          you.

But the afterglow is short-lived. Jamie is
in   sudden PAIN. He GRIMACES,   MOANS,
clutching his stomach.

His face begins to blanch and perspire as
the pain wracks him.

                    ELAINE
          What is it?

He can't answer. She lays her hand on his
stomach, and its warmth feels good.

                    ELAINE
          Can I do anything?

                    JAMIE
          (struggling)
          I'll—be okay in a minute.

He WINCES as another pain hits him like a
kick in the balls.

                    ELAINE
          Sharp pains?

He nods.

She gets up, and while he balls up into the
fetal position, holding his guts, We can HEAR
her PADDING ABOUT (o.s.), filling a GLASS
and returning with WATER and a BOTTLE of
MIDOL.

                    ELAINE
          See if this helps.

He downs the PILLS, and she CARESSES his
FOREHEAD, wiping SWEAT from his BROW. Ironic
role reversal.

                    ELAINE
          Just lie still.

She curls up behind him, holding onto him.
She kisses his bare shoulder, chaste,
motherly. He is breathing easier.

                    ELAINE
          Better?

                    JAMIE
                  (nodding)
          Thanks. That's what I get for
          pigging out.

She kisses his ear, and keeps stroking him.
ELAINE Let's go to sleep.

                              FADE TO BLACK

                              CUT TO:

INT. JAMIE'S BEDROOM - MORNING

Jamie and elaine are still asleep. It is
9:15. Jamie squirms.

ANGLE - CLOSE ON JAMIE as he SNEEZES AWAKE.

His eyes OPEN, and he does a double take, looking around the room with wide eyes, SNEEZING again.

INT. ANOTHER BEDROOM - DAY - LONGER ANGLE - DISTORTED LENS

Jamie is lying alone on a DIFFERENT BED in a DIFFERENT ROOM, naked under a FLOWER-PRINT sheet. The room is shadowed with heavy CURTAINS that are partly open, revealing an unfamiliar CITYSCAPE.

Somehow, the room reminds us of a jungle, with sculptures, animal figures hiding in the hard-to-pierce SHADOWS. But there is something FEMININE and MYSTERIOUS about the room.

ANOTHER ANGLE - JAMIE'S P.O.V. as he looks around the room. Nothing is familiar to him. We hear the SHOWER RUNNING (o.s.), and notice the CLOCK RADIO: 7:15 a.m. A BOUQUET of ROSES sits open on the NIGHTSTAND.

A MAN'S VOICE speaks.

                    VOICE (O.S)
          You awake, babe?

Jamie's P.O.V. SWINGS to face the doorway leading into the adjoining BATHROOM, and we HEAR the SHOWER being CUT OFF.

RESUME JAMIE'S BEDROOM

He is sitting upright in his own bed, looking straight ahead, blindly, disoriented, frightened.

                    JAMIE
          (whispering to himself)
          It's happening again...

Elaine STIRS.

RESUME OTHER BEDROOM - JAMIE'S P.O.V.

A MAN comes out of the BATHROOM, just a TOWEL around his waist. He is very well-built and good-looking. He smiles right into the camera. It is The Man Who Wasn't There. The Intruder.

                    MAN
          How can anyone look that good
          this early?

He approaches the CAMERA, reaching out his HANDS to us.

RESUME JAMIE

His face expresses SHOCK.

                    JAMIE
          No! No!!!

Elaine groggily comes awake next to him.

                    ELAINE
          What?

RESUME JAMIE'S P.O.V. - OTHER BEDROOM

The man PULLS BACK from the CAMERA, as if from a kiss.

                    MAN
          God, you are such a turn-on!

He takes the woman's HAND gently, and begins to KISS it. His lips press moistly against her fingers, and his kisses get wetter. He LICKS her fingers, and puts them in his mouth. Her MOAN goes DEEPER as she REACTS. She LIKES this.

He leans down below the frame line, kissing and licking amorously. We HEAR a WOMAN'S PURR

as our VIEW drifts up to the CEILING. Then,
in the P.O.V., the EYES CLOSE to BLACK.

                    MAN (V.O.)
          The morning's the best, isn't
          it?

RESUME JAMIE'S BEDROOM

                    JAMIE
          God, no!!!

Suddenly his body is thrown back against the
bed!

Elaine, frightened, reaches out to him, but
is afraid to touch him.

                    ELAINE
          What do you want me to do?

All of his muscles are tensed; his hands are
claws gripping the sides of the bed.

                    ELAINE
          Jamie, what is it?

He JERKS, as if being roughly PENETRATED,
his BODY invaded. It makes him SCREAM.

RESUME P.O.V. - OTHER BEDROOM

As the Man is atop him, THRUSTING. But the
BODY we see moving under him is a WOMAN'S.
We HEAR her REACT.

                    MAN
          You feel great!

Her enthusiasm builds with his, and their
MOANS become whimpers. Their lovemaking
grows more intense, overwhelming... and
Jamie feels it!

RESUME JAMIE'S BEDROOM

He is now helplessly making the whimpering
SOUNDS from the other bedroom. He is BUCKING
uncontrollably. Elaine's fear is turning
into disgust from the seemingly kinky sexual
nature of Jamie's FIT.

                    ELAINE
          Stop it! Jamie, stop it!!!

But he can't. He can't even HEAR her.

There is a knock on jamie's front door
(O.S.). Elaine looks from the frenzied, out
of control jamie toward the living room, not
knowing what to do.

The POUNDING on the door gets LOUDER.

               VANESSA'S VOICE (O.S.)
          Jamie? Anybody home?

                    ELAINE
             (frantic whispers)
          Jamie, please! There's
          somebody at the door!

He keeps reacting, oblivious to the real
world around him. More KNOCKING.

               BOOTH'S VOICE (O.S.)
          Daddy! Let us in

We hear a key in the door, and a frantic
elaine wraps the sheet around her naked body,
slamming shut the bedroom door.

INT. JAMIE'S LIVING ROOM - DAY

The DOOR OPENS, and Vanessa and Booth ENTER,
smiling, ready to awaken DADDY. Booth is
giggling excitedly.

Lucy sees them, and goes to SCRATCH on the
BEDROOM DOOR.

                    BOOTH
          Hi, Lucy! Rise and shine,
          Daddy!

He runs laughing toward the bedroom, pulling
Vanessa behind him.

RESUME BEDROOM

Booth and Vanessa ENTER, confronted by the
frenzied   scene.   Jamie   is   BUCKING
frantically, as Elaine hurriedly climbs into
her clothes.

The SMILES on Booth's and Vanessa's faces
DROP; Elaine doesn't know what she's gotten
herself into.

Booth thinks there's something wrong with
his Daddy, and runs over to the bedside.

                    BOOTH
          Daddy, stop! Stop it, please!

He turns angrily to elaine, and starts
hitting at her, flailing with little boy
fists.

                    BOOTH
          You hurt my Dad! Leave him
          alone!

                   ELAINE
          I didn't do anything!

Outraged, Vanessa grabs the boy, covering
his eyes as she pulls him out of the room.

                   VANESSA
          God damn you, Jamie!

Jamie is just coming out of the spell as his
ex-wife and son storm out of the apartment.
He is weak and shaking, horrified to have
transposed so nakedly... in front of these

intimates.

                    JAMIE
          (a whisper, to himself)
     It's a woman...

Furious, Elaine won't even look at him as
she finishes dressing. Jamie looks at her
with total embarrassment, as she STORMS OUT
of the room, and FOLLOWS.

INT. JAMIE'S KITCHEN - DAY

Elaine is in the kitchen, taking her
groceries out of the refrigerator. Jamie
enters, keeping his distance.

                    JAMIE
          Listen, I, uh... something
          really weird is going on...

                    ELAINE
          (unable to look at him)
          Tell me about it.

                    JAMIE
          I'd like to explain it to
          you—

                    ELAINE
          Listen... this is just too
          weird too soon, okay?

                    JAMIE
          I'm really not a creep, you
          know...

                    ELAINE
          That's not for you to decide,
          is it?

She turns to head out, and he reaches to take
her arm.

                         JAMIE
              I'm really sorry...

So is she, but it's difficult for her to deal
with all of this right now. They really did
seem to have some chemistry the night before,
and now she has pangs of regret as well.

                        ELAINE
              So am I. Just because I spent
              the night with you doesn't
              mean you can fuck with me. I
              really don't need these
              problems on the first date,
              you know? I'm sure you can
              find women to indulge you in
              those slimy little newspapers
              in the boxes outside the post
              office!

She takes her STUFF and EXITS, the DOOR
SLAMMING SHUT in her wake. Jamie stares
blankly behind her, as LUCY ENTERS. He looks
at Lucy, depressed and shaken.

                        JAMIE
                     (to Lucy)
              At least I've got you...

Don't be so sure. She looks at him, turns,
and leaves the room, leaving him alone...

                                        CUT TO:

INT. JAMIE'S BATHROOM - DAY

He looks depressed as he SHAVES in front of
the MIRROR. The RAZOR seems a dangerous
instrument in his condition; his eyes are
hollow, receptive as he goes about his
mindless morning task.

Halfway through, he suddenly SNEEZES. The
RAZOR SLIPS, making a shallow CUT on his
FACE! But he is OBLIVIOUS. A DROP of BLOOD

splashes in the sink, the red SEEPING out
into the foamy water.

He is staring, transfixed, into the mirror,
as his body RELAXES. He stands TALLER, a
million miles away, TRANSPOSING again.

The WATER continues to RUN, STEAM drifting
up around him, hypnotic. His FACE FLUSHES,
and he SMILES. His SKIN PRICKLES, and the
gentle, loving SOUND/MUSIC PLAYS.

This time, it makes him feel WONDERFUL...

Clumsily and sightlessly, he BACKS into a
SITTING POSITION on the toilet, unable to
remain standing. He stares blindly ahead as
the room FILLS with STEAM, his reflection
hiding behind the vapor, as he continues to
TRANSPOSE...

JAMIE/WOMAN'S P.O.V. - THE WOMAN'S BEDROOM -
DAY

At her DRESSING TABLE, seeing through HER
EYES, through a BOUQUET of ROSES. We HEAR
her VOICE-soft, airy—as she SINGS. No song
in particular, just heartfelt, joyous, happy
MUSIC.

There is a tiny MIRROR on the table, but it
only gives us tiny, tantalizing GLIMPSES of
parts of her body, never her FACE. Her hand
comes up to SPRAY PERFUME on her neck, and
she GIGGLES slightly. It TICKLES. She rubs
it in, sensually.

There is a clever little WOODEN BOX
surrounded by romantic little THINGS that
don't make much sense. Her beautiful,
tapered HANDS lovingly place the items in
the box: a ZOO of tiny STUFFED ANIMALS, a
high school RING with a thick ROLL of BLACK
TAPE around the band, a PLASTIC SHARK, a
CHOCOLATE TRUFFLE, and a quickly drawn

SKETCH of THE MAN'S FACE, which she KISSES
REPEATEDLY, leaving LIP PRINTS all over it.
She picks up the last item, and ties a note
to it with a piece of yarn: a FLOWER, with a
single PETAL left on it.

The note reads: "He loves me".

Closing the box, she scribbles another note:
"To whom it may concern—I love you, too!"

CU JAMIE IN ROOM

As in the opening. He is looking down at his
hands, embarrassed, uncomfortable. It takes
him a moment or two to be able to speak,
suddenly feeling very emotional.

                    JAMIE
          "I love you."
                    (long beat)
          Those simple words were
          suddenly so potent and
          meaningful... it... well, it
          embarrassed me. These silly
          little trinkets meant more
          than diamonds to her. And to
          me.
                    (breaks off)
          Until that moment, I didn't
          know you really could feel
          with your guts and your
          heart. I know I never had
          until then. It felt so weird,
          so new and... deep... and
          good... I had no idea until
          that moment how shallow my
          life had been, and it...
          humiliated me...
                    (beat)
          It felt like... growing up.

He looks up with a hopeful expression, as if
asking for understanding. He's not going to
get if from the detectives.

RESUME JAMIE'S BATHROOM

He shivers as the experience passes through him and leaves him limp. He can't believe what he's just felt.

                    JAMIE
               (into the mirror)
          Who are you?

INT. COUGAR CHEMICAL LAB - DAY

Wally is MOVING quickly with us through the lab as A GROUP of DOGS is gathered around him, JUMPING for doses of his PRIME RIB FLAVOR; they love it, and won't—can't—leave him alone. Jamie ENTERS, and Wally excitedly CALLS OUT to him from the cacophonous CANINE clutch.

                    WALLY
          Jamie, they love it!

Jamie is distracted, but the four-letter-word that is suddenly so meaningful to him registers.

Wally squeezes out of the dog frenzy, concerned about Jamie, leaving the animals to their artificial FEAST.

                    WALLY
          What's the matter?

                    JAMIE
          Nothing. I'm just thinking.

                    WALLY
          Okay, you're not a little
          weird this morning. Nothing's
          the matter. You're just
          thinking.

Jamie looks at Wally, needing to talk with

someone about the strange events that are
happening to him.

                    JAMIE
                 (intimate)
          Wally...

                    WALLY
          Never mind. I don't want to
          know.

                    JAMIE
          Wally, something very strange
          is happening to me.

                    WALLY
          And did you go to the doctor?
          No...

                    JAMIE
          I went to the doctor.

                    WALLY
                 (surprised)
          And?

                    JAMIE
          And doctors don't know shit.
          All they do is guess.

Wally sits down at his bench, folds his arms,
watching his friend, waiting for the news.
Jamie is silent for a few BEATS, STRUGGLING
to figure out how to tell.

                    JAMIE
          You know these... spells I've
          been having?

                    WALLY
                 (concerned)
          They getting worse?

Jamie is unable to answer the question, and
just ignores it.

                    JAMIE
          It's... a woman.

Wally BRIGHTENS. Man talk! Dames!

                    WALLY
          A woman! Jamie,
          congratulations! That's
          great! What's she like?

                    JAMIE
                (playing along)
          Well, she's—she's pretty
          wonderful...

                    WALLY
          What's she look like?

                    JAMIE
     (looking him straight in the eye; beat)
          I have no idea.

                    WALLY

          Okay...

                    JAMIE
          Wally, listen to me. It's
          like I'm receiving
          transmissions from somebody.

                    WALLY
          What, you mean like,
          possessed?

                    JAMIE
          No, not like possessed.
          There's a woman... I don't
          know who or where she is,
          but—I can see what she
          sees...
                (embarrassed)
          Feel what she feels...

                    WALLY
                 (Groucho eyes)
            And what does she feel?

Jamie doesn't laugh. Wally sees how serious
he is.

                    WALLY
            You're serious...
            (Jamie nods; Wally's skeptical)
            Well, how do you know it's a
            woman?

Jamie BLUSHES, embarrassed, no longer sure
he wants to talk about it.

Jeanette APPEARS at the doorway, interested
in the conversation.

                    JAMIE
            Never mind.

                    WALLY
            Look at you, you're turning
            red! What happened?

Jamie and Wally both turn to see Jeanette
standing there, listening.

                    JEANETTE
                 (leaving)
            I think I'll powder my
            nose...

Once she's gone, Wally gets closer,
confidentially.

                    WALLY
            Tell!

                    JAMIE
                 (awkward, looking away)
            Last night, she was... she
            had, urn, intercourse... and
            I... well, I... felt it...

                    WALLY
              (taking a step back)
          You felt her get fucked?

Now Jamie is really sorry he said anything.
Wally looks at him like he's missing a cog.

                    JAMIE
          Never mind.

                    WALLY
              (tentatively)
          Tell me about her...

                    JAMIE
          I'm not crazy, Wally! This
          shit is for real!

                    WALLY
          I'm on your side! I just
          asked you to tell me about
          her!

Jamie looks at him, just thinking.

                    JAMIE
          I'm going to lunch, okay?

                    WALLY
          It's only 10:30.

                    JAMIE
          Then call it brunch, okay?

And he EXITS.

EXT. CITY PLAZA - DAY

Lunchtime. Jamie is sitting on the rim of a
FOUNTAIN, eating a healthy pita sandwich.
The plaza is a beehive of activity, with the
INHABITANTS of the surrounding HIGH RISES
spilling out for lunch around the hot dog
carts.

Jamie takes a bite of the sandwich and tosses it to the swarm of PIGEONS making a nuisance of themselves.

He watches without seeing, passive, blank, his mind elsewhere... and he begins to TRANSPOSE.

His BODY SETTLES as he sets down the sandwich, and pays no attention when the pigeons start to swarm over it.

He CROSSES HIS LEGS in a feminine manner, but it's subtle.

He SMILES and seems to SHED the massive weight on his shoulders, happy in the afternoon sun. He gently LAUGHS.

He is looking into the water in the FOUNTAIN, staring back at his own reflection, and begins to SING, a soft, meandering MELODY.

JAMIE'S P.O.V.

As he watches his reflection RIPPLE and DISTORT, we can HEAR the distant SOUND of THE WOMAN'S VOICE, singing the same TUNE as Jamie, in perfect unity.

The SOUND/MUSIC joins in, and he reaches into the water as OPTICAL BUBBLES BURST and the scene shifts, the MUSIC churning with the WATER.

                              DISSOLVE TO:

INT. A BATHROOM - CONTINUING JAMIE'S/WOMAN'S P.O.V.

The Woman's lovely HAND is SWIRLING the WATER in the BATHROOM SINK, helping it to go down a sluggish DRAIN. She LOOKS UP toward the medicine cabinet MIRROR, at an angle with

will not allow us a view of her reflection.
Her ARM reaches out, pulls the MIRROR OPEN...
In that brief moment, we catch a split-second
GLIMPSE of an absolutely gorgeous, naked
WOMAN (JACQUELINE DUPRES), reflected in the
MIRROR from the waist up. The lightning flash
image is indelibly etched in our sight.

She has large BROWN EYES, white, almost
PORCELAIN SKIN, shoulder length AUBURN HAIR,
and is just breathtaking...

But as soon as she FLASHES BY, the FRAME
begins to SHIFT again.

RESUME JAMIE

He gasps at the sight of her, coming out of
his spell.

RESUME JAMIE'S P.O.V.

The bathroom gives way to the fountain, and
JAMIE'S   rippling   reflection.   Total
frustration.

RESUME JAMIE

He is unwilling to let her go.

                    JAMIE
          Don't go!

He reaches frantically into the WATER for
her, splashing messily, shattering his own
reflection.

                    JAMIE
          Come back!

People around him are getting splashed, and
pissed, from JAMIE'S actions. One man
SPLASHES BACK, drenching Jamie, bringing him
suddenly back to the real world.

Jamie looks around with surprise to see people walking away, glaring and hurling epithets at him.

                              DISSOLVE TO:

INT. LABYRINTH - NIGHT - STEADICAM P.O.V. SHOT

We are in an old, deserted, mysterious WALKWAY, moving sinuously, hearing our own BREATH and the PADDING of our BARE FEET.

The Hallway twists and curves, with WALLS of damp, mossy, and crumbling BRICK, lit by recessed lights every 30 feet or so.

How did we get here?

We MOVE slowly, hesitantly, uneasily down the creepy corridor and its alternating POOLS of LIGHT and DARKNESS, looking in all directions... as if there might be a way out. Every so often, light spills through a ROW of IRON CAGE BARS.

We HEAR another set of FOOTSTEPS (o.s.), and SWING AROUND.

No one there, so we continue... a little faster. Another set of footsteps keeps in time with us, padding along the wet stone floor.

A SHADOW RUSHES BY: a glimpse of a GIANT CAT? We move FASTER, building up to a RUN.

And then, the LIGHTS sputter OUT. We RUN, constantly TURNING to see who or what is chasing us through the nearly impenetrable darkness. We HEAR BREATHING right over our shoulder, but it is hardly human!

We RUN up against a DEAD END of IRON BARS, and SWING AROUND for a frightened look behind, as the silhouetted FIGURE of a MAN rushes up quickly from behind, his LONG SHADOW suffocating us!

We STRUGGLE with the CAGE DOOR as he is just about on us, and CRASH THROUGH, just at the last moment!

We run desperately through the seemingly endless, slimy CORRIDOR, the MAN getting closer, his breath and footsteps nearly deafening!

And then, we RUN UP AGAINST a double set of heavy IRON BARS!

We turn around, just in time to see the MAN LOOM UP over us, an impossibly long and deadly BLADE in his hands, PLUNGING right at us! It is the MAN who was making love to Jacqueline!

XCU - THE MAN

We RUSH IN on his face, lit by the glint of the BLADE, and his visage of horrible victory suddenly DARKENS as we see the REFLECTION of US in his EYES: A TIGER, snarling and ROARING horribly!

The Man SCREAMS as the P.O.V. CAMERA overtakes his FACE!

                              SHOCK CUT TO:

INT. JACQUELINE'S BEDROOM - NIGHT

XCU her FACE. The beautiful BROWN EYES SNAP OPEN, filling the frame with her terror. We HEAR her GASP.

                              SHOCK CUT TO:

INT. JAMIE'S BEDROOM - DAY

CU JAMIE, as his EYES SNAP OPEN. He's been
DREAMING her DREAM with her, and his heart
is pounding.

                    JAMIE
          Shit!

Once he gets his bearings and begins to calm
down, he feels cheated. All he got was her
dream.

EXT. CITY STREETS - EVENING

Jamie has a bag of groceries in his arm, as
he rushes up the street from the bus stop.

EXT. JAMIE'S APARTMENT - EVENING

Juggling the bag of GROCERIES, Jamie unlocks
the door and lets himself into the building.

INT. JAMIE'S APARTMENT - EVENING

INSERT - HAND AND CANDLE

Tight shot of JAMIE'S HAND lighting a CANDLE
in the dark.

WIDER ANGLE

There are CANDLES placed strategically about
the room. ROMANTIC MUSIC-like the MUSIC we
HEAR at Jacqueline's place—plays in the
background. A DOZEN ROSES sit unfurling in a
vase on the table. Jamie, stuffy from the
roses, LIGHTS the last CANDLE and PULLS OPEN
the CURTAIN, pausing for a moment to gaze
out into the clear, blue-black sky.

He sits on the couch; there is a little
AROMA-DISC MACHINE on the table. He inserts

a DISC marked "Chocolate", and switches it ON.

Then, he pops the cork on a BOTTLE OF CHAMPAGNE, and POURS two glasses.

With Lucy watching from the corner, Jamie settles back into the cushions of the couch, trying with all his might to summon up the Woman. So far, nothing is happening.

He looks at the end table, sees BOOTH'S FACE smiling at him from a picture frame. It holds his gaze for a few BEATS before he guiltily turns the snapshot face-down.

Again, he settles back, trying to drain his mind and conjure her up.

JAMIE'S P.O.V.

He slowly scans the lit candles, the room... the music is soothing, almost hypnotic.

RESUME JAMIE

He wants her so badly. He is trying to bring himself down into a calm, alpha-like state of receptivity.

                    JAMIE
          Come on... come back to me.

Quiet, serene, willing her back. Slower, quieter. Past the CANDLES and CHAMPAGNE, we MOVE IN ON HIM. It's never going to happen.

                              DISSOLVE TO:

SAME SCENE, SAME ANGLE - LATER

But we've DISSOLVED his OPEN eyes CLOSED. They BLINK OPEN, as if from sleep.

QUICK CUTS

The CANDLES, now mere puddles of WAX, WINKING
OUT. The RECORD caught in its CATCH-GROOVE.
An empty CHAMPAGNE GLASS, knocked over. Time
has passed.

RESUME JAMIE

We PULL OUT, to find him NOT seated in his
living room, but rather STANDING in The
Woman's BATHROOM.

INT. WOMAN'S BATHROOM - NIGHT

He ENTERS the bathroom, leaving the door open
behind him, and stands in front of the full-
length mirror.

IT IS AN ARTFUL, UPSCALE ROOM, WITH LOTS OF
TILE: A STRANGE BUT SOMEHOW MELODIOUS CROSS
BETWEEN ART DECO AND THE JUNGLES OF ROUSSEAU.

RESUME JAMIE'S APARTMENT

Jamie is in two places at once, still sitting
on the couch, his eyes wide, Lucy on his lap.
We know at once that he is transposing again.
His BREATH deepens.

JAMIE'S   P.O.V.   -   THE   WOMAN'S
BATHROOM/JAMIE'S LIVING ROOM

The view fluctuates maddeningly between the
two locations. As the vision BUBBLES between
the two, as if the brain is trying to decide
where to live, we can make out her ROBE
dropping to the floor, getting glimpses in
the MIRROR.

We can make out that she is beautifully
shaped. She slaps her stomach, checking
herself out.

Finally, seeing through her eyes, she steps

right up to the mirror, and the reflection
of her face fills the frame. The vision gives
way to her completely, with crystal clarity.
She looks piercingly right into the CAMERA!

RESUME JAMIE

Completely enchanted, possessed, gripping
Lucy unconsciously, making her SQUEAL.

RESUME JAMIE'S/WOMAN'S P.O.V. - THE WOMAN
She is taking inventory of her appearance.
It is a very intimate, private moment.

She pulls her hair back, tries various ways
of framing her face, then makes a comical
grimace.

Then she tries framing her nose with her
fingers in different ways, as if imagining
different noses. And then, for the first
time, we hear her speak. Sort of.

She playfully BARKS like a DOG, as if to
jokingly say to herself, "God, girl, you are
such a bowser!" It makes her giggle at
herself, and then, putting on a joky, sultry
pose, she half-closes her eyes to sexy,
feline slits, pulls her hair across her
face... and... PURRS deep down in her throat.

And then:

                    JACQUELINE
          You wish.

There is no ego here; her voice is lilted by
the trace of a French accent. She leaves the
mirror with a self-deprecating wave.

RESUME JAMIE

Sweat appears on his brow and upper lip, his
eyes unblinking, his breathing coming
harder.

RESUME THE WOMAN'S BATHROOM - JAMIE'S /WOMAN'S P.O.V.

The shower curtain is YANKED OPEN to REVEAL a large, old-fashioned, claw-foot porcelain tub. She begins to SING, that lovely, loving VOICE, happy, soothing, comforting.

Her hand turns on the water and feels for the right temperature, and when it's right, she climbs in for a shower, the WATER cascading over us. Then she POURS a quick shot of CHAMPAGNE into the TUB.

She LATHERS UP, covering her body in thick SUDS. Her hands busily work the suds over her hands, her face, her BODY.

RESUME JAMIE

Ecstasy.

RESUME TUB - THEIR P.O.V.

She has the SHOWER MASSAGE in her hand, rinsing the SOAP from her body. Then she switches from RINSE to MASSAGE, and the water PULSES mightily over her shoulders and back. She slowly eases down to lie on her back in the luxurious tub. She runs the pulsing water all over her body, before her LEGS ultimately PART.

RESUME JAMIE

His body is moving in erotic waves, his heretofore wide eyes falling helplessly closed.

RESUME BATHROOM - THEIR P.O.V.

She aims the pulsating water between her legs, and distant purring sounds begin as she can't keep from slowly gyrating.

ANGLE - LUCY - ON JAMIE'S LAP

She is purring, asleep, but as Jamie MOVES, she wakens.

ANGLE - JAMIE

He moves with the Woman, gyrating, matching her rhythm, making sounds of his own. Lucy, a little freaked, jumps down, and watches from a distance.

Jamie takes deep, ragged breaths, oblivious to his surroundings, until the waves of climax crashes over him. It is powerful, draining, and his body slumps against the couch.

His eyes open, and he returns from Oz to his lonely little world, out of breath.

                    JAMIE
          Jesus!

And as he tries not to come back home, just catching his breath, the DOORBELL RINGS. He is not up to getting it.

                    JAMIE
          No.

The persistent person at the door KNOCKS loudly, almost angrily. Jamie is in no condition to answer it. Then, a VOICE calls out: it is VANESSA.

                    VANESSA (O.S.)
          Jamie?

                    JAMIE
                (to himself)
          Oh, shit...

And he tries to get his proverbial shit together enough to answer the door, but it takes time. He tries to throw a towel over his telltale trousers, embarrassed, drained, and confused.

She KNOCKS again.

                    VANESSA
          Jamie!

But by the time Jamie gets to the door, she is gone.

INT. HALLWAY OUTSIDE JAMIE'S APARTMENT - NIGHT

Vanessa is at the STAIRWELL already, heading down.

                    JAMIE
          I'm here, Vanessa.

She STOPS, looks up to him. She points to the floor in front of him, and he looks down to see an ENVELOPE there. He bends down and picks it up.

                    VANESSA
          I didn't mean to drag you out
          of bed.

                    JAMIE
          It's okay.

                    VANESSA
          I wouldn't want to spoil any
          fun.

                    JAMIE
          Look, we're divorced. I don't
          have to meet your approval
          anymore.
                    (re: envelope)
          What's this?

                    VANESSA
          I assume you can still read.

He takes out a legal document: a RESTRAINING
ORDER, forbidding him from seeing Booth,
because of his questionable moral nature.
Jamie is angry as he reads enough of it to
see what it is.

                    JAMIE
          You can't keep me from seeing
          my own son!

                    VANESSA
          Like the last time you saw
          him? Oh, yes I can!

                    JAMIE
          Listen, it wasn't what you
          think!

                    VANESSA
          I don't want to hear what you
          were doing! You can fuck
          whoever you want, wherever
          you want, whenever you want
          to now! Have a nice day!

And she LEAVES. Jamie watches her go for a
moment, before SLAMMING the DOOR SHUT.

INT. COUGAR CHEMICAL LAB - MORNING

Monday morning. The group is arriving, ready
for the new week. Jamie actually looks happy
when greeted by Wally and Jeanette; we can
only guess why. He is clean and neat, clean-
shaven, HUMMING The Woman's SONG.

                    WALLY
               (clearing his throat)
          Well, another day, another
          hundred and eighty-seven
          dollars.

                    JEANETTE
          Before taxes.

                    JAMIE
          Morning, guys.

                    WALLY
          (hesitant to broach the subject)
          How are you feeling, Jamie?
          Everything okay?

                    JAMIE
          Yeah, I'm okay. How about
          you?

                    JEANETTE
          What Mr. Jagger here means
          is, did you have any more of
          those episodes?

He waits a meaningful beat. He doesn't want
to have this intensely personal secret life
invaded. No intruders.

                    JAMIE
          Episodes?

                    WALLY
          You know, like feeling the
          girl get fucked. Jeanette
          knows.

                    JAMIE
          No. No, no more of those...
          hallucinations. It must have
          been the shock of the
          macrobiotic diet, like the
          doctor said. All I needed was
          a good hamburger.

Wally and Jeanette look askance at one
another.

                    JEANETTE
          Have you been keeping the
          crystal with you? It's
          probably that. I brought you
          something special, in case
          you needed it.

She takes out a little silk PILLOW.

                    JEANETTE
          It's a dream pillow. Just put
          it under your pillow at
          night, and I can dream with
          you and protect you from
          psychic harm. It works.

                    WALLY
          Jeez! Keep out of his dreams,
          Jeanette!

                    JAMIE
          I'm okay. Really. And thanks
          for your concern.

                    JEANETTE
          Better keep that, anyway.

                    WALLY
          So, listen, Jamie. The twins
          are visiting my folks, so
          Anna wanted me to invite you
          over for dinner.

                    JAMIE
          When, tonight?
                    (Wally nods)
          No, I—I can't tonight.

                    WALLY
          Forget it, Jamie. I'm not
          letting you out of this. You
          know Anna. She invited a
          girlfriend. I told her you
          were gay, but she won't
          believe me.

                    JAMIE
          Wally, please don't try to
          set me up, okay? I can't come
          tonight.

                    WALLY
          Why not? It'll be fun! F-U-
          double-N fun! You got
          something better planned?

Jamie FLUSHES, embarrassed.

                    WALLY
          He is feeling better! You're
          seeing somebody! Well, who is
          she? Do we know her?

                    JAMIE
                 (blushing)
          You don't know her.

                    WALLY
          Well, what's her name?

Jamie falters for a moment, fumbling, before
righting himself.

                    JAMIE
          I'd rather not say.

                    WALLY
          Why, you afraid I'll call her
          up and tell her who you
          really are?

                    JEANETTE
                 (watching Jamie squirm)
          Cut it out, Wally. The man's
          entitled to a private life.

                    WALLY
          New rules?

Jamie guiltily evades Wally's eyeline. Then,
suddenly:

                    WALLY
          Oh, shit! It's her, isn't it?

                    JAMIE
                  (guilty)
          Who?

                    WALLY
          You know who I mean. The girl
          in the hallucinations! You
          met her, and fell in love!
          Gorilla your dreams!

Jamie doesn't say anything, but his face is
a set of open books.

                    WALLY
                  (to Jeanette)
          Isn't this the most romantic
          thing you've ever heard?
                  (wanting confirmation)
          It is her, isn't it?

Even without his assent, it is obviously
true.

                    WALLY
          You know I'm gonna keep
          bugging you until you tell me
          all about it.

                    JAMIE
          I know.

Suddenly UNDERSTANDING dawns on Wally. He
gets SERIOUS.

                    WALLY
          Listen, I know this is a
          stupid question, but have you
          even met this dream girl
          face-to-face?

Jamie can't look at him, but guiltily tries

to cover his fumbling stutter.

                    JAMIE
          How crazy do you think I am?

                    WALLY
          I don't think you're crazy.
          But I'd be lying if I said we
          weren't worried about you.

                    JAMIE
          Don't worry about me, okay?
          I'm all right.

                    WALLY
        (putting his hand on Jamie's arm)
          If you're still having those
          hallucinations, maybe you
          ought to go back to the
          doctor, don't you think?

                    JAMIE
        (angry, yanking his arm away)
          What makes you think I want
          it to stop?

                    JEANETTE
                  (gently)
          Jamie... you haven't met her
          face-to-face, have you?

He just looks at her, unable to answer. She
grinds out her cheroot in Wally's agar-
filled Petrie dish, and puts her hand on his
face.

                    JEANETTE
          Listen to me. This is the
          most perfect case of
          spontaneous biocommunication
          I've ever seen.

Suddenly, Jeanette doesn't seem like such a
crackpot to Jamie.

                    JAMIE
          Biocommunication?

                  JEANETTE
          Telepathy. E.S.P. Come on-a
          my house tonight. I'm an
          expert on this shit.

What does he have to lose at this point?
Wally smirks.

INT. JEANETTE'S HOUSE - NIGHT

A fat, late-middle-age, bald man is red and
huffing as he works out to a "Buns of Steel"
video playing on the TV. This is Jeanette's
HUSBAND, the POLYP. He never speaks.

Jeanette CROSSES FRAME with an armload of
BOOKS, topped by a box of chocolate-covered
graham crackers, the ever-present cheroot in
her mouth. We FOLLOW her out of the DEN, and
INTO:

INT. JEANETTE'S KITCHEN - NIGHT

She DROPS the PILE of BOOKS on the table
where Jamie is waiting, and then settles in
next to him behind an overflowing ashtray
and a Jolt Cola.

                  JEANETTE
          It isn't bullshit, Jamie.
          It's not crackpot stuff, and
          it's not New Age mumbo jumbo.
          Serious science,
          parapsychology, university
          grant shit. I mean, look at
          this stuff. Choco-Graham?

She tosses books on the table in front of
him, showing him page after page of
DOCUMENTATION. He declines the graham

cracker.

                    JAMIE
          Okay, books. Great.

                    JEANETTE
          Yeah, books. Scientific
          evidence, studies. Look at
          this: Duke University
          studies, Dr. Joseph Rhine,
          1930 to 1933, over 100,000
          tests conducted in the most
          disciplined scientific
          manner, proving results that
          extra-sensory perception is
          real. They ran tests with
          five different cards, even in
          separate rooms, where chance
          would be maybe five guesses
          out of 25. He got results
          with subjects consistently
          getting 15 to 18 right out of
          25! Consistently!

                    JAMIE
          You know, that's real
          interesting, Jeanette. But
          I'm not talking about
          guessing stars and squiggles
          here. I'm getting somebody
          else's senses sent to me!

                    JEANETTE
          And I'm trying to show you
          that biocommunication is
          real! Long range telepathy is
          a true, documented
          phenomenon! Look.
              (tosses book: *The Probability of the
                   Impossible*;)
          Thelma Moss ran tests at
          UCLA-UCLA!-on what she called
          "emotional E.S.P." She
          combined powerful, emotion-
          inducing sounds and images,
                    (cont'd)

                    JEANETTE
                  (cont'd)
        showed them to subjects in
        one room, and had "receivers"
        in another room describe them
        with near perfect accuracy.
        When she got such incredible
        results in those tests, she
        tried it again between
        subjects in Los Angeles, New
        York City, and Sussex,
        England, and if anything, the
        long-distance results were
        better than room-to-room
        tests!
        (this is starting to interest
         Jamie, so she keeps rolling)
        Then later, at Duke
        University again, they had a
        test where one person was
        sitting in a room and
        describing what another
        person was seeing as they
        drove through the
        countryside... over 1500
        miles away!
                  (beat)
        Somebody's calling out to
        you, Jamie. Somebody needs
        you real bad. For real.

Jamie NODS. He knows it's true.

                    JAMIE
        But how? And why me?

                    JEANETTE
        Back around the turn of the
        century, a physicist named
        William Cookes had a theory;
        he thought telepathy was
        caused by high frequency
        vibrations of ether,
                  (cont'd)

                    JEANETTE
                    (cont'd)
          generated by molecular action
          of the brain of the agent,
          and received by the
          percipient. You. Meaning,
          you're both tuned in to the
          same channel. Metaphorically
          speaking.

Jamie REACTS.

INT. JAMIE'S KITCHEN - NIGHT

We PAN ACROSS the LIT CANDLES in f.g. to see
Jamie already far into the depths of
transposition. The AROMA DISC revolves,
CHAMPAGNE uncorked, a BOX OF CHOCOLATES
half-eaten, etc. The HALF-MELTED CANDLES are
puddled on the tablecloth, and soft strains
of CLASSICAL MUSIC drift through. A pile of
Jeanette's BOOKS lie scattered open on the
table.

The ritual has worked; his deep breathing is
becoming more natural, everyday breath. His
wide eyes stare unseeing at the candles
before him. All receptors are open.

Blind to the candles, he stares ahead, and,
oddly, grabs one of them, and JAMS its
burning TIP against the white tablecloth.
The FLAME goes OUT in a gurgle of MELTED WAX.
He MOVES the CANDLE, as if with a PURPOSE.

ANGLE ON TABLE

Soon we understand. He is drawing with the
candle, red, waxy LINES on the linen. It
seems to be an ANIMAL of some sort.

RESUME JAMIE

He stares ahead, his hands working independently of him. His eyes are blank and distant.

EXT. ZOO - LATE AFTERNOON - JAMIE'S/WOMAN'S P.O.V.

INSERT - SKETCH PAD

There is a wonderful rendering of a ferocious TIGER'S FACE being DRAWN by the Woman's HAND. Unexpectedly, TWO TEARDROPS fall onto the drawing, making the PASTELS RUN. She suddenly flips the pad shut, revealing where we are:

In the heart of a lush ZOO. A placid TIGER lies yawning in the bottom of the enclosure, quite at odds with the ferocious BEAST in her DRAWING.

RESUME JAMIE IN KITCHEN

His eyes still wide, he lays his hands on his drawing, which is a fair facsimile of hers.

RESUME ZOO - THEIR P.O.V. - TRACKING

We see through her eyes as she gets up and walks down an asphalt path.

The VIEW that greets us around a wooded CORNER is surprising: a BIG CITY SKYLINE, with a large BAY on one side, and lush, green MOUNTAINS across the bay.

This is the same city we saw in JAMIE'S first VISION (on the highway in Wally's van)!

She approaches a BLACK DODGE VAN, and we GET IN with her, checking her RED EYES briefly in the rearview mirror, and the scene BUBBLES AWAY, leaving us with the crude drawing on

JAMIE'S table.

RESUME JAMIE

His eyes are slick with her tears.

He looks down at the DRAWING, his only
tangible link to the woman he's falling in
love with. He's surprised to see it there,
not realizing that he drew it.

He lightly traces the wax lines with his
finger, feeling her any way that he can.

                    JAMIE
          Can you feel me, too?

Standing by an empty food dish at the edge
of the kitchen, Lucy MEOWS for some dinner,
but JAMIE'S mind is elsewhere.

He feels very lonely, abandoned in this
functional, but not homey, cubicle. But he
is hopeful; he has seen the skyline of her
city.

                    JAMIE
          Please, come back.
          (girding the courage to say it)
          I love you.

He looks across the room, his gaze settling
on a picture of Booth stuck to the
refrigerator. He doesn't know why it makes
him feel guilty. But it does.

                              DISSOLVE TO:

EXT. JAMIE'S APARTMENT BUILDING - NIGHT

Jamie walks up and ENTERS the building.

INT. HALLWAY - JAMIE'S APARTMENT BUILDING -
NIGHT

Jamie looks up at the three stories of
stairs, then heads up.

JAMIE'S P.O.V. - APARTMENT STAIRWELL

We see through his eyes as he heads up the
well-lighted stairwell, intercutting with
the angle on Jamie.

And then, it begins to HAPPEN. We bubble and
churn, TRANSPOSING to The Woman's P.O.V.

INT. ANOTHER HALLWAY - LOFT - NIGHT - HER
P.O.V

JAMIE'S hallway gives way to this one: a
grungy, faintly-lit affair, with a bare
LIGHTBULB dangling at every floor.

The slap-dash wooden STAIRWAY CREAKS with
her steps, and it looks very FOREBODING and
DANGEROUS.

It is an industrial warehouse turned into an
ARTIST'S LOFT. We reach the TOP, and pause a
BEAT in front of a heavy industrial DOOR that
is AJAR. Then, we ENTER with her.

INT. LOFT - NIGHT - CONTINUOUS

It is filled with a slovenly collection of
easels, art supplies, sculptures, paintings,
and ramshackle, second-hand furniture. It is
difficult to see beyond the walls of items
that break up the massive space.

We can HEAR SOFT VOICES at the other end of
the loft. We slowly make our way through the
STUFF in the DARK, unfamiliar room, until we

can make out the KING-SIZE BED in the corner.
Something is going on there.

We head over to a LAMP on the dresser. The
Woman's HAND comes forward and switches it
ON, bathing this corner of the room in soft,
YELLOW LIGHT. Then we shift our attention to
the BED.

The Man we've seen her with is in the bed
with a beautiful GIRL, barely old enough to
vote. Both are nearly UNDRESSED.

The Man quickly SITS UP, and his face relaxes
into a SMILE, as if covering his little
peccadillo.

                    MAN
          Look... look what I got for
          us.

WE DON'T KNOW IF HE'S COVERING UP, OR IF IT'S
SOMETHING THEY ARE BOTH INTO. HE HOVERS FOR
A MOMENT, REELING A LITTLE UNEASILY.

The GIRL TURNS to us and SMILES, then
GIGGLES, a little embarrassed.

                    GIRL
          Hi.

The Man quickly STANDS, solicitous, taking
The Woman's HAND and leading her back to the
bed.

                    MAN
          Come on... get in here with
          us.

We HESITATE, then allow him to lead us back
to the bed. He pats a spot between them, and
we move onto the bed. The Man is getting
excited; his face and the Girl's fill the
frame.

                    MAN
          Doesn't she have a beautiful
          face?

The Girl smiles again, still embarrassed,
but willing.

He takes the Woman's HAND in his, and lays
it on the Girl's shoulder, and strokes it
with her hand.

                    MAN
          Feel her skin.

Their faces fill the screen. The Man is
obviously turned on; his plan seems to be
working. He POINTS to the wall next to the
bed.

                    MAN
          Look.

We look. There is a MIRROR on the wall,
reflecting the entire bed scene of the THREE
of them. It is a highly-charged erotic
tableau, with the fully dressed Woman
bookended by the virtually naked Man and
Girl. We cannot read The Woman's face, but
pulses are pounding.

                    MAN
          Kiss her...

It's an excited whisper. The Girl nervously
licks her lips as we get even CLOSER to her
face, so close we can see perspiration
forming on her brow, and the shine of her
saliva from her tongue.

But suddenly there is PANDEMONIUM, as the
Woman explodes in a JEALOUS RAGE, whipping
around, picking up and THROWING everything
in the room. She throws the PHONE at the Man,
then the LAMP, which SHATTERS against the
wall in a shower of SPARKS and shards. It is

a noisy, frightening explosion of her temper, completely unexpected!

But his is the greater FURY.

He leaps from the bed, backhanding her (THE CAMERA), and the screen FLASHES BRIGHT WHITE as he connects! He LASHES OUT again, this time KNOCKING HER against the WALL MIRROR, with another FLASH of LIGHT on IMPACT!

As we STARE into the DOZENS of REFLECTED IMAGES of her FACE in the shattered MIRROR, we can SEE the Man coming up from behind, before the vision begins to BUBBLE AWAY to BRIGHT WHITE LIGHT.

                              DISSOLVE TO:

INT. JAMIE'S APARTMENT HALLWAY - OVERHEAD LIGHT - NIGHT

Jamie is collapsed against the wall, his eyes wide, as the vision drifts away, just at the most important part! His FACE is RED, as if being STRANGLED, and he GASPS for BREATH.

                    JAMIE
                  (shouting)
            Leave her alone!

An apartment DOOR OPENS, and a TENANT looks out, baseball bat in hand. Jamie turns to the Tenant, then runs up the stairs to his own apartment.

INT. JAMIE'S APARTMENT - NIGHT - CONTINUOUS

He slams the door in his wake, then leans his back to it, his mind working a hundred miles a minute.

INT. JAMIE'S BEDROOM - NIGHT - LATE

Later that night. Total silence, as we CUT to various still-life tableaux: the CLOCK RADIO at about 4:00 a.m., the PICTURE of BOOTH, JAMIE, and half of VANESSA, a PILE of Jeanette's PARAPSYCHOLOGY BOOKS on the floor, the remains of a BOX OF CHOCOLATES, etc.

Then, we see Jamie on the bed. He is asleep, but not at rest. He turns, troubled, uncomfortable.

But soon, the tension washes off his face. He is overtaken by calm, and it is a lovely moment. He smiles. His body shrugs off the tension, and drifts into repose. Gradually at peace, he tumbles headlong into slumber.

                              SHOCK CUT TO:

LATER

Jamie's eyes snap open as he bolts from sleep.

                    JAMIE
          What?

INT.   WOMAN'S   BEDROOM   -   NIGHT   -
JAMIE'S/WOMAN'S P.O.V.

The Man is hovering over us, his face defining "Innocence". He REACHES gently toward the CAMERA (The Woman's FACE), and STROKES it.

                    MAN
          It didn't mean anything. It's
          just flesh, you know that. It
          isn't like we haven't talked
          about it...

The Woman is silent. He hovers experimentally before lowering his naked frame onto her BODY. The Man knows now is not the time to talk about it, if he wants to sate his libido. He stops, his face close to camera, and looks at her body, getting aroused.

                    MAN
          Just flesh...

But as he is about to ENTER her, her ARMS suddenly FLASH into the FRAME, her two hands gripping an enormous, glinting KNIFE!

There is a horrible, piercing SCREAM as she brings the BLADE up through his BELLY and under the STERNUM, brutally PLUNGING it relentlessly DEEPER into his horrified, squirming BODY.

As he struggles, her LEGS WRAP AROUND HIM, and she shoves it deeper. It is a shocking attack of sadistic fury!

BLOOD runs down the blade from his gaping chest, and red rivers flow down her arms to puddle on her bare stomach. The Man is jerking, gurgling, fading.

RESUME JAMIE

His hands are clenched in a single, white-knuckled FIST, aping the Woman's. He gulps for breath in the throes of the vision, feeling her sick fury.

RESUME P.O.V. SHOT

She jerks the blade from the bone and flesh, and his body crumples on top of her in a bloody, lifeless heap. She tosses the knife to the floor, and, struggling with the dead weight, shoves the corpse off of her and over the side of the bed, where it falls with a dull thud.

RESUME JAMIE IN BED

He is completely shaken, sick with emotion,
unable to bear the hideousness and brutality
of the murder. Awash with revulsion, he
suddenly lurches over the side of the bed
and VOMITS.

INT. JAMIE'S BEDROOM - NIGHT - LATE

He lies in his bed, arms crossed over his
face, his bed starting to slowly REVOLVE in
the center of the room.

EXT. ALLEY BEHIND BUILDING - NIGHT - P.O.V.
SHOT

We COME OUT of a STAIRWELL into a rather
grimy ALLEYWAY, lugging something behind:
something heavy, in a GUNNYSACK. It could
only be the BODY.

We approach the Woman's VAN; she OPENS the
rear GATE, and with great difficulty, hefts
the bag into the back. Part of it (a limb)
is sticking out, keeping the door from
closing, and when she shoves on it, it makes
a sickening CRACK.

She slams the door, and the SCREEN FLASHES
WHITE.

                        FADE IN FROM WHITE

INT. INTERROGATION ROOM

Jamie looks up into the camera, on the edge
of madness, hysteria.

                    JAMIE
          The woman I knew could never
          have... done that. She taught
          me how to feel, and then—I
          don't know...
                    (beat)
          I can't tell you how... dirty
          it made me feel. I could feel
          his blood running down my
          arms, all hot and thick and
          sticky. Nothing I can say can
          make you understand how...
          sick, so filthy and... I
          don't know—depraved. Like a
          murderer. I just felt so
          empty, and cheated, and
          scared. I just didn't know
          how to feel anymore.

                    DETECTIVE
          About her?

                    JAMIE
          About anything. All the
          visions—everything—just
          stopped dead.
     (he reacts to his ironic choice of words)
          I was on my own, now, and I
          didn't know how to handle it.
                    (beat; cont'd)
          I couldn't eat, I couldn't
          sleep... I couldn't even
          think. I just kind of went
          dead inside. I was in love
          with her... but this had me
          all fucked up.

EXT. CITY STREET - DAY

Jamie WALKS through the anonymous masses,
alone, his mind far away. He stops for the
RED LIGHT as a BUS moves through the crowded
intersection. There is a SNARL of TRAFFIC...
and in the opposite lane is a red SPORTS
CONVERTIBLE... with Vanessa   and   Booth

inside!

Jamie is shaken from his reverie, and it
takes a second for it to register. Then:

                    JAMIE
          Booth! Booth, son, over here!

ANGLE - VANESSA'S CAR

Vanessa looks up. Booth sees his daddy, and
unfastens his SEAT BELT, standing up on the
seat.

                    BOOTH
          Daddy! Daddy!!!

Vanessa shoves him back down in his seat.

                    VANESSA
          Keep that seat belt fastened,
          young man!

Jamie runs out into the street, and the light
changes. Vanessa puts pedal to metal, and
Jamie is suddenly stranded in honking
traffic.

                    JAMIE
              (calling out)
          Daddy loves you, Booth!

But the car is already out of sight.

INT. COFFEE BAR - NIGHT

Jamie ENTERS, sits in a CORNER at the
uncrowded coffee house. Very alone. The TV
above is blasting a ball game, and Jamie
couldn't be less interested. The WAITER
approaches.

                    JAMIE
          Black coffee...

Though the TV is on, he's not really watching; his deadened eyes just settle on the bright screen in the dark room... for escape.

There is a commercial break: just another CAR COMMERCIAL... for a DODGE VAN. He doesn't know why he is subtly hypnotized by the spot, but he can't look away from it.

TV SCREEN

The VAN drives up, the GRILL and DODGE LICENSE PLATE filling the frame dramatically, with a swell of MUSIC.

INCLUDE JAMIE

It hits him like a ton of bricks. It is the same kind of VAN the Woman drives!!!

FLASHBACK - THE VAN IN THE PARK

The Woman is climbing into her van, checking her hair in the rearview mirror.

RESUME JAMIE

The "DODGE" PLATE fills the TV screen, and Jamie is mesmerized.

RESUME FLASHBACK - THE VAN

We go back seconds EARLIER, past the van, seeing just the corner of the LICENSE PLATE.

RESUME JAMIE

The commercial ENDS and Jamie is still staring at the TV, not seeing it.

RESUME FLASHBACK

We OPTICALLY BLOW UP the CORNER of the LICENSE PLATE until it fills the FRAME. We

can't see enough of it to get the number, or
even the state... but we do see its color:
GREEN LETTERING on a WHITE BACKGROUND.

RESUME JAMIE

He sits up, his eyes brightening, getting
excited... on the verge of developing a PLAN!
Then, as the Waiter brings his coffee:

                    JAMIE
          I'm going to find you!

And he's out. The Waiter sips the coffee.

INT. JAMIE'S KITCHEN - NIGHT

ENCYCLOPEDIAS, MAPS, and AUTO CLUB LEAFLETS
litter the tabletop. A big, rumpled MAP of
the U.S. pinned to the wall.

Deep in excited concentration, Jamie pores
over color pages of U.S. LICENSE PLATES,
trying to match up the COLOR PATTERNS.
Florida, Idaho, Washington, and others have
white plates with green lettering.

FLASHBACK - THE WOMAN'S CITY'S SKYLINE

The sight as she left the zoo, the mountains
and bay in b.g.

RESUME JAMIE

He is checking the license plates against
the map.

                    JAMIE
          The coast. It's along the
          coast.

He starts to cross off the unlikely
candidates with a fat FELT MARKER. Not Idaho.
Maine? Florida? He crosses Florida off, too.

                    JAMIE
          No mountains like that in
          Florida.

FLASHBACK - JAMIE'S BEDROOM

We OPTICALLY BLOW UP the CLOCK RADIO: 9:15
a.m.

FLASHBACK - THE WOMAN'S BEDROOM as she is
about to be made love to. OPTICALLY ENLARGE
on the alarm clock: 7:15 a.m.

FLASHBACK - THE ROCK CLUB

The Club Manager points to his WATCH, calls
out "10:00 o'clock!"

Jamie is transposing at the table, and we
COUNT the EIGHT CHIMES he's receiving from
Jacqueline.

RESUME JAMIE

                    JAMIE
          The west coast!

He crosses Maine off the chart. He goes down
the list of states and plates. California is
close, but no cookie. Oregon is out: blue on
orange.

WASHINGTON! Bingo!

He gets excited; it is his first sign of hope
in a hopeless romance. He CIRCLES the picture
of the Washington PLATE in the BOOK, and
throws a TABLE KNIFE at the map on the wall.

INSERT - WALL MAP

It HITS, sticking right in the middle of
Seattle.

INT. AIRLINER - DAY

Jamie, clean-cut and well-dressed, is poring
over his notes, taking an occasional nervous
look out the window, noting for the first
time his fear of flying.

INSERT - WHAT HE IS STUDYING

An Auto Club TOUR BOOK OF WASHINGTON is open
on top of a pile of maps, and the tiger-
scored tablecloth. Jamie is leafing through
the book, searching for a list of ZOOS...

EXT. SKY - DAY

The JET roars across the SKY.

INTERROGATION ROOM - JAMIE

He is far away, remembering things that are
painful to think about. We let him think for
a moment, then:

                    DETECTIVE
          Come on. It's just too easy.
          You set out to Washington
          because of a piece of a
          license plate? Give me a
          break.

                    JAMIE
               (looking up)
          I'm not asking you to believe
          me; I don't really give a
          shit.

                    DETECTIVE
          But why Washington?

                    JAMIE
              (it's so obvious)
          It was the west coast, there
          was a zoo there, and the
          colors on the license plate
          matched.

                    DETECTIVE
          I don't understand what you
          were going to do. Turn her
          in? Play knight in shining
          armor, what?

                    JAMIE
          I don't know. I just knew
          that I had to find her.

                    DETECTIVE
          Well, what did you expect to
          do once you found her?
              (no reaction)
          Were you in love with her?

Jamie looks up into the camera, and—almost
defiantly—nods.

                    JAMIE
          Yeah. I loved her.

                    DETECTIVE
              (skeptical)
          A murderer.

                    JAMIE
          I didn't know—maybe it was
          just a dream we shared. Maybe
          it was self-defense. I didn't
          know. I hoped so.

It's eating him up.

EXT. SPACE NEEDLE - DAY

It looms large in b.g. as Jamie steps into
CU.

                    JAMIE
                 (whispering)
            I'm coming

EXT. SPACE NEEDLE OBSERVATION DECK - DAY

He stands at the edge of the deck, fighting
acrophobia, the WIND blowing him as he walks
around the full circle. He stops, gripping
the rail, and looks out over the vast,
unfamiliar city spread out before him. Then,
a CRASH of DARK REALIZATION...

                    JAMIE
                  (hushed)
            It's the wrong city...

INT. JAMIE'S HOTEL ROOM - LATE DAY

Quiet and lonely. Jamie is SITTING on the
BED in the tawdry little room, SURROUNDED by
his PACKED BELONGINGS. He has the PHONE in
hand, and DIALS a NUMBER. It is picked up,
and we hear his son BOOTH'S delighted,
confident, adorable voice on the other end.

                 BOOTH'S VOICE
                (OVER PHONE)
            You have reached the
            Caldwell-Evans residence.
            Please leave a message for my
            mommy Vanessa or Booth Taylor
            Evans at the beepy noise...

It breaks Jamie's heart.

                    JAMIE
            Hi baby boy. I just wanted to
            call you from out of town and
            tell you how much I love you.
            I can't wait to see you,
                  (cont'd)

                    JAMIE
                  (cont'd)
          Skeezix, and pull a silver
          dollar out of your nose. See
          you when I get back, okay?
          And we'll go out to a movie
          or something, how's that? I
          love you, honey. And say hi
          to Mommy for me. Bye bye...

INT. VANESSA'S APARTMENT - EVENING

The room is lit by TV light. The sound is
down, and Vanessa is sitting on the couch,
the HEAD of her SLEEPING young SON in her
LAP. Listens to the end of Jamie's message
over the ANSWERING MACHINE, just letting it
PLAY, Booth snoring in light oblivion. And
then, CLICK.

EXT. STREET IN FRONT OF HOTEL - PIONEER
SQUARE - NIGHT

Cheap but tidy, the place is 30 years old,
but with most of the neon still intact.
There is heavy TRAFFIC on this main drag.
Jamie comes out onto the street, bag in hand,
not really caring where he's going. He sets
blindly out across the street, his mind
racing.

Jamie crosses the street, and there is a
terrible SCREECH of TIRES. A PICK-UP TRUCK
SKIDS sideways, trying in vain to avoid
Jamie... but it is too late. He is KNOCKED
to the ASPHALT.

The DRIVER rushes out of the car to Jamie,
who is dazed and SCRAPED, but not badly hurt.
But his anger has boiled over.

                    JAMIE
          Fuck!

                    DRIVER
              (scared and defensive)
          Are you okay?

Jamie is too pissed at himself and everything
going on to notice the driver.

                    DRIVER
          You just stepped right out
          between those cars. I guess
          you didn't see me, huh? Hop
          in, let me take you to a
          doctor...

Jamie gets to his hands and knees, angrily
kicking his battered suitcase to the
sidewalk. We TRACK AROUND HIM as he LOOKS
UP, and

SEE WITH HIM the LICENSE PLATE on the PICK-
UP. He FREEZES when he sees it.

                    DRIVER
              (reacting)
          What?

It is a British Columbia commercial PLATE...
GREEN LETTERS on a WHITE BACKGROUND!

The Driver bends down to give Jamie a hand,
but he STANDS, waving away the help.

                    JAMIE
          I'm okay.

                    DRIVER
          You sure? You look a little
          banged up there.

                    JAMIE
          I'm all right!

                    DRIVER
          Okay with me, pal.

Jamie REELS a bit, but smiles, suddenly
figuring it out.

                    JAMIE
                 (to himself)
          Canada!
                 (to Driver)
          That's why it wasn't on the
          chart!

                    DRIVER
                 (humoring him)
          Sure. Anybody knows that.
          Canada's right off the chart.

A bit shaken, the Driver is eager to take
his leave, and does so, driving off through
the gathering CROWD.

Jamie WATCHES, unable to take his eyes off
the diminishing LICENSE PLATE.

EXT. VANCOUVER - DAY - TRAIN DEPOT

A high, spectacular VIEW of the CITY. The
sky is crisp and ice blue, and the beautiful
city SPARKLES. There are snow-capped
MOUNTAINS in b.g., and the SKYLINE is at once
familiar to us.

We CRANE DOWN across the DEPOT as the TRAIN
PULLS IN, filling the FRAME. The CROWD
DISEMBARKS, Jamie among them. Almost afraid
to check out the skyline, he hesitantly looks
up and takes it in, his hopes rising. And
with good reason...

INT. TRAIN STATION - SNACK BAR - DAY

He joins the MELTING POT of WHITES,
ORIENTALS, CANADIAN INDIANS, etc., sipping
COFFEE at the crowded COUNTER and poring over
a STACK of TOURIST PAMPHLETS. An INDIAN in a
Pendleton is next to him, looking at his copy

of Thelma Moss's *Probability of the Impossible* through rheumy, bloodshot EYES, a CUP of CLOUDY COFFEE perched precariously in less-than-steady hands. Rough night.

Inevitably, the Indian SPILLS HIS COFFEE, and watches it dribble to the floor through smashed, red-rimmed eyes. Jamie gingerly moves away one seat.

After a couple woozy beats, the Indian grabs a section of NEWSPAPER from the floor, and starts to mop up the coffee with it. Jamie tries not to watch.

ANGLE - NEWSPAPER ON COUNTER

It swishes the coffee around more than soaking it up. But...

JAMIE sees something that snaps him to attention.

JAMIE'S P.O.V. - THE COUNTER

We SEE the coffee-soaked front page of the newspaper: a PHOTO and HEADLINE that jolts our attention. We recognize the MAN in the PHOTO as the MAN in the VISIONS! COFFEE is seeping into the picture... like blood.

INCLUDE JAMIE

He grabs the paper as the Waitress mops up the mess with a towel.

                    WAITRESS
          I'll get that...

                    JAMIE
          Wait a minute.

He keeps hold of the PAPER and tries to read the messy article.

ANGLE - NEWSPAPER HEADLINE

"Artist's Mutilated Corpse Found in Own Loft". It identifies the Man as DENNISON HOOPER.

RESUME COUNTER

                    JAMIE
          Holy shit...

Jamie is galvanized; the Indian nodding off at the counter. He pores over the story, stares at the portrait of the Man, the picture of his loft, the details of the commemorative gallery showing of his work.

EXT. STANLEY PARK - DAY

Jamie is wandering aimlessly, absorbed in a handful of newspaper accounts of the murder. He is at the edge of the park, oblivious to the SNOW-CAPPED MOUNTAINS in the b.g. But we recognize them immediately.

We TRACK WITH HIM around the CORNER, and he looks up, startled to find himself suddenly in the STANLEY PARK ZOO! He sees he is where his first VISION took place!

                    JAMIE
          Oh, God...
            (a beat, then whispering)
          Honey, I'm home...

There is a roar (O.S.), and Jamie spins around, running along the path. We track with him as he rushes to become suddenly face-to-face with the tiger that the woman painted in the vision!

An art class is gathered, painting the sleeping tiger. He is unbearably close now.

EXT. CITY STREET - GASTOWN - EVENING

It used to be the wrong side of the tracks,
but gentrification has led to a string of
successful cafes, galleries, and expensive
shops.

Jamie approaches a particular GALLERY, with
a huge PHOTO of Dennison Hooper, Artiste, in
the window.

INT. KROSTIC GALLERY - EVENING

The room is filled with unusual ART, and
bustling with PATRONS. News of the murder
has brought out the flies, there to buzz
about Hooper's strange, sexually obsessive
works caught between the cracks of photo-
realism and drug-like surrealism.

Most of the gallery is filled with Hooper's
works, with the less fortunate, still-living
artists hastily shunted aside.

Jamie ENTERS, very much out of his element,
excited, nervous.

He surveys Hooper's paintings; their sexual
nature has more meaning to him than to the
others. He is pale, queasy as he sees a
stylized PORTRAIT of a man and woman making
love in a pool of their own BLOOD.
"Menstruation" is typed simply on the little
title card.

A PATRON jammed in with the crowd around him
begins to speak to him.

                    PATRON
          He certainly has come into
          prominence.

Jamie just nods.

                    PATRON
          A week ago, he'd have painted
          your bathroom wall for a
          couple hundred dollars, and
          now they're asking eighteen
          thousand for this. He's
          lucky. Getting killed was the
          best thing that ever happened
          to him.

The painting and the conversation are making
Jamie queasy.

                    JAMIE
          Please, where's the rest room?

                    PATRON
          There's one in back, but they
          won't let the hoi polloi use
          it.

Jamie couldn't care less. He rushes through
the crowd, holding his mouth shut, and ducks
behind the door, slamming it in his wake. We
HEAR him VOMIT (O.S.), and so do a couple of
others, who try to pretend they don't.

He comes out PALE and SWEATING, his back to
the paintings on the wall.

JAMIE'S P.O.V.

Moving in slow motion, the CROWD becomes
VULTURES and PREDATORY CATS checking one
another out. Then, they become just another
gathering of pompous, foolish humans.

INCLUDE JAMIE

He backs away from them, leaning his back
against a painting we haven't seen here...
it is a huge 5'X5' version of the STYLIZED
COUGAR HEAD commissioned for Cougar
Chemical!!!

A DEALER rushes up to him, yelling.

                    DEALER
          You don't lean on art!

STARTLED, HE JUMPS AWAY FROM IT, TURNING TO
LOOK AT WHAT HE WAS LEANING ON, AND IS
SHOCKED TO SEE SOMETHING SO FAMILIAR. HE
KNOWS IMMEDIATELY THAT THIS WAS PAINTED BY
THE WOMAN!

He can barely hold himself up as he looks at
his first tangible link to her. He looks at
the TITLE CARD: "Pussy" by Jacqueline
Dupres.

                    JAMIE
          (to himself, savoring the words)
          Jacqueline... Dupres...

The Dealer looks at Jamie with disdain. This
riffraff does not belong in his gallery.
Jamie can't take his eyes off the painting.
JAMIE I need to find her.

                    DEALER
          I'm sorry, but Mme. Dupres is
          a very important client...
          and we must respect the
          artist's privacy. Are you
          interested in this piece?

                    JAMIE
          Very...

EXT. GASTOWN STREET - NIGHT

He makes his way out of the gallery, and we
move with him down the street to a group of
PHONE BOXES. There is no phone book in the
first booth, so we rush with him to the
second. Better luck.

He opens the PHONE BOOK.

INSERT - PHONE BOOK

His hands flip through the pages, settling on the end of the "D" section. His finger runs down the list nervously: a couple Dupre, DuPrez, but no Jacqueline or J. or any other Dupres.

RESUME JAMIE

He hoped for better, but expected the worst. Gastown is closing down around him; he looks around for some direction. Without him even noticing, a BLACK DODGE VAN zooms past him. We can't see who is driving, only the silhouette of a WOMAN. But Jamie misses it. Then he stops. He SMELLS the air. Is he transposing again?

No SOUND/MUSIC. He TENSES, waiting for his senses to shift into overdrive. He presses his back against the wall and jams his eyes shut. But there is only the smell.

In a moment, he opens his eyes, surprised not to be transposing. But he keeps SMELLING something, sure he's transposing. He looks around, then SEES IT, across the intersection.

In the middle of a block of cutesy tourist shops on the corner is an especially notable one: a GINGERBREAD HOUSE with an old-fashioned SIGN over the door: "THE CHOCOLATE FACTORY"!

He has come full circle, from his first dream of chocolate, to its source in Jacqueline's city. He is drawn irresistibly to the shop.

EXT. CHOCOLATE FACTORY - NIGHT

He comes out of the shop with a fancy, expensive box of CHOCOLATES under his arm.

EXT. CHINATOWN STREET - NIGHT

He makes his way through the energetic all-business early-morning bustle of Chinatown. His senses are heightened; the sights, the smells, the sounds are all exaggerated. Jamie seems clear, directed.

EXT. GASTOWN INDUSTRIAL STREET - NIGHT

It is a row of brown brick warehouses, lofts, import-export houses. Jamie steps out onto the corner, and looks up to SEE the LOFT where the Man—Dennison Hooper—was found dead. We RECOGNIZE it from the newspaper photo.

He tries in vain to peer through the crusty old

windows, and then tries the DOOR. It CREAKS OPEN, and he looks up the crumbling, shadowy STAIRWAY. That was easy...

INT. STAIRWELL LEADING TO LOFT - NIGHT

There is only MOONLIGHT as Jamie makes his way up. He KNOCKS timidly on the heavy DOOR, but there is no sound. It is distressingly QUIET. He looks at the POLICE SEAL across the door.

                    JAMIE
          Hello? Anybody here?

Dead SILENCE.

After a thoughtful beat, Jamie suddenly surprises us by mightily KICKING the DOOR OPEN, leaving the police seal dangling from the splintered JAMB. He stands still, and there is still no sound, except for the

REVERBERATIONS through the large, empty loft beyond.

INT. ARTIST'S LOFT - NIGHT

Jamie ENTERS, taking it all in. It is obvious that the Police have gone over the loft exhaustively. There are TAPE and CHALK MARKINGS all over the room, GLOWING in SHAFTS of BLUE MOONLIGHT.

There are rows of standing EASELS in the decrepit but roomy area, most of them displaying Hooper's PAINTINGS, in various stages of completion. All of them are quite bizarre.

One large PHOTO holds his attention for much too long: a full-color photographic PORTRAIT of Dennison Hooper and Jacqueline Dupres, standing intimately close, naked, like John Lennon and Yoko Ono as the Two Virgins, but sexier. It upsets him.

Jamie wanders through the paintings as if through a graveyard. He SHIVERS at a painting of a man mounting a cat creature. It seems a favorite theme.

He stands for a moment in the center of the room, just taking it all in... feeling the room.

He walks along the row of dirty, crusted, industrial school-style WINDOWS, silhouetted against them.

CLOSER ANGLE

He wipes a circle of dirt away with his hand, looking out at the city.

We MOVE IN with him, looking across to the factory on the other side of the street, then look down to the street below.

The BLACK DODGE VAN is parked there!

A woman looks up from the driver's seat from under her sunglasses... We rush in on her face; it is Jacqueline Dupres!

She SEES Jamie's silhouette, FREEZES for a BEAT, then fires up the ignition and slams into gear, peeling away.

Jamie REACTS.

                    JAMIE
          Don't leave!

He RACES through the loft, knocking easels over in his wake.

EXT. STREET IN FRONT OF LOFT - DAY

She peels around the corner, just as Jamie comes stumbling outside in the bright MOONLIGHT.

But he SEES the LICENSE PLATE!!! He FREEZES, staring at her dust, the LICENSE NUMBER his mantra .

                    JAMIE
                 (repeating)
          BMS 087, BMS 087...

EXT. VANCOUVER DEPARTMENT OF MOTOR VEHICLES
- DAY

Establishing shot.

INT. D.M.V. - DAY

Jamie reaches the WINDOW, carrying a BAG with his BOX of CHOCOLATES. He is IMMACULATELY

GROOMED, looks HEALTHIER, more HANDSOME than we've ever seen him. His quest has made him grow into a romantic, almost heroic figure, and his dauntless masculinity is attractive; he wears it well.

The CLERK is a WOMAN, fiftyish, efficient, and surprisingly friendly.

                    CLERK
          Hi. What can I do for you?

                    JAMIE
          Um... I got hit by a car last
          night, and I got the license
          number. I need to get the
          driver's address—

                    CLERK
          Oh, my! Are you all right?

                    JAMIE
          Oh, yeah, just some
          bruises...

                    CLERK
          Where you can't see them.
          Lucky you.

EXT. D.M.V. - DAY

Long shot. The city is bustling as Jamie bursts jubilantly from the building.

EXT. RESIDENTIAL STREET - DAY

We MOVE WITH JAMIE as he heads down the unfamiliar street, following a MAP as he checks STREET SIGNS. His heart is racing; he's getting closer.

He takes a breath when he hits The Corner and sees the sign:

ANGLE - STREET SIGN

He's found it: "Sea Orbit Lane".

RESUME JAMIE

We SWING AROUND JAMIE to REVEAL the DEAD-END STREET the Woman lives on. It is short, lined with BROWNSTONES, some of them EMPTY, undergoing renovation and gentrification. This is a neighborhood that is returning to the affluence it knew 100 years ago.

He tugs on his jacket and adjusts his tie, and heads up the short street.

He starts out at a strong pace, but slows more and more as he gets closer, his heart visibly pounding. And then, he's reached it. He looks up at the nicest home on an expensive street, covered with vines, beckoning yet mysterious.

Her house...

ANGLE ON JAMIE

Now what? His mouth is dry, his forehead sprinkled with perspiration, his face pale. HE STANDS THERE FOR A LONG TIME, NOT SURE HE IS ABLE TO GO THROUGH WITH THIS, NOW THAT HE IS AT LAST HERE…

But unable not to go through with it.

He goes to the door, and makes himself ring the bell. We hear the soft chimes (O.S.).

No one answers. He forces himself to ring again, then knocks.

Nobody's home. At first he's relieved, but the relief soon gives way to crushing disappointment.

EXT. STREET IN FRONT OF BROWNSTONE - NIGHT

Later that night. Jamie is reading about Hooper's murder in the paper, munching on a carrot, sipping a Diet Coke, WATCHING Her House from the STEPS of the empty, torn-apart HOME on the other side of the street.

Occasionally a CAR sweeps him with its HEADLIGHTS, and his blood rushes, but it is invariably a FALSE ALARM.

It's getting COLDER, and he pulls his JACKET tighter around him.

                    TIME-LAPSE DISSOLVE TO:

EXT. SAME SHOT - DAWN

The next morning. Jamie is asleep on the stoop in BRIGHT SUNLIGHT, the empty Coke can crushed next to him. We HEAR a LOUD GRINDING NOISE (o.s.) as a huge dinosaur-like SHADOW falls across Jamie.

REVERSE ANGLE

MEN are noisily dumping trash into what turns out to be a GARBAGE TRUCK, waking Jamie. It takes a moment to wipe away the webs and remember where he is; then JOLTS into consciousness, upset to find that he fell asleep.

The TRASH MAN gives Jamie a live-and-let-live look, grunts, and pulls the truck away. Jamie watches as the TRUCK pulls out of the frame to REVEAL Jacqueline's DODGE VAN sitting in front of her brownstone!!!

He tries to gather his thoughts, but before he can even think clearly, Jacqueline's DOOR

OPENS, and she APPEARS! It is all too fast and too suddenly REAL for him to handle it. She is dressed all in WHITE, striding into her car, pausing for a moment for a disinterested GLANCE his way. And for the briefest of moments, their EYES CONNECT.

Was that a look of recognition?

And she is GONE.

We MOVE IN ON JAMIE. The ache of excitement and pain is all over his face, the seeming sudden hopelessness, the obvious division between them, the two sides of the tracks. Her casual dismissal of him hurts a lot.

INT. EMPTY HALF-RENOVATED BROWNSTONE ACROSS THE STREET - NIGHT

It's the TOP FLOOR of the three-story, walls-down, wide-open BROWNSTONE across from hers. Jamie's SUITCASE is open on the floor, and his belongings are all over the room, which looks like a bombed-out ruin.
Jamie the squatter is sitting on the window sill, watching and waiting. We look over his shoulder to see the BLACK VAN pull up across the street.

EXT. STREET IN FRONT OF WOMAN'S BROWNSTONE - NIGHT

She gets out of the van and enters the house. We pan up to follow her path, and get to the second floor just as a light comes on upstairs.

RESUME JAMIE IN WRECKED BROWNSTONE

Scared and excited, he is smoothing into the nicest clothes he has with him.

EXT. WOMAN'S BROWNSTONE - FRONT DOOR - NIGHT

Jamie crosses the street, the box of candy under his arm. He flushes with first-date excitement as he boldly RINGS the BELL.

                    JACQUELINE (O.S.)
                      (distant)
          Just a minute!

The sound of her VOICE galvanizes him; it is sweet, musical, French-accented.

We HEAR BARE FEET padding down carpeted stairs (o.s.), and the DOOR OPENS.

She is suddenly face-to-face with us, in a terrycloth robe, without make-up, wrapping a towel around her hair, a disarming SMILE on her face. She is achingly beautiful.

                    JACQUELINE
          Sorry, I was in the shower.

INCLUDE JAMIE

He can't speak. It is too much to have her suddenly standing in front of him after all he's gone through, to confront the woman he loves... the murderess...

                    JACQUELINE
          Yes?

He looks at her. He has seen, felt what is under that robe. He can barely deal with the nearness of her.

                    JAMIE
          Jacqueline Dupres?

She NODS, without a trace of recognition.

                    JAMIE
          Do you know me?

                    JACQUELINE
                   (confused)
          Have we met?

                      JAMIE
          (embarrassed; shaking his head)
          Sorry. I guess not. Delivery
          for you...

                    JACQUELINE
               (smiling, delighted)
          Really? What is it?

He SMILES, and holds up the BOX for her.

                    JACQUELINE
          I can't imagine...

She takes the package, and a startled, ICY
CLOUD crosses her face as she sees the
"CHOCOLATE FACTORY" logo. She LOOKS UP at
him, icicles shooting from her eyes. He knows
at once he has made a mistake.

The DOOR SLAMS in his face.

INT. WRECKED BROWNSTONE - NIGHT

Jamie ENTERS, furious with himself for being
so stupid.

                      JAMIE
          You dumb shit! It reminds her
          of him!

Frustrated, he slams his FIST against the
WALL, hoping it will hurt. It does.

He walks over to the window facing her house,
keeping well out of view.

Her SILHOUETTE comes into view against the
second-story bedroom curtain, running a comb

through her wet hair. And then, the LIGHT
goes OFF.

EXT. CAPILANO SUSPENSION BRIDGE - TWILIGHT -
DREAM SEQUENCE - STEADICAM P.O.V.

We are STANDING at the edge of a long, WOOD-
AND-ROPE SUSPENSION BRIDGE over a
frighteningly high WOODED GORGE with a
trickling STREAM below.

Lush, beautiful woods surround us, with
breathtaking vistas of snow-peaked MOUNTAINS
lit by the setting sun.

It is obviously a DREAM.

We look out onto the bridge. A MAN stands
halfway out, looking down into the valley
below. We can't see who he is, only that he
is shirtless.

We MOVE TOWARD HIM, and the BRIDGE begins to
SWAY. The Man is oblivious to us, and it is
a frightening, vertiginous view.

As we approach him, he TURNS TO FACE US; it
is Dennison Hooper.

He LOOKS RIGHT AT US, surprised, and a PAIR
of HANDS brings up a LONG KNIFE in both
FISTS, PLUNGING it into his chest, leaving
its hilt sticking out!

But the Man is unfazed! He PULLS IT OUT, and
LUNGES at us, furious! He REACHES OUT and
GRABS US with powerful arms, and throws us
off the bridge!

The P.O.V. shot CONTINUES as we FALL, and
FALL, and FALL toward the WATER below!

We can SEE our REFLECTION as we come crashing
toward the stream; it is Jacqueline Dupres'
face reflected in the water, eyes filled with

TERROR! Just as we are about to HIT, we:

SMASH CUT TO:

INT. WRECKED BROWNSTONE - DAY

Jamie bolts awake. We MOVE IN ON HIM. The
sun is up outside the window behind him.

EXT. STANLEY PARK ZOO - DAY

A beautiful, cold, crisp morning. A HANDFUL
of JOGGERS are going through their paces
around the park.

ANGLE - JACQUELINE DUPRES - TRACKING

She runs alone, drenched in perspiration.
She looks great wet.

ANGLE - JAMIE - FOLLOWING

He is jogging way behind her, keeping his
distance.

Up ahead, we SEE the Woman disappear into
the greenery.

Jamie is nervous, having lost sight of her.
Keeping safely behind, he doesn't know which
way she has gone, and slows to a labored
walk, his clothes drenched in sweat.

He stops where the paths cross, and looks
around at the water fountain. She is nowhere
to be seen, and he bends to DRINK long
draughts of water between racking breaths.

He STANDS.

ANGLE - JAMIE'S P.O.V.

XCU of Jacqueline's angry face!

                    JACQUELINE
          Why are you following me?

INCLUDE JAMIE

He CHOKES on the water. He can't speak,
choking and out of breath; she sternly awaits
his answer.

                    JACQUELINE
          I want to know why you've
          been spying on me!

                    JAMIE
               (labored)
          I'm... not... following...
          you.

                    JACQUELINE
          Do you think I'm an imbecile?

He just shakes his head, rather than try to
answer her.

                    JACQUELINE
          What do you want?

She glares unflinching into his eyes, but he
cannot hold the gaze, and looks at his feet,
trying to think of what to say, to take
advantage of his crumbling opportunity.
He can't control what comes out of his mouth
next.

                    JAMIE
          I think you're the most
          beautiful woman I've ever
          seen.

That throws her off-balance for a moment,
though she doesn't believe him. He must be a
COP or a BLACKMAILER.

                    JACQUELINE
          Nice try.

                    JAMIE
          It's true.

                    JACQUELINE
          I want an answer.

                    JAMIE
          I told you...

                    JACQUELINE
          Tell me why you brought me
          those chocolates.

He doesn't know what to say.

                    JAMIE
          I thought you'd like them...
               (knowing she needs a better answer)
          I... needed to meet you.

                    JACQUELINE
          How do you know me?

                    JAMIE
          I've... seen you around.

                    JACQUELINE
          Where?

                    JAMIE
          The gallery. Here. I saw you
          sketching at the zoo. A
          tiger. I... I'm an admirer...
          of your work. You did the
          logo for Cougar Chemical...

She looks at him, thinking, trying to figure
him out. He's talking about things before
the murder. She is cagey, suspicious; maybe
he's just a fan.

                    JACQUELINE
          Why didn't you just come up
          and say hello? Why are you

                    following me? I could call a
                    policeman and have you thrown
                    in jail!

                              JAMIE
                    I don't know... look, I'm
                    really sorry. I was stupid...
                    but I just had to meet you.

                              JACQUELINE
                    Well... we've met.

And as far as she is concerned, that is that.

                              JAMIE
                    Yes.

He musters an I-blew-it smile. She calms a
little.

                              JAMIE
                    I like your painting very
                    much. You're very talented.

                              JACQUELINE
                    Merci.

She starts to leave, and Jamie can't bear
that it all might end here at the Stanley
Park water fountain.

                              JAMIE
                    I'm not one of those creeps
                    who follows beautiful women
                    around and drives them crazy.
                    I'm not a stalker.

She tries to figure him out. We can't read
her mind, and he just can't let go.

                              JAMIE
                         (gently, persuasively)
                    Look, I know I made a
                    mistake, and I'm really,
                    really sorry. I realize I
                    make a lousy first

                    impression... but... could
                    you just give me a chance?
                    Could we pretend that your
                    best friend introduced us at
                    a party? Can I just talk with
                    you, see you once?

When she doesn't say anything immediately,
he takes it as desperate encouragement, and
continues before she can decline.

                         JAMIE
                    Lunch, someplace nice, your
                    choice.

                         JACQUELINE
                    (almost laughing with the
                       audaciousness of it)
                    No! I am glad you like my
                    work, but I don't think that
                    would be a good idea.

                         JAMIE
                    Just talk, I promise. We need
                    to talk.

                         JACQUELINE
                    You need to talk. I don't.

                         JAMIE
                    Look, I know you just want me
                    to leave you alone, but I
                    just can't let you go like
                    this. I've come a long way to
                    find you...
                         (she REACTS)
                    Please. Just lunch. In a
                    public place.

                         JACQUELINE
                    My life is complicated enough
                    right now.

                         JAMIE
                    I know.

                    JACQUELINE
                 (suddenly on guard)
          What do you know?

                      JAMIE
          I mean, everybody's life is
          complicated these days. Mine,
          too.

                    JACQUELINE
                   (considering)
          Why me? Why don't you go
          stalk some movie star
          somewhere?

                      JAMIE
          I know how special you are.

                    JACQUELINE
          You don't know anything about
          me.

                      JAMIE
          I do.
                    (covering)
          I know you wish I'd leave you
          alone.

She NODS, and almost smiles.

                      JAMIE
          I swear, I know how you feel,
          and I don't blame you. But
          honestly, I promise I'll
          leave you alone. I'll never
          bother you again, if that's
          what you want. I'll even
          leave Vancouver and never
          come back... ever. Just let
          me take you to lunch first.

                    JACQUELINE
                  (thinks a beat)
          You're right about one thing.
                  (he brightens)

You make a terrible first
impression.

EXT. HARBOUR CENTRE - DAY

The huge complex stretches high into the
Vancouver sky.

INT. HARBOUR HOUSE RESTAURANT - DAY

Jamie and Jacqueline are at a window table
in the slowly-revolving restaurant at the
top of the building.

It is awkward, somewhat formal between them,
and he can't help but watch her while she
eats, making her uncomfortable when she
looks up over a forkful of salad.

                    JACQUELINE
          Your spinach is wilting.

                    JAMIE
          I just can't believe I'm here
          with you.

                    JACQUELINE
          I don't know if I can take
          much more adoration...

                    JAMIE
          I'm sorry... I must seem like
          such a geek to you...

She doesn't answer that, and he keeps staring
at her. Who can blame him?

                    JACQUELINE
          Are you just going to keep
          staring at me? Is that why
          you've been following me
          around?

Suspicious, she is wary, eager to finish the
lunch she is sorry she accepted in the first
place.

                    JAMIE
          (trying to work into the inevitable)
               I've never known anybody like
               you.

                    JACQUELINE
               Everybody I know has...

He shakes his head, getting very serious,
his hands nervously fiddling with a couple
COINS, even unconsciously the magician. Is
it time? Will it ever be? He sees her
watching his hands, and looks down to see
what he's doing.

He puts the change on the table, and looks
up at her. This is it.

                    JAMIE
               Listen... I've got to talk to
               you about something.

ANGLE - JACQUELINE'S HANDS

They grip her fork and knife so tightly her
knuckles go white.

RESUME JAMIE AND JACQUELINE

She FREEZES, steeling herself.

                    JACQUELINE
               I've been waiting for this...

Her heart is pounding, and she looks trapped,
a little frightened at the moment of truth.

                    JAMIE
          (with difficulty)
               I... have to tell you why I
               love you...

She CHOKES, coughing into her napkin.

                    JACQUELINE
          What?

                     JAMIE
             (unable to look at her)
          I can't say it again.

                    JACQUELINE
          Please don't.

She looks out into the city spread out below
them, her mind racing, confused, many
emotions welling up within her. It's time
for Jamie to spill the beans, but it isn't
what she's expecting.

                     JAMIE
          I know you better than you
          think.

                    JACQUELINE
          How long have you been spying
          on me?

Heads turn, and PEOPLE are watching. Jamie
SHRIVELS.

                     JAMIE
          It's not what you think.
          Don't be afraid of me...
               (looking around)
          Can we go somewhere a little
          more... private?

                    JACQUELINE
          I'm not afraid of you...

EXT. VANCOUVER STREET - DAY

They walk in silence through the city hustle
and bustle. Finally, when they reach a more
private spot, Jamie stops her, his hand on

her arm, not knowing quite how to start.

                    JAMIE
          Sometimes... sometimes I'm...
          well... inside you.

She SLAPS him, and he grabs her hand. He is
committed to taking control, stronger,
knowing this is the last chance.

                    JAMIE
               (sternly)
          Listen to me. I'm not crazy,
          and I'm not a pervert. I
          swear to you, I'm on your
          side.

His sudden strength frightens her, and Jamie
sees himself moving into a position of
control. If it doesn't come out now, he will
surely never get another chance.

                    JAMIE
          Sometimes I can feel the
          things you feel, smell the
          things you smell... sometimes
          I even see the things you
          see. I don't have any control
          over it... it just...
          happens.

She looks at him like he's crazy, but he
won't let go of her.

                    JAMIE
          I know I sound like a
          lunatic, but it's true! It
          started when I tasted your
          chocolate...
               (she REACTS)
          I thought it was just a
          dream, but the zoo... your
          paintings... your dreams...

He relaxes his grip on her, feeling guilty
as her fear grows. She is silent, wondering

what all of this means. She doesn't run away,
maybe because she senses it would be useless.
Or... that it's true.

Jamie doesn't know how much to tell her, but
isn't foolish enough to let her know that he
knows about the murder. But she's smart
enough to figure that out for herself.

                    JACQUELINE
          What dreams?

                    JAMIE
          Always being chased. In
          corridors, on some kind of
          suspension bridge... and the
          cats...

That horrifies her, and she steps back,
knowing now that he must know...

                    JAMIE
               (covering)
          Mostly they don't make sense
          to me... but I got to know
          you better than anybody knows
          you. For some reason, we're
          psychically linked. And
          that's why I love you.
               (beat)
          And I... was hoping you could
          feel... me...

They look at one another for a long beat,
both minds racing, not sure how to handle
one another. Then:

                    JACQUELINE
          I'd like to go home now. I
          need to be by myself...
          please.

                    JAMIE
          I'll walk you...

She is already walking, not even
acknowledging him.

EXT. RESIDENTIAL STREET - EVENING

It is getting dark, as they walk in awkward
silence, near the corner of her street. Then
she looks up at him.

                    JACQUELINE
          I'd really rather be alone
          right now...

Jamie looks heartbroken.

                    JAMIE
          Just let me walk you to your
          door.

They STOP, right at the corner of her street.

                    JACQUELINE
          Please, just leave me alone!

He backs way off; all he can do is go along
with it. It's over. They look at each other,
a long silent beat, then Jamie just gives
up.

                    JAMIE
          Okay. I'm sorry...
          Jacqueline. I understand.

And he turns to leave her to her street.

But he suddenly TURNS BACK to face her, and
roughly SHOVES HER against the wall!

                    JACQUELINE
Don't touch me!

But it's for her own good. He's SEEN
something in front of her house.

                    JAMIE
                 (frantic)
        Sssshhh!

Now she knows he's crazy—maybe dangerous—as
he holds her against the brick wall. She
struggles, and he holds his hand over her
mouth. She BITES his hand, but he won't let
go.

                    JAMIE
                 (getting pissed)
          Quiet! Look!

He PEERS AROUND the corner of the building,
and so does she.

ANGLE - STREET IN FRONT OF HER BROWNSTONE -
NIGHT

There is an unmarked POLICE CAR in front of
her house, parked across from her VAN. TWO
DETECTIVES sit in the car, waiting.

RESUME JAMIE AND JACQUELINE

It is all driven home now. Her eyes are wide
with fear and distrust.

                    JAMIE
          Those are cops. You can't go
          home now.

                    JACQUELINE
                 (nervously)
          Why should I be afraid of the
          police?

He just looks at her; they don't have time
for these games.

                    JAMIE
          I keep telling you, I'm on
          your side. You've got to
          trust me.

                    JACQUELINE
              What do you know about me?

                      JAMIE
   (as much to convince himself as to convince
                       her)
              I know that you had to do
              it...

Now what? It would be a foolish waste of time
to doubt his story now, though she still
finds it incredible.

                      JAMIE
              Let me help you.

She has no choice. Suddenly, the unmarked
car's HEADLIGHTS come ON, and the ENGINE
FIRES UP!

Jamie GRABS her arm and RUNS, dragging her
briskly into the night. Terrified, they are
running, as the CAR SQUEALS around the corner
in their wake!

ANGLE - ALLEY

They duck into an ALLEY, running full tilt,
and as they reach the END, and duck around
the corner, the CAR comes screeching behind
them.

VARIOUS STREETS AND ALLEYS

AS THE FRANTIC CHASE ENSUES. FINALLY, AT THE
END OF ANOTHER ALLEY, THEY LEAP INTO A
DUMPSTER, AND SCRAMBLE INTO THE GARBAGE.

The COP CAR PULLS UP, and the DETECTIVES JUMP
OUT and look around.

ANGLE - IN DUMPSTER

They are in the midst of the most repulsive
garbage, holding down their gorge in

tension.

RESUME COPS

There is the long SHADOW of another
PEDESTRIAN at the other end of the street,
and they leap into the car and TAKE CHASE,
allowing Jamie and Jacqueline to rise and
peer out of the dumpster, eating their dust.
They look at one another. Who do you trust?

                    DETECTIVE'S VOICE
          Yeah, but why you?

INT. INTERROGATION ROOM - NIGHT

Jamie LOOKS UP at the detective, snatched
from his painful reverie.

                    DETECTIVE
          I mean, you never even met
          her before, right? This just
          doesn't make sense. Why you?
          Out of millions of people,
          why you?

                    JAMIE
          You think I don't wonder? You
          think I don't spend every
          minute thinking about that?
          At first, I thought it was
          the chemicals at work—some
          kind of somatic reaction,
          some kind of sensory opening-
          up or something. Or maybe her
          art brought us together.
          Psychometry.

                    DETECTIVE
          Psychometry. Sixty-four
          dollar word.

                    JAMIE
          It means the ability to read
          about an object's owner by
          holding or touching the
          object. You know, that
          nightclub magician kind of
          thing. But it's real. By now
          I'm an expert in this stuff.
          Maybe her art was my window
          to her.
               (just really getting it)
          You know, it all started when
          General Cougar unveiled the
          painting she did.

He just shakes his head. The Detective waits
for him to go on. Not giving him input.

                    JAMIE
          Or maybe it's simpler than
          that. Maybe it's just because
          she was so full, and I was so
          empty. Maybe.

EXT. HOTEL VANCOUVER - DAY

Establishing.   Jamie   and   Jacqueline
cautiously ENTER.

INT. HOTEL ROOM - NIGHT

They ENTER and LOOK AROUND. Jacqueline keeps
a skittish distance from him, and watches
nervously as he DOUBLE LOCKS the door.

There is only one queen-sized BED in the
room, and we can see that it is on both their
minds. He sits on the corner of it, and she
stands in the corner farthest from him.

                    JAMIE
          You want anything, room
          service, whatever?

She just shakes her head, vulnerable,
helpless and feeling manipulated. He keeps
looking at her.

                    JACQUELINE
          Stop staring at me!

                    JAMIE
               (looking away)
          I'm sorry...

She looks at him with an accusing glare.

                    JACQUELINE
          What do you want from me?
          Money?

Jamie shakes his head, genuinely shocked.
How can he make her believe how much she
means to him?

                    JACQUELINE
          Sex?

                    JAMIE
               (hurt)
          Everything I've told you...
          everything I will ever tell
          you is the truth. I will
          never lie to you. I love you;
          I want to help you!

                    JACQUELINE
          Even knowing what I've done.

After a moment, he nods, looking down. He
can't answer, remembering the nausea, the
guilt, the pain... and her fury.

                              DISSOLVE TO:

SAME PLACE - LATER

Jacqueline is ASLEEP under the covers.

Across the room, Jamie has fallen asleep
watching her in a CHAIR, in his clothes.
She is DREAMING... being CHASED in her sleep.
Jamie is sharing the dream, their movements
and whimperings in UNISON.

We PUSH IN ON JAMIE to CU, and hold for a
few beats before bringing in the SUN. Without
cutting or dissolving, SUNLIGHT COMES UP to
indicate MORNING. We FADE IN TRAFFIC SOUNDS
(o.s.), and Jamie AWAKENS (still in CU).

We PULL OUT to REVEAL the EMPTY BED!
Jacqueline is GONE! Jamie BOLTS up, until he
HEARS it... the SOUND of the SHOWER (o.s.).
He sits there listening to her behind the
bathroom door, and can only but imagine what
is going on inside; the running water
conjures up all those erotically-charged
VISIONS he has experienced.

He slowly STANDS, and can't help but approach
the BATHROOM DOOR. He stands there for
several beats, leaning against the wall,
listening, remembering, imagining. It is
almost unbearably frustrating for him.

He gently TAPS on the door. Again. There is
no answer. Louder.

                    JAMIE
          Jacqueline?

No answer. He knocks loudly, beginning to
worry.

                    JAMIE
          Jacqueline, are you all
          right?

Still no answer. He tries the door, and it
is LOCKED! He RAMS it with his shoulder, and
it finally GIVES; he DIVES into the thick
STEAM within.

INT. BATHROOM - DAY

Steam is pouring from the shower. He YANKS
OPEN the shower curtain!

                    JAMIE
          Jacqueline!

Jacqueline is huddled at the end of the tub,
the shower drenching her. She turns and faces
Jamie, wide-eyed, as if just yanked from a
trance. He sees her there, naked, the WATER
running down her body, and—after the first
glimpse—looks away, embarrassed.

She is shivering, frightened, vulnerable.

He reaches in and turns off the shower,
drenching his sleeve. Then he helps her out
of the tub, the savior, and chastely wraps
her in a towel, and helps dry her off.

                    JACQUELINE
          Thank you...

This is a switch; she's thanking him. His
dream of being her knight in shining armor
has a chance...

Still half in a trance, she allows him to
help dry her off; then, suddenly present,
she looks him in the eye, taking his hand in
hers. Wordlessly, she grips the hand, her
nails digging into his skin, nearly drawing
blood, then buries her face in his chest.

She wraps her arms around him in a desperate
HUG, and weeps into his chest.

Slowly, he brings his arms up around her,
afraid that any sudden move will end this
dream. He STROKES her wet hair.

                    JACQUELINE
             (voice muffled by his chest)
          I'm scared...

                       JAMIE
          I won't let anything happen
          to you.

She looks up into his eyes, reading him. Is
that trust dawning? She reaches up and
gently, hesitantly, traces his face with her
fingertips... each contact is an electrical
charge... hearts are beginning to beat more
rapidly... breathing less regular...

He reaches up to touch her hand, then ever-
so-gently touches it to his lips. She lets
him. He touches the tears on her face, kisses
away the wet fingertip.

                    JACQUELINE
                    (a whisper)
          Take care of me...

He's hesitant to make the big move, and can't
believe it when she does. She brings his face
down to hers, looks into his eyes, incredibly
vulnerable, then grazes his lips with hers.
Soon the hesitation gives way to a desperate
passion, and they are kissing deeply.

Jamie is not sure he can deal with this,
feeling guilty, as if he had manipulated this
whole event. He doesn't want to take
advantage... but driven by a need to be close
with her confidante, Jacqueline lays her
HAND gently against his FACE.

Jamie lifts her hand, sees the bleeding MARKS
from her FINGERNAILS, and KISSES them. He
tenderly LICKS them clean, and we are
reminded of an earlier moment between
Jacqueline and Hooper.

As Jamie takes her FINGERS into his MOUTH,
her breathing goes throaty, reacting more

than she wants to, frightened by her passionate response. He is in power; he knows her secrets...

The dam breaks, and their fears and hopelessness give way to a desperate EMBRACE on the bathroom floor.

Their nerve-endings reaching through the flesh, skin RIDES skin in a combustion of energy. It is an intimate encounter so filled with raw, primal emotion and release that it frightens them, and just becomes more incendiary and overwhelming.

But it isn't really sex. They are drained, scared. Her eyes are wet, and she shivers, holding him close.

> JACQUELINE
> I need you... your help...

It is more than he could dream for.

> JAMIE
> I'm here...

EXT. QUEEN ELIZABETH PARK - DAY

They walk silently through the devastatingly beautiful rolling green hills and wildly colorful gardens. It is quite at odds with the darkness of events in which they are embroiled.

They come to a KOI POND and she stops and KNEELS, looking into the reflective waters. After several beats...

> JACQUELINE
> I am so tired...

And she sits on the grass by the pond. He sits next to her.

She lies back, warmed by the sun, and closes
her eyes. He gently rests his hand on her
forehead, and strokes her hair.

                    JACQUELINE
          And the world closes in.

He lies down on his side next to her, up on
one arm, watching her.

                    JAMIE
          I won't let anything happen
          to you.

Exhausted, she brings her hand up and lays
it on his. Jamie is elated; could this
finally be trust?

                    JACQUELINE
          Thank you.

She looks at him, embarrassed to find him
staring at her with such emotion.

                    JAMIE
          You are so gorgeous...

                    JACQUELINE
          And you love me so much.

It's a curious thing for her to say. His mind
darkens for a moment, until she reaches up
and KISSES him. This time it is intimate,
though not filled with erotic passion.

JACQUELINE Thank you.

She closes her eyes, and seems to be drifting
off. Jamie looks into the pond, the day going
dreamy on him.

ANGLE - THE POND - JAMIE'S P.O.V.

He stares at his reflection; it ripples, and
his face becomes Jacqueline's: soft and at

peace... But enigmatic. Until a koi pops up
to ripple the reflection away.

                    JACQUELINE
          What time is it?

                    JAMIE
          I don't know... five, six
          o'clock.

She sits up.

                    JACQUELINE
          Will you take me home?

                    JAMIE
          What about the police?

                    JACQUELINE
          That's why I've got to go
          there. I don't have
          anything... car, purse,
          money, clothes...
                    (looking away)
          Then... maybe we can go
          away... together.

Jamie REACTS, and she looks hopefully up into
his eyes. He doesn't know how to respond.

                    JAMIE
          You trust me?

                    JACQUELINE
                    (beat)
          I have to...

                    JAMIE
          We've got to be careful...

                    JACQUELINE
          Of course.

EXT. STREET IN FRONT OF WOMAN'S HOUSE - DAY

They carefully peer around the corner to see the POLICE CAR with the TWO DETECTIVES in place.

ANGLE - JAMIE AND JACQUELINE

They pull back out of sight.

                    JAMIE
          Shit! Listen, you go around
          back, and I'll go up like I'm
          just dropping by for a
          surprise visit, and try to
          find out what they want...
          and what they know.

She looks petrified, but knows she has to trust him, much as she doesn't want to. He grips both her hands and squeezes them, and heads down the street, before she has a chance to say anything.

Jacqueline SNEAKS around behind the half-renovated brownstone across the street from hers.

WIDE ANGLE

Jamie nervously walks up the street toward her brownstone.

BACK OF WRECKED BROWNSTONE

Jacqueline ENTERS, trying to find a perch from which to watch. She ENTERS the back door of the half-renovated house.

FRONT OF JACQUELINE'S HOUSE

Jamie goes past the cop car, trying to ignore it, and RINGS THE BELL with forced nonchalance.

INT. WRECKED BROWNSTONE - NIGHT

We MOVE WITH Jacqueline through the levels
of the house. She quietly moves to the second
floor... until her foot sends a LOOSE BRICK
crashing to the ground floor. She STOPS,
holding her breath.

When all seems clear, she moves on.

RESUME JAMIE AT JACQUELINE'S DOOR

He KNOCKS; still no answer. He turns to SEE
both CAR DOORS COME OPEN.

RESUME JACQUELINE - WRECKED BROWNSTONE

She moves through the rubble and into Jamie's
hiding room! As she approaches the WINDOW,
she stops, notices all of the personal
effects of someone who lives there: Jamie's
open SUITCASE, CLOTHES... BINOCULARS...

She is shocked to see it there, and goes to
inspect the items.

She finds Jamie's WALLET, and leafs through
its contents; right on top is Jamie's Cougar
Chemical PICTURE I.D. CARD. As it registers
in her brain, she walks across the room to
the WINDOW, where she can see her house...
and Jamie... quite clearly.

ANGLE - HER HOUSE - JACQUELINE'S P.O.V.

Two MEN IN SUITS are talking with Jamie, but
we can't hear what they are saying.

ANGLE - JACQUELINE

We PUSH IN on her vulnerable, pensive

expression.

We CIRCLE HER, PULLING OUT to INCLUDE the scene down on the street, as the cops continue to talk with Jamie. Soon, Jamie WALKS AWAY, and the Cops climb into their car and DRIVE OFF.

EXT. YARD BEHIND WRECKED BROWNSTONE - NIGHT

Jamie comes hurrying behind the empty building, excited.

                    JAMIE
               (whispering)
          Jacqueline!

She APPEARS from the DOORWAY, and Jamie FREEZES. He looks from her to the second story, wondering what she has seen, but she plays dumb, so he goes on.

                    JACQUELINE
          What happened?

                    JAMIE
          They wanted to know who I
          was, if I was a friend of
          yours. I just played the dumb
          cousin, and they went for it.
          They wanted to know if you
          had any family, where they
          might be able to find you,
          and I told them that you
          often stayed with your
          parents in Edmonton.

                    JACQUELINE
          And now they're off to
          Edmonton?

                    JAMIE
          All I know is they're not
          hanging around here. They're
          gone, Jacqueline.

                    JACQUELINE
              Thank you. Jamie.

Hearing her speak his name—especially so
intimately—thrills him.

EXT. STREET IN FRONT OF HER HOUSE - NIGHT

They are afraid to leave the shadows.

                    JAMIE
              Maybe we ought to go in the
              back way, just to make sure.

She nods her agreement, letting him take the
lead.

EXT. BACK OF WOMAN'S HOUSE - NIGHT

She UNLOCKS the door, and, with a meaningful
look between them, they go in.

INT. JACQUELINE'S HOUSE - FOYER - NIGHT

They ENTER. Jamie is nervous, actually
entering her domicile after all this time
and excitement. It is dark at the foot of
the STAIRS, and she is leading the way,
looking around for evidence that the police
have been inside.

He just stands at the foot of the stairs,
nervously watching her, his heart racing.

                    JACQUELINE
                (turning to him)
              Come on in...

He can't believe that she's inviting him into
her HOME. But she LEADS him UP THE STAIRS...

INT. HER LIVING ROOM - NIGHT

The large ROOM is quite remarkable, and he
GASPS with recognition. The walls are
PAINTED MURALS of ANIMALS in their JUNGLE
habitat.

One wall is a TIGER in lush savannas; another
is a LIONESS and her CUBS; the MATE is
directly across the room, devouring the
remains of a slain ZEBRA.

The FURNISHINGS also express the jungle:
AFRICAN WEAPONS, SPEARS, BOWS, and other
artful appointments, combined with
expensively comfortable furniture. It is
like no other room, with jars of
PAINTBRUSHES, EASELS, PAINTS, etc., all
over.

                    JAMIE
          Jesus...

He's here. Seeing it for real, all of it at
once, in person, is an unnerving experience
for him. She moves closer to him, and he puts
his hands comfortingly on her shoulders.

                    JAMIE
          It's going to be okay. Don't
          be frightened.

He looks into her eyes, and they hold his
gaze, standing intoxicatingly close to one
another. He takes her hands in his, and she
SQUEEZES them... a little scared.

                    JAMIE
          I'd do anything for you.

                    JACQUELINE
          I know.

                    JAMIE
          I love you.

                    JACQUELINE
          I know.
               (nervous, pensive beat)
          I... I love you...

He sighs with relief and disbelief. She puts
on a brave but tender SMILE, and he moves
closer.

                    JACQUELINE
               (almost a whisper)
          Jamie, I...
               (beat; he waits for it)
          I did see things... feel
          things. But I didn't know
          what it was. I thought I was
          going crazy...

It is more than Jamie could have hoped for;
he REACTS, nearly overwhelmed.

                    JAMIE
          You're not crazy,
          Jacqueline... What... what
          did you see?

                    JACQUELINE
               (almost afraid to go on)
          I don't know... Images, and
          flavors, something... Faces,
          chemicals. A child, a little
          boy. Loneliness...

Jamie RESPONDS; they are linked. He leans
forward and gently touches her LIPS with HIS.
When she doesn't object, he takes her in his
ARMS, and the gentle, protective KISS
becomes more PASSIONATE... the culmination
of months of obsession.

When finally they break the kiss, their eyes
are shining. She is actually shivering in
his arms, emotional, vulnerable, frightened
by all of this, as the world is catching up

to them.

                    JAMIE
          You're shivering...

                    JACQUELINE
          I could use something to
          drink.
                    (needing to break away)
          You want something?

He just nods. He couldn't care less about a
drink right now.

She leaves his side and goes over to the
little bar at the far end of the room. Trying
to calm his racing heart, he takes a seat on
the thick, squishy couch in the middle of
her jungle.

ANGLE - AT BAR WITH JACQUELINE - JAMIE IN
B.G.

Shivering nervously, she gets out two
glasses and pours the drinks. Then, taking a
glance at Jamie, who is looking at the
painted murals, she sees her PURSE on the
bar.

She REACHES for it, fumbles in it for...
something we don't see.

                    JACQUELINE
              (soft, vulnerable)
          I'm glad you're here with me.

It is the most wonderful thing she could say
to him.

                    JAMIE
              (as she brings their drinks)
          Me, too...

She sinks into the couch next to him, and
sips her drink, just watching him...
shivering. The ICE CUBES in their glasses

CLINK from the force of her heartbeat. She hands Jamie his drink, and he sets it down on the table in front of him.

Jamie is so close to her. He can't resist reaching out and touching her. He runs his hand through her HAIR, pulling her face to his, breathing her, feeling her, experiencing her.

It becomes a long, romantic KISS.

She finally has to come up for air, and takes another sip of her drink, hoping he'll follow her lead.

He does. He belts the drink down, and GRIMACES.

                    JAMIE
          Bitter.

Distracting him from the drink now, she comes in to kiss him, encouraging him to taste her instead.

She pulls him down into the marshy COUCH, and their embrace is horizontal. All of the events have led to their need to LINK; all they have is each other. Both their lives are shattered, and they clutch at one another for solace.

Soon, Jamie is on top of her, and CLOTHING begins to loosen and fall away. When Jamie is in the all-too-familiar position, he FREEZES for a moment, as GOOSEFLESH strokes him and departs.

                    JACQUELINE
          What?

                    JAMIE
          Just a little dizzy...

                    JACQUELINE
              (her breathing more irregular)
          Me, too...

He just shakes his head, and their passion
builds... and the fantasy is about to be
fulfilled. She pulls him onto her.

INSERT - THE BAR

Jacqueline's PURSE lies open next to the
bottle... and so does a PILL BOTTLE, lying
on its side. Several XANAX TABLETS have been
dumped into his drink!

RESUME JACQUELINE AND JAMIE

Her hands run all over his body, pulling him
closer, inspecting him, and she throws a leg
around him, as flesh presses flesh.

He KISSES her wounded HAND, and it makes her
SHIVER; she gently pulls it away and brings
her mouth to meet his.

Their kisses are DEEP, their groping needy.
The dream is about to come true, their
bodies, sheened in passion, are about to
merge in blissful physical surrender... as
his DIZZINESS soars...

And then...

Jacqueline's HAND slides under the sofa
CUSHION, as if just to grasp, but in a
lightning movement, both HANDS are suddenly
GRIPPING the HANDGUN that is jammed under
Jamie's jaw!

                    JACQUELINE
          What do you want?

Jamie's WALLET drops from her clothing, and
he REACTS, understanding immediately. She
never felt what he felt; she cheated him,
found out his secrets in the brownstone

across the street. He can only choke on the
gun, totally taken off-guard.

                    JACQUELINE
          How long have you been
          watching me from over there?
          What are you waiting for? Why
          don't you just throw me in a
          cell and get it over with?!
          Or do you just want to fuck
          me?!

It sounds horrible coming from her, dirty,
scalding.

                    JAMIE
          I'm not a cop and I'm not
          trying to blackmail you! I
          love you!

                    JACQUELINE
          Do you? Did you feel it, the
          knife? Did you feel it
          jamming in with all your
          might? Could you feel him
          jerking and fighting? Did you
          feel the blood running down
          your arms into a puddle on
          your stomach?
               (pulling back the hammer)
          Is that what made you love
          me?

                    JAMIE
          You had to! He made you do
          it!

She snorts a humorless laugh, and he takes
the moment to summon the strength and courage
to PULL AWAY from her and GRAB her WRISTS!
She SQUEEZES OFF A SHOT; a BULLET RIPS
THROUGH his CALF!

Making a DOUBLE FIST, he KNOCKS the GUN from
her grip, sending it FLYING across the room!

He LEAPS across the COFFEE TABLE after it, sending things crashing to the floor.

A caged animal, she JUMPS on top of him, and they STRUGGLE. The GUN is just out of reach! She CLAWS for his wounded LEG, and JAMS HER THUMB into the BULLET HOLE! Jamie SCREAMS! She TUMBLES over him, grappling for the GUN! She GRABS it and FIRES; the SHOT goes WILD, and PLASTER FLIES from the FACE of the TIGER. Jamie rolls across the carpet, reeling, his senses dulled by the drug, grabbing an African SPEAR from the corner, swinging it wildly at her.

It CONNECTS with her ARM, breaking in two from the impact! Was the CRACKING her BONE as well?

The GUN FLIES, and lands BETWEEN THEM!

FRANTICALLY, LIKE A JUNGLE CAT, SHE GRABS THE BLADE END OF THE SPEAR, AND LEAPS ON HIM WITH FURY.

She SLASHES his sleeve open, and BLOOD flows as they battle their way across the room toward the gun.

Running on instinct, he bashes her across the side of the head with a two-handed FIST; she SCREAMS like a struck animal and falls to the floor. Her hands SLIDE DOWN the length of the SPEARHEAD, and BLOOD FLOWS.

Rushing to his feet, Jamie dashes for the gun, but his LEG gives out, and he crashes to the floor.

She SLASHES at him with the BLADE, missing the meat, but PINNING his PANTLEG to the floor!

She PICKS UP an African CARVING and THROWS it at him, gashing his temple and knocking him back.

She SCRAMBLES for the GUN as he struggles to
pull the blade out, his head bleeding.

He suddenly GRABS the CARVING in his hand,
ready to throw it.

                    JAMIE
          Jacqueline!!!

His cry brings back a flash of humanity to
her face, as she looks quickly at him, and
the heavy wood CARVING he is ready to throw.
But with a deft TWIST and a SLEIGHT of HAND,
magic Jamie makes the CARVING DISAPPEAR!
Catching the half-second she is thrown off-
guard, his other hand in a single lightning
movement PULLS the SPEARHEAD FREE and THROWS
it at her!!!

She throws her HAND up, and the BLADE goes
THROUGH HER HAND!

The GUN tumbles to the floor, as she STARES
with animal disbelief at the BLADE sticking
out both sides of her hand.

Seizing the moment, Jamie LUNGES for the gun.
He's on his KNEES, shaking, both hands
clutching it, aiming it at her.

                    JAMIE
          I don't want to hurt you!
          Don't make me do this!

Her eyes are wide, insane, and he doesn't
know what to do.

With frightening strength, Jacqueline YANKS
the BLADE out of her hand. Blood DROOLS from
the WOUND.

                    JACQUELINE
                  (creepy)
          You don't know me. You should

never have come here...

And she slowly STANDS, gripping the BLADE.
She takes a step nearer, testing his resolve.

                    JAMIE
          Don't do it! I just want to
          help you!

                    JACQUELINE
          I can't let you know what you
          know!

Another step CLOSER... He RAISES the
trembling GUN.

ANGLE - JAMIE'S P.O.V.

She takes another STEP CLOSER, beginning to
LOOM over him, the BLADE poised higher.

REVERSE ANGLE - HER P.O.V.

Looking down on him; he seems a pitiful,
broken man, destroyed by his romantic
obsession.

                    JAMIE
          Jacqueline!!!

He PULLS BACK the HAMMER.

                    JACQUELINE
          You love me...

RESUME JAMIE'S P.O.V.

SOMETHING is HAPPENING! Things start
SHIFTING, and the ominous SOUND/MUSIC is
back, as the BURSTING BUBBLES APPEAR!

His P.O.V. is being replaced by hers!!! He's
TRANSPOSING again, at the worst possible
time!!!

P.O.V. SHOT - THROUGH HER EYES

The effect is total now! He SEES himself
cowering! ! !

                    JAMIE
          Not now!

He is having trouble aiming now, seeing
himself in the second person. His AIM WAVERS,
adjusting to the MIRROR-EFFECT and REVERSE-
IMAGE problem of correcting his fire.

JAMIE AND JACQUELINE

She looks confused, cocking her head. Jamie
seems as if his body has been EVACUATED; his
eyes are BLIND. She seems to understand what
is happening, and steps boldly closer.

RESUME P.O.V. SHOT

She moves CLOSER, and Jamie's battered BODY
tries frantically to aim through her eyes at
the CAMERA (Jacqueline)!

JACQUELINE as curious as she is determined:

                    JACQUELINE
          Is it happening now?
               (she sees that it is)
          It's real...

A mad trace of victorious SMILE at the corner
of her lips.

RESUME JAMIE - P.O.V. SHOT

                    JAMIE
             (frantically trying to aim)
          Don't do it!!!

The BLADE COMES UP in her hands in front of
CAMERA, poised to SLASH as we approach!

His SIGHTLESS EYES widen, trying to see, but only look back as a mirror through her eyes. Just as she SLASHES DOWN, Jamie FIRES!

ANGLE - JAMIE AND JACQUELINE

She is THROWN BACK by the FORCE of the BULLET, and they BOTH SCREAM in matching ANIMAL CRIES of pain, Jamie feeling it as much as she. But she LUNGES again, and Jamie FIRES!

RESUME P.O.V. SHOT

We COME FORWARD again, and he is forced to FIRE again. Both BODIES are thrown back by the force of each shot, as he experiences HER being HIT with each SHOT!

With a COSMIC ROAR, and with a RED-WHITE FLASH at each BULLET IMPACT, the ROOM starts to go DARK, and begins to REVOLVE into a SPIN.

We HEAR jagged, dying BREATHS, and a heavy, slowing HEARTBEAT thudding to a HALT as the image churns into a whirlpool, her life swirling down the drain like her PAINTS.

There are vivid EXPLOSIONS of LIGHT and COLOR, accompanied by unbelievable SOUNDS.

Then, silent BLACKNESS for several BEATS.

Finally, as if the CAMERA were OPENING ITS EYES:

                                        WIPE TO:

INT. LIVING ROOM - NIGHT - P.O.V. SHOT

Looking up at the CEILING, which is also a mural of staring jungle animals.

ANGLE ON JAMIE

He slowly comes back to life, clutching his chest. With much pain, he slowly sits up and looks around.

The silence is JARRING, and he is a WRECK.

Jacqueline's CORPSE lies across his legs, staring at him, her body unpleasantly revealed from under bloody, disheveled clothing.

He struggles to STAND, barely able to balance on one leg, looking down, heartbroken, at the Woman at his feet. We PULL AWAY, and he is dwarfed by the room and the act.

ANGLE - JAMIE - OPENING SHOT - INTERROGATION ROOM

We can see now that he is still in Jacqueline's living room; that's where he's being interviewed by detectives.

IT IS NOT MUCH LATER, AND HE TRIES TO WAVE AWAY THE THICKENING CIGARETTE SMOKE.

                    JAMIE
               (to camera)
          And I knew what it felt like
          to die...

The DETECTIVE pushes the bright LAMP away, and SIGNALS the UNIFORMED OFFICER at his side to TURN ON THE LIGHTS. They come on, and Jamie looks away from the mess that other cops are going over.

The Detective just sighs and stubs out the last cigarette in the pack in the carved AFRICAN BOWL on the battered COFFEE TABLE.

                    DETECTIVE
          You know, that's not an easy
          story to swallow...

Jamie is exhausted, won't even look at him.

                    DETECTIVE
          I said, it's pretty hard to
          believe what you just told
          me.

                    JAMIE
          I heard you. I just don't
          give a damn
                    .
The Detective just looks at him, considering
the long, complicated, unbelievable tale
he's just heard. He looks like he actually
believes it.

Jamie looks at the Detective; does he see
the belief? The Detective BREAKS EYE
CONTACT, looks away before betraying
compassion.

He looks at the other MEN, who don't offer
their opinions. They're glad he's in charge.
They all turn to see ORDERLIES hoisting the
bloody, sheet-wrapped CORPSE on a stretcher,
looking to the Detective for orders.

                    DETECTIVE
          Get 'em on the ambulance.
          Both of 'em.

Jamie WINCES as one of the MEN helps him to
his feet.

                    DETECTIVE
          (sharply, as if with compassion)
          Get a stretcher!

And they ease Jamie onto a stretcher. The
Detective and the Officer with him watch
silently as Jamie is carefully picked up and
taken out and down the stairs.

The Detective lets out a long SIGH, and
without looking at his partner, says, almost

with embarrassment.

                    DETECTIVE
          Looks like self-defense to
          me.

And he LOOKS UP at his partner, as if to dare
him to disagree. The Partner just NODS.

EXT. STREET IN FRONT OF BROWNSTONE - NIGHT -
HIGH ANGLE

A small CROWD has gathered around the COP
CARS and AMBULANCE. Both STRETCHERS are
being loaded into the ambulance, and the
others are climbing into their VEHICLES and
solemnly SLAMMING the doors and driving
away.

It is a long, sad view from a distance.

As the vehicles DISPERSE, so does the
gathered crowd, though more slowly.

We continue to PULL slowly BACK, until we
see that we are looking out of Jamie's CAMP
in the BROWNSTONE across the street.

We MOVE BACK INTO THE DEPTHS of the dark,
shadowy room, past the litter of his
belongings, as the crowd in the distance
continues to dissipate, and settle on
something draped over the battered suitcase:
The TABLECLOTH, with the WAX DRAWING of the
TIGER that Jamie made while transposing.

                    THE END

Afterword

By Tobe Hooper

After I finished reading *A Life in the Cinema*, it was well past midnight. Time for bed, I thought optimistically. On the long road to sleep, I finally found myself in that place where the dream world starts pulling you in slowly, and the music fades in. I got stuck in this weird and lucid netherworld all night.

From that place, this is my POV.

The great pinwheel of miracle and wonder spins in a storm of images, feelings, and mysterious syntactical wonderment that floodtides into my super unconsciousness forcing open doors hidden in the gray matter apertures for the esoterically twisty tunnels that lead to the dreamy creamy dark and gleamy fantasy zone.

Not too safe here … and that's really cool.

And there it is again! *The taste of sweat, and the smell of sex.*

(Thank God.) Or is it the smell of chocolate? … now the *taste* of chocolate …

I'm losing it—there's no question about it. I'm tasting chocolate, but someone other than myself is eating it. And if that isn't fucked enough, I'm seeing through *HER EYES!*

Has love … come … for me? Chosen *me?* Images of chocolate flutter away and then a lustful mist glums and glooms, turning into palm trees. Through the smog, there's the Hollywood sign.

Visions of Jean Harlow II ... Alabaster breast satin-covered static electrically charged nipples spark and crackle as they rise heavenward. The sex? ... sometimes it's good here in the Hollywood rectum spectrum, a place where proud people and monuments are razed to the ground, replaced overnight by new versions of the same with even less spirit. Don't you just love the smell of exposed living—the steaming gut of artist being double-fucked in the morning? What about you, STARFUCKER?

STARFUCKER ...

And now a secondary wave of images and emotions comes jiggedy roaring after me ...

His Insignificant Life and Very Important Death

There are wondrous things happening here with primal jelly and very good baby food. It's a miraculous thing after death. Now BABY SHOWERS—I'm actually watching aged sex in a convalescent home. The din in here is overbearing. Help ... CUT ... !

FLASHBACK: Just before going to bed.

After I finished reading *A Life in the Cinema*, the excitement of provocative fear was clouding in on me. I have this weird vision of horsefucking the macabre. I find myself in this idiosyncratic, beguiling mind place, having experienced Mick Garris' book. And I like very much this spectrum of sensations. An enticing projection of intellect and heart, into the bubble of primal jelly where lust, fear and kink-twisted horrific acts merge in harmony with the ray of light and astonishing hope. Mick's magic wand, so to speak, penetrates the skin of the big "IT", near impossibly hitting a vein of the *pure stuff*—the nectar of sweet secretions that feed the awesome well of answers and wonder—the real stuff that implodingly explodes nourishments for the elusive spirit of the arts. It's the stuff of greatness, the stuff that dreams are made of.

Tobe Hooper, 2000